SEASONS OF DUST

SEASONS
OF
DUST

IFEONA FULANI

HARLEM RIVER PRESS
NEW YORK
& LONDON

'The Ancestors' by Kate Rushin from 'Black Back-Ups' published by Firebrand Books, 141 The Commons, Ithaca, New York 14850. Copyright © 1993 by Kate Rushin.

Published for **Harlem River Press** by **Writers and Readers Publishing, Inc.**
P.O. Box 461, Village Station
New York, NY 10014

Writers and Readers Limited
9 Cynthia Street
London N19JF
England

Text Copyright © 1997 Ifeona Fulani

Book Production: Neuwirth and Associates
Cover Design: Terrie Dunkelberger

Cover Art: Dawn Scott

For Michael

ACKNOWLEDGEMENTS

My thanks to Judith Hamilton, Michaelle Archer, Marie Hitchins, Sandra Polynice, for their unfailing support and encouragement. Thanks also to Dr. Carolyn Cooper for introducing me to the Cassidy system for writing Jamaican Creole, which has influenced my own writing of Jamaican speech.

I went all the way to Africa
Searching for the mythic past
I found it on a homemade altar
Watching from a fading photograph

'The Ancestors' *by Kate Rushin*

PROLOGUE

JAMAICA 1990

MORNING COMES SOFTLY HERE.

I take my morning cup of Earl Grey tea amid that softness. With river noise in my ears I savour the tea's astringent tang and watch as dawn spreads gently out before me, stretching way across the valley, edging the purple-green hills with golden light.

Such a different life.

This time yesterday I was walking down the hill to catch the bus for Kingston. At Three Miles I clamboured aboard the Mandeville bus in a rush-hour jostle of elbows, knees and glares. Normally, I avoided travelling at this time but I was going to visit my mother for the first time since coming home and it had to be done early.

She answered my knock looking displeased.

"Is soh long yu tek fi kom sii mi? Look how long. Yu shud bi shame." As she spoke she held the door open just enough for me to enter. She was unprepared, in a housecoat with hair twisted up in Chiney bumps.

I liked her that way. She was more natural, almost defenceless.

We sat on the veranda, away from her husband, hardly speaking. Birdsong filled the silence while we sipped at glasses of powdery-tasting iced tea. The day was perfect, the sky so clear that in the distance I could see the contours of our home parish.

"Why did you leave England?" I asked, breaking the silence.

She thought for a moment, then kissed her teeth.

"Inglan wasn't nice agen. It get too tuf fi blak piipl, soh mi just seh, choh, mek mi goh home. I feel plenti betta ya-so."

I nodded sympathetically and resisted the temptation to probe further.

"Soh, yu finally tear yuself way from yuh faada!" she said.

"I did that a long time ago," I answered calmly. No anger today. This is a peace-making mission.

"Mi knuo seh im fill up yu hed wid lie bout mi. Mi knuo seh im turn yu mind gainst mi."

"No. No. My mind was set long time ago." Immediately I regretted the words. Her eyes grew defiant, her mouth set hard. I sensed her trembling and knew she was uneasy.

"Can you see Rocky Gap from here?" I wanted to change the subject.

"Yu must hiir my side!" she said angrily. "Yu doan knuo di stori till yu hiir mine."

"I know. I know. There's no rush. You can tell me next time I come."

"Yu komin agen, den?"

"Yes. Of course. Yes."

She sank back in the white wicker chair, visibly relaxing.

So many stories, woven and entwined like the strands of the coconut coaster on which my glass of iced tea rested. So hard to pick out a strand and say, this is the main one, the important one which holds the others together.

The river beyond my garden gurgles gleefully like a child at play. Not far from my head, a hummingbird darts among the red flowers of a hibiscus bush, plunging deep into their scarlet cups to drain every drop of nectar. Alighting on a slender branch, the bird rests, poised for flight yet perfectly still for just one moment.

Part 1
SEASONS OF DUST

JAMAICA

1950-1953

Chapter 1

AT LAST THE RAIN CAME. Ray Erskine stood in the downpour, watching the red dirt dissolve into pools around his feet. Soon, streams of red water were coursing down the hillside, reminding him of blood. Not the dark, deathly blood that spurted from the veins of slaughtered animals, but the hot lifeblood pounding through his veins and beating in his head with a driving, restless pulse.

Water seeped into his boots as he surveyed the hazy landscape. Nothing but fields as far as the eye could see. Fields rolling down the hillside and across the plains to touch Wide River which stretched like a fat serpent, rising in the east and fading languidly into the sea in the west.

Lord, he was glad of the rain! For weeks he had worked the caked earth with dust invading his eyes, his nostrils, his mouth. Each day at twilight he climbed the hill to his house passing Maas Stanley, his neighbour, on the way. Together they bemoaned and cursed the drought, praying that rain would come to swell the tomatoes, carrots, scallions and melons in their fields.

As the storm gathered momentum he collected his tools and left the field, heading along the main road through Rocky Gap and up the hill.

He was twenty-six years years old, of medium height and slender build. Large eyes burned with vitality and his slim face, with its full mouth and cleft chin looked headstrong, an impression confirmed by the rapid, purposeful motion of his walk.

He strode uphill past a cluster of small houses concealed from the road by a screen of trees and flowering bushes. Only the sounds of people living betrayed their presence, sounds of children's voices, of metal vessels clattering while women hurried to finish cooking the evening meal before the premature darkness brought on by the rain descended completely. Ray was racing against the darkness himself, hastening to escape the chilling rain.

His house stood in a clearing at the top of the hill. By the time he reached the gate, the fields and trees which surrounded the house on all but one side were completely obscured by darkness. On the fourth side, where the ground dropped steeply down to the sea there was a blue-black void. As he paused in the back doorway to remove his boots he could hear Esme and Ruby talking. The murmur of their speech was comforting, like a familiar song. He loved to come home to their company in the evening, to receive their care and attention and to eat the meal prepared for him.

Yes, he thought, catching the scent of food. Biif soop; just di ting fi a nite like dis.

"Ray, wat a piice ov rain!" Esme greeted him as entered the small kitchen. "An look how yu wet up!" She was a short woman, but stocky and strong. She moved around briskly, in no way hampered by the large belly which proclaimed her pregnancy. She filled a basin with water for him to wash up, took away his wet clothing, and began setting the table for them to eat. Soon he was seated in front of a deep dish filled with soup, meat, dumplings, yam and sweet cassava.

The kitchen was smoky from the coal stove which normally resided in the back yard but which Ruby had brought in from the rain. A kerosene lamp on the table gave enough light for Ray to see the food in front of him and the faces of the women seated across from him. The lamp threw shadows on the kitchen walls and silhouetted Esme's head, which seemed to bob up and down, enormously distorted and unnaturally mobile. Rain beat loudly on the metallic roof of the house.

Ray felt cosy just listening to the rhythm of raindrops, protected and at ease in the smoky little room.

The house consisted of two rooms, a kitchen and a small verandah at the front. At the back, a short distance away from the house, was a bath house and further away still, a pit latrine hidden behind a clump of hibiscus bushes. Ray had built the house with his own two hands. Two short years ago he had been just another farm labourer toiling under a burning sun to earn a mere pittance each week, dreaming of one day owning land, of building a house, of settling down and making something of his life. The chance to make good his dream came in the form of a contract labour scheme. With dozens of men from all over the island, he had signed up for a year of hard labour constructing roads in the city of New York. For one year he had worked every bit as hard as he had done in the fields of Rocky Gap, suffering cold weather, bad food, incivility and prejudice. He had been glad for the money, but glad to leave America also. Who told him America was the land of freedom, hope and opportunity? It seemed to him that coloured people in that place were treated worse than animals! It looked like slavery had never been abolished there. He had thought Jamaican whites were high and mighty, but they were nothing like those Americans! Only God knew how coloured Americans put up with them.

Returning to Rocky Gap with a wallet full of dollars in his pocket, Ray had purchased three quarters of an acre of land where his house now stood and the few heads of livestock which grazed there. The remaining dollars had purchased an acre of land down the hill, now divided into three fields. It was a mean piece of land, mean as the man who had sold it to him for well above its true worth. The stony, dry earth demanded sweat, toil and even drew blood from his hands in return for a yield of crops. There were times he hated the ground he owned and worked upon, cursed the dirt and stones, but he strove ceaselessly day after scorching day and forced a living out of the reluctant soil.

Ray had returned from America with another, less tangible asset: experience. He had travelled, gone abroad! This (and the money he brought back with him) made him an object of desire among the young women of the district. He had always been popular; he had good looks and pleasing ways and he loved a good time. He never missed a dance, he would even travel as far as Balaclava with his girl on a donkey cart if there was a good band playing on a Saturday night. And when it came to sweet talk, there was none could beat him; his tongue was made of honey. A girl really had to have a grip of her senses to resist Ray Erskine.

Ray had known Esme's family for as long as he had lived in Rocky Gap. The Partridge family was one of the largest in the district, headed by the tyrannical patriarch Doc. Doc begat fourteen children by two wives, and who knows how many others outside. His first wife had died of pneumonia, leaving ten children behind her while his second wife Sara, Esme's mother, died giving birth to Harold, her fourth child in almost as many years. Of course, bad-minded gossips claimed that both Doc's wives died of fright. Ray, who had heard many stories about him from Esme, and who was a little afraid of the man himself, was inclined to share this view.

Ray's first contact with the family came through Matthew, the eldest Partridge son. They became acquainted playing cricket, for which they shared a passion, and friendship followed quickly. Through Matthew, Ray was absorbed into the younger generation of Partridges almost like another brother.

Ray's own family came from Red Hill, a small community some three or so miles away from Rocky Gap. All he knew of his father was that he had disappeared when Ray was an infant leaving Mama to raise two sons and a daughter, of whom Ray was the youngest.

Mama was a tall woman with big hands and feet and skin the colour of molasses. People said that after Ray's father deserted his family, her mind turned against men, for she was never known to have another sweetheart. She eked out a living labouring on one of the large farms in the district. Wearing an old wide-brimmed straw hat on her head, her long skirts hitched up around her waist, she worked in the fields in all weathers, back bent, weeding or digging. She could wield a machete like a man and consequently could manage heavy, better paid work that traditionally was reserved for men.

Mama had no ambitions for herself.

"Mi? Mi kyaan evn write mi nyame! Is oonu why mi wuk! Is oonu is mi fyoocha!"

She held high hopes for her children, especially Becca. Her daughter was not going to do any farm work, not as long as she, Mama was alive! She must go to school, make something of herself! All her children must get an education, must have a chance to better themselves. This was what she worked for, slaved for.

Becca was Mama's favourite child, her eyeball. Becca helped her in the house, helped her in the field, and also did well at school. When she won a scholarship to the high school in Northfield Mama's chest swelled with pride. Becca became the model for Ray and Tiny, the yardstick against which their behaviour was measured. Between scoldings, beatings and other means of motivation, Mama hoped with all her heart that Tiny and Ray would do as well as Becca.

Ray had been in primary school for three years when the worst drought in years struck the western parishes of the island. Deprived of rain from March to August, every living thing turned brown and shrivelled up in the ground. Every farmer sustained ruinous losses. Dust blew everywhere, dressing crops, bushes and trees in a red-brown film until Red Hill resembled a village cast in clay.

Rain came eventually, and farmers began to plant. Heavy downpours watered the soil, flooded the newly planted seeds and roots, washing away nearly everything in the ground.

Mama's employer laid off one-third of his workers, Mama included. With all the farmers in the district facing the same predicament, she could not find work anyplace. Her small savings soon disappeared, used up to buy food and seeds to plant in her own food patch. With no money for fees, she was forced to stop sending Ray and Tiny to school.

Pride prevented her from borrowing money from anyone in Red Hill, and besides, many of her neighbours were in similar difficulties. They were all faced with the prospect of hunger.

Mama humbled herself and begged help from Nathan Caldwell, a distant cousin who lived in the north of the parish. Maas Nathan's farm was well-established and prosperous. Moreover, he had not suffered such severe losses as farmers in the south. He lent Mama the handsome sum of five pounds, which she promised to pay back as soon as she could.

Just about the time her former employer was beginning to take back workers, Mama got sick. She had fever, she raved in delirium, she could not keep down food. Her strong body shrank to skin and bone. Neighbours brought goat head soup and fish tea, and every kind of bush remedy to give Mama strength. The children prayed fervently to God to spare her life and save them from being orphaned. Physically nourished and spiritually reinforced, Mama threw off the fever and began to recover.

By the time Mama was on her feet again, all the borrowed money was gone.

As soon as she was able to make the journey, she went back to Maas Nathan and was granted another loan, this time on the condition that she sent one of her sons to help on his farm. Mama returned to Red Hill and went straight back to bed, weakened by agitation of mind.

What was she to do? She could not manage without the borrowed money; yet she knew that compliance with Nathan meant committing one of her sons to virtual slavery. Every soul in Red Hill would condemn her; she would never hear the end of how she had sold her pickni for five pounds. But what else could she do?

She took Ray aside and told him she was sending him to stay with Maas Nathan for a while. She made a small bundle of his clothes and put him on a donkey cart heading north, giving instructions to the driver to leave him at Nathan's farm. Becca and Tiny watched Ray's departure, each of them wishing they had been chosen to go. Silent and glassy-eyed, Mama watched the cart until it disappeared from sight over the brow of Red Hill.

"Yu tink yu kom fi stay fi a wile? Is so yu tink? Mi sorri fi yu! Is wuk yu kom fi du bwoy, wuk!"

For the whole of his first week at Maas Nathan's farm Ray cried. He cried for Mama, for Becca, for Tiny, even for Red Hill itself. The unfamiliar place, the strange people, and most of all the hard labour, overwhelmed him. He woke most nights shivering and lay awake till daybreak grieving.

Why him? What had he done to Mama? Why had she sent him

away when he was the youngest and the smallest? His brother was tiny in name only; he was in fact older and also bigger physically. He felt that Mama had thrown him away like an unwanted dog, and he could find no understanding for her actions in his heart.

Life on the farm was hard. Ray rose each day at dawn to feed the animals and then worked in the fields. He learned how to fork the ground, how to plough, how to weed and fertilize crops, when to plant and when to reap. As the weeks and months passed, the skin on his hands grew tough and his arms strong from lifting and carrying loads.

Comfort had come to Ray in the person of Miss Lea, a woman of roughly Mama's age who worked as a helper in Maas Nathan's house, cooking, washing and ironing. Miss Lea had taken in the blank eyes, the unsmiling face, the rigidity of his young frame and had responded with compassion.

"Poor maddaless pickni!" she would say, and shake her head with a sigh. How could a woman send away her child? she wondered. She had a daughter Ray's age and nothing, no circumstance, could bring her to part with her. As for Maas Nathan, he was just as bad. He was a widower, it was true, and not used to looking after children, but he could do much better by the child. The poor boy was left to fend for himself like a yard dog, taking food where he could find it, and sleeping on Maas Nathan's back porch on a bed of sacking. What a disgrace!

The nurturing instinct was strong in Miss Lea and it drew her to Ray. She took him under her wing. She saw to it that he ate proper meals. She made sure he bathed regularly and changed his clothing, which she washed, ironed and mended. She gave him small gifts from the kitchen, a piece of cornmeal pudding, a gizzada, or a sweet, hard, coconut drop. Her kindness thawed Ray's heart. Grateful for her attention, he opened up to her. He became her friend and unofficial helper and lost the feeling of being alone in the world.

By the age of fourteen Ray was a youth of considerable physical strength and skill. He had made the best of his years on Maas Nathan's farm. He had learned everything he possibly could about crop cultivation and animal husbandry and he dreamed of one day owning a farm of his own. He had made friends among the other workers, particularly with Don, a youth a few years older than he who shared his love of sport. It was Don who taught him to play cricket, Don who took him fishing and birdshooting, Don who took him to his first dance.

Don was ambitious too. One of his uncles had migrated to Cuba and become wealthy. Don planned to follow in his uncle's footsteps, if not to Cuba, then maybe to Panama or America. He involved Ray, a more than willing collaborator, in his plans to escape from the hard toil and scant rewards of the farm labourer's life.

It was Don who began to question Ray's continued presence on Maas Nathan's farm. It was common knowledge that Ray had come there to work in return for a loan made to his mother, though the precise amount of the loan was not known. How long would it take to work off the loan? An obvious question, and an important one which had not occurred to Ray until Don asked him. Ray didn't know the answer, Miss Lea didn't know either. Perhaps the best person to ask was Mama but Ray hadn't seen her since he left home five years earlier. She hadn't once come to visit him, and he, having hardened his heart against her, had not gone back to visit her either. He decided to confront Maas Nathan on the matter.

Maas Nathan was vexed by Ray's enquiry but his response was clear: "Bwoy, mi wasn't gwain tell yu dis, God's troot. Mi neva want distress yu. Mi did sen go tel yuh madda seh shi fi kom an tek yu fram laas yiir. An shi did sen bak an tel mi fi kiip yu, kaas shi kyaan manij fi tek yu now. Shi seh shi hav yuh bredda a-giv er trubbl an shi no want no more bwoy-pickni roun er fi badda er. An shi seh dat sins yu no hav nowhere els fi go, yu fi stay yasso, same way."

As he listened to Maas Nathan speak a burning heat rose up in Ray and spread up through his veins to his head. He felt to put his fist through Maas Nathan's face, to smash the plump, dark flesh of his jaw and see the blood flow. Instead, he ran from him, ran from the farm into nearby woodland, sobbing.

What kind ov madda mi hav? Shi noh hav haart? Shi nat flesh an blood? Den how shi triit mi soh, lakka animal widout sens nor feelin?

He found no answers as he leaned against the guava tree weeping.

What kind ov man is Maas Nathan? If mi wuk aaf mi madda debt from laas yiir, how kom im doan giv mi nuo pay yet?

For hours Ray remained under the tree, drawing comfort from its silvery trunk. By the time he returned to the farm he knew what he would do. The following Friday evening, on the pretext of going to a dance in the neighbouring district, Ray left Maas Nathan's farm for good with only the clothes he wore and a few shillings given to him by Don in his pocket.

He was twenty when he arrived in Rocky Gap. For six years he had roamed the parish, remaining in no place for very long.

Finding work and a place to stay was easy. Getting to know people, making friends was much, much harder. People in that part of the island were clannish, it was a known fact. Outsiders were distrusted, even if they were from a neighbouring district. Ray grew used to isolation; he was so accustomed to it that to him, loneliness was a normal everyday feeling.

He could never explain why he eventually chose to settle in Rocky Gap. Perhaps it was the gentle, rolling landscape. Perhaps the calm rhythm of life in the village soothed his restless spirit. Perhaps it was the pleasure of playing with one of the best cricket teams in the parish. Or maybe he was held by bonds of association with the Partridge family.

※ ※ ※

The rapid pit-a-pat of rain on zinc; food, warm and heavy in his belly; the dimly lit room and soft shadows on the wall: all this induced in Ray a mood of contemplation. He was thinking about the drought, assessing the damage already done to the crop, wondering how much good the rain would do at this late stage.

Man, the life of a cultivator was tough! He sighed, allowing himself a moment of self-pity. It was not humanly possible to work harder. Yet here he was, facing the possibility of destitution, with a pregnant woman to provide for and a baby due at any second.

His eyes followed Esme as she moved around, creating order in preparation for the close of the day. He hadn't planned to settle down so soon. He hadn't planned on woman, house, child quite so soon.

Esme, ripe with allure, had simply stepped into the centre of his life, taken hold of it and reshaped it.

Ray had been courting Rosa Partridge when her younger sister Esme caught and held his attention. At that time Esme was a quiet, contained young woman, whose dark brown eyes darted knowing, side-long glances, making Ray feel that she knew his secrets. Her sand-coloured face was wide at the cheekbones and narrow at the jaw, with slanted eyes which gave her a catlike appearance. Her short, plump body gave an impression of strength confirmed by her movements which were brisk and energetic. Nevertheless she was a very feminine woman. Her close-fitting blouses emphasised the fullness of her breasts and her skirts gathered tightly at the waist to show the wide flare of her hips. She smelt like a sweet, powdery flower, exuding an aura of sensuality which few men could ignore.

Ray had known Esme without paying her much attention until the Easter fair at Wide River, about a year after his return from America. The fair was a major annual event, attended by everyone in the parish with the means of getting to the small town. Older folks travelled in buggies and donkey carts, while others rode horses or bicycles, or shanks pony, according to their means.

On the morning of the fair groups of young people set out on foot to walk the distance from Stony Gap to Wide River. All of them were dressed to kill but Ray was sharper than a flick-knife in a brightly coloured shirt with a pattern of parrots and palm fronds, neatly pressed trousers, two-tone shoes purchased in New York, and a Panama straw hat. He took to the road with a group including Rosa, who clung to his arm, Matthew, Jimmy, Paul, Harold and their sweethearts, Elvira, Molly, Sarah and Esme with her companion, Junior Brewster. As they walked along the dusty narrow road leading out of Stony Gap they passed other groups who chattered and sang as they walked, like flocks of brilliantly coloured, babbling birds gathering together in preparation for migration.

The road to Wide River followed the line of the coast, and the sea could be glimpsed, a glistening deep turquoise blue shining through trees which separated the beach from the road. It was a beautiful morning, the sunlight brilliantly clear, the air not yet hot. Majestic flame-of-the-forest, their blossom startlingly scarlet against the blue of the sky, lined the road like giant soldiers. Pink bindweed climbed up tree trunks, intertwined with huge yellow buttercups. Delicately tinted orchids hung on slender stems from branches of trees already laden with lush, green foliage and even more luscious fruit: breadfruit trees with large, lustrous leaves and heavy, green globes; ackee trees with vermillion pods waiting to pop and reveal their yellow fruit; huge mango trees covered with yellow-brown blossom, like miniature trees themselves. Who could fail to feel joyous on such a morning, with nature exploding in abundance all around, and the promise of a day of pleasure just a few short miles ahead?

Ray's party arrived in Wide River well before noon. They headed for the centre of town, to a large clearing bordered by trees and bushes where the fair was to take place. A circle of stalls had been erected around the clearing and vendors were plying all manner of wares, foods and beverages. There was fried fish and bammy, mackerel rundown rich with coconut milk and served with green bananas. There was curry goat and rice, jerk pork, roast yam and saltfish, fried plantains, johnny cakes and roast breadfruit. There were gizzadas filled with gooey, sugary grated coconut, ginger cake, ginger beer, lemonade, carrot juice and rum punch. There were vendors selling dress material, trinkets, eau-de-Cologne, khus-khus water, bay rum and liniment. There were stalls piled high with straw hats, frothy crochet runners, embroidered tablecloths and handtowels. Vendors tried to tempt passers-by with smiles and soft persuasion calculated to ensure that nobody left that day with money in their pocket.

The fair was opened in the early afternoon by the parish priest, an unhappy-looking Englishman with shiny, yellowy skin. After exhorting the revellers to behave with Christian decorum, he blessed them and declared the fair open in the names of God, the King and the British Empire.

The fairground was filled with people from all over the parish and neighbouring districts—black people, red people, yellow people, brown people, white people. Men who had not met since the last fair slapped each other on the back in greeting, exchanged news and stories and drank rum punch together. Women passed each other smiling politely and saying how-you-do, or stopped to admire each other's dress, to chat a little before moving on. Young men eyed pretty women, bold women eyed the young men, pick-pockets eyed everyone. Old people armed themselves with food and drink and sought comfortable, shady places to sit, while groups of children roamed from stall to stall, using guile or sleight of hand to obtain their share of the sweet things so temptingly displayed.

In the late afternoon a band took up position under an awning and began to play. Within moments people had gathered to dance. The band opened with a selection of the waltzes and quadrilles favoured by the older folk. Then came the lighter, livelier mento and the popular calypsos which drew all ages to dance. Men with straight backs and heads held high moved snaked-hipped and graceful. Women dipped and swayed with one hand on waist while the other lifted their skirt high, winding up and down in a teasing motion belied by modestly downcast eyes.

Ray was among the first to start dancing, with Rosa as his partner. He loved to dance, loved the traditional songs and popular tunes the band played. He was inexhaustible. The dancing became spirited and Rosa retired to catch her breath. Her place was filled by Esme who, like Ray, was tireless. Her campanion, Junior, had two left feet and no sense of rhythm. She left him to keep Rosa company and moved towards Ray, her face glowing in anticipation of pleasure.

She was dazzling that afternoon. Her sister Molly had made her a new dress of soft red cotton, a deep, vibrant red which complemented the yellow tones of her skin. The fabric hugged her breasts and flared out from her small waist, emphasised by a wide black belt. Her hair, pressed and curled especially for the occasion, shone with pomade, while her lips, striking red in her sand-coloured face, smiled in acknowledgment of her allure.

Ray liked the way she leaned against him as they danced. He felt a tension in his throat and congestion in his groin and had no doubt at all that Esme was aware of the effect she had on him. The band played a popular calypso and they danced body to body, movements guided by the lilting tempo of this Caribbean music, sometimes throwing back their heads to laugh at the clever, suggestive lyrics of a song, next moment engrossed in the perfect synchronisation of their limbs. They were well-matched and they took pleasure in it, to the annoyance of at least two spectators.

"Look pon yuh sista winin up erself gainst Ray," muttered Junior angrily to Rosa.

Rosa was too proud to demean herself by appearing jealous, though she was smarting in anger at her sister and, if truth were told, at Ray. She moved away from the dancing, turning her back on the revellers, unwittingly giving Esme and Ray permission to continue.

"Wait til I kech dat likkl bich!" She muttered as she walked away, imagination fired with malice. She felt slighted by Ray's lack of consideration for her feelings. She would never expect anything different of her sister, but she expected better of Ray.

Eventually Esme and Ray retired from the dance, hot and thirsty and needing to rest their feet. Ray bought rum punch for them both and found a place for them to sit away from the crowd, on a fallen tree trunk. They fell into an easy, flirtatious banter.

"Soh tel mi; what goin on bitwiin yu an Junior?"

Esme laughed and shook her head.

"Nottn too serius."

Any member of her family overhearing this exchange would have been astonished. Everyone in the family believed that Junior and Esme would settle down together eventually. Junior himself would not have believed his ears, for he had been courting Esme quietly but steadily for months and thought of her as his future wife. What had come over her? And why did Ray believe her? He had seen her with Junior countless times and up until that moment had assumed they were a couple, as did everyone in Rocky Gap.

Perhaps it was the rum, perhaps it was the heat and excitement of the dancing. Suddenly, Esme decided she wanted Ray, never mind Junior, never mind Rosa. She had always liked him. She liked his ambition, his adventurousness, the way he was willing to work hard to get what he wanted from life. She sensed in him a fiery, volatile spirit which excited and attracted her.

At that moment Ray was not certain what he wanted from Esme. She had tantalised him while they were dancing and he would have liked to take her into the bush to see if she could fulfill her mute promises. Rosa crossed his mind and he felt a twinge of conscience. There was bound to be a scene between the sisters later; the thought of this made him hesitate. Knowing the family as well as he did, he had no wish to be the cause of animosity and he had no wish to get caught up in any hostilities.

The matter was resolved by Esme. Sensing his hesitation, she leaned heavily against him and rested her hand on his thigh, making a direct appeal to his senses. In response, Ray pulled her to him, his hand travelling up the hollow of her spine to touch her neck, follow the line of her shoulder and rest softly on her breast. They kissed, a warm sweet kiss of exploration. Then, as though by mutual agreement, they rose and went to find a more private place.

Chapter 2

"**M**AAS STANLEY DAAG WAS OVA here agen.**" Talking to no-one in particular, Ruby's nasal voice rose above the sound of the rain. "Im chase di fowl-dem roun di yaad, a-baak an a-jump up an down like im kraizi." She paused a while, hoping for a response, then continued.

"One ov di hen soh fraid, shi run til shi drop ova di hill. Yu shudda hiir er a-sqaak an a-mek nise!" Another pause, this time for dramatic effect. "Poor likkl ting." Ruby's voice faded away dolefully.

Immersed in thoughts of his own troubles, Ray had little sympathy to spare for a hen.

"Yu mus taak to Maas Stanley bout dat daag, yu knuo Ray." Esme pulled out a chair and sat down, leaning back and stretching out her legs in front of her. "Evri odda day im kom ova di fence an du som damij. An Maas Stanley neva yet pay fa eniting im daag du."

She watched his face. He was distracted, she could tell. The crease between his eyebrows, the unfocussed gaze; the way he sat with elbows on the table and shoulders hunched, were signs of worry, of some anxiety not yet shared with her. He had been troubled for some time, worn out and exhausted by the drought. Now it was raining, she thought his heaviness would lift.

She felt weary herself. The energetic movement of the child inside her robbed her of sleep at nights, and the physical burden of it drained her normally formidable energy. The child was due at any moment but she avoided facing the prospect of its birth, as though denial would somehow delay the event. She sat with her hands on her belly as if to control the child's moving limbs by her touch. It a-kom soon, she thought, too soon. She was not ready.

The months during which Ray had courted her, the months before she knew she was pregnant, were the happiest of Esme's life. They had spent every spare moment together, walking in the woodlands or seeking out-of-the-way places where they could lie together, explore each other's bodies, make love. Not to mention the dances and cricket matches and the evenings spent on Molly's verandah just talking.

During that time Ray was building his house. Esme felt certain from the start that when the house was completed they would get married and move in together. With this future in mind she encouraged and helped him wherever possible. She advised him how the rooms should be laid out; where the kitchen should be, which direction the verandah should face, where to locate the bathhouse and the latrine. To tell the truth, she would have liked a bigger house, but Ray was careful with his money, did not want to waste it on extravagances such as additional, unneccesary rooms.

Word soon travelled around Rocky Gap that Esme and Ray were carrying straw, and only Junior Brewster and Doc Partridge were averse to the match. Junior wore his broken heart on his sleeve, hanging around Molly's house for weeks after the Wide River fair, hoping to waylay Esme and persuade her to come back to him.

Doc Partridge, however, had objected to Ray on principle.

"Is dat blak monkey bwoy yu tek up wid?" Doc's voice was loud and cutting; it cracked like a whip and could hurt like one at times. Esme had expected Doc to raise the issue of Ray's colour sooner or later and she had prepared herself not to react.

"Yu noh hav nuo ambishun! I only hope yu noh plan fi giv mi nuo monkey granpickni!"

Doc Partridge's contempt for black-skinned people was well known. He made no secret of his bigotry, even though his two wives and several of his numerous mistresses were dark-skinned. His own skin was a pallid yellowish shade, the colour of faded coconut matting. If he knew that black-skinned people despised his colour as much as he did theirs he did not care. It bothered him not one whit that to their eyes he might look unfinished, like half-baked bread.

Esme made no effort to change her father's opinion or to argue with him. She simply continued to see Ray. In fact, she hardly let him out of her sight. She found time in the day to watch him working. She met him in the evenings, to spend the quiet dark hours in his company. On Saturday evenings they joined up with other couples going to spree in Wide River or nearby Northfields. She went to cricket matches on Sunday afternoons, travelling to neighbouring districts with the Rocky Gap team in whatever way they travelled, whether by foot, by cart or by truck, carrying food and drink for Ray and herself in her basket.

The times Esme enjoyed most, the times she recalled and relived when unhappy circumstances arrived, were those nights spent in company on the beach, eating fish roasted over impromptu fires, bathing in the warm, dark, velvet waters of the sea, then lying with Ray on the sand and gazing up at the star-filled sky.

Esme discovered she was pregnant only four months after their first dance. It was not a welcome development, but Esme, being a practical woman, wasted little time in regret. Part of her gladly acknowleged that a child would bind her closer to Ray. She did not long for motherhood or see fulfilment in the addition of children to her life. Rather, she saw having a child as part of the process of catching and keeping Ray. She knew instinctively that the sweet times she and Ray shared would become fewer and fewer but she told herself that this was how it had to be, bracing herself mentally for the changes which would inevitably follow.

By the time the house was finished the parish was already in the grip of drought. The water tank Ray had sunk so proudly in the ground stood empty and Esme was faced with the task of preparing a newly built house for occupation with water begged from a neighbour and carried in buckets three hundred yards uphill. Esme was no stranger to hard work; she worked like a labourer, with Ruby, her helper, until the new floors gleamed and all traces of dust and rubble had been removed from the house and its surroundings.

They had very little furniture to start with. Ray had made them a table and a wooden bed and they bought a brand new mattress in Wide River, but the other few pieces they possessed, they had begged. A pretty, dark-stained dressing table with a curved front and oval mirrors had come from Doc's house. He let Esme have it only because it had belonged to her mother. He didn't want that monkey-boy using anything of his, he told Esme. Aunt Hyacinth grudgingly gave them two rickety old chairs which had stood in her yard for years. Ray made wedges to balance them; dem wi' du til wi kyan du betta, he said. Esme agreed, feeling already blessed with plenty.

As the end of her term approached Esme grew impatient with the discomfort of pregnancy. She refrained from grumbling in Ray's presence, but when she and Ruby were alone, she complained at length.

"Mi noh knuo if mi kyan eva go tru dis agen," she grumbled. "Mi kyaan sliip, mi kyaan stan up, mi kyan haadli waak widout bendin ova!"

Ruby was sweeping out the kitchen with brisk, rhythmic strokes. She murmured sympathetically in response, even though privately she thought Esme was having an easy time. No vomiting, no health problems and an understanding husband as well!

"But yu lucki, Miss Esme, yu noh hav nuo problem. It look like yu just gwain drop di baby. Like yu mek fi briidin." Ruby bent over to scoop up the kitchen debris and stepped out into the heat of the yard to dispose of it. Esme leaned against the doorpost and sighed petulantly.

"If yu kud fiil how dis baby foot a-jook mi inna mi belly, yu wudn't taak bout luck!"

Noh badda long out yuh lip afta mi, gyal, thought Ruby. Yu tink mi gwine fiil sorri fi yu? If yu neva want pickny, wat yu go tek up wid man fa?

She stepped back into the house almost brushing past Esme.

"Yu noh tek aafta yu madda at aal, at aal," she said cheerfully. "Evri time shi faal prignant, it was non-stop sikniss an problem. Shi jus neva mek fi it, an shi did hav too meni of oonu. Nuo wonder Harold did kill er!"

"Ruby, yu is a wikkid bitch! Yu a-taak bout mi madda jus fi frighten mi!"

Hearing a tremour of genuine fear in Esme's voice, seeing a shadow cross her eyes, Ruby realised she had gone too far. She hadn't really intended to upset Esme, aggravating though she was. She patted Esme's back, adopted a soothing tone and told her to lie down and relax, take a nap; she would feel better after a rest.

Esme lay on her bed trying one position after another in a ceaseless search for comfort, feeling thankful that the bedroom was cool. Its small window, permanently shaded by a short length of plaid cloth, let in a sea breeze which blew right onto the bed.

Dat Ruby was a bitch fi troo! She was thinking. What mek er bring up Madda name if not maliss? Jus wach mi an shii!

Esme hardly ever thought of her mother. Sara Partridge died young giving birth to Harold, her fourth child and Esme's junior by two years. People still talked about how Doc Partridge had buried two wives in the space of seven years, and how he had grown fearsomely miserable and feisty after the second one passed away. Esme couldn't remember her mother, but she remembered those years with Doc. He was left with fourteen children to raise and he was determined to do it alone.

"Mi done wid marrij di day Sara bury," he was fond of saying. "Mi decide on dat day seh mi nat givin anodda woman di chance fi ded pon mi!"

Some people said Sara died from overwork. Doc already had ten children when she married him, a heavy handful for any woman, and Doc gave her little or no assistance with them. And then she had four of her own, almost one after another, draining her strength.

After she died Doc wasn't able to cope with them either, for all his bravado. Molly and Rosa, the two eldest girls helped to mind the young ones and run the house, but they also had to go to school. A succession of domestic helpers came and went; none stayed longer than a few months. The burden of work, the number of children and Doc's cantankerous nature drove them away.

People in Rocky Gap noticed Sara's children going to school with uncombed hair and soiled clothes, looking rough and uncared for. Rumours began to circulate about how Doc was neglecting the young ones and how the older ones were ill-treating them. These rumours reached the ears of Sara's elder sister Hyacinth, who lived just outside Rocky Gap with her husband Maas Jimmy Henry, one of Rocky Gap's more prosperous sons. Maas Jimmy owned a hardware store in Wide River and lived with Hyacinth and their three children in a large house he had built with his own hands. He owned the five acres of farm land on which his house was built and he owned acres more in Rocky Gap itself. By anyone's standards he was a prosperous man.

Maas Jimmy and Miss Hyacinth were well respected in the district by all but Doc Partridge.

"Dem piipl is hipocrit, yaa!" Doc never minced words. "Dem go a-church on Sunday and praise God an gwan like dem holy, an di rest ov di week dem praise Mamon an worship moni!"

The truth of the matter was that Maas Jimmy and Miss Hyacinth were God-fearing people who prized the virtues of industry and discipline above all others. They were zealous in their desire to praise the Lord and do His will, and tireless in their execution of good deeds and charitable acts within their community. When the condition of Sara's children was brought to their atention they resolved to do their duty as Christians, to take the children and give them a home and to raise them to know God.

Miss Hyacinth liked Doc no more than he liked her, and she expected to have difficulty persuading him to part with the children. Doc, however, was a practical man when it suited him. He sat on his verandah facing his sister-in-law and listened while she explained to him in a nervous voice why she and her husband felt they should take his four youngest children off his hands.

Miss Hyacinth was nervous because she knew he was perfectly capable of insulting her or chasing her off his property with curses, or both. To her relief he did neither of those things. Instead he nodded his head thoughtfully when she had finished speaking. He admitted he could hardly manage to look after so many children and he agreed that the young ones needed a woman's care. Less than an hour later Paul, Elvira, Esme and Harold left their father's house to live with Aunt Hyacinth and Maas Jimmy.

The children had no choice other than to adapt to their new circumstances without fuss or protest. Resistance would have been pointless, drawing down scoldings and beatings. They were fed, clothed and sent to school and they were expected to help around the house and yard when not in school.

This was neither new to them nor surprising nor even unpleasant. They had much greater difficulty adjusting to the ways of a religious household. Each day began with prayers and each meal was preceded by grace. On Sundays everybody went to church looking clean and groomed in Sunday-best clothes; the girls in floral print dresses and straw hats, the boys in starched white shirts and ties, long trousers and shoes which Paul was made to polish to a high shine.

Doc's children were compliant enough with Miss Hyacinth's desire that they should learn prayers, sing hymns and read the Bible regularly, but their aunt sensed that their efforts were not sincere. She knew it would be a hard task to bring these children to God. She blamed their blaspheming father for their ignorance and prayed that his children would grow to see the light of God. In the meantime, she and Maas Jimmy applied a firm discipline which was intended to wither any budding inclinations to sin.

Esme however, needed special treatment. Or so said Aunt Hyacinth.

"Dat pickni, shi hav di devil in er, smaal though shi bi! Jus luk in er two eye! Yu noh sii Satan shinin, bright an bold as sin?"

Yes, sin! In Aunt Hyacinth's mind six years old was not too young for sin, not at all, and Aunt Hyacinth saw it as her duty to ensure that Esme learned godliness and humility.

Esme never properly understood what her sins were or why she needed to learn humility. Neither did Aunt Hyacinth explain why Esme was given ugly sacklike dresses made out of nasty worn-out old clothes, and not Elvira. Or why she had more chores than the others. Or why she always got the pot bottom, the stick-up, burn-up food and the bony chicken back.

Or why Aunt Hyacinth beat her to within an inch of her life with a bamboo switch for taking a mash-up gizzada from a plate in the kitchen. A plate piled high with nearly two dozen perfect, newly baked gizzadas.

From that day Esme hated both gizzadas and Aunt Hyacinth. Perhaps the devil possessed her indeed, because from that day Esme showed the world that she knew how to carry malice. She let it glare from her eyes, shout in the tone of her voice, the set of her mouth, the sway of her walk. And no amount of beating could get it out of her.

Until she was old enough to walk the distance from Maas Jimmy's house to Rocky Gap, Esme saw very little of her father. This was neither a cause for celebration nor for regret, for even when she lived with him she had had very little direct contact with him. He was a name, a memory, hardly a person at all. It was Molly she missed. She had a special feeling for this sister, who was more like a mother to her than a sibling. Molly visited Miss Hyacinth's house regularly, sometimes with Matthew, or Paul or Rosa, but mostly alone. Molly was the link between the Partridge children at Maas Jimmy's and the rest of the family back in Rocky Gap. Doc relied on her for news of his children, and through her he sent whatever he had to contribute to their welfare: sometimes it was food from his fields, eggs or a chicken and, occasionally, money.

Esme loved Molly, admired her, but most of all, she envied her sister's accomplishments, for Molly was a talented and skilled seamstress. She ran a small but profitable business from her father's house initially, then later from her own house. She was independent, she had money, but she was lonely.

"Find a man an sekkl down!" This was the advice of her sister Sara, which Molly chose to ignore: she wasn't ready to take up that particular burden. She decided instead to take Esme to live with her.

Looking back, it seemed to Esme that her life really began after she moved in with Molly. Like a newly freed slave, she revelled in the freedom of choosing how to pass her time. She took charge of Molly's tiny house, willingly undertaking tasks which she had performed resentfully for Aunt Hyacinth. She discovered she too had a knack for sewing. She had left elementary school able to read a little and write a little and she had no ambition to continue her education. She was glad to find something she enjoyed doing which could also earn her money.

Esme took full advantage of the new, freer conditions of her life. She grew closer to her older brothers and sisters, particularly Matthew. She followed Matthew everywhere and hung around with him at the places where he met his friends, so she could get to know them too. Soon she was walking out with Vernon Palmer, one of Matthew's buddies, much to Molly's alarm.

"Mind yuself wid dat Palmer bwoy!" she warned Esme. "Mi noh want yu turn into nuo slak fuck-a-bush gyal inna fi-mi house. Mi noh wan nuo baastad pickni in ya eida!"

There was no need for Molly to worry about Esme: she was no-one's fool where men were concerned. She was attractive and she quickly acquired a number of admirers, but she was far more curious about her effect on them than about the young men themselves. Yet their admiring glances warmed her, their foolish sweet talk amused her. She felt important in their company, significant and desired and alive.

Esme was past twenty when Junior Brewster began to court her. From the first time he visited Molly's house Junior made it clear that he was seriously interested in Esme. Of medium height but strong and muscular, Junior was solid, slow and quiet. He reminded her of a big tree with spreading, sheltering branches. He was known to everybody in Rocky Gap and he was respected for his steadiness. Older people loved him. What a *mannersable* bwoy, they would say. Him not like di rest. Him hav *discipline*. Him hav *self respek*. These virtues, these cardinal qualities had drawn Esme to him like a hungry mouth to food, as though somehow she could ingest and digest and thus possess some of his ease of being, not recognising that it came simply and directly from being loved.

When Molly learned that Esme was giving up Junior for Ray, she could not believe it. For days she and Esme argued.

"Is dat wild-eye bwoy yu want deh wid? Yu gwine giv up a diicent bwoy like Junior fi *him*? Gal, yu sik wid yuh hed!"

"Is fi-mi life, an mi want mek sumting ov it," Esme argued back. "Junior noh hav nuo ambishun! Im gwain kyarri on same way, same likeim faada an fi-him faada before dat. Mi noh want dat kinda life at aal, at aal!"

Once Esme's mind was made up, that was that; she was her father's daughter in that respect. She saw a brighter future with Ray and held to that vision in the faces of Molly and Doc Partridge.

❈ ❈ ❈

The night the rain came, Esme slept fitfully beside Ray. Comfort eluded her. She tossed from one side to another, sat up, lay on her back, trying to find a position in which to rest. Deep into the night she started awake, jolted by a sharp pain low in her belly. Half-sitting, half-lying, she felt moisture seeping between her thighs to make a wet, warm circle in the mattress beneath her. Panic gripped her and she shook Ray roughly until he woke.

"Ray, wake up! Mi waters bruk! Wat du yu, man! Wake up!"

Ray dressed as fast as he could and hurried to wake Ruby, who slept at the back of the house. Rain fell gently, patting on the ground outside, slapping against the leaves on the trees he passed as he ran through the night to fetch Miss Amy, the midwife and Molly.

The child was born just before dawn, a plump little girl with a head of thick black hair. It was an easy birth, but it would have been hard to convince Esme of that as she lay limply in the bed, holding the baby to her. She was shattered, and weary, and she felt more than a little resentful of the child suckling so vigourously at her breast.

"Maasa God," she declared, "if mi haffi go tru wid dis nex time, no bodda mek mi hav eni more!"

Molly and Ray were sitting at the side of the bed, Ray watching the baby with amazement glowing in his face.

"Yu only a seh dat now," said Molly soothingly. "Yu soon chienj yuh mind!"

Esme watched the baby nursing, small jaws pumping, eyes shut tight. She touched the soft, new cheek with a finger and an unfamiliar emotion caught at her throat. She looked at Ray and almost smiled at the happiness in his face.

"Is fi-yu daata dis," she said to him. "Look pon er, noh? Shi is di ded stamp ov er faada!"

Chapter 3

BY THE TIME ESME REALISED things were going wrong with Ray, it was already too late to fix them. What registered first was a feeling of neglect. Ray, who used to love to come home at the end of the day, was spending hardly any time at home.

When she thought about it, she realised the problem began after the hurricane. Hurricane Charlie, they called it, the worst to hit the island in decades. It had ravaged the district, ripping roofs and walls from houses, felling trees and causing widespread floods. She would never forget crouching in terror under the lintel of the doorway to the kitchen, holding Tessa tightly to her. The house trembled, seemed fragile in the face of roaring winds which battered its walls for hours without cease. Tessa cried the whole time and Ruby, beside herself with fear, wailed and bawled, praying to God for mercy and deliverance.

No lives were lost in Rocky Gap, but terrible damage was done. Their house had miraculously remained intact, but their neighbours and relatives had been less fortunate. Maas Stanley's house had no roof or windows and he lost cattle and goats. His marauding dog had disappeared without a trace, sucked up into the eye of the hurricane.

Every farmer in the district lost crops to the high-velocity winds and flooding rain.

Standing in his scallion field the morning after the hurricane abated, surveying the remains, Ray felt his heart contract and sink like a boulder in his chest. Every plant lay flattened. Scallions almost ready for reaping lay spattered on the soil and the field was littered with debris borne downhill by streaming rainwater. From where he stood he could see into neighbouring fields and they all looked the same. The scale of destruction overwhelmed him, draining his spirit and robbing him of the will even to begin to clear the ground.

The men of Rocky Gap came together and formed work groups to lend assistance to those who needed help with rebuilding and repairs. Maas Jimmy's house had been severly damaged and Ray was one of a group of men helping with repairs. He worked his land until mid-afternoon, then went over to Maas Jimmy's to work until dark. Maas Jimmy made sure his helpers had food and drink after they had finished for the night and they would linger in his yard, talking, mulling over the effects of the hurricane, commiserating with each other, sometimes laughing and joking according to the mood of the evening. The men were there on Sundays also. They gave all their free time until the job was completed and then moved on to another house.

While Ray was working at Maas Jimmy's Esme would sometimes make her way there with Tessa, the baby. She sat in a corner of the yard chatting with her sister Vera until Ray was ready to leave. She enjoyed the camaraderie of the evening work sessions, whose atmosphere reminded her of the excursions she used to make with Ray and Matthew in the days before motherhood. She sat under a mango tree out of reach of the sun with Tessa on her lap, sharing gossip with her sister Vera, who still lived with Aunt Hyacinth and Maas Jimmy.

It was Vera who told her the men were saying she came to Maas Jimmy's to keep Ray under surveillance.

"Dem seh yu kyaan let im outta yuh sight; yu haffi hold on to im trousis foot," Vera told her, laughing at the thought. "But mi noh blame yu," she continued. "Yu kyaan trus eni man dese days."

"Iinhi?" Esme responded sarcastically. "So mi fi siddung inna yaad day in, day out? Mek dem knuo is *fi-mi* aanti yaad dis, mi bredda an sista dem liv right ya, soh if mi want fi kom an rest an chat likkl bit, what it hav fi do wid Ray? Dem too fast, yaa!"

Some weeks later, around Easter time, the work groups disbanded, having completed all the repairs they could manage. Around this time Ray began to stop at Peter's rum shop on his way home in the evening, to take a drink or two or maybe play a game of dominoes. The company of other men, their easy talk and occasional arguments warmed and lifted his spirits in this otherwise depressing time. By the time he left the bar and headed up the hill for home, he walked with spring in his step, whistling or singing as he went.

Esme hadn't minded the evening working sessions all that much. At least she knew precisely what Ray was doing and why. She felt differently about his evening stops at Peter's. It vexed her to know that he was relaxing in company, drinking and amusing himself while she was waiting in the house, waiting for him with nothing but a baby and stupid Ruby for company. Why couldn't he bring home his drink and relax with her?

Why had things changed? she wondered. Why couldn't they just pick up the old pattern their lives had followed before the hurricane?

A quiet voice began to whisper from within, tempting her with ugly thoughts. She ignored the voice to begin with, afraid or unwilling to hear its seductive message. It grew more insistent, gathering volume like a wind approaching from the sea until it filled her head and she could hear nothing else.

One afternoon as she was sitting in the yard preparing ackees for the evening meal, the voice shouted loud in her head. All at once she saw the truth of it with staggering clarity. Yes, of course; how could it be otherwise? Ray had another woman, he must have. As her hands separated the firm, yellow flesh of the ackees from their scarlet outer casings then detached the shiny black seeds from their centre, conviction grew, took on shape and detail converting the suspicions of her uneasy mind into full-blown fact.

Looking at her reflection in the old brown-tinged mirror in her bedroom she hardly recognised herself. What had happened to the shapely, seductive girl who had so effortlessly stolen Ray from Rosa?

Pregnancy had added weight and thickened her body. Even her face had a heavy look, made more so by the constant frown she now wore and the downward curve of her mouth. She was barely twenty-three, but she looked older. To her own eyes she was already mash-up.

She tested the notion of Ray's infidelity on Molly. They were sitting on Molly's verandah watching Tessa attempt to creep down the steps into the yard.

"Yu knuo what mi hiir?" she began casually, "mi hiir seh smaddy sii Ray komin outta bush wid Veda Walker."

Molly looked at her sister, startled and suspicious. "But who kud tell yu a ting like dat? Dem want mek mischiif in yuh life, is certain."

"Maybe not," responded Esme calmly. "Is Ruby dem was taakin to an dem neva knuo seh mi inna di hous a lissen."

"Well, mi noh knuo. Yu mus watch out fi dem bad-minded piipl who jus want fi sii yu an Ray mashup. Yu knuo how dem stay! Dem liv like puss an daag in fi-dem yaad, an dem kyaan stand fi sii how yu an Ray liv gud!"

"Yu tink a soh?" asked Esme.

"Iinhi, a soh!" replied Molly emphatically.

In her movements around Rocky Gap Esme kept a look-out for signs to substantiate her suspicions. She began to make regular trips to the field during the day, a development Ray initially mistook for a sign of renewed affection. She reviewed all the likely rivals in her mind. She had mentioned Veda Walker to Molly but only because that was the first name that sprang conveniently to her tongue. She had no reason to suspect Veda. In truth, she had no real reason to suspect any woman in Rocky Gap. Her only grounds, her only clues were Ray's persistent absence at evening time and his lack of interest in making plans for their wedding. With each passing day the vacuum inside her grew more demanding. Like a hungry, malevolent spirit it needed something to feed on to keep it alive, while she, its creator and host, required something to blame for its existence.

Tessa had grown into a plump toddler and was learning to walk on fat, wobbly legs. She followed her mother around the yard crawling with the speed of a land crab, or running in short unsteady spurts to grab her mother's skirts. Tessa laughed delightedly when she toppled over and fell on her plump behind. She gurgled and chortled obligingly, charming everyone who came by her.

Ray loved her with that special, tender, incredulous love that fathers sometimes have for their daughters. Every evening he bathed and put on fresh clothes, then sat and played with Tessa, dancing her on his knees, throwing her in the air, teasing her until she convulsed with laughter, arms waving, feet kicking, face creased with smiles. Esme's love was less joyful, less obvious. Anxiety, the negative drift of her mind and her resulting weariness of spirit robbed her of joy in her child. She felt perpetually tired, resticted not only by the chores and responsibilities of motherhood, by also by plain lack of energy.

"Mi lov mi baby yu knuo but bwoy, mi kyaan stan dis siddung-inna-hous bisniss!" she confided to Molly. "Mi taak to Ruby til mi tieyad an kyaan stand er eni langa! Somtime mi just wish mi was single agen. Dem times, mi neva hav nuo worries!"

"Baby is nuo eesi ting, yu knuo Esme," replied Molly, busy with sewing. "Espeshali if yu gwain look afta dem gud!"

"But dat is aal mi do! Mi haadli sii Ray! Mi haadli get fi go eni place! Is just hous an baby, hous an baby fram one day to anodda! Laad, man, mi kyaan tek it!

"Is dat yu eatin up yusself bout?" asked Molly bluntly. "Yu did expek sweet life, dancin an sportin worl widout end? Daalin, a noh soh it goh! Man wi nice yu up til dem ketch yu. Evriting is swiitniss til dem hav yu where dem want yu. Den when dem reddi, dem jus gaan bout dem bisniss!" She put down the dress to thread a needle.

"Mind yu," she began, biting off a length of thread with her teeth, "Ray wuk haad. Yu kyan haadli blame im if im stop by Maas Peter now an agen fi tek a drink an relax. But yu si mi? Mi noh badda mi hed bout man, evn dough all ov oonu hav mi aaf as ole maid!" Squinting into the light, she poked the thread through the eye of the needle.

"Nuo matta how dem gud an how dem nice, man mek haad wuk fi woman. But since yu done mek pickni wid dis one alredi, yu might as well sekkl yuself an mek di best ov it. If yu karri on misrabl wid im, de nex ting yu knuo im get up an liiv yu fi anodda woman fi tru!"

Molly's words lingered in Esme's mind like a haunting refrain. Of course, she had realised from the start that the good times with Ray would not go on forever. But they had ended so soon, like an eagerly desired but too small serving of some delectable food, before she had had enough. In moments when clarity penetrated the mesh of emotion she could see she was the creator of her misery. But she was too weak to withstand her own demon. Her will was malnourished; it lacked the vigour, the strength and the optimism she needed to control it. Instead she let loose her resentment on Ray.

Communication between them degenerated into terse, monosyllabic exchanges. To his bewilderment, Ray found himself living with a stranger whose moods and tempers were beyond his understanding, who snubbed his attempts at conversation and who stiffened under his touch if he reached out to her. Her behaviour confused him.

The preceding year had been pure toil for Ray. Like Sisyphus pushing his rock uphill, Ray was locked in a struggle against the forces of nature. Day after day he laboured, replanting crops and tending them, striving to make them yield, hoping that he might recoup some of the losses caused by the hurricane.

Esme's strange behaviour weighed on his mind, adding to his worries. The change in her baffled him. She had been so supportive in the beginning. She was a sweet influence in his life then: lover, comforter, harbour. He had felt at the centre of her life, the focus of her attention and care, which she had given without reserve. Now, her coldness numbed him, her sarcasm hurt him and her bitterness increasingly made him angry.

Particularly in bed. Every night he lay beside her turned back. He had to persuade her to let him touch her and plead with her to make love with him. If she complied it was with the minimum of responsiveness. Was it surprising that they quarrelled? Nothing loud enough or angry enough to lead them to the root of their conflict, but terse, bitter exchanges which gradually, block by block, formed an impenetrable wall between them.

Chapter 4

WHEN TESSA WAS EIGHTEEN MONTHS old Esme found she was pregnant again and immediately sank into depression. Hoping to remedy her condition, she drank bush tea of every kind. In spite of gripping pains in her gut and bowel, the teas failed to take effect and she grew angry, with the kind of anger that festers in the stomach. Bad thoughts clouded her spirit, colouring everything negative: everybody and every circumstance. Worst of all, she felt nauseous all the time. Ordinary domestic odours made her retch — cooking smells, floor polish, the smell of rum on Ray's breath when he came home at night.

Ray also suffered, contaminated by Esme who moved around the house enveloped in a toxic silence. If he spoke to her she barked back at him, if he touched her she shook off his hand as though he were the poisonous one. He resolved to spend more of his evenings at home in the hope of placating her, but night after night they sat on the verandah in the warm dark, not speaking, their silence covered by the evening call of insects and birds and the occasional quiet rustle of leaves.

Ray wanted to talk to Esme, to break the taut barrier of silence separating them. More than anything he wanted to know what this thing was that was eating her up and threatening to consume him too. He needed to tell her the problems sitting like weights on his head. But how could he when she sat across from him, remote and chilly yet magnetic as a polar star?

He was afraid of her. She had laughed with scorn when he told her he suspected his field hand was robbing him. She turned her head away when he said he saw signs of the onset of another drought. He felt she had withdrawn from him all love, all care, all concern. He felt lonely.

From the time he first began to cultivate his land, Ray had hired Bobby Brewster to work with him full-time. Bobby was a tough, simple-minded little man with leathery red-brown skin and watery red eyes, the consequence of habitual rum drinking. He could be heard excercising his tongue most nights at Peter's, whose rum-and-water was Bobby's favourite lubricant.

Every night at Peter's rum shop there was a core of regulars who stopped by to wet their throats and ease off some of the day's accumulated weariness. In the daytime the shop sold general provisions and served Rocky Gap's women as a general store, but after sunset the shop was male territory. Men sat on wooden crates and rough benches in front of the shop, under the wide branches of a mango tree which, to the relief of Peter's patrons, had survived successive storms and hurricanes. Men felt at ease at Peter's. Here the talk ranged from local gossip to national and international politics. It was here many of them learned what was going on in the world, for none of them owned a radio and few could read a newspaper. Men brought back news from neighbouring areas of who was selling land, who was buying it, who was sick or dying, or getting married. Personal problems were also aired: money problems, work problems, woman problems. Peter knew the state of heart of virtually every customer and was frequently advisor to a worried man who had nowhere else to take his troubles.

Peter's provided Ray with a temporary refuge from the problems he felt converging on him. All the men who drank at Peter's worked the ground; anxiety about the weather, concern about prices, about crop yields, were the worries they all shared and discussed daily. On the heels of one such discussion Matthew Partridge drew Ray to one side and quietly told him he had seen Bobby Brewster digging in one of his fields late one evening, long after the end of the working day.

Ray began to keep a close watch on Bobby. He took to walking along the far side of his fields occasionally, the side by which Bobby left the field, as it was down the slope of the hill and nearer to his house.

On one of these excursions Ray met Bobby leaving the field with a heavy sack over his shoulder.

"What yu doin a ground soh late, Bobby?" asked Ray, blocking his path.

"Mi did liiv som ov mi tings behind, soh mi did just go bak fi dem." Bobby tried to push past Ray.

"Hold on a likkl," Ray held onto Bobby's shoulder. "What yu hav inside dat sak?"

"Jus a few tings, Ray sah, notten fi worri bout."

"Mek mi look." Ray pulled the sack off Bobby's shoulder, out of his resisting hands.

Inside the sack were half-grown carrots, onions, scallions, cho-chos and who knows what else, caked in earth, obviously dug up in haste. Bobby's face took on a surly look under Ray's angry gaze and he mumbled something about mekkin fuss over notten, an what man need man haffi tek. "What man need man haffi tek?" Ray yelled angrily. "Man, yu brazen, iinh? Well hiir dis, mi noh want nuo tief workin fi mi, so galang bout yu bisnis!"

Ray was ready for a fight and felt almost cheated when Bobby slunk away, head hanging and cursing profusely under his breath.

It was difficult for Ray to find a man to take Bobby's place. Most grown men in the district either owned or rented land which they worked for themselves. Only a few like Bobby, who were either simple or otherwise handicapped were available for full-time employment, and they were much in demand. Ray found that he had exchanged the weight of anxiety about Bobby's thieving for the burden of extra work. Fatigued in body and in spirit, his good intentions towards Esme were defeated by the need which drew him to Peter's with increasing regularity.

On a Saturday night not long after the incident with Bobby, the group of men seated under the tree was large and boisterous. It was the first Saturday of the new year and the holiday spirit could be heard in the animated voices and free laughter of the group. Some of them had been to Wide River that day and were recounting the latest news. The best story came from Maas Stanley, about a young girl who was caught trying to leave the meat market with a crocus sack full of stolen meat between her legs. A detailed analysis of the crime followed, seasoned with raucus speculation as to how the bag and its contents arrived at their resting place. Ray laughed until he couldn't sit up straight, even added his version of what had taken place, yet when the noise subsided he shook his head, regreting the fact that you couldn't tell a thief from a decent man these days and wondering what happened to conscience.

Bobby, who was sitting in the shadows, jumped to his feet and threw his empty glass at Ray. Every voice hushed and all eyes turned to Bobby, watching for his next move.

"Yu luv kaal piipl tief, inh?" Bobby rested his hand against the trunk of the tree to steady himself. Rum thickened his tongue and slurred his speech, but his eyes were fixed on Ray's face and the hostility in them was unmistakable. "Yu jus kom inna di distrik di odda day, nobaddi knuo where yu kom fram, an yu tink seh yu betta dan evribaddi else kaas yu hav two likkl piice ov land. But wi all knuo seh yu a tief too!"

"Kom, Bobby, noh bodda wid dat, man! Peter, giv im anodda drink, noh?" One of the older men intervened and several voices murmured their agreement, including Peter who poured another drink for Bobby.

Bobby would not be stopped.

"Is *yu* tief Junior woman! Is *yu* mash up di bwoy life! Evribaddi did knuo seh Junior an Esme did deh! Is yu turn er fram im! But wach; yu neva knuo seh yu a bring dun krasses pon yuself! Well, jus wach an sii!"

Ray sat stunned, as though he had been hit on the head. He was the centre of attention, aware that the next move was his, yet he was unable to speak. A familiar, chill vapour crept down his spine, spreading until his back was rigid with it, his chest was filled with it, his hands clammy from it.

Peter's voice broke the tension in the atmosphere like a warm breeze on a cool night.

"Cho, man, yu kyaan kaal tekin weh a woman tiefin. Woman noh hav mind ov dem own? Mi knuo seh di man doan baan yet who kud tek fi-mi wife unless shi wan go! If a man soh much as taak to er widout shi giv im permishun, shi trace im till im baal!"

Everybody laughed at this. Peter's wife Maudie was well known, as much for her strong mind as her caustic tongue. Ray alone remained silent. With a few choice words Bobby Brewster had revealed his true position among these people and robbed him completely of peace. It was so clear. The men under the tree were all connected to each other in some way: by blood, by marriage, by longstanding friendship, by shared experience of life. He was a relative outsider, a newcomer. What had made him think he belonged among them, was accepted by them?

He had hardly given a thought to Junior Brewster since getting together with Esme. Did people feel he had wronged Junior? He now wondered. Junior was born and bred in Rocky Gap, he was one of them. Did that mean these men he drank with, sported with, would take Junior's part, even now? As he followed this line of thought Ray felt a chill settle in the bottom of his belly but did not recognise it as fear.

The conversation turned to predictions for the year ahead. It was election year and views were divided as to whether the current government would be returned to power.

"Mi noh kyare which one win," pronounced Peter, resting his elbows on the bar to take the weight off his feet for a while. "Aal ov dem stay same way. Dem prance round Kingston, mek big spiich, big promis! Dem no knuo what a gwan down yas-so. Rain a-fall, but dutty tuff! Kolad man in di kontri a-wuk wiself dry fi fiid white man a Kingston! An dem tink seh a so it fi go! Mi seh, mi noh blame a singl one ov dem man who gan a Inglan. After aal, wi might as well wuk fi dem ova deh as ova yasso. At least den wi kyan sii what wi wukkin for!"

"Mi hiir seh plenti man migrate laas yiir," added Matthew Partridge. "Mi noh blame dem, to rahtid! Look how meni man in de distrik wuk till dem drop, an still kyaan manij fi mek a hous fi put ova im pickni hed! Might as well dem go ova deh an wuk likkl moni fi kom bak wid!"

"Mek dem gwan, yaa," Maas Stanley waved his hand as though dismissing all those would-be migrants. "Dem kyan goh, but mi a tell oonu one ting. Mi not liivin fi-mi kontri go wuk inna eni koal place! Dat-deh kontri mek fi white man, it noh mek fi kolad man, an wi noh suppose fi stay deh eni time!"

"A trut yu a taak," chipped in Ray, coming back to life. "Wen mi was in Nyoo Yaak, mi jus kudn wait fi liiv! Mi seh, mi kount evri day! An di problem is nat de koal; dough mek mi tel yu, dat koal is wikkid! Nuo man, di problem is di piipl! Di white one-dem noh want wi deh, an di kolad one jus as bad! Mi seh, dem hav a briid ov white man ova deh wi kill yu if yu soh much as look pon im. It no matta what kola yu bi: so long as you not white, yu is worse dan daag to dem."

The listeners kissed their teeth and murmured their disgust.

"But what kyan wi do?" continued Ray. "Wi kyaan do eni betta. If di onli way a man kyan mek two penni is fi goh America or Inglan goh wuk, mi seh, mek im goh an wish im luk."

"Cho, man, Inglan kyaan bi soh bad," argued Matthew. "Aafta aal, wi is al paat ov di Kommonwealth, an wat's more, fi-dem Queen is fi-wi Queen too! Nat like America, where dem ongle knuo kolad piipl as slave!"

There were grunts of agreement and a few remarks in support of Matthew's viewpoint, following which the conversation returned to the subject of the year just past. Without exception the men under the tree agreed that '52 had been one of the worst years ever. Recovery from the devastation of Hurricane Charlie had taken months of effort and drained all their resources. Recovery had not yet been achieved for many of them, for although there had been no further disaster, their savings had been depleted. The men speculated on the year ahead, wondering what it would bring in the way of improvement. Some were optimistic, following their naturally hopeful tendency. Others could see no signs of change; maybe these ones had not had enough rum as yet to lift their spirits away from the umpromising reality of the present. All agreed on one thing,though: money was as scarce as fowl in a hungry man's yard.

Ray was unable to get back into the spirit of the evening, try as he might. Rum normally soothed his fatigue, normally made him talkative, but not tonight. He rose to his feet bade the men under the tree good evening, and walked over to the bar to settle his account with Peter.

"Gaan alredi?" asked Peter. "Stay likkl longa, man! Yu look like yu kud tek a koppl more drink."

Peter reached for the bottle and Ray's glass, but Ray stopped him with a shake of his head.

"Noh bodda yuself wid Bobby an im taak, Ray," said Peter quietly. "Yu knuo how im stay from time. Two drink an im redi fi kuss im mummah!"

"Mi hav nottn but problem, Peter, nottn but bad luk." Peter's sympathetic tone tempted Ray to confide in him. "Bwoy, bad luk worse dan obeah," Ray continued; "when it staat, nottn kyaan stop it."

As he walked to his house troubled thoughts crammed Ray's mind. The musical night noises of birds and insects failed to penetrate the anxious jangle. He went over the events of the past two years — the Easter fair at Wide River, his courtship of Esme, her pregnancy. The seeds of their present trouble must have been sown over that time, but when?

"Maasa God, why mi life soh full ov kraases? From mi was pickni is nottn but tryal me haffi diil wid." The sound of his own voice startled him. He laughed bitterly; things must be bad if he was talking to himself.

His thoughts turned to money matters, to the grinding labour of making his ground yield crops and profit. Why had he chosen this life? he asked himself. He could have learned another trade, like carpentry or masonry. He had always known farming was hard work. He had always known about the hot sun burning down on the tender, naked space between covered head and clothed back; about drought which turned the soil to stone and dust; about floods which turned whole fields into rivers of mud; about pests which ate away seeds and roots; about chigger lying in wait for human flesh to inhabit, about macca springing from nowhere to jook and sting. He had always known that a cultivator's life was labour of the hardest, most gruelling kind. The prospect of a future of years like the one just past, repeating its disasters without limit or end, was dreadful.

Esme. He shook his head as though trying to dislodge an obstruction. Lord knows, he had spent enough time trying to figure out what was wrong with her! His head was bursting. Thoughts overflowed, became words which his tongue released into the night. Foolish as it seemed, words eased his distress. Or maybe it was the night, warm and bright with light from a globular moon which invited confession and gave back comfort.

"Mi noh knuo what doh er! Fram mornin till nite shi a walk round di place lakka vex duppy. Man, shi soh misrabl, shi mek di baby bawl! An dat mout shi hav, it lash worse dan eni pissl. Shi gwan like shi want punish mi fi somting, but what? If mi do er eniting, mi noh knuo is what."

The previous week he had paid Molly a visit, a sure sign of serious concern, for he rarely visited his sister-in-law. She was too stiff for his taste and moreover, he felt she disapproved of him. Yet Molly had listened to him attentively before giving her opinion.

"Is di prignancy," she pronounced firmly. "It kom too soon afta di first one."

Ray couldn't see why that should be a problem. In his opinion Esme had Ruby to help her round the house; he supported her, he provided for her. Esme was lucky. She had life easy compared to many women he knew.

Molly was insistent; there was no other problem that she could see. Except, perhaps, his tendency to spend time away from home. "But Molly," he protested, "mi kyaan just run home at nighttime an siddung inna yaad soh! Mi did try it, jus fi sii if it wud mek tings betta, but it neva mek a blaastid diffrence! Nuo man, mi kyaan liv soh! Mi kyaan wuk soh haad widdout relax."

He had sought Peter's advice some weeks previous to the conversation with Molly, with even less satisfatory results.

"Look ya, Ray, mi knuo Esme from shi was a yung gyal, an evn den shi kud mek up er face an long out er mout lakka lizzad! Is one misrabl woman dat! Shi tink shi kyan tek long mout an rule yu! Wat yu mus do is lan two bitch lik pon er bihind, mek er sii yu nat rompin wid er!"

Ray had shaken his head at that piece of advice.

"Man, mi kyaan do dem tings. Mi noh knuo how fi ruff-up woman. Mi fraid wi kech fight an mi lik er bad, kaas fi-mi tempa wikkid, mi kyaan kontrol it."

No one had any real solutions to offer. But then, no-one really understood what Esme was like at home — not Peter, not even Molly.

She put on a good face for everyone else. Only he saw the everyday devil in her, and she was making him as miserable as she was. He couldn't remember the last time he felt good or happy around her. Not since the hurricane. The hurricane had spoilt everything, had mashed up more than the eye could see. He hadn't lost his house like some, but he had lost all three fields of crops. The yard around his house seemed naked now, stripped of banana trees, plantain trees, and the tallest, oldest mango tree. With them his happiness had vanished, like Maas Stanley's dog, carried clean away.

"Mi kyaan blame dem man who a go try dem luk inna Inglan, mi kyaan blame dem at aal." He was talking in earnest, right out loud,without restraint, so absorbed that he had stopped walking. He stood on the narrow track, hands outstretched as though entreating the bush, the trees, the stars and the moon to understand.

"Mi hiir seh dem hav plenti job deh, an pay gud wages too. Whole hiip a dem a get passport fi goh. In a diffrent time mi wud giv it a try too. But mi no hav moni fi pay passij fi miself an Esme an two pickni. Mind yu, mi hiir seh is best if de man go first. Im kyan find a job an place fi liv den send fi im woman an pickni aafta. Mi haffi kansida dis, serius, kaas if mi stay yasso dis life gwain kill mi bifore mi time. If is not drowt is hurrikien, if is not hurrikien is tief, if is not tief is worm an fly nyam up yuh crop. An if is not dat, is dyam blaastid woman!"

He started walking again, muttering quietly now, sighing and shaking his head.

"It kom in like woman is krasses. Neida mummah, nor sista, nor wife is eni use. Dem swiit yu up fi a likkl time, but bapse! Likkl trubl kom an kwik time, evriting chienj!"

Ray arrived home to find the house in darkness and realised it was very late.

"Dem mussa sliip," he thought, relieved that he didn't have to face Esme's accusing face. He walked through the main room and into the bedroom, feeling his way. The bed was empty, neatly made up and covered with a spread. Tessa was soundly asleep in her crib at the far side of the bed. A kerosene lamp on the dressing table gave out a soft, flickering light.

But where is Esme? he wondered. He walked back through the living room and into the kitchen, half knowing Esme would not be there so late. Opening the kitchen door, he scanned the backyard. No sign of Esme. He could hear Ruby snoring noisily. But where the hell was this woman? he muttered.

He was anxious now. This had never happened before. Even in these bad times, she was always there when he came home. He always knew when she was going out, where she was going, and when she would return. Maybe she was visiting Molly, he told himself, or her father. Maybe she was down by Maas Jimmy to see Elvira. No, he told himself. None of them would keep Esme from her home so late.

He was unsure what to do, whether to go down to Rocky Gap to look for her, or whether to just sit and wait. The thought that she had left him flitted across his mind, a faint shadow. He let it pass. He went back into the living room, lit a lamp, and sat down by the table.

"Choh, man," he muttered, rising to his feet again. "Mek mi goh look fi er! Eniting kudda happen!"

At that moment he heard Esme's foot on the front step. The door opened and she walked in boldly, no trace of apology in her demeanour. She paused in the doorway, looking at him.

"Where yu komin fram soh late?" he demanded, anger swiftly following relief. She froze, defiance settling on her face, bottom lip jutting out.

"Yu tink is ongle yu hav place fi go a evenin time?" She shot him a look of pure venom and moved towards the bedroom. He grabbed her arm to make her stop and shook it to make her look at him.

"Yu liiv mi pickni asleep an gaan? What happn to yuh sens? Yu noh realise dat eniting kudda happn to er?"

"Mi liiv er in di hous wid Ruby," Esme spat back at him. "In eni kase, sins when yu a worri bout pickni? Yu gaan bout yuh bisnis weneva yu pliis. Yu noh evn knuo whedda shi sik or shi well, whedda shi eat or shi staav. Yu noh kyare bout er!"

Ray shook the arm he was holding to silence her.

" Hush yuh mout, woman! Hush yuh foolishnis!"

She thumped his chest with her free hand.

"Oonu is daag, yu hiir mi! Daag! Mi ongle sorri mi hav anodda one fi yu in mi belli! Mi shudda dash it way lang time!"

In the flickering yellow lamplight Esme's eyes gleamed with malice. A spark flared in Ray's head. Trembling, he gripped Esme's shoulder tightly. Esme tried to pull away but before she could free herself, his fist smashed into the side of her head. She staggered but regained her balance and faced him squarely.

"Yu raas, yu! Yu animal! Yu tink mi fraid fi yu?"

His fist smashed again, this time into the soft flesh of her cheek, jarring against bone. He punched into her arm, her side, her belly. She fell to the floor, screaming. He dropped to the floor beside her, beating her with his fists, not stopping even though she screamed. He kept on beating and kneading until a clap of thunder burst in his ears, cracking open his skull. Pain slowed his fists. A drop of blood trailed down his cheek and splashed onto Esme's white cotton blouse, forming a scarlet star.

He looked up fearfully, like a man expecting retribution, to see Ruby standing over him, his cricket bat gripped firmly in her hands.

Part 2

IN MY FATHER'S HOUSE

LONDON

1955–1961

Chapter 5

M Y FAVOURITE PHOTOGRAPH OF MY parents, their wedding portrait, was taken a few weeks before Dada's departure from Jamaica for England. It shows Dada slim and upright in a tailored suit as sharp as a blade, face glowing with the brightness of dreams. Standing beside him, Madda wears a sober costume and an expression to match; that special combination of stubbornness and bad temper which she wore most of the time, but which sat on her face like a shadow on the photograph.

I haven't seen that photo for years. I don't know whether he has it or she has it, or whether it was lost, tossed away, yet another piece of debris discarded in the process of change.

My father, Ray Erskine, migrated to England in the early 1950s. He was part of that wave of Jamaicans who responded to the call for help from the seat of Empire. He and hundreds like him left their impoverished rural parishes, left their women and children to go to rebuild a Mother England ravaged by war.

It must have been hard, starting life afresh in this strange, cold country. He still talks about his first months in London: how foreign the place was, how unfriendly the people and how cold the weather. He arrived in

February to a city covered by a sheet of grey ice. He thought he was prepared, having already experienced winter in New York. He could not have imagined anything like that winter. Everything froze. Trees like frosted steel, grass like slender nails, pavements of lethal pewter. He froze too. Feet, hands, face, clothing, even the breath on his lips.

Like a man replaying a cherished recording of a favourite song, Dada repeated the tale of his early days in London countless times. How for the first few months he stayed with Clarence, the cousin of a friend from home, sharing Clarence's bedsit in a dilapidated house in Fulham. How he disliked Fulham! How he hated the stark, treeless road on which he lived! How the noise of the congested high street where he caught the bus each day to go hunting for work grated on his ears! Fulham was so ugly it hurt his eyes and made his head ache.

He missed Jamaica. He missed the sunrise over the sea in the morning, the smell of fresh fish frying in coconut oil, the taste of freshly roasted breadfruit. Memories of home would creep up on him like tears as he sat huddled in a bus seat, staring out of a window misted over with his breath at the shops along the high road, at the people walking with shoulders hunched as though to keep the cold from penetrating to their very hearts.

Yet he still loved the idea of England; England the mother country, the land of opportunity. The idea had a powerful hold on him, on all who came with him. It inspired them, sustained them like manna and kept them on the trail of that most nebulous of rewards — a better life.

He had heard that work would be easy to find, but the work which was easy to get, he did not want. The buses or the railways did not appeal to him. Neither did factory work. Mi dun wid slaveri, he would say. In Jamaica he had been a farmer, but he was also a skilled carpenter. He decided on the building trade and just kept searching until one of the large building contracting firms took him on.

He still talks about his first experience of work in his new country. He makes a big drama of it. How he borrowed money to buy the basic tools he needed. How he reported for his first day of work one chilly, April morning wearing layers of borrowed sweaters and long-johns under his trousers. How he walked across the muddy building site to the foreman's office, feet gradually turning numb as the moisture seeped through the thin leather of his Kingston-bought shoes.

"Is hell to bi di ongl kolad man in a wukplace!" Clarence had warned him. Clarence and his friends all had stories to tell about black men being persecuted by white workers.

"First ov aal, dem nat gwain taak to yu, nat evn a good maanin! An yu kyaan tek yuh eye aaf dem. Dem wi tief yuh tool, an piss inna yu tea fi spite yu!"

At lunchtime that first day, one of Dada's new workmates pointed to a prefabricatd cabin at the far end of the site and told him he could get lunch in there. Glad at the thought of a temporary shelter from the cold, Dada hastened across to the cabin. He entered a smoke-filled room and a dozen pairs of eyes turned to look at him.

"And what do *you* want, matey?" The question came from a burly looking fellow whom Dada knew to be the site foreman.

"S-sorri, suh," he stammered without knowing why he was apologising. "Mi kom fi mi lunch!"

The diners burst into laughter, slapping tables with their hands and stamping their feet.

"Have trouble reading, do you?" asked the foreman with mock concern. " That sign on the door says 'Management Canteen'. We don't have no nigger managers round here, you know!"

The laughter in the canteen felt like lashes on his skin. He backed out, burning with shame, rage and hurt. "Dem baastad!" He would say. "Dem wud do eniting, evriting in dem powah to shame blak man. Dem nevva want wi niir dem. Not pon di site, not pon di striit, not in dem kontri at aal! Dem tink wi was saaf; dem tink wi wud tek fraid an run way. But wi, wi jus laaf pon dem. Aal dat shit jus mek us determin to stay an show dem who is monki an who is man!"

Less than one year after his arrival in England, Dada sent for my mother. I followed nine months later. I was four years old at the time and plump as a soft cornmeal dumpling. And sharp. I took in everything and retained most of what I saw. I remember Aunt Vera waving to me as I boarded a BOAC jet at Palisados Airport with Miss Iris, a family friend who was travelling to London to join her husband. I remember arriving at London airport and being sucked into its crowds, its noise and excitement. Dada and Miss Iris' husband were waiting for us. Dada swept me up and hugged me to his chest. I burst into tears, confused. Who was this strange man grabbing hold of me like he owned me? It was two-and-a half years since I last saw him and I did not recognise him. He told me he was my Dada and he had come to take me home. I told him I lived in Jamaica and I wanted to go back there. He put me down, tears in his eyes.

The home to which Dada took me was a large room at the front of a three-storied Victorian terraced house in a street in Paddington, just off the Harrow Road. The house had many rooms, each of which sheltered a complete household, some with one person, some with two, some with one or two children as well.

The room was my parents' first home together in England, and they both prayed for the day when they would move out of it.

"Laad God," my mother lamented, "it neva once kraas mi mind seh mi was komin to Inglan fi liv inna hog-sty!"

The shared bathroom and toilet were permanently filthy, the shared kitchen not much better. Virtually every day Madda grumbled about the condition of the stove, and how she had to clean it before she could start cooking. What kain ov naasti piipl were dey livin mangst? she used to wonder out loud at the top of her voice. Dada regularly exchanged insults with the Irishman in the room directly above ours, who every weekend staggered noisily into the house in the early hours of the morning, singing loudly as he stomped up the two flights of stairs to his room.

They both had jobs, and both worked long hours. I was enrolled at a primary school not far from where we lived. In the morning Madda took me to a childminder where I stayed for the two hours or so before school. Dada collected me on his way home in the evening. Every day was strange and bewildering, but exciting too. Even at that young age I think I was stimulated by change, curious about the new. In the evenings I used to sit on the front steps of the house and watch cars and people passing in the road. I wanted to play in the street with our neighbours' children, but Madda would not allow me. She didn't want me to mix up with those people too much, lest their nastiness rub off on me, she said. I had to content myself with spectating.

The world I observed from the doorstep included Jamaicans, Trinidadians, Barbadians, Irish people, Poles, Spaniards, and of course, the English. Madda was on a nodding aquaintance with a woman named Mavis from St. Kitts who lived across the road. Whenever she saw me on the step, Mavis would wave and call to me, her accent thick and strange.

"How Inglan triitin yu, Tess chile?" she would say, and I would reply, "Fine thanks Miss Mavis!"

Dada sometimes went out drinking with a fat, genial Trinidadian named Happy Wallace, who remained a friend of our family long after we left Paddington. Apart from these two, my parents were suspicious of everyone. I was curious about the people I saw in the street. Many of them looked like us, dressed like us. Where did they come from? Did they like it here? I wanted to ask them but I never did.

From the doorstep I watched the season change from summer to autumn to winter. Leaves shrivelled and fell from trees, days grew shorter and colder. Cold weather transformed familiar people into bulky, hunched creatures who scurried on their way, heads down, shoulders rounded to protect their chests from the wind. I retreated indoors and watched the world through the window in the relative warmth of our room.

For months after my arrival I was caught up in the dance of adjustment. London, Paddington, Bravington Road. Summer, autumn, winter. School and classmates, home and Madda. Adjusting to Madda was hardest of all. I am sure I loved my mother. I can't recall my feelings very clearly but most five-year-olds love their mother, don't they? I'm sure I was no different. I'm sure I loved her and wanted her to love me, as any five-year-old would.

In those days she was working as a seamstress in a small garment factory in Harlesden. When Dada and I got home in the evenings, Madda would be in the kitchen, still in her work clothes, preparing dinner. We ate together, she cleared up, I bathed and went to bed. On Saturday mornings she slept late, and Dada would bring her coffee in bed before leaving for work. I would snuggle down with Madda until she was ready to get up. It should have been cosy, mother and daughter sharing a little warmth together on a weekend morning, but it was not. Even as I tried to get close to her soft warm body, Madda would turn her back and lie in silence with the bedclothes pulled up to her chin.

On Saturday afternoons we went shopping for fresh food and groceries in the busy streets of Ladbroke Grove. She loved to shop. Actually, she loved to spend money, but in those early days, when she and Dada were saving every penny to buy a house, all she could spend money on was food. She preferred to shop at the small grocery stores run by Greeks or Spaniards which stocked West Indian foods but she would also spend hours strolling through the market, exhausting my short legs looking for bargains.

Although in later times she would say that she never liked England, that she was never happy here, I believe that she enjoyed the early years. I know she enjoyed having money to spend. When she and Dada talked about the future and the house they would buy I could feel her excitement. The future was always full of promise. As in the movies she sometimes took me to see at the cinema in Notting Hill, a happy ending was bound to arrive eventually. "Afta aal," she used to say, "wi kom fi mek life an wi haffi do betta dan bak home. Mi dun wid pit tailet, wid cachin waata inna pail. Chigger na see fi-mi foot agen, nor hot sun fi-mi face. Dem-deh day paas."

Their search for a house took a long time, and led them to all parts of London. In those days, buying a house was a Herculean task for black people. Yet Dada always used to say, "Is kolad piipl kom to Inglan an shuo di aadnari white man how to buy hous."

They looked at houses in Harlesden, Fulham, Willesden and Wandsworth. They looked in Kilburn, Clapham and Finsbury Park. Facing colour prejudice ("We have to think of the neighbours, you must understand") and limited by distrust of their own people ("Mi noh waan liv eni place where dem hav too meni kolad piipl") it was a full year before they found somewhere to buy.

I loved the house the first time I saw it. It was my dream house; a huge, two-storied, double fronted Victorian villa, approached by a red-and-blue tiled path, and five stone steps. There were big, sun-filled bay windows overlooking a front garden stocked with flowers and shrubs. On the pavement outside the front gate, a flowering hawthorn tree drizzled pink blossom, covering the ground with fragrant confetti. At the back, twin rose-bordered lawns twenty feet long were divided by a crazy-paved path, and a spreading apple tree stood at the end of each lawn. I saw myself climbing the apple trees to pick their delicious fruit. I saw myself picking roses and arranging them in the house for Madda. I saw us sitting comfortably in the large room overlooking the back garden, happy and at peace, like any English family. The quiet, tree-lined street had a charming ambience of order and propriety, of the kind foreigners believe exists everywhere in England but the English know do not. That fantasy caught all three of us, trapped us. We fell in love with the house and with the future it promised.

We moved in summer when the days were long, hot and sunny. I saw my parents grow plump with pride at taking possession of their own home. Madda almost beamed as she wondered possessively through the large, empty rooms, enjoying to the full the freedom of ownership. They invited the few people they knew to pass by, and on the first Saturday Mavis came to visit. She sat on a hard upright chair left behind by the previous occupants, listening enviously as Madda and Dada enthused about the area and its amenities, the street, even the neighbours whom they hadn't yet met. Madda showed Mavis each room from the cellar upward. I followed them, listening while she explained to a wide-eyed Mavis her plan for each room; which ones would be rented out to help pay the mortgage, which ones we would keep for our own use. Madda had grand schemes for furnishing our part of the house. She had seen a sumptuously plush three-piece suite with matching cocktail bar and stools in a furniture shop on the Harrow Road and she had set her heart on buying them on hire purchase. And she simply had to have the walnut bedroom suite with the king sized bed and built-in bedside tables. Mavis just listened, visibly impressed.

Our first tenants came by word of mouth, the word having been spread around the West Indian community in Paddington. We were fortunate that the previous owners had left behind enough furniture and curtains to make the four rooms upstairs comfortable. There was such a demand for the rooms that Madda and Dada frequently argued about who they should take: should they take couples, children, Irish, English, African or Indian tenants?

"Mi noh waan nuo pickni fi run up an dun an mek nise inna mi hed!" Madda declared flatly.

"If evribaddi did tink like yu, how wi wudda manij get place fi liv wid Tessa?" argued Dada.

Madda remained adamant. They agreed they would rent to coloured people in preference to whites and that they would rent to Jamaicans in preference to other West Indians, despite a fear that coloured people would try to avoid paying rent. Neither of them wanted Africans or Indians.

"Mi kyaan tek dem at all!" declared Dada, "dem too naasti!"

"Dem kyan gwaan, yaa," said Madda dismissing them all, "dem tink dem betta dan wi."

Our joy in the house was enhanced by glorious summer weather. Day after day of warm sunshine transformed London. The gardens in the streets around us were ablaze with summer flowers. Red roses, pink roses, white roses, yellow roses. Snapdragons, huge hydrangeas, fuchsia hedges laden with tempting buds which popped when I squeezed them. Even the common yellow-hearted daisies which speckled our lawn looked pretty. On Sunday mornings Dada tended our garden, weeding, cutting and planting, singing as he worked. He bought a second-hand lawn mower to cut the grass and I would follow merrily behind him, scooping up the fallen blades and piling them onto a heap at the end of the backyard. The farmer in him was happy, revealed in the careful, colourful neatness of our garden.

We had very little contact with our neighbours to begin with. We passed them in the street from time to time, they would greet us, we would respond, and that would be that. One day an elderly woman from the house across the street called to me as I swung on our front gate. She asked me where we came from.

"Paddington," I answered smartly.

"Before that!" She persisted.

"Kingston!" I replied ambiguously, knowing she wanted to hear the name of some dark, foreign place, yet spitefully denying that satisfaction.

She shot me an irritated look and retreated into her house.

The number of people coming and going through our front door must have must have looked odd to our neighbours. There was a rapid turnover of tenants in those early months. Some left complaining the rent was too high for the facilities provided. Others were given notice because of unacceptable behaviour. Like Pat, our first (and only) white tenant.

Pat was tall, thin and unhealthy-looking, as though she was raised on a diet of chips fried in lard. She was a nurse at Whittington hospital, a short distance away. Her irregular comings and goings aroused Madda's suspicions to the extent that she took to peeping through the window whenever she heard Pat's step by the front door.

"What dat ugli, maaga gyal doin wid so meni man?" she wondered, seeing Pat come in with yet another escort. "It siim like evri time shi kom in shi hav a diffrent one!"

"Noh soh dem nurse kyarri on!" Dada said. "Wen mi was here aloan, mi kudda hav as meni of dem gyal as mi did want, if mi did want em. Main yu," he added hastily, "mi was neva intrested in dem."

After three weeks of Pat, Wilfred, a middle-aged Jamaican lodger, told Ray the he was leaving, "kaas mi neva kom to Inglan fi liv in hous wid nuo prositute."

Madda laughed fit to bust when she heard.

"Bakside!" she cackled. "Yu tink shi's a pros fi tru? Dis one mi haffi chek out!" She went straight upstairs to talk to Pat.

"How dare you speak to me like that!" I heard Pat shriek. " You people come here, you've just come down from the trees, you can't read or write and you think you can insult decent people?"

I didn't like Pat, but I trembled at her foolishness. Who but an idiot would talk to Madda like that?

"Who di raas yu tink yu taaking to, gyal?" Madda's voice was low with threat. "Rememba is inna *my* house yu deh! Yu betta moov yu mawga pussi outta mi yaad quik quik quik!"

By the end of the week Pat and her belongings had gone.

"Wi shudda knuo is soh shi stay," said Dada afterwards. "Afta aal, no decent Inglish gyal gwain rent room wid kolad piipl. Noh tru?"

A few days later Lily Williams, the most elegant woman I had ever seen, arrived. Tall and slim with slicked-back hair and red, red lips, she looked like a movie star. Much more beautiful than Ava Gardner, much more glamorous than Jane Russell.

I sat on the stairs watching her move in with suitcases, boxes, bundles.

" Hello! Yu liv here too? Kom, help mi wid dese tings!"

She smiled and I was smitten. I followed her up and down the stairs to her room helping as best I could, until she had brought up all her things. I sat on her bed and watched her while she began to dust out the wardrobe and the drawers of the dressing table in preparation for unpacking. I counted the dresses she hung in the wardrobe, the pairs of shoes she lined up under the bed, took note of the toiletries and cosmetics she spread out on the dressing table and was satisfied. She had much more of everything than Madda.

I became Lily's devoted slave. I waited on the stairs for her to arrive from work each evening. I would give her time to take off her work clothes and relax for a while then knock at her door, knowing that I would be welcome inside. She accepted my admiration graciously, like the goddess she was. Everyone admired her, even Madda, who liked very few people. The two women soon became friends, to my complete chagrin. They were always chatting, in the hall, in our kitchen, sometimes in Lily's room, sometimes in Madda's. They talked about anything and everything. Like where to buy good salted pig tail, where to find fresh fish, cheap fabric, things like that. Sometimes they got serious and discussed personal matters. I learned new things about my mother just listening to them talking. She told Lily everything about her family, her father, even Dada. At times during their conversations their voices dropped to a whisper and I knew they were discussing something really intimate. But I think their favourite topic of conversation was sickness. The subject came up whenever they sat down together for any length of time. They discussed in great detail all ailments they had ever suffered, how, why and with how much pain. They speculated on the diseases they might contract in the future how, when, and for what reason. Fatal illnesses fascinated Madda particularly, to the extent that she bought an encyclopedia of health from a door-to-door salesman. They pored over the colour photographs together for hours, stomach-churning pictures of cancerous breasts, gangrenous limbs, weird disfigurements caused by disease. White piipl siknis, Madda used to say. Wi haffi bi kyareful how wi mix wid dem. Wi kyaan get too kluos or wi mite kech dem naasti siknis.

I was an eavesdropper, a jealous voyeur peeking into the world of adult women, often disturbed at what I overheard. Yet I was always there, listening.

Chapter 6

SEPTEMBER CAME, AND WITH IT came time for school. I was enrolled
at St Michael's Primary, a small Church of England school attached
to a chapel of the same name. Having endured weeks without contact
with other children, I went to school gladly.

The first thing I noticed about St Michael's was its sweet, musky
odour, a curious combination of age and polish. The smell matched
the shine of the varnished wooden wall panelling and complemented
the gleaming parquet flooring. The shine on the floor impressed me,
calling to mind one of Madda's dictats: "In a diicent place, floor must
shine, furniture must shine, window must shine." (These were words
usually barked in dissatisfaction with my housekeeping efforts.)
Someone had taken time to create that shine and had put in years of
effortful care into maintaining it. I took pleasure in it. Many mornings
I sat cross-legged on the mirror-like floor, gazing dreamily down at my
faintly reflected face, lost in the shadowy world of the shine for the
entire duration of morning assembly.

On that first day, I realised that I was the only black child in the
school, a chocolate drop misplaced in a jar of mint imperials. I soon
became the focus of a great deal unaccustomed attention which, I

admit, I enjoyed at first. Children gathered round me in the playground asking one question after another to hear me speak, because my accent fascinated and amused them. Some of them asked to touch my hair, while others just grabbed one of my three fat plaits and pulled.

Teachers were equally curious, though less direct. I would sometimes notice my class teacher talking to one of her colleagues and looking at me while they spoke, and I knew they were talking about me. I tried to ignore the brash bullies, the ones who forced their hostility on me. I avoided them in the playground, or walked away if any of them approached me directly. Once, I got into a playground fight with a stupid boy who spat at me and called me names. In a fit of rage I kicked him in the shins and pushed him to the ground, but we were separated by the teacher on duty before I had the chance to really thump him. No one bothered me after that day.

School was the herald of a new phase in my life, one which introduced me to independence outside and inside the home. Each afternoon after school I unlocked the big wooden front door of our house and entered its peaceful emptiness with a thrilling sense of freedom. I liked the quiet, the stillness, the feeling of having the entire house to myself. It was my task to wash up the breakfast cups and plates, which I did standing on a chair at the kitchen sink. That done, I played hopscotch on the garden path, or sat on the front doorstep pretending it was my throne, or watched the street from my bedroom window like a monarch surveying her kingdom. During that brief space of time I felt grown up and powerful; like the princess I often pretended to be, I was free to do what I chose.

My best friend at school was Anne Pendleton who sat at the desk in front of me in class and lived in the house next but one to ours. Anne had red hair and freckles, slightly protruding teeth and wore glasses. She reminded me of a cute baby rabbit, but our classmates poked fun at her endlessly. Our friendship began after an incident in the playground, when four girls backed Anne into a corner calling her "carrots" and "four-eyes", pulling her hair and jabbing at her with their fingers. One of the bullies snatched Anne's glasses from her nose and ran away with them, leaving her crying and unable to see. I chased the thief, grabbed the glasses from her, barged my way through to Anne and handed them back. After that incident Anne regarded me as her protector, a role I gladly assumed. We became inseparable, sitting together in class, playing together in the playground, walking home together after school.

Anne invited me home to tea, and fearing that Madda would forbid it, I went to Anne's house without telling her. Mrs. Pendleton smiled politely as I followed Anne into the house. ("So *you're* Anne's new friend!" she murmured.) She was plump and neat, with red hair like Anne. I thought her the typical English mother, though I later learned that the Pendletons were Scottish. Mrs Pendleton sat at the table with us while we ate Marmite sandwiches and cup-cakes. She asked me about my family, enquiring about where we came from, what my parents did for a living, who the other people in the house were. I'd grown used to being questioned and I was anxious to please, so I replied politely.

I was on my very best behaviour. I ate everything I was offered, nibbling daintily through numerous tea-cakes until Anne kicked my ankle under the table, and holding my teacup with my little finger crooked as I'd seen Lily do, I enjoyed my first experience of afternoon tea. I hoped I'd be invited again, in spite of the uncomfortable feeling I got each time Mrs. Pendleton's critical glance alighted on me.

Madda found out about my secret outing one day when Mrs. Pendleton stopped to talk to her in the street. She pretended to be vexed about it but I knew that she was secretly pleased that contact had at last been made with neighbours. Maybe it was the Pendleton's example, or maybe it was just time, but other people began to talk to us, rather guardedly, but civilly enough. Soon, Dada was having discussions about gardening over the fence with the man next door. The old lady in the house opposite became quite friendly, but not for long. She asked my mother one question too many and was firmly put in her place. Madda, who had been quick to sum up the old lady (dat ole witch, she called her), resented intrusions into her privacy and had no inhibitions about being rude to offenders.

Two weeks before her seventh birthday Anne handed me a small envelope with my name written on it enclosing an invitation to her birthday party. I was delighted. Other children in my class had given parties, but this was the first I had been invited to. I proudly showed Madda the pretty pink card when she came home that evening, and carefully explained to her that I needed a party dress to wear, and a present to take for Anne.

The Sunday afternoon before the party, I watched as Madda unfolded a length of maroon nylon fabric embossed with white polka-dots. She spread the fabric over the dining table, and took up her scissors to cut. I knew without asking that this was going to be my party dress. My heart sank. I wanted something pink with frills and a stiff, paper nylon petticoat to wear underneath it. I wanted red patent leather shoes and long lacy white knee socks to wear on my feet. Yet I knew my mother well enough to keep my disappointment to myself. Any complaint from me would have brought down bitter words on my head, and the possibility of not going to the party at all.

On the morning of the party, a Saturday, Madda and I went shopping at Nags Head, a street corner where the Holloway Road and Seven Sisters Road crossed. On Saturdays vendors set up stalls selling everything from green bananas to framed pictures of the Royal corgis. The tropical food stalls attracted crowds of West Indian shoppers from all over North London. On this particular Saturday Madda stopped by a barrel laden with cheap lingerie. Her hand fell on a pile of girls' panties, the kind made of thick cotton jersey, almost as thick as the navy blue knickers we wore at school for gym. She picked out three pairs and paid for them.

"Yu kyan tek dese to yuh paati," she said, handing me the brown paper bag.

I was appalled. How could she expect me to give this bag and its ugly contents to Anne? What would the Pendletons think of me? I would die of embarrassment. Yet I took the bag obediently, forcing back the protests that filled my mouth like bitter-tasting medicine.

I dressed for Anne's party without pleasure. I put on the new frock and looked at myself in the mirror on Madda's dressing table. The frock was too long, and the colour did not suit me. She had plaited my hair in three sections and had tied a big red bow at the front in a babyish style I disliked. I had polished my black shoes until my right arm ached but they refused to shine. To my own eyes I looked wrong and I knew the other party guests would think I looked silly. For a moment I considered not going to the party at all, but I feared my mother's scorn even more than I feared the ordeal awaiting me at the Pendleton's.

I rang the Pendleton's doorbell wishing I was somewhere else. Mr. Pendleton answered the door and showed me into the front room, which I entered reluctantly, clutching the brown paper bag in my hand. All the furniture had been pushed against the walls, leaving a large carpeted space in the middle. Anne sat on the sofa in the window recess opening presents, helped by her mother. Party guests, boys with Brylcreemed hair and white shirts, girls in pretty pastel dresses, sat in chairs around the room.

"Hello, Tessa," Mrs Pendletom greeted me, and Anne looked up from her task to smile at me. Mutely, I handed my gift to Mrs Pendleton.

"You've brought a present for Anne!" she said, smiling politely as she took the odious package from me. "Anne dear, say thank you to Tessa!"

"Thanks, Tess!" said Anne, taking the bag and opening it.

"Knickers!" exclaimed Mrs Pendleton, holding up one of the hideous objects for everyone to see. "You can *never* have too many knickers, can you dear?" She added, with unmistakable sarcasm.

Anne nodded, looking doubtful, while I bit my lips till the blood came holding back tears of shame. Anne took my hand kindly and drew me into the room, where I joined in the organised activities like a good sport. I played games and devoured cakes and sandwiches and jelly and ice cream, as though filling up the pit in my stomach carved by dread of what the other children would say about my ridiculous gift and frumpy appearance when I was gone.

On returning home, I found Madda getting ready for an evening out. She was in her bedroom ironing the clothes she was going to wear. One of my favourite things, a circular black skirt of taffeta covered with lace, was draped over the ironing board. I sat at the foot of the bed, watching her.

"Insted ov tekin aaf yu clothes, yu siddung lookin at mi?" This was said without as much as a glance in my direction. I said nothing and did not move.

"What yu skrewin up yuh face foh, pickni? Yu noh knuo seh yu ugli enuf aalredi?"

She looked at me this time, a mocking half-smile on her face.

I must be trying to look like you, I retorted in the safe silence of my mind.

I jumped up, heading for the door but Madda stopped me, taking hold of my arm and turning me to face her. She peered into my face inquisitively, as though trying to read me.

"Somting burning yu up tonite. What is it?"

"Is y-yu!" I exploded. "Y-yu mek mi wear dis s-stupid dress an you mek mi kyarri dem stupid b-baggy to di paati! Yu mek mi fiil like idiot!"

"But if enibadi sii mi triyal! Where dis pickni kom fram, Maasa God?" She burst into peals of laughter, slapping her thighs as though I had cracked the funniest joke of all time.

"You tink seh mi noh unnerstan yu?" she said, suddenly serious. "Yu want to mix up wid dem white piipl an kyarri on like yu is one of dem. But yu betta get it into yu natti hed dat yu an dem is diffrent! Noh badda biliiv dem like yu, kaas kolad piipl kom in like dirt to dem! An if yu hav eni sens, yu stop folla dat gyal Anne bout di place right now, kaas where shi goin in fi-her life yu kyaan goh. Shi ugly and er hiir red, but shi white. When shi redi, shi same one gwain turn round an kaal yu neaga! So yu betta wach yusself an shii!"

"Yu doan knuo what yu taakin about!" I yelled at her as I stormed out of the room, slamming the door after me.

In my own room I tore off the offending dress and flung it on the floor. I threw myself on the bed crying in a fit of rage, shame and help-lessness, my spirit calling to some nameless power to wreak retribution on my hateful mother.

I cried until the anger dissolved and was replaced by a numb feeling of apprehension. I had shouted at Madda! Lord, what would she do to pun-ish me ?

I discovered the next day that the chosen weapon was silence, administered with a wooden face and that oh-too-familiar pushed-out mouth. I felt bad inside; I felt uncomfortable in the house for days. My mother's displeasure permeated the atmosphere like a bad smell. My only escape was between the covers of books borrowed from the school library or the public library. The Secret Seven and Babar the Elephant distracted me, providing temporary refuge from my mother's anger.

Chapter 7

SHORTLY AFTER MY SEVENTH BIRTHDAY Madda received a letter bearing the news that her brother Matthew and sister Molly had booked their passage to England and would be with us in May. Like ants in a frenzy of nest-building, my parents threw themselves into fixing up the house in preparation for their arrival.

Dada painted and decorated the rooms downstairs. New carpets were fitted in the hall, the living room and the master bedroom. One afternoon I came home from school and was greeted at the front door by the powerful, throbbing voice of Jim Reeves. Following the sound, I came upon Madda in the living room, swaying to the music and gazing lovingly at a big shiny new Blue Spot radiogram. Dada, who had passed his driving test some months previously, bought a car, a long, sleek Vauxhall Cresta. Second-hand, (but no-one would have guessed) it graced the front of the house with gleaming elegance. Adorned with new things inside and out, by the time my aunt and uncle arrived, our house looked like the home of prosperous people.

We set out to meet them at London Airport in our new car, all of us excited at the adventure ahead of us — a long car ride, the hustle, bustle and glamour of the airport, and in Madda's case, the prospect of seeing her brother and sister again.

My mother astounded me that day. She wept when she saw her sister and brother. She hugged them and kissed them with tears and a joyful smile. I was amazed because I could hardly remember a time when Madda hugged me, or kissed me. Dada too was happy, shaking hands energetically with Uncle Matthew and slapping him heartily on the back, both of them laughing. Laughter and talk filled the car on the journey home; the new arrivals could hardly contain their enthusiasm for London.

They had chosen a good time to come. London looked pretty, softened by the young green of trees putting out new leaves, warmed a little by the delicate spring sun. Seen from the car, the suburban streets we passed looked clean, neat and attractive. As for Bayswater, Oxford Street and Regents Park, Uncle Matthew and Aunt Molly had never seen anything as big, rich or grand as the buildings which graced these areas.

"Man!" exclaimed Uncle Matthew as we rode down Oxford Street, "dis is one rahtid citi!"

"It nat bad," said Madda. "Mind yu, nat aal of it stay soh! Dis is di paat de rich piipl dem liv in. Yu haadli si a kolad man down yasso."

"Yu haadli si a kolad man eniwhere!" Dada added. "More an more ov wi komin ova, dough. Tank de Laad fi dat!"

Aunt Molly moved into my room, filling it with her suitcases and boxes. On that first night she sat on the bed gazing about her and shaking her head as though bemused.

"Is ongl now mi kyan truli seh mi unnerstan all di excitement bout Inglan," she declared over dinner. "Yu miin to seh, kolad piipl kyan buy big hous like dis ova ya, when inna Jamaica, blak man kyaan evn driim ov buyin hous in town! What a disgrace pon Jamaica!"

"Tings too ruff inna Jamaica, yaa! Haad wuk wi kill yu bifore yu mek likkl progress" Dada said. "It nat iisi ova here, but if yu willin fi wuk an if yu kyan biir di koal an di rain an di dyam misrabl piipl-dem, yu kyan mek a decent livin."

"Is som ov dat diicent livin mi want fi mi wife an pickni-dem!" Uncle Matthew was fired up and rearing to go.

"Yu betta staat look fi job faas, den!" Madda was nothing if not practical.

They settled into a long talking session. I sat on the arm of Dada's chair, taking in all the news from home, which Aunt Molly and Uncle Matthew delivered with elaborate detail. How my grandfather was still so vexed with Madda for marrying my Dada he didn't even send her a greeting. How Aunt Elvira was selling crochet runners by the dozen and saving the money to buy a plane ticket. How Dada's land had been rented out to Roderick, so-and-so's cousin who was so lazy, he let the land run to bush. Listening to the animated flow of talk I was taken back to a shadowy, dimly remembered world, like a dream recalled long after the images had faded and only feelings remained. I saw my parents came to life as though revived by a potent, magical tonic. They glowed, laughing and happy, as though some lost vital element had been restored to them.

Aunt Molly had the appearance of a schoolteacher, sensible, neat and somehow trustworthy. She had a reticence about her, almost a lack of confidence, but I had the feeling that she was kind. Uncle Matthew, now, was quite different. He was large and loud and very vocal. He did most of the talking that evening. He was a born storyteller; every bit of news was embellished and dramatised, every detail revealed with relish. He sat on the edge of his seat, eyes sparkling, hands waving as though excited by his own story.

"Man, time tuff ova desso, mi naa tell yu nuo lie!" said Matthew rounding off his performance. "Is ongl di big faama dem a mek moni. Smaal man like wi a faal! Evri man who kyan fain di passij moni want to emigrate!"

"Oonu siim to bi doin aal rait in Inglan," remarked Aunt Molly, eyes lingering on the new carpet and the new furniture, "but tell mi, how oonu manij wid a hous dis size!"

"Inglish hous noh smaal like Jamaica hous, yu knuo Molly" explained Madda. "In eni case," she added a little boastfully, "wi kyan afford it."

"Wi tek in tenant to help pay di morgij," Dada said. "Is soh aal ov wi haffi do. Kolad man kyaan rent a decent place so iisi, an evn a pigsty kaas plenti moni ova here. Evri kolad man haffi strive fi buy im own place soh him famli kyan liv diicent."

"Well, if mi faada kud see di two of yu now, im wud choke on him spit!" said Uncle Matthew, and Dada smiled a proud smile. And so the conversation meandered into the night, long after I had gone to bed.

Uncle Matthew got a job at Dada's workplace and began work with no delay. Aunt Molly, who had no dependants back home to worry about, was more interested in "gettin to knuo London", as she put it. It turned out that she had an adventurous streak. When the spirit moved her, she borrowed Madda's coat, tied a scarf over her head ("fi keep di briiz outta mi ears") and set off for a day of sightseeing. Alone, she took the bus to Oxford Street to look at the shops, to Baker Street to visit Madam Tussaud's and to Buckingham Palace to look at the Queen.

"Molly gyal, yu betta dan mi!" Madda would say. "Yu jus riich Inglan an alredi yuh knuo di place betta dan wii who deh ya likkl while!"

"Well, mi kyaan unnerstan how oonu liv in a place an noh knuo it. Yu mus knuo it as best yu kyan!"

Sometimes Aunt Molly took me with her on her excursions, and on one occassion, one warm Sunday afternoon, she led us all to Battersea Funfair. Dada, his friend Happy, Madda, Molly, Matthew, and Lily from upstairs and me all packed into the Cresta. At Battersea Park we joined the throng of fun-makers, moving from ride to ride, stopping only for candyfloss, popcorn or a soft drink. I clutched at Madda when cobwebs and skeletal fingers brushed my face in the shadowy tunnels of the ghost train and I could hear Lily shrieking and Uncle Matthew laughing behind us. I screamed as I hurtled down the helter skelter on a coconut mat, giving myself up to the momentum of the ride, safe between the wooden walls of the downward-spiralling channel. How the men loved the bumper cars! Matthew and Lily together in one car, Madda with Happy, Dada and me with Molly, the men at the wheel. They rammed into one another like rival bulls locking horns, laughing as the impact of rubber against rubber jolted their targets in their seats. Our car took a lot of bumps; Happy and Uncle Matthew ganged up on us, coming at us from both sides. Dada grew frustrated, trying to dodge and getting jolted instead. By the time the ride ended he was angry. As we headed off toward the big dipper I held on to his hand tightly, hoping to soothe him with this modest show of affection. We boarded the big dipper, and as it charged up and down on its tracks we clung to each other, me yelling wildly, Dada laughing with exhilaration, all anger dispersed.

He wanted to take Madda into the tunnel of love, and took her arm to lead her towards the entrance but she shrugged off his arm and headed towards the fortune teller's tent. He called after her, but she ignored him, joining the queue outside the tent. Matthew and Lily, Happy and Molly paid their money and got in the love-boat leaving Dada and me outside, Dada looking thunderous. I knew that the day was spoiled for me and for Dada, and I blamed Madda. Dada wouldn't even hold my hand; he paced up and down, impatient for the others to finish their ride. The tunnel of love was sweet, I could tell by the smiles of the returning voyagers. Madda eventually rejoined us and as we headed towards the car Uncle Matthew teasingly tried to extract the fortune teller's predictions from her. She shook her head mysteriously, giving nothing away.

When cricket season came, the adults took days off from work to go to watch the West Indies beat England in the test match. I went to school reluctantly on the those days, feeling excluded and envious. I left the women preparing food for the day out: fried fish, rice and peas and chicken, bottles of ginger beer and home-made rum punch, delicacies I never got to taste. They returned in the evening and settled in the living room with the french windows open to let in the fading summer evening light. Clothes crumpled and voices hoarse from shouting encouragement for their team, the men continued to argue the merits of the match, while Madda and Molly bustled about putting together snacks and Dada poured drinks for everybody.

They were happy then. The seeds of the new life, planted on their arrival in this country, had sprouted and grown, producing first blossom. They had no reservations about enjoying their prosperity and sharing it with family and friends. If Madda was a little ostentatious at times, so what? Everyone knew how hard she and Dada worked for what they had. Only a mean-spirited person would have judged her for it.

With the arrival of my aunt and uncle my quiet times alone in the house had gone. I became increasingly exposed to the demands of the adults around me. I washed dishes, dusted furniture, vacuumed carpets, ran errands. My parents spent less time at home as they were both working overtime. For Dada this meant longer working days in addition to Saturday morning work. For Madda, it meant an unwelcome introduction to Saturday work. Our weekly marketing excursions ceased. Instead, I followed Lily or Aunt Molly to wherever they went to do their shopping. They were easier to be with, I have to admit; they indulged me with sweets, ice lollies, ice cream, but I missed going out with my mother.

Aunt Molly's Saturday shopping ceased when she began going to Saturday church.

" Yu goin to *church?*" Madda could not believe it.

"*Church?*" said Uncle Matthew who could not believe it either. "Is man shi gone deh fi look, yaa!"

Each Saturday morning Aunt Molly dressed with meticulous care. She spent an age in the bathroom and emerged smelling like the perfume section of a chemist's shop. After much primping and preening she stepped gaily through the front door, hat perched skittishly on head, Bible under arm. Poor Aunt Molly. Even before I overheard Esme and Lily gossiping about her I sensed that Uncle Matthew was right; Aunt Molly was out seeking something more than God on Saturday mornings. Yet the idea of Aunt Molly with a boyfriend was hard for me to assimilate. To my eyes, Aunt Molly was old and plain, even in her best clothes. Not like Lily, who charmed and dazzled, spreading her beauty around her with laughter and high spirits. Who could get romantic over dull, quiet Aunt Molly?

It all became clear when Cecil came to visit. I answered a knock on the front door one Sunday afternoon and there he stood, tall, dark and lanky in flannel suit and tie, with hat clenched in both hands.

"Good h'afternoon" he said politely. "H'is Molly here, please?"

Aunt Molly came foreward, all eyeballs and smiles, took his hand and led him into the sitting room where Uncle Matthew and Madda were.

" I want yu all to meet Ciisl," she said proudly. "Ciisl, meet mi sista Esme an mi bredda Matthew an mi bredda-in-law Ray."

Cecil shook hands and said howdi, then picked up The News of The World from an armchair, sat down and began to read.

Esme and Matthew exchanged glances.

Uncle Matthew cleared his throat.

"Which paat ov Jamaica yuh come from, Ceesl?" he asked conversationally.

"H'I come from Kingston, the centre of civilisation on our little h'island." replied Cecil, looking up from his paper. "However, my mother hailed from Portland and my father from St Anne," he concluded, without a trace of a smile.

"Bakfoot!" Exclaimed Madda under her breath. "What is dis!"

"Ceesl is a civil servant." Aunt Molly explained.

"Ahoa!" said Matthew enigmatically, rolling his eyes towards heaven.

Cecil stayed long enough to drink a cup of tea and look around the garden, and then left.

Madda and Uncle Matthew teased poor Aunt Molly about him mercilessly.

"Look what Molly kom a Inglan an find! A speaky-spoky swivl servant wid a maaga nek!"

"Molly, yu tink im kyan manij di bisniss?" Uncle Matthew was very concerned. "Im look kina feeble to mii. Yu betta go easi wid im!"

Cecil came to visit every Sunday and on that basis he was accepted as Aunt Molly's man. He and I became firm friends. I admired him, because unlike my parents, he was educated, and was interested in books, in knowledge, and in something he called culture.

"You must grow up to be cultured, Tessa, cultured. Read Shakespeare! Read literature! Listen to music. H'I mean to the classics, h'only the classics!"

Cecil took it upon himself to correct my speech, which was beginning to lose its Jamaican accent.

"Please, child, please! H'I don't ever want to 'ear you speaking Londish!" Londish being his name for Cockney.

"Yu jus mind yu doan en up taaking fool-fool like im!" Warned Madda.

When a room upstairs became vacant, Aunt Molly moved into it and for a short space of time I was alone again in my room. I enjoyed the temporary solitude, and spent every spare moment I could reading.

I was already a voracious reader of library books, comics, anything I could lay hands on. Dada was proud of my reading, which he mistook for studiousness; he called me his bright princess, his top-of-the-class-girl. The material I read was more entertaining than educational but I did not disillusion him.

In the time between Uncle Matthew's departure to a room he rented in a house nearby and Aunt Elvira's arrival, our part of the house seemed empty. We could have taken in any number of new arrivals from home during that time, as someone new landed every week, or so it seemed. Our house became their Mecca. From Friday evening until Sunday evening, we had visitors coming in and going out, visitors for whom we had a never-ending pot.

"Laad Esme, mi luv yuh cookin," they all said, "yuh food taste just like food bak home!"

Whether it was Friday night liver, Saturday soup, or Sunday rice and peas and chicken, the meal could always stretch to feed however many mouths were present. All of this meant more work for me, as I had to help prepare the food and wash dishes afterward. I didn't enjoy helping with the housework, but I knew better than to protest: I enjoyed slaps on my head or backside even less.

Chapter 8

AUNT ELVIRA ARRIVED IN ENGLAND with the coming of spring. We threw a party for her to which every relative, every friend came to eat curry goat, drink rum and black or lager and lime, and dance till daybreak. Judging from their reaction, our neighbours did not approve. The old lady from the house opposite stopped me in the street the next day to ask me what was the cause of the rumpus. I told her it was to celebrate the arrival of my aunt, at which she rolled her eyes heavenward, and muttered, "Not another one" under her breath. So I told her my mother had fourteen brothers and sisters in all, and that they would all be coming over. I left her looking pale, both hands pressed to her chest as though to still her panicking heart.

Aunt Elvira bore a striking resemblance to Madda, except that she wore glasses, almond-shaped frames with winged tips which looked like they might take flight from the bridge of her nose at any moment. She laughed and talked constantly, like Uncle Matthew. Her report of news from Rocky Gap lasted for weeks. Every time she sat down with an audience, whether to eat or simply to relax, whether there was one person listening or ten, she had another chapter to recount.

She resembled my mother so much and yet was so different; I was fascinated by her. She should have been an actress with her big personality, big voice and her gift for drama. She could take an unremarkable incident and embellish it in such a way that her audience was rivetted. The time was to come when Madda would curse her "dyam blasted mout", but in the beginning she was sheer entertainment and everyone, even Madda, enjoyed her.

Aunt Vera wasted no time finding work as a machinist in a garment factory off Seven Sisters Road. She was not a natural seamstress like Madda and Aunt Molly; she had acquired the necessary skills before leaving Jamaica just so that she would be employable in England. She had big plans. She had a sweetheart in Jamaica she wanted to bring over as soon as possible so that they could get married and settle down. She wanted to buy a house for them to settle down in. She was going to save every penny she earned. With her first paypacket she opened a bank account into which she deposited funds each week without fail.

"Mi kyaan afford fi waste time an moni sportin and spreein!" she told me one night as we lay in bed. "Yuh Madda, shi luv spen moni, bwoy! Shi always had a boasi striik in er. Shi must hav pretti frock an pretti shoes fi shuo aaf, evn when er pickni goh a skool inna mashdown shoos!"

Perhaps it was because I resembled her a little, or maybe because we shared a room, but Aunt Elvira and I very quickly became close. I enjoyed our conversations in bed at night, her stories of life back in Jamaica. She talked to me as though I was grown up and fully comprehended what she had to say. But most of all, she earned my gratitude by taking my side against Madda.

"Esme, yu noh sii seh yuh pickni frock dem too shaat fi er?"

"Esme, yu must komb yuh daata hiir evri day! Yu kyaan send er to skool lookin lakka ole neaga pickni!"

She irritated Madda, who would stick out her bottom lip and sulk. At first I feared Madda would find ways to hit back at Aunt Vera, but I came to realise that she was a little afraid of her sister, and with good reason. Aunt Vera was outspoken to a fault. If she was annoyed, she didn't care what she said or whom she offended. And she could quarrel and cuss! Anyone who upset her on a bad day would not only hear about their own shortcomings, but also those of their mummah, their puppah, their bredda, sista, husbands or wives, as appropriate. She and Uncle Matthew were always catching up and quarrelling, loud, intense arguments after which Uncle Matthew would stay away until loneliness or hunger for Madda's cooking got the better of him.

Dada and Aunt Vera got on like a house on fire. Of all the people who came around us he was most comfortable with her. They would chat companionably while he worked in the garden, or in the kitchen while she helped him prepare Sunday dinner. It was clear to everybody that he appreciated her attention.

"Enibaddi wud tink di two of oonu deh!" I heard Madda mutter more than once, seeing the two of them together.

Apart from Dada, Aunt Vera and Cecil were my favorite adults. I admired Aunt Lily and I liked Aunt Molly, but I shared a special bond with these two. For a time I nurtured a fantasy of the two of them falling in love and getting married which collapsed when it became apparent that they did not get along at all. In and out of his hearing Aunt Vera was scathing about Cecil's rather eccentric ways, which upset him, upset Aunt Molly and upset me too.

"Molly, weh yu get dat jingbang fram! Mi certin im noh knuo which paat ov im fi do what!" Whereupon Aunt Molly would tell her to move herself and keep her nasty mouth out of her business; strong words, coming from Molly.

Aunt Vera's outspokenness soon landed her in trouble trouble at her workplace. She came home one evening, mouth set in one long straight line, veins standing out on her forehead and went into our room to lie down. At dinner time she was visibly calmer and bursting with her story.

"Bwoy, mi neva kom kraas such a briid ov ignorant piipl yet! Dem woman at mi wukplace, dem sii mi day in, day out for trii month now. Yu tink dem wud realize by now dat, dough mi skin kola diffrent, mi is still human bein like dem! Well, oonu lissen to dis!" She rested her hands on her hips and drew a deep breath.

"As how di sun was so brite dis maanin an look like di day gwain waam, mi put on a lite frock an a kaadigan. Mi mussa did look too nice fi dem, kaas, kom tea-time dis aftanoon, hiir Miss Rita, di one on di ovalockin mashiin:

"Elvira" Aunt Vera's voice became falsetto cockney, "'Tell me, is it true that you black people have tails?' She look strate inna mi face when shi say it! Mi kud hiir de odda bitch-dem a-laaf afta mi. So mi jus look pon er an ask er if shi want si mi tail." Aunt Vera paused a moment to savour the reaction of her audience.

"Bifore di bitch kud blink, mi tun mi bak pon er, pull up mi frock, pull dun mi draws an shuo er mi bakside, shuv it up rite in er face! De bitch shok, she nearli drop aaf er chiir! Den mi go strate to Missa Isaacs, di baas, an mi tell him seh mi kyaan wuk wid dem-deh piipl! An yu knuo what im seh? Im seh dese Inglish not civilise! Dem triit evri odda piipl like animal, an is dem is animal! Im seh im knuo from experience, kaas im is a Jew, an dem triit Jew like dut! An him seh mi kyan go wuk in im odda factri in Tottnam if mi noh want stan wid dem-deh bitch eni longa. So mi seh yes, mi gwain staat dere Monday!" Aunt Vera drew a deep breath and sat back in her chair.

"Yu haffi shuo dem seh yu nat gwain tek foolishnis," said Dada, "oddawise dem wi tek yu mek jackass. Mi noh knuo how lang it gwain tek dem fi get use to wii, but dem betta get use to wii fa wi nat gwine stop kom!"

Uncle Matthew was mad when he heard.

"Dem a-tek pure advantage ov wi! Look how wi wuk haad! An fi what? Fi less dan di white man who nat evn doin as much."

Uncle Matthew was always getting into fights at work. Dada had persuaded him to join the trade union, arguing that this was the only way he and other coloured workers would be able to bring complaints against unfair treatment and unequal pay. Dada always used to say that the coloured man must use the union to fight for his rights, but Uncle Matthew was more angry, more militant. He was always ready to fight but he preferred to use his fists.

Most Saturday nights my parents went out dancing. They dressed to kill for these sessions, and for Madda, getting ready was part of the fun. Lily, who often went with them, was the same. Aunt Vera, who had no taste for nightclubbing herself, used to say that the two of them, Lily and Madda, were bad influences on each other.

They had been out to a club the night Dada threw the dressing table stool through the front window. I remember it as clearly as if it were last week. A group of them had gone to a club in Notting Hill, one of their favourite night spots. It was mid-November, Madda's birthday, to be precise, and she had bought a new dress for the occasion, a beautiful black moiré gown which buttoned down the front with large red buttons. She looked stunning in it.

That night Aunt Vera and I both woke up with a jolt in the early hours of the morning to the sound of the front door slamming. It crashed against its frame so forcefully that the whole house shook. I heard Dada shouting at the top of his voice, ranting like a madman and cursing bad words.

"Yu hoor yuh! Yu tink mi neva sii yu winnin up wid dat bumbo claat bwoy! Yu fukkin hoor yuh !"

Aunt Vera jumped out of bed and pulled on her dressing gown. I could hear Cecil, poor ineffectual Cecil, trying to calm Dada, telling him he was waking the whole house, waking the whole street; what would the neighbours say? We heard a crash, closely followed by the bell-like sound of glass falling to the ground. Then there was a thud as something fell heavily to the floor. Aunt Vera ran into Madda's bedroom with me following at her heels.

I saw Madda lying limp on the floor in front of the shattered bay window with Dada kneeling over her body, his hands at her throat, pumping with all his might. Cecil and Lily were on him pulling at his arms, pleading with him to let go. I heard a voice screaming "Dada, stop it! Stop it!" without realising it was mine.

Aunt Vera grabbed Dada's chin from behind and yanked back his head. Pain made him loosen his grip on Madda's throat so that Cecil and Lily could pull him off her and pin him to the floor.

Madda turned on her side and just lay there, the full skirt of her dress bunched around her thighs, her legs like pistils protruding from the petals of a crushed black flower. Cold air seeped through the broken window into an atmosphere already chill.

"Get bak to yuh bed!" said Aunt Vera sharply.

I went back into my room, climbed into bed and lay there trembling, waiting for Aunt Vera.

Day was already bright by the time Aunt Vera came back to bed. I was wide awake, but she didn't speak. She simply rolled over on her side and closed her eyes.

For days after the house was silent, the atmosphere thick with tension. The tenants moved quietly around like the duppies from Aunt Vera's ghost stories. I hardly saw my Dada. He came home late from work every night and shut himself up in the living room, and when I eventually did see him he avoided my eyes as though ashamed. He and Madda barely spoke to each other for months after their fight. He made a bed on the living room couch and slept there. Madda, whose throat was badly bruised, could barely speak at all. She made the most of her injuries, bearing them with all the pride and defiance of a wounded heroine.

Only Aunt Vera carried on as normal. She talked to Dada, she talked to Madda. She took over cooking the family meals as Madda had stopped; another form of protest. Everyone else in the house had sided against Dada, but it was hard to tell whose side Aunt Vera had taken. As for me, all I wanted was for my parents to talk to each other again so that my life would get back to normal and that the cold, hungry feeling in my stomach would go away.

Nobody told me what caused the fight. When the old woman across the road stopped me in her usual inquisitive fashion to ask me about the fracas and enquire what was the problem between my parents, I was able to tell her in all truthfulness that I didn't know. Eventually I pieced a story together, like an amateur detective, by eavesdropping on adults talking in whispers in the hallway, on the stairs or in the kitchen.

The story was quite simple. My parents and their group were at a night club drinking and dancing and having a good time. While Dada was dancing with Lily and with Aunt Molly, Madda was dancing too long and too close with a man they had known back home in Jamaica. Dadda got mad and dragged her away from the man and out of the club. The rest I already knew.

Eventually our lives returned to a kind of subdued normality, largely due to Aunt Vera's efforts. Madda's bruises healed and her voice returned. Tenants began to walk and talk normally. Dada moved back in with Madda. But although peace was restored, I knew that things would never be the same again.

Not long after the fight Aunt Vera moved to a house in Tottenham where she had rented a bedsit in preparation for the arrival Samuel, her sweetheart. Soon after that, Aunt Molly and Cecil rented a place together in Finsbury Park, not far from us. I missed them all, but Aunt Vera's departure left a particularly large gap. Without her I felt lonely and curiously exposed. The house felt dead; the jollity was gone and fewer people came to visit. I lost my best companion, Dada lost his confidante and we were both left at Madda's mercy.

Still, we visited Aunt Vera and Aunt Molly frequently, as the sisters took it in turns to provide Sunday dinner. Since our house was no longer at the centre of things, the family circle grew wider to include new places to visit and new people, relatives from home, friends of my aunts, friends of my uncle.

※ ※ ※

Aunt Vera's sweetheart Samuel was the ugliest man I had ever seen. His face fascinated me. It wasn't that he had unpleasant or distorted features, or even bad skin. It was the breadth of his face and forehead, the wide spread of nose and mouth, the way light refracted from the planes of his face, that made him look sinister.

"Laad, Vera, im ugli bad!" was Uncle Matthew's pained reaction. " Mi figat seh a so dem Palmer blak an ugli. Yuh miin yuh kudn't do betta dan dat?"

"Moov yu feisty self!" retorted Aunt Vera. "Soh im noh pretti; soh what? Him wuk haad an im act decent. Mi content wid dat!"

"Bet yu neva mek Doc set eye on im!" said Matthew, at which Aunt Vera dug an elbow into his ribs.

Whenever my grandfather's name came up in conversation I sensed a powerful character. I imagined a wrathful tyrant who was always watching and waiting for his children to err, eager to judge and punish. They all seemed to fear and respect him, but it was Uncle Matthew who most evidently held him in awe.

"My faada," he used to say, "raise wi to be equal to eni man! Niida white man, red man nor neaga kyan tek advantage of Partridge briid! Is soh im tell wi time an time agen."

"Inna fi-wi distrik," he boasted, "wi is important smaddi! Dat miin seh ova yasso, wi is important smaddi too!"

"Yuh faada was important smaddi, but dat no miin seh yu is enibadi!" said Dada, intending to take him down a peg.

Annie, Uncle Matthew's wife, was a quiet smiling woman of whom Uncle Matthew was inordinately proud.

"Mi glad fi hav er wid mi, yu sii! Look how shi brown an pretti!" And his hands would smooth Aunt Annie's straight black hair lovingly. I used to see his hands touching pretty, black Lily in the same way.

" An she mek four pretti pickney fi mi. Mi noh must luv er?"

"Soh where di four pickni-dem deh?" said Dada, irritated. "Yu betta mek haste an send fi dem bifore Annie giv yu four more!"

The crisis at home subsided like a passing storm and school regained its former prominent status in my world. I was doing well at school at that point. I was the best in my class at reading and I was the first in my class to get a gold star for learning the multiplication tables from two to twelve. My life fell into a quiet rhythm. I went to school; I came home; I washed the breakfast things, tidied the house, ran errands for Madda. I even had time to read, now and again. Anne Pendleton invited me to her house to play less frequently than she used to. In fact, since my parents' big fight the whole street cooled towards us. The family living opposite stopped talking to us, and our next-door neighbours no longer exchanged pleasantries over the garden fence. We felt we had been expelled from a club by the unanimous consent of the other members. We suspected all along they had never really wanted us among them. Now we knew they had barely tolerated us and were only too glad of an excuse to reject us.

I recall a certain bright afternoon when the early summer sun bathed our house in honeyed light. Fading blossoms from the hawthorn tree in front of our gate covered the pavement with a mottled pink carpet which felt bumpy under my feet. As I approached the house, I noticed that Madda's bedroom curtains were drawn. Strange, I thought; someone must be home.

I opened the front door and stepped into a silence which on this golden day felt cool and heavy. I turned the handle of Madda's door, usually my first port of call when I came home. It was locked.

"Madda, Madda! Yu in dere? Yu aal right?" I called through the door. There was no answer, not a sound, but I sensed the room was occupied. I walked through the house, out of the back door and into the garden and sat on the steps, chin resting on my hands, elbows resting on my knees. I had a clear view down the passage running through the house from front to back. As I waited for my mother's door to open, I felt icicles form in my belly and turn into teeth, which gnawed at my gut.

The door opened and Madda came out in her dressing gown, followed by a man I'd never seen before. He wore a suit and a hat, that much I took in before I looked away, not daring to look at his face. Madda let him out of the house and returned to her room without once looking in my direction. What was going on? What was my mother doing? I wondered. Like a nervous young animal, I was quick to sense danger.

I was still sitting on the step when she emerged again, this time fully dressed and calling my name. I stood up and went to her.

"Mek mi a kup ov koffi," she said when I stood before her. She paused a moment, face expressionless and then said, "yu betta not seh eniting to yu faada," after which she went back into her room and shut the door. I felt my life begin to unravel, like the crochet runner on her dressing table which I had inadvertently ruined by pulling on a loose thread.

No, I thought, I'd better not say anything. What would Dada do if he found out? He would kill her, I was absolutely certain of that. An image of her lying on her bedroom floor with Dada crouched above her, hands pumping at her throat flashed across my mind. Wasn't she afraid? Frightened thoughts chased each other around my head as I made her coffee, as I sat eating dinner with her and Dada that evening, as I sat at my desk in class the next day.

The man began to telephone in the mornings after Dada had gone to work, and she lay on her bed cooing down the phone to him in a fake sultry voice. Sometimes I heard her trying to persuade him to come to the house. Perhaps his conscience bothered him, or perhaps he feared that such flagrant risk-taking might attract discovery. Perhaps his sense of decency was stronger than hers, because he rarely came.

Madda knew no such caution. She fell into the habit of leaving work early on Wednesdays and taking me with her to an early show at the cinema in Finsbury Park. He would be there when we arrived, waiting in the lobby beside the fake marble statue of Cupid.

At first he tried to charm me with sweets and popcorn but I refused to talk to him. I felt justified in not responding, sinking petulantly in the plush cinema seat whenever he tried to make conversation with me across Madda's solid body. Eventually he gave up and spent his time fondling Madda's hand while I focussed on the screen, trying hard to ignore them.

For weeks, months, my father remained unaware of Madda's secret life. I don't know how. I thought she reeked of guilt. I saw sin branded across her forehead in blazing letters and it puzzled me that no-one else noticed. I felt sorry for Dada, I wanted to hug him and tell him I loved him, as if my love could make up for the awful thing Madda was doing. But we were not that kind of family; we did not make demonstrations of affection. So Dada just carried on, unaware that his life had become a field of mines just waiting to explode.

Roughly one year after the big fight, I fell ill with Asian flu and had to stay home from school. Madda grumbled at the inconvenience, but she took time off from work to look after me. As I now realise and appreciate, my mother was a resourceful woman and she managed to turn the situation to her advantage. He came to visit nearly every day! Either he didn't work, or he took time off too, but he came to our house virtually every day of my illness.

I didn't actually see him on these visits as I was bedridden in my parents' room. But I heard his tread on the front door step, heard his knock at the door, his voice in the hall. He would arrive around lunchtime, in time to eat. Madda prepared a meal for him every day and my father ate the remains when he came home in the evening. He and Madda would disappear into my room for hours, leaving me burning with fever, with anger and with shame for my mother who clearly knew no limits.

Dada, always the more caring parent, was particularly attentive during my illness. Every evening he brought home a gift for me: chocolates, a comic book, a bottle of Lucozade. Dada's attention pleased me as much as Madda's behaviour disturbed me, and I felt all the more sympathy for him as a result. Most evenings, I lay in their bed watching the two of them together with a strange feeling of disconnection. They did not talk to each other much. Dada got home quite late, washed and changed his clothes while Madda served up the evening meal. Most evenings they ate in their room with the radio playing, filling the silence with noise. What conversations they did have were spare and to the point. Madda, of course, always tended to be taciturn. He might venture a comment on some item of interest heard on the news; she might have something to tell him about a tenant, or gossip passed on by one of her sisters. But most of the time they did not converse.

Chapter 9

SOMETIMES CHANGE COMES QUIETLY, ONE season passing to another, evident only after the transformation. Leaves lying dead on the ground; earth cold and white with frost; green young shoots sprouting on wizened branches. At other times change moves like a runaway steamroller, forceful and violent, flattening everything in its way.

Suddenly it seemed as though half of Rocky Gap was living in London; in Fulham, Paddington, Finsbury Park, Tottenham. Our circle of relatives and friends kept on increasing and my parents were once again at the social centre of a growing community of Jamaicans, many of whom were connected by blood or by friendship from back home.

Aunt Vera married Samuel just before Christmas. They had a brief registry office ceremony followed by a big party at our house. The neighbours complained about the noise to the police, who came banging on the door at around one in the morning, demanding that we turn down the noise. Dada, who was quite tipsy, was ready to argue, but Cecil intervened, dealt with the police, and persuaded Aunt Vera to turn down the music.

Madda stopped speaking to Aunt Vera for a long time after that party. They quarrelled as only sisters can, out in the garden, arguing in heated whispers so that I, concealed behind the garden door and straining my ears to hear, could not figure out the problem. Aunt Vera was telling Madda off, I could make out that much. I caught the words, "dutti slaknis" and I heard Madda tell Aunt Vera to "piss off an mind her own bisnis," with which she turned on her high black suede heel and marched right back into the house.

Madda could hold a grudge for as long as it suited her. After a suitable length of time she would haughtily resume relations with the offending person, but until she was ready she would maintain an absolutely hostile front. So it was with Aunt Vera. It was months before I saw her again.

※ ※ ※

Something was wrong with my mother and I didn't know what.

Madda wasn't getting up in the mornings in her usual brisk way. She lay in bed like a tragic heroine, eyes closed, handkerchief to her mouth, spitting occasionally into the chimmy she kept under her bed. She stopped drinking coffee, she stopped eating bun and cheese, and she retched at the sight of fried food. Her disposition degenerated from ordinary grumpiness to a scary, near-snarling visciousness. I pored over the Home Health Encyclopedia, carefully pondering the myriad of ailments with symptoms resembling Madda's. What could it be? Nothing as everyday as flu or bronchitis. Tuberculosis seemed like a possibility but I finally decided on rabies. Madda going mad from a mad dog's bite; it seemed to fit, somehow. And what should I do? I had vivid fantasies of nursing a repentant Madda on her death-bed and equally powerful fears of contracting the disease and dying with her. Self-preservation triumphed over self-sacrifice and I kept out of Madda's way as much as I could.

On one of Aunt Molly's frequent visits, I overheard she and Madda talking in low-pitched voices.

"Gyal," Madda whispered, "when mi seh mi fiil sik, I miin sik like daag! Same way mi was sik wid de one mi did loos. An funni, when mi was prignant wid Tessa, mi neva sik evn one day!"

So that was it. Madda was expecting a baby!

Madda and Molly whispered together, Madda and Annie (who was also pregnant) whispered together, and when they all met up they plunged into deep discussions about pregnancy, about childbirth, this one's experience, that one's misfortune, who did dash way a baby and how, and so on.

Around this time Cecil stopped appearing at our Sunday gatherings. Aunt Molly began to change visibly; almost overnight, she faded and shrank into herself like a deflated balloon. What happen to Molly and Cecil? everyone was asking in whispers.

When Madda asked her directly Aunt Molly admitted Cecil had left her.

"So what *realli* happn, Molly? Im was kiiping anodda woman?"

"Nuo," said Aunt Molly, folding her lips firmly to signal reluctance to discuss the matter. "Wi just kud nat gree," she added finally.

The truth came out in pieces, which Madda fit together.

"Well mi-diir, it siim like im did hav anodda woman aal alang. Some yung gyal from im wukplace! An im gwaan till di gyal faal prignant an kom a dem yaad fi tell Molly an harass er. Yu eva hiir eniting go soh yet? Dem Christian! Dem is pure hippocrite!" Madda kissed her teeth long and hard.

"An yu knuo di worst paat? What mek Molly baal di livin eye waata? Di gyal was a white gyal! Ascordin to Molly, one ugli, krass-eye sinting no diicent man wud look pon two time!"

"Same ting mi did tell oonu," said Uncle Matthew. "Dyam swivl ser-vant! Im tink seh im betta dan wi, but mi knuo wi too gud fi him! Mek di ole Jan Crow gwaan, yaa!"

I was embarrassed for Cecil, I missed him, and I felt angry on his behalf. Uncle Matthew's remarks were unfair! To my mind Cecil had never behaved as though he believed himself better than us. He was intelligent, thoughtful and kind, the complete opposite of Uncle Matthew. Only he took any interest in my progress at school, only he bothered to hear me read or look at my writing. No-one else cared.

Maybe boredom led Madda to patch up her differences with Aunt Vera or maybe it was sympathy for her sister, but as soon as Madda learned that Aunt Vera had been sacked from her job for fighting with another worker, she found her way to Aunt Vera's house in Tottenham. It was our first visit to the house and Madda was curious. It was not as big as ours, nor was the street as clean or as quiet. Yet stepping into the hall was like entering a familiar place. The house smelled of good cooking, of chicken well browned and stewed down with plently of seasoning, smells which made my mouth water and my stomach rumble hungrily. I had forgotten how good a cook Aunt Vera was.

Aunt Vera was all smiles and chatter as she showed us around, and Madda was generous with admiring oohs and aahs. After plying us with tea and seating us on a new red plush sofa still cased in its crisp plastic cover, Aunt Vera told the tale of how she came to lose her third job.

"Yu memba how mi did liiv Missa Isaacs an get a nex job in Finsbury Park? Well, mi was doin fine, gettin on aal right wid evribaddi an evriting. Den guess what happn?"

"What?" said Madda, knowing only too well.

"Mi get in a quarril wid di soopavisa! Di woman find fault wid evri likkl ting mi doh! Nottn mi doh was right, evn when I kud sii dat fi-mi wuk was niita dan sum ov di white-gyal dem wuk. An shi neva seh nottn to dem, nat one word! So push kom to shov, an mi tell er plain seh shi prejudice! An when shi mek fi turn er bak, mi grab hold ov er an spin er to face mi. An guess what?"

"What?" Said Madda dutifully.

"Shi miss er step an faal an lik er bak pon one ov di ovalakkin machiin!"

"Vera, man! Yu must wach yuh tempa! Yu kyaan fight evribaddi!"

"Shi shudda buss er aas!" said Aunt Vera, unrepentant. "Plenti ov dem odda gyal in deh kyaan evn sew tree stitch strate, yet shi neva seh nottn to dem! Is just mii shi want provoke!"

"But Vera, yu noh realise seh a soh dem stay!" said Madda. "Dem lov fi troubl wi! Dem kyaan ignore wi at aal! It kom in like wi is chigger unda dem skin, an dem haffi scratch, scratch, scratch till dem get wi out!"

"Yu knuo what burn mi most ov all?" continued Aunt Vera. "Is dat Samuel! Aal im kyan taak bout is di moni! Im done kuss mi alredi, bout how mi is too kantankerous and kyaan get along wid enibaddi! Mi knuo seh wi niid de moni, mi knuo seh wi hav morgij an aal kind ov debt, but mi is nobaddi slave an mi naa tek no bad treatment from eni bakra, not evn di Queen of Inglan erself!"

"Vera lissen to mi! Yu betta lern fi rilax likkl. If yu waan fi stay inna dis kontri yu haffi learn fi diil wid di piipl-dem! Man kyaan sit pon kow bak an kuss kow skin! More dan dat, if yu mek dem worri yuh brain, dem wi giv yu presha! Yu sii mi? Me naa mek nuo white man nor woman put mi inna grave bifore mi time!"

It didn't take Aunt Vera long to find another job, but even before she began work in the new place her sisters were placing bets on how long she would last there.

Madda's doctor had advised her to stay home and rest until the baby came, but she was a bad invalid. She could not give up her social life. Our visits to the cinema with the man Brewster continued. We visited Annie, who was also on maternity leave, and called on Aunt Molly and Aunt Vera in the evenings. Dada frequently came home to an empty house.

"How kom yu suppose to stay home an rest and yu a-run round all ova di place!" he protested.

"Soh what is wrong wid goin to mi sista yaad or mi bredda yaad? Yu expek mi fi siddung aal day by misself?"

Dada refrained from arguing with her. Even at the best of times it was wise to avoid provoking Madda and these were not the best of times.

Not long after my ninth birthday Madda gave birth to my brother Stephen. The first time I saw him he was feeding, cradled in the crook of her elbow. Everything about him was round; tiny nose, large forehead, eyes shut tight as he focussed all his attention on the important task of sucking. Dada said he was the dead stamp of me, which pleased me no end. Resemblance bonded me to him far more tightly than our shared parentage. Seeing miniature versions of my features in his face, I felt a surge of feeling for the tiny bundle that Madda held in her arms.

I loved him from that first moment. When Madda brought him home I doted on him, eager to hold him, to change his nappy, to bottle-feed him, to cradle him in my lap. Madda, permanently weary, indulged my infatuation gladly. "Choh man!" she would grumble, "Dis siddung-inna-yaad-a-watch-pickni bisnis too borin!" She grumbled to Lily, to Aunt Molly, to Aunt Vera. "It wudn't evn bi soh bad if mi had likkl compani, smaddi to paas likkl time wid."

"But Esme," said Auntie Molly, "yu noh hav Annie just nearby?"

"Annie!" Madda said scornfully, "shi kom in like hen inna fowl roost; shi spin roun an roun in di one room, just a laaf an skin up er teeth, like shi hav someting fi glad bout!"

"Esme, man, ease up yusself! Mek yusself content. Yu hav Ray fi provide fi yu, an yu hav evriting yu need, yu even hav Tessa fi help you. Mi kyaan unnerstan why yu inna hurri fi run bak to wuk!"

"Ray fi provide fi mi?" she said with sarcasm. "Mi haffi provide fi misself, mi-diir! Mi kyaan rely pon im! An mi knuo seh dem wi tek mi bak at mi ole wukplace; soh mi no gwain waste time. Mi goin bak quik quik!"

"But Ray is yu husban!" persisted Lily. "Yu mus kyan rely pon yu husban."

At which Madda kissed her teeth and changed the subject.

Dada wanted Madda to stay home with Stevie, but she was adamant "Puss kyare fi dem pickni betta dan yu!" he shouted. She accused him of wanting to keep her prisoner, of wanting her as his slave. He walked out of the house slamming the front door behind him. They didn't speak to each other for days.

When Stevie was three months old Madda found a childminder for him and returned to work.

※ ※ ※

Aunt Vera spent Christmas in hospital, sick with an ulcer. The day she was discharged Madda collected her from hospital in a taxi and took her home. Aunt Vera looked shockingly thin, a weak, greyish shadow of her normally plump, lively self.

"Docta seh is worri kaas it," Aunt Vera flopped onto her bed. "Im seh mi haffi tek life more iisi, rilax more. But how mi kyan rilax wid a damn man like Samuel aroun mi? Im kyaan do nottn! Im kyan bareli mek tea an fry egg fi imself fi eat! So mi haffi hakkl misself fi goh wuk, fi kom home an kook, wash an iron, an dat dyam blaastid man, im jus kom home, nyam, belch, an cok up im fut, seh im a-rest!"

Tears filled her eyes, the veins on her forehead stood out and her voice shook. I sat beside her and held her hand while Madda moved quietly around the room clearing away clothes and tidying up.

"Esme," asked Aunt Vera quietly, "what mi gwain du?"

"What kyan I tell yu, Sis?" Madda sat down on the bed looking at Aunt Vera, as though willing some of her own steely strength into her. "Yu haffi tek it iisi, like di docta seh. Yu haffi stop worri bout moni. Why not rent out two ov di room upstair, tek in two tenant; dat wi help wid di morgij."

"Mi noh want nuo strainja traipsin in an out ov mi hous, yaa! Mi waant mi privici an mi waant a room fi do likkl sewin, so mi kyan tek in homewuk when mi reddi. Rememba, dis hous not big like fi-yu."

"Well," said Madda "kansida it, kaas di likkl moni yu will get wi help tek som ov di presha aaf yu bak."

Not long after, Uncle Matthew came by the house to ask Dada to help him move into Aunt Vera's house.

"Man, is di salushun to fi-wi problem an to Vera problem!" he told us. "Famli mus help dem one anodda, noh tru?"

"Shud be soh, but is not ofen soh," Dada replied. "Yu sure seh yu an Vera gwain gree? One ting mi knuo, is dat from mi knuo yu, an from mi knuo shii, di two ov oonu kud neva gree fi longa dan ten minit."

"Choh man, is soh wi stay! When wi faal out, it no mean nottn! Wi a-fall out an gree bak aal ov wi life. It noh mean nottn!"

Dada helped with the move, but he remained sceptical about the prospects of domestic harmony between my aunt and uncle.

"It look like is more trubbl Vera tekkin pon er hed. An mi shure seh Matthew an Samuel nat gwain get along eida. Still," he added, "is a fact dat if it wukout, evribaddi will bi betta aaf."

Chapter 10

I WAS LYING ON MY bed, trying to read and at the same time keep an eye on Stevie who was getting into everything. He opened the wardrobe door and peered inside, grabbing at a dress hanging above his head. Quickly losing interest, he tottered over to the dressing table and tugged a drawer, chattering to it as though persuading it to open. He tugged at the dressing table runner, bringing down my comb, brush and tin of talcum powder with it. I put down the book and rushed to rescue my belongings, irritated.

I heard a knock on the front door while I was prising my hairbrush out of Stevie's grip. I heard Dada opening the door and I heard footsteps follow his down the hall, into the sitting room. I wondered who this visitor could be; a friend or relative would have gone into my parents' room. I put Stevie in the middle of the floor where there was nothing he could damage and redoubled my effort at reading.

Ten minutes later or so Dada called me. I picked up Stevie and carried him into the living room. My parents sat side by side on the sofa with long, solemn faces, and a middle aged white man occupied an armchair. All three of them watched me enter the room and put down Stevie.

Dada spoke first.

"Tessa, dis gentleman kom from yuh skool. Di hedmaasta send im fi tell us yu havin problem at skool."

"Not exactly, Mr Erskine," the man interrupted. "Tessa's class teacher and headmaster felt I should talk to you to find out if Tessa is having problems at home." He turned toward me, speaking quite kindly. "You see, dear, your schoolwork has deteriorated; you are late for school nealy every morning; you sometimes fall asleep in class. We are worried about you, because you are one of our brightest pupils."

"But how kyan shi bi late fi skool evri day!" burst out Dada. "Yu si how niir wi liv to di skool? An shi hav whole hiip ov book aal ova di place. When shi lok up in er room we tink seh shi a study. If shi nat studyin, what is shi doin? To tell yu di trut, sah, dis is shockin news to wi."

Dada's words reverberated in my ears, confusing me. Both he and Madda were watching me accusingly. Why doesn't one of them tell him? I wondered. Why doesn't Madda tell him I have to take Stevie to the babyminder, all the way to Finsbury Park, before school? Why doesn't she tell him that I can't get to do any proper reading because I have to collect Stevie in the evenings, and when I get home with him, I have to watch him, even while I am tidying the kitchen and getting dinner started? I waited, every cell in my body begging my parents to explain these things to the man.

"Well, my dear," he continued, "you'll have do better in future. I can see that you have a good home and good parents. Lots of childen aren't as fortunate as you, you know! You must pull your socks up!"

"Well, sah," said Dada, "I feel shame dat yu haffi komplain bout mi chile, God knuo." Madda nodded balefully. "Maybi now yu taak to er, shi will buk up and bihave erself at skool!"

I was burning with shame as I walked out of the room. By the next morning I was burning with anger too. As I marched down the road behind Stephen's pushchair I was so caught up in my feelings that I barely noticed the familiar streets, the morning traffic, people I normally greeted.

They didn't stick up for me! My parents let that man believe that I was lazy! I felt humiliated. I felt empty inside and as lonely as any child abandoned by her parents. It wasn't fair. I worked so hard for them, did my best for them and what did they do? They didn't stick up for me!

That evening Madda barely addressed one word to me and even Dada was cold. I did my chores as normal. I helped prepare dinner, I washed up the dishes afterwards, I put Stevie to bed. I told myself I didn't care about them, I didn't care about their coldness; I didn't want to talk to people who didn't stick up for me.

Less than a week later, I threw a large bunch of house keys up into the tree outside our front gate. With a soft jingle the keys settled on a wide branch and remained there, stuck. I had been entertaining Stevie who watched from his pushchair, clapping his hands together and giggling gleefully when the keys flew up in the air then fell, gleaming as they fell into my waiting hands.

Unable to get into the house, I waited on the doorstep, fretting about what Madda would say. Boy, would she be mad! The bunch had master keys to all the house doors and to the gas meters also. Why I had possession of them, I don't know. But I knew for certain I would be punished for losing them, as sure as my name was Tessa.

Madda reacted much as expected. She snapped at me, calling me a stupid fool then pushed out her bottom lip and withdrew into her room, closing the door firmly behind her. At that point I knew the punitive silence I was already enduring would be extended, but I was already used to it. I could deal with it. Shut away in my own room, I imagined myself somewhere safe, somewhere cosy and snug and big enough to include Stevie.

Dada's reaction was shattering.

"Yu damn iidyat!" he shouted at me. "Yu no hav no sens?" I froze. Dada had never yelled at me before. I stood speechless as me moved towards me, fumbling with his belt, but I didn't realise what he was doing until the buckle struck the corner of my mouth, cutting my lip and grazing a tooth. I tasted blood in my mouth, then the buckle sank into my arm, biting through clothing into my flesh. I tried to dodge him but Dada held me by the arm, lashing me repeatedly until his arm grew tired and he stopped.

The sound of Stevie screaming reached me, like a noise from a far-off place. He was standing in the doorway, screaming because I was screaming. The lashes stopped, but I carried on screaming, standing in the middle of their room, my arms wrapped around my chest. My parents turned their backs and left me where I stood.

Eventually, I went back into my room and lay on the bed. Poor little Stevie followed me, still crying. He climbed up on the bed and
hugged me, howling, tears and snot running down his face. He looked
so pitiful I felt as sorry for him as I did for myself.

An idea leapt suddenly into my mind like a brilliant flash of light
illminating a dark space. I sat up, inspired, surprising Stevie who immediately stopped crying. I acted instantly, put on shoes and coat, put the
few coins I had in my coat pocket. I carried Stevie into the hall and
placed him in front of Madda's door. He would soon start to bang on
it, demanding to be let in, but he watched me as I opened the front
door and stepped out, obviously wondering whether or not he should
follow me.

I was running away! Why had I never thought of it before? Children
in the story books I read were always doing it. My parents deserved it,
they deserved to lose me. I would go a long way away and never return,
and they would suffer painful remorse and agonising guilt. It would
serve them both right; him for beating me and her for not stopping
him. I would never, ever forgive them.

I headed in the direction of Tottenham without thinking. It was a
route I knew well, the way to Aunt Vera's house. As I walked down the
hill towards Tottenham Lane I tried to figure out where to go. No use
going to Aunt Vera, I decided. She would feel sorry for me, but she
would send me straight back home, probably to more trouble. I kept
walking. The late spring night was dark and chilly. My mind played
vivid scenes of my parents discovering my disappearance. They would
realise how callous they had been and would be smitten with shame;
they would search for me everywhere, in a frenzy of regret. These fantasies fed my anger and propelled my legs, like fuel driving an engine.
As I passed a police station I visualized my parents being arrested and
taken away in handcuffs. And suddenly I saw what I should do. I
should go to the police and register a complaint!

The duty officer listened to my story, his face expressionless. He took
down my name and address, my parents' names and phone number.
He told me to sit in the waiting area, and disappeared into another
room. I must have been sitting there for about an hour when Madda

arrived with Lily, both of them looking grave. The duty officer handed me over to Madda with some inappropriately jovial remarks. She walked out of the station without even looking to see if I was following. I took hold of Lily's hand, hoping that she would offer me some comfort, but none was forthcoming, not even a squeeze. Lily merely looked at me reproachfully. I was alone and adrift; no-one cared about me, it seemed. I was hurting; not only the welts on my body but my chest hurt, a tight, squeezing pain around my heart. Now I can see it was a growing pain, in a way. For that night I became aware for the first time of how lonely, how painful and how unjust life could be.

My parents punished me with weeks of silence. I was accustomed to Madda's long sulks but Dada had never behaved that way before. I could hardly bear it. I did everything I could to placate him. I took him coffee in bed in the morning. I made him tea when he came home at night. I swept out his car, I cleaned his shoes. He remained unmoved. Even worse, he told everyone in the family I was an ungrateful wretch and he would never forgive me for going to the police as long as he lived.

Poor Stevie couldn't figure out what was happening. The bad atmosphere upset him and he became clingy, wanting me to hold him all the time. I was glad that somebody wanted my company, even if it was only a tot who needed to be comforted.

My parents weren't talking much to each other either. Even before I got into trouble, the atmosphere at home was tense. When the two of them were at loggerheads everyone around them felt it. They generated a tension that was tangible, like a mist of microscopic barbs.

They quarrelled over every little thing, especially when Madda bought a new dress or pair of shoes. I remember some black suede sandals she bought, high-heeled and with thick straps which criss-crossed up the front of her feet and around her ankles. They looked wonderful on her full, muscular legs. When Dada found them in her closet, looking blatantly new and expensive, he dashed them on the floor, demanding to know if she thought he was Eddie Fisher. Must bi, he yelled, kaas yu spendin moni like Elizabeth Taylor.

They quarrelled when Madda and Molly went to Selfridges' sale, and she came home with a fur stole. "It was a baagin," she said, "it was chiip; it isn't riil mink."

"Yu knuo when last I spend moni on a soot?" he yelled, and stormed out of the room slamming the door behind him.

There was a really big row when the gas man came and emptied the meters and there wasn't enough money in them to meet the bill. "Is who tiif out di moni?" Madda wanted to know. She thought it was one of the tenants. "Is mii," said Dada, "when mi neva hav moni fi put in mi pokit. An why? Kaas mi wife own de Bank of Inglan, shi haffi dress like di Queen an mi haffi wuk lakka slave fi kiip er, an waak street wid nat a penni in mi pokit!"

Stevie always cried when they quarrelled, cried so I could hardly comfort him. I was often left alone with him in those days. Madda went over to Aunt Molly's most evenings after work and Stevie and I would be alone in our part of the house until Dada came home. He quarrelled with Madda about that too, one Sunday afternoon.

Aunt Molly and Lily were with us in the living room. They were discussing Uncle Matthew and Aunt Annie, who was expecting another baby.

"Aal shi fit fa is fi briid," Madda was saying, "briid an skin up her tiit lakka fool!"

"Mi noh knuo how dem mek babi soh fast," said childless Aunt Molly. "Dis nex one gwain mek six dem hav! Laad G-man, where dem gwain put aal dem pickni? Dem gwain drive Vera mad!"

"It noh look like dem gwain bring ova dem odda pickni, iida." Dada said. "Afta aal is ongl labourin Matthew doin; im nat gettin nuo big moni fi dat, an Annie-shi nat wukking at all. Soh how dem gwain save moni fi pay pickni passij?"

"Aal dem shud neva hav soh much pickni," said Aunt Molly kissing her teeth, "since dem kyaan look afta dem!"

"Noh badda taak!" agreed Madda. "If it wasn't fi Vera, dem wudda aal pak up inna one room! An when yu aks Annie why she a-briid so faas, shi just ki-ki and seh 'Laad, Esme, dem just kiip kommin; what mi fi du?'" Madda' voice rose an octave in a crude imitation of Annie. "An shi neva did tek kyare ov di one dem shi hav bak home, yu knuo. Dem use to run up and down all ova di place lakka leggo biis. Doc always use to qwarrel wid Matthew ova it. 'Is picknii yu a grow or faam animal?' im used to aks Matthew."

The women all laughed, but Dada frowned. "Oonu liiv di woman alone!" he said. "From what mi si, she a tek good kyare o' di one-dem she hav wid er. Shi noh haffi wuk kaas she noh mad fi moni an belongins; shi just mek erself content an manij wid what shi hav."

"Mi kyaan unnerstan how dem kom from Jamaica to Inglan, fi liv pon pittance!" Madda said. "When flea hav moni im buy im own daag; mi neva kom here fi scrape nor scrabbl! Mi done wid dat di day mi liiv Jamiaca! Is *life* mi want, an *life* me gwain mek, an mi willin fi wuk fi it!"

"Iinhi?" interjected Dada. "Yu willin fi wuk fi it? Yu mean yu willin fi *mii* fi wok fi it fi yu!"

"How yu miin?" Madda sat up straight in her chair. "How yu miin? Yu want to seh dat mi noh wuk too! Well lissen daalin, mi wuk as haad as yu, an mi haffi mind pickni as well!"

"Which paat of yu wuk as haad as mi! Yu eva go pon bildin site yet? Yu eva wuk outside when it a-rain an it a-snow? Hush yu mout yaa woman! Yu noh evn mind yu pickni dem! Is strainja a-mind yuh baby! An yu daata haffi mind erself kaas yu nat evn faat pon er, let alone mind er! Puss tek betta kyare ov dem pickney dan yu!"

He was standing over Madda at this point, jabbing his finger at her to emphasise each point he made. Madda jumped to her feet too and pushed her face into his.

"You tink yu kudda manij yu-one? You tink yu-one kudda buy house, buy kyar, buy eni ov dis?" The movement of her arm, took in everything in the room. "Is *mi* drive yu, *mi* nurse yu, *mi* mek yu kom to sumting! Yu figat seh yu did kom fram nowhere an neva hav nobaddi? An now yu want kuss mi seh mi noh du nottn? Yu si oonu ole neager who noh kom from nowhere? Oonu damn ungrateful!"

I thought Dada was going to hit her, and so did Aunt Molly, for she jumped up, pushed Madda back into her chair and took hold of Dada's right arm. His chest was heaving and he glared at Madda, hands clenching and unclenching.

"Yu tink yu kom from somewhere?" he finally said in a quiet voice. "Well, let mi tell yu dis; yu kom from di same place as mii; bush! An rememba dis; is *mii* bring yu, *mii* pay yuh passij fi kom ya! Oddawise yu wud still deh pon yu bihine inna Rocky Gap red dut! Soh mi no knuo what kind ov fuckries yu a-taak!" He spun on his heel and strode out of the room.

"Dat shit!" Madda spat the words after him. "Im tink im own mi? Im betta wach out!"

" Mi did tel yu from di beginnin, but yu neva pay me no main." Said Aunt Molly. "Mi did knuo aal along dat it wud kom to dis one day!"

I knew then I was the only person on Dada's side. Aunt Vera was his pal, but she was Madda's sister. He got on well with Annie, but she never did or said anything much; having her on his side wasn't much of an asset. Most of the people close to us were connected to Madda. I was the only one. Even at a time when I didn't like him very much, I felt that he needed my loyalty.

Chapter 11

S tevie grew into an appealing, inquisitive toddler whose nose was always where it should not be. By the time he was eighteen months old, he was could converse fluently. True, his vocabulary consisted largely of half-words, grunts and noises, but he strove so hard to express himself, that he usually made himself understood. Despite the difference in our ages we were very close. I was his nurse and caretaker, he was my companion. During the awful time following my attempt at running away, Stevie comforted me. When misery reduced me to tears, he would cry too. When anxiety made me feel so listless that all I could do was lie on my bed, Stevie would lie beside me, curling his small body around my back and putting his arm around me. Looking back, I wonder if I showed him enough affection in return. Many of the things I did for him I resented. When he wanted to play, I usually wanted to read and would grow irritated with him for preventing me. Sometimes he cried when I pushed him away. Sometimes he just looked a me through big round eyes, and then carried on playing alone.

A curious thing about Stevie was that he was very slow to walk. At the age of two he could stand up unsupported but when he tried to take steps he would fall on his bottom howling with shame. When I picture

Stevie at his childminder's house, confined to a cot like a pet animal in a cage, I realize his legs were weak from lack of use. It was a blessing, then, when the childminder gave notice that she was giving up looking after children and going back to work.

It took Madda two weeks to find someone new and in the time she took off work to look after Stevie, she entertained Brewster liberally. I came home from school one afternoon to find the house in darkness and Stevie sitting in the hallway wearing only a nappy and a grubby vest, cheeks criss-crossed with shiny tear-tracks.

"Stevie, what are you doing alone out here?" I spoke loudly, knowing that Madda was in the bedroom and wanting her to hear me.

"Madda in-side! In-*side*!" said Stevie, pointing to the door of her room. I picked him up and carried him into the kitchen, where I proceeded with my chores, ears cocked to hear my mother's door open, to hear Brewster leave our house.

On his next visit, just a few days later, I came home to find him sitting comfortably in the living room playing with Stevie while Madda looked on, a sickeningly sloppy expression on her face. She remimded me of a love-sick cow. Her favourite LP was playing on the radiogram, Brook Benton singing slushy ballads. Sloppy songs, her sloppy face, that man in our living room, they all made me mad. It was worse, almost, than knowing he was in my mother's room, in her bed. The living room was family space. How dare she bring him in there?

The following week he was there again, all smiles and charm. They were drinking rum and the sleazy smell of liquor tainted the air. What if Dada came home early and found them? I wondered. Somewhere in my mind, buried, unacknowleged was half a hope it would happen. Yet I knew it was unlikely. In all the time I could remember, Dada had never once come home from work early. I worried more about the neighbours seeing Brewster coming and going so often. I was glad it was November and darkness fell early. No-one would see him when he left, unless they were deliberately looking out for him.

To my relief, Madda found a childminder towards the end of her second week at home, and returned to work the following Monday.

Extraordinary things happened that November. Some would call it a fateful month. Madda, who followed her stars closely, definitely would; she belived strongly in fate. She was born in November and she often used to say it was her month, her time of year.

The week following her birthday she won £900 on the football pools. Dada, who checked their coupons every Saturday evening, went over hers again and again. There was no mistake; Madda had won the second dividend! £900 was more money than she, or anyone we knew, had ever possesed at any one time. Delirium prevailed in our house for a while. Madda and Dada laughed and whooped for joy, so much so that Lily and Wilfred and Doris came downstairs to find out what was going on. Madda was so excited she telephoned Molly, Vera, Matthew, her cousins, her friends to tell them. Stevie caught her mood. He bounced up and down on the spot laughing and whooping in imitation of Dada.

The cheque from Littlewoods arrived on Thursday morning while Madda was dressing for work. She sat on her bed in her underwear and stockings, scrutinising the orange envelope as though afraid of its contents. She opened it carefully, removed the cheque and pressed it to her lips before replacing it carefully. Noticing me watching her she shot me a look I could not read and stood up to finish dressing.

The following Monday morning, the postman knocked on the door with a telegram. We knew the instant we saw the yellow envelope that it contained bad news. "Is who ded? Is who ded?" I could almost hear my parents' thoughts.

"Aieeeee! Laad! Laad! Laad!" cried Madda when Dada read her the message in the telegram. Her sister Sarah had sent to tell her that their father had died in his sleep the previous Friday.

Madda sat on the bed, tears pouring down her face. Dada sat beside her not touching her, but trying to comfort her with his presence. Stevie looked from Madda to me, perplexed. I felt awkward, not knowing know what to do. I could not remember my grandfather and I did not feel like crying. I went to the kitchen, made Madda a cup of coffee and carried it to her. She held the big, white enamel cup and saucer in her hands while tears dripped from her face into the hot brown liquid.

She stayed at home that day, and I stayed with her. She telephoned her sisters and her cousins to give them the news. That evening Dada drove to Aunt Vera's house, picking up Aunt Molly on the way. When we arrived, the sisters burst out crying, wailing and bawling. Uncle Matthew, who had only heard the news that evening, just sat with his head on his hands. I had never seen so much grief. They must really have loved their father, I thought. I could recall dozens of conversations about Doc Partridge; talk of how feisty he was, stories of his quick wit and sharp tongue. Stories about his womanising. Stories about his harshness to his children. Uncle Matthew claimed he still had scars from beatings received years ago, and yet here he was, mourning.

An argument developed between Uncle Matthew and Madda over who (if anyone) should attend Doc Partridge's funeral back home. Madda had money, said Uncle Matthew, she could afford to go. Fi what? argued Madda. Shi neva like funeral from time. Is betta shi use di moni on a set up fi Doc, soh dat aal di famli kud pay dem respeks. The others agreed with Uncle Matthew but they knew their sister; if she did not want to go to the funeral, nothing human would persuade her to.

They held a wake for Doc Partridge at our house nine nights after his death. Everybody connected to Rocky Gap came. On the day of the wake Madda and my aunts cooked up a hurricane. They curried goat, roasted yam, fried fish. They made saltfish fritters, coconut toto and cornmeal pudding. They grumbled about not being able to get bammy and breadfruit, and fresh soursop to make juice. Instead they bought bottles of ginger beer and made rum punch. That evening, the house was crammed with people, many of whom I had never seen before. Everyone was smartly dressed out of respect to the dead man. There were speeches from Matthew, from Dada and others who knew him, singing his praises and excusing his faults. The food was eaten, the drink consumed. The radiogram played calypsos, and people sang the old-time songs Doc Partridge had loved.

I was in there among them while they sang, while they cried, laughed, danced. I doubt that Stevie understood what was going on, but that didn't stop him from singing and dancing too. As the night passed and the number of people dwindled, the gathering grew quieter, calmer. Someone started singing a hymn and soon everyone joined in, singing one hymn after another. I was amazed to hear my parents singing hymns. They never went to church, never prayed, not even to say grace before meals. Aunt Vera and Uncle Matthew were the same; Aunt Molly was the only church-goer in our immediate family. They were a constant source of surprise to me, my parents. I was always learning new things about them.

For days after the wake the atmosphere in our house was quiet. Madda's grief had been shared and released and she was calm. The ritual mourning of my grandfather's death had a healing effect on all of us. It seemed as though all the anger, rage and pain in our home had been dispersed, purged. Christmas was approaching, a new year to follow; maybe the next year would be a happier one for us, I hoped and I prayed.

On New Year's Eve a big dinner dance was being held at the Unity Club, my parents' favourite nightspot of the moment. They loved the club for the hot new Jamaican music played there, for its hot Jamaican food, and for the big personality of the Jamaican who owned and ran it. Everyone in their close circle was going: Lily, Matthew, and Molly were also going, even stay-at-home Aunt Vera and Samuel were going. I watched my parents dressing jealously. Stevie and I would be seeing in the new year with the tenants upstairs, Doris and Wilfred, no fun at all compared to dinner and dancing at the Unity Club.

The revellers set off in high spirits. From our bedroom window we watched them leave the house, descend the steps, pass through the gate and group around the car. The night was frosty-cold, silvery gray and crisp. Madda wore her fur stole. She stood for a second in the glow of a streetlight, poised like a mannequin in a store window, perfectly dressed, from the sculptured curls piled on top of her head to the stiff, wide skirt of her dress to her feet, criss-crossed in black suede. All of them, gathered together for a moment, formed a monochrome tableau, faces robbed of colour by the night, cool, elegant and remote.

When they came home it was already day; the cold, flat light of winter mornings was visible through the edges of my bedroom curtains. Stevie was fast asleep beside me, one leg thrown over me, one arm wrapped around me. They came in quietly, as though worn out, exhausted. I heard Lily's feet on the stairs. I heard the door to my parents' room open and close. It would be hours before Madda got up, I thought, snuggling down in my bed.

Not much later my parents' door opened and Dada's feet echoed in the hall, then in the kitchen. A cupboard door banged, and Dada's voice muttered a curse. I started as something crashed on the kitchen table and I jumped out of bed, fear taking hold of me. In the kitchen I found my father hunched over the table, his head buried in his hands.

"What's the matter, Dada?" I asked, tentatively touching his shoulder. He didn't speak; neither did he move.

"You have a headache?" I asked timidly. Slowly, he raised his head and looked at me. His mouth was trembling, out of control. He could hardly speak.

"Yuh Madda lef me," he muttered hoarsely, then dropped his head into his hands, sobbing.

I stood beside him trying to digest the news. I wanted to comfort him, to do something to stop his crying, but all I could do was hold on to his shoulder and all I could say was, "Don't cry, Dada, don't cry."

That New Year's Day nobody came to visit, nobody called. The house was cold and silent. Dada stayed in his room most of the time, huddled under the bedclothes, ignoring Stevie who kept banging on the door calling for Madda.

"Whe' Madda? Whe' Madda?" he asked. He looked for her in every room, and resorted to tears when he couldn't find her. I bathed him, dressed him, fed him. Later, when I heard Lily moving about, I took him upstairs, to find out what had happened at the Unity Club.

"Chile," she said sadly, "what mi fi tell yu? Yuh Madda an faada kech up in di club last night. Im box er an kuss er in front ov evribaddi. Shi just waak out, strait outta di klub in di daak, koal nite. An when shi liiv, shi tell im seh shi nat kommin bak to im soh long as shi liv."

I asked where my mother had gone.

"Mi noh knuo, chile," she said sighing. "Mi noh knuo. Mi noh knuo what gwain happn."

She was with Brewster, of that I was certain. But she had to come back home. She and Dada quarrelled all the time and then made up again. She couldn't just leave Stevie. And what about me?

Aunt Vera telephoned to ask if I knew about my mother, and I told her I did. She asked if I was OK, if Stevie was OK, if we had food to eat, and so on. She inquired about Dada. She wanted to talk with him, but he refused to take the phone. Aunt Vera told me to make Dada bring us to her house but I didn't even ask him to. Don't disturb me, he had said. I want to be left in peace.

We lived in a limbo of uncertainty. The public holiday came to an end, but Dada did not return to work, staying in bed most of the time. When we ran out of food, he got dressed and went to the shops, and then returned to bed. He hardly spoke to anyone. Uncle Matthew came by, but Dada wouldn't see him.

Aunt Vera came by and tried to talk to him, but he wouldn't see her either, until Aunt Vera said she was going to take Stevie and me home with her for the time being. Then he erupted in fury, cursing bad words, cursing Madda, Aunt Vera, the whole Partridge family. "Galang outta mi hous an liiv mi an mi pickni, he shouted." Aunt Vera left.

Doris and Wilfred were kind to Stevie and me during that awful time. They sent down food for us, they stopped on their way in and out of the house to check on us. My school was on holiday, so I was able to be with Stevie full time. I could cope with Stevie, with cooking and all that. The hardest thing was keeping warm. I lit parraffin lamps in all our rooms, as I always did, but I was cold all the time, and worried. I was worried about Dada and I was worried about my mother.

She called a week after New Year's Day. Fortunately, Dada was out of the room when I answered the phone. She had called before, she said, but Dada had hung up as soon as he heard her voice. Was she coming home? I asked. She didn't think so, she said. What about Stevie? I asked. What about me? You must go to school and take Stevie to the childminder as usual, she said. She would come and look for us as soon as she could.

Dada came back into the room at that point and demanded to know who I was talking to. Madda, I said timidly. He snatched the phone from me and slammed it down on the receiver. "Don't mek me ketch yu taakin to her agen," he yelled, looming angrily above me. "No, Dada," I said, just to keep the peace.

I went back to school, Stevie went back to the childminder and Dada went back to work. Madda stayed with Brewster. She came to the house one day when no-one was there and took most of her clothes, the washing machine, the fridge and the radiogram. The old woman across the street told us that Madda had driven up in a van with two men. It was mean of her to take the household things, the old lady said disapprovingly.

That same evening, Dada moved our old radiogram from his bedroom into the living room. He played song after song, all of them sad, and cried for hours. Stevie and I cried too, we couldn't help it. Tears filled the room. Tears were in the kichen, in our beds, in our food, in our throats. Tears were everywhere.

Part 3
NATIVE SON

LONDON
1980–1983

Chapter 12

THE FIRST TIME I SAW Loretta, I was standing by the entrance to the market at Camden Lock, queueing up for one of those sausages in pitta bread you can get down there. It was a sunny Sunday morning and all the trendies, drabbies, hippies and punks of North London were gathered in Camden Town. A solid column of people snaked its way along the road leading from the underground to Camden Lock market. The sausage queue extended into the road, constipating the traffic trying to force its way through to Chalk Farm. The sausages were delicious, big, brown and meaty, tasting of herbs and charcoal. The smell of them grilling made my mouth water and my guts cramp with hunger. I had to wrap my arms tight in front of me to muffle the growl coming from inside of me.

People from the street were pushing and shoving their way into the market. Man, they were so keen, digging their elbows into me to get me out the way, crushing my feet as they passed, you'd think they had real bargains on those stalls instead of a whole load of overpriced clothes and crap. You can get better stuff in Oxfam just down the road. It amused me to watch them, though. Hampstead types in multicoloured sweaters from Guatemala, floaty Indian skirts, African baskets hanging over their shoulders. Women mainly, lots of them with babies and toddlers perched on their hips or dangling from their hands. Punks were there too, dressed in every shade of black, chained, studded, some of them so skinny and pale I almost felt sorry for the bastards. I can't stand them. I don't have much to do with them if I can help it. They can't stand us either. A gang of them cornered me one night, in front of the bakery on Southend Green, and started to beat the shit out of me. They'd have mashed me to a pulp if a squad car hadn't crept up just as one big bastard was ramming his boot into my side. Must've been the only time I've ever been glad to see the Babylon.

This Loretta, she was so cute, the minute I clapped eyes on her the pain in my guts stopped. Dreadlocks hanging like fine rope down to her bum, white T-shirt, tight white jeans, Doc Martens and black leather jacket. Very nice. When she turned her head, big hoop earrings knocked against her cheek and drew your eyes to the velvet mole resting on her cheekbone like a pretty, black insect on a creamy brown flower. I wanted to touch that cheek, to brush the warm skin with my finger and gently smooth away the blemish.

I couldn't believe it when she walked towards me, unmistakably straight in my direction. Watching her push her way towards me gave me the jitters and made my hands turn clammy. I looked around, pretending not to see her, turning my head as though I was looking for someone in the crowd. She stopped right in front of me, so close I could pick up the sweet warm scent coming from her.

"You're Roy's friend, Steve, ain't yuh?" The husky, sexy voice went perfectly with slanted black eyes. Exotic, my mate Dave would say. He's one of those white boys who likes black girls. Thinks they're different, more exciting than white girls. He'd go crazy over this one. I could go crazy over her myself.

"Yeah, I know Roy," I answered, deadpan, looking her in the eye and trying to sound cool. She looked straight back at me, bold as they come.

"I've seen you around quite a bit, you know. I've been looking for a chance to talk to you. I like your style." She smiled a little, just enough to make her eyes slant a bit more and my heart drop into the pit of my empty, hungry stomach. Jesus. What was I gonna say now?

"You goin' by Cuffie's on Sat'day?" she asked, sparing me the agony of speaking.

"Yeah," I answered. Bush Doctor was playing down there on Saturday night. No way I'd miss that.

"Well, maybe I'll see you there," she said, moving away, smiling over her shoulder at me through the curtain of her locks. My guts bellowed so loud, the blonde piece in front of me turned round and smiled, one of those oh-I-know-what-you're-feeling smiles. I hugged my stomach and stared coldly back at her.

I could hardly wait for Saturday night. I saw myself myself dancing with her, welded close, swaying sexily to a lovers tune. The thought was so nice, I laughed out loud, which made the girl in front turn and look at me again. I couldn't wait to tell Roy about Loretta.

Roy was my spar, my best mate. Known him since school, years now. I met him down at the Sobell Centre where I used to play ice hockey.

"Man, you nuh fraid dem bus yuh foot wid dem stick?" his first words to me. He was fresh from yard then and the patois was strong in his speech. He sat and watched the hockey game.

"Bwoy, dat game faas!" He was impressed. I played for Islington Youth, and I used to train every night. I was good, so fast on the ice no-one could catch me, and pretty nifty with my stick too. I thought I'd play for England one day. My dad put an end to all of that, though. He hassled me into giving up the game. He'd have a go at me nights I came in late from training. I was fifteen, and if I came in later than ten at night he'd carry on as though I was some kind of criminal who did nothing but roam the streets robbing people and mugging old ladies.

"Why yu kyaan studi yuh book like diicent pickni?" he'd rant, half-drunk. He never seemed to worry about the kind of example he was setting, with his drinking and his raving. It never seemed to matter to him that I was really good at sports, not just hockey table tennis too, and boxing. I could've made it big with any one of them. Even after old Brooksie the games teacher from school called at the house and told the old fool that I'd been chosen to play for the borough, he still carried on. He wouldn't let me go to away games. He'd say I was lying, that I just wanted to get up to no good with my no good tiifing fren dem, even when we were going to Wales to play in a tournament, and a coach came to pick me up at home. When it pulled up outside our house at half past five in the morning, I was ready, kit packed and everything, and that bastard wouldn't unlock the front door so that I could get out. He ranted on about how me good fi notten and how him wastin time an moni pon me. He grabbed my stick and cracked it across his knee. It split in the middle with a noise like a gunshot. I couldn't believe he'd broken my stick. I wanted to take it and smash it into his head, crack some of his bones. I'd bought that stick with my own money, money I'd had to scrounge and hustle, 'cos he never gave me any. I wanted to kick down that door, locked up and bolted like a jail, kick it down and get out of that house for good. I didn't have the nerve then, though. Instead I gave up hockey and told Brooksie I didn't want to be in any teams. He didn't believe me, but I didn't see how I could have explained to him that I had a psychopath for a father. He must have sensed something, though. He asked me if he should get the educational social worker to talk to my dad, but I said nah, don't bother. I knew it wouldn't make a scrap of difference.

Roy lived with his mum and two sisters in a house just off the Kentish Town Road. Mrs Henry had painted her house a strong, luminous shade of pink. As soon as you turned the corner and saw it glowing in the middle of a terrace of chilly white, you knew West Indians lived there. Greeks would've painted it blue. Irish or Indians wouldn't have painted it at all.

I used to spend a lot of time round by Roy. For one thing, it was more like a home than our house. Mrs Henry let Roy do whatever he pleased. He came and went whenever he liked and she never hassled him. Maybe that's why he liked staying in so much, just chillin out in his room upstairs, listening to music, or watching TV with his mum and his sisters in the living room. Half the time my dad thought I was out on the streets getting up to no good, I was over at Roy's.

I went over there the night of Cuffie's dance. I'd spent a lot of time sprucing myself up, but I could've looked a lot better. Same old jeans, washed-out T-shirt and sneakers. Only my dreads, thick and springing back from my forehead like a lion's mane, made we worth a second look.

Roy had dreads before me. As soon as he left school he began to grow his. He was really into the Rasta thing. Talked about Jah and Babylon and going back to Africa all the time. Roy saw oppression everywhere: in people's faces on the street, in every TV programme, every movie we went to see.

"Dat is di ting bout downpression, mi bredda. When it deh pon yu, yu noh sii it. Yu fiil it; yu fiil it to yu haart, but unless yu open yuh eye-dem, open dem gud, yu nat siin where it come fram."

I used to go with him to meetings over in Ladbroke Grove sometimes. We sat with the bredren and the elders, smoking and reasoning about everything you can imagine — politics, Babylon and Africa, about women, youth, families, about the Bible, Rastafari and Selassie-I, passing round a spliff while we talked. It felt good being amongst them, the arguing and laughing and the smoke drawing me in. The Rastamen made a lot of sense in the beginning, but I kind of gave up on them when things started to get rough for me. I got to the stage when I'd wake up in the morning and look around my room, with its peeling wallpaper and dingy windows covered with an old sheet, barely keeping Haverstock Hill at bay, look at the mattress on the floor where I slept under some funky-smelling blankets I'd got from Oxfam. I'd get up and pour myself some cornflakes, moisten them with milk that was always slightly sour, or maybe open a can of baked beans. I'd hear Dave in his room listening to some moron DJ on Radio One, and Brian in his, humping some girl he'd brought home from the pub last night, and I'd feel stuck.

This was my life. I didn't own anything worth owning, didn't have any money or prospects of any. No-one was gonna give me anything, either. A lot of the time I couldn't even muster enough money to pay the tube fare to Finsbury Park. So how the fuck was I ever gonna get back to Africa and find my roots?

I thought Roy would pull out his locks with envy when I told him about Loretta, but he didn't.

"Yu like dat daata?" he asked, his eyes widening with mild surprise.

"Well," I said, feeling like I had to explain myself, "who wouldn't!"

"I-man lookin fi I ebony queen. The daata - she not quite ebony."

I get it; Loretta wasn't black enough.

"I-man like a cultural daata. A one who know erself, er African self. The dreadlocks cool, still."

That's big of him. The woman looks like a living dream, and that's all the he can say about her. Still, I should've known what to expect with Roy. He's one serious dread. Even before he began to sight up Rasta, he was into his roots. He always talked pure patois, broad and plain, as a matter of principle. Teachers use to pretend they couldn't understand him. White boys jibed at him and made fun of him in the playground. Mind you, that stopped after one of them got his head busted for going a bit too far. They left him alone after that. Nowadays, everybody's talking patois, trying to sound Jamaican. Some of the white boys think it's hip; they talk 'bout rice an peas an ting as though they have it for dinner every Sunday.

We took the North London Line to Kilburn and hung out with some of Roy's bredrin by a Jamaican fast food place, drinking carrot juice and smoking a spliff until closing time. By the time we set off for Cuffie's, I was feeling so mellow not even the cop squads prowling the high road could rattle me.

The bass vibes grabbed us before we even turned into the street where Cuffie's house was. We followed our noses to the house, led by a sweet aroma drifting tantalisingly in the air, whetting my appetite for the spliff I had in my back pocket. A small crowd stood outside the front door, waiting to go in, youths, dreads, a few whites. I could tell from the slow progress of the queue that inside was rammed. Bush Doctor was a popular DJ in these parts; he had something for everyone with his wicked mix of reggae, oldies and even the odd African tune.

Inside was as hot as Kingston in a heatwave, and dark as a London Underground tunnel. I felt sweat break out under my arms and at the back of my knees. Body heat, mingling with smoke and beer fumes, hovered over the swaying heads of people dancing. Bodies were packed comfortably against each other on the floor, or leaning on their backs against the wall, knees and torsos moving with the riddim. I followed Roy, who was inching his way patiently through, shoulders first, down the hall and into the front room, to his favourite spot against the wall where he could receive the full force of the sound. I preferred to be near a window, so I could beat it quick if the Babylon came down on us, but I stuck with Roy all the same.

I saw Loretta leaning against the door-frame, eyes scanning the crowd in the room, cutting through the smoky dimness like two laser beams. She looked flushed, feverish almost, and so alive I felt the charge from her in my guts. She saw me and smiled, then plunged into the dancing mass on the floor, can of Red Stripe held high above her head. I was pleased, scared and excited all at once. I wanted to sniff my underarms to make sure she wouldn't smell the sweat that was soaking through my T-shirt, but I managed not to. I wished I'd put on some deodorant, though. Roy must've seen her coming, 'cos he turned and gave a knowing half-smile and held out his hand for the spliff, before stepping into the crowd and disappearing.

The music was too loud to talk, so I nodded at her when she reached me, and shaped my features to look as though I was mildly pleased to see her. The Paragons were blasting through the speakers, "The Tide is High", a wicked old tune. Loretta came up close and we started dancing, swaying pelvis-to-pelvis, knees knocking together every now and then. She was wearing a short, tight red dress under the black leather jacket and that same jasmine flower scent. Man. The soft, warm pressure of her breasts made two damp circles on my chest. I felt my hood stiffen in my briefs, snaking up against my belly. Did I feel as good to her as she did to me? I wondered without worrying, enjoying every sensation, every moment.

Next day we went for a walk on Primrose Hill. She brought her kid Kaya, a cute little girl.

"Kaya's a great name," I said and started humming Bob Marley's song of that title. I was just making conversation.

"Thanks," she said, not looking at me. Her eyes were on the distance somewhere, looking at God knows what.

"How old is she?" We were strolling aimlessly over the grass, me pushing Kaya's pushchair.

"Two an' a bit." She was quiet, like she didn't want to talk or say much.

"Where's her dad?"

"Oh, 'e fucked off when 'e found out I was pregnant." She turned her eyes on me. "I didn't mind. 'E was no big deal." She went quiet again. I wondered if the kid got that name because her dad was a dread. I wondered if she had a weakness for dreads. I wondered if she thought I was Rasta, but I didn't dare to ask her in case she said yes. Then what would I say?

Walking got boring after a while, so we headed for Marine Ices. I had just enough money to buy the two of them a cone each, pistachio for Loretta and chocolate for Kaya. We sat at a window table and I watched Loretta licking her cone with big hungry sweeps of her tongue. She stared out the window most of time. Every now and then her eyes dragged themselves from the view of Chalk Farm Station to Kaya, who was doing her best to plaster the table with chocolate ice cream.

"Oh, stop it, will ya, Kaya!" she droned, sounding bored to death, and went back to staring out the window.

I must've got it wrong, I thought, looking at her profile. I thought this girl had the hots for me. The way she was winding up on me at the dance last night, I thought she was ready to jump my bones at the first opportunity.

Nah. I couldn't have got it wrong. I don't make mistakes like that. Something's up with her today. Maybe she's got cramps, or something like that.

I walked her to the bus stop and waited till her bus came, chatting rubbish to Kaya, who seemed a lot more interested in me than her mum. When the bus came round the corner I said bye and turned to walk off, but she grabbed my arm, all sweet and smiley and said she was sorry, she had things on her mind, and would I meet her again tomorrow? I said yeah, great, same time same place? and walked off feeling good that I hadn't been wrong about her fancying me.

I saw her nearly every day after that. She'd meet me outside the hospital where I worked and we'd go for a stroll in my lunch hour. There was nothing else to do all day, she said, and she hated being cooped up indoors with the kid. Nighttime wasn't too bad, she said. At least there was something to watch on telly at night.

Getting her to talk about herself was harder than making conversation with a cop. Information came out in bits and pieces. She lived in a council flat in Swiss Cottage. She got it on account of Kaya, but her older sister Diane lived with her. Diane was manageress of a clothes shop up-West. I figured that was how Loretta came by all those wicked clothes.

I didn't mind seeing her often, but those afternoon outings were costing me money. Nothing big, mind you, but my pay wasn't all that big either. I found myself going round my dad's more often than usual to see my sister Tess, who in those days was still living with him. I could always count on her for a fiver or even a tenner if she was in a good mood. How she could ever be in a good mood living in that house with dad and his wife, I can't figure out. Man, a magistrate's court was livelier than that house! I'd got the hell out of it as fast as I could. I left school and left home all in the same week. My dad would've have thrown me out if I hadn't left, in any case. He'd been going on for months about how I was a waste of time. How I was going to leave school with no "O" levels. As though having a few bits of paper was going to make any difference to my life! He was getting me down and I knew he could only get worse. He'd find new things to harass me about, he'd invent faults, pick holes in my character, he'd make my life a misery. One Saturday, I went out in the afternoon, telling my stepmother I'd be back later, but I never went back. I moved in with this girl I'd been seeing, Angela, who had a cosy little flat in Finsbury Park.

Now Angela is a story unto herself. She was a lot older than me, eight years or so, a big woman, all plump juicy chocolate flesh and soft, hungry lips. I'd started going with her when I was fourteen. Anyway, when things started getting hot at home, she told me I could stay with her, so I took her at her word.

We had a good time together in Angie's little flat. I hardly ever thought about my dad or Tess and certainly not my stepmother, and it was nearly a year before I went back home to visit. I kept getting messages from Tess that she was worried about me. She kept asking Roy for me. He knew where I was, but he never told her. I know he wanted to. Now and again he'd hit me with some heavy reasonings about responsibility to your family, and that kind of garbage. I'd tell him plain, what's the point of being responsible to a father who thinks you're trash? What's the point of being responsible to my stepmother who pretends I don't exist? Yuh sista check fi yu, he'd say, yu should rispek dat. Yeah, I know. But she was living with them. She's cool as far as they're concerned. They thought the sun shone out her bum. Me, I have to fight my own fight, tread my own path. I gotta put family behind me. I've got my own life to live.

Chapter 13

I'VE NEVER BEEN ONE TO make a big deal over women. Girls have been chasing me since I was in primary school, yet I've only had two real girlfriends. Not counting girls I've just gone out with a few times, or slept with once or twice.

Angie was the first. I lived with her for three years, almost, and I have to admit, she spoiled me. She cared for me like I was something precious. Washed and ironed my clothes. Spent hours in the kitchen cooking meals I liked. Let me have Roy and Cicero and the other lads round for dinner and a smoke. I appreciated it, even at the time, I really did. I'd thank her and she'd just smile her wide, juicy smile and say she enjoyed it. And she was good about money too, never nagged me about giving her housekeeping money or paying bills. Just as well, since I was out of work most of the time. I'd get jobs, but I hardly ever lasted more than two or three months in any of them. I'd either get the sack for being late in the mornings or skiving, or I'd get fed up and walk out. Then I'd sign on down at the social security office and chill out for a while before looking around again.

When I wasn't working I'd spent time at the Sobel, getting into training, playing hockey or table tennis, getting fit again. Sooner or later I'd get another job, usually through the job centre. There were some real feisty gits working in my local employment office. They had it in for me, I'm certain. They'd send me to the worst jobs on their books. I'd refuse nine out of ten of them, but in the end I always had to take something. Some of them were real arsehole jobs. Packing shelves at Sainsbury's. Cold store assistant at Marks and Spencer's. Loading bay assistant. Messenger.

Funny enough, the job I hated most was the one I stayed longest in: temporary porter at the Royal Imperial Hospital. My job was to roll stiffs from the wards to the mortuary on a trolly. No joke. I'd roll them from the ward to the theatre and back again, and a few days later, from the ward to the mortuary. Or now and again, from the theatre to the mortuary. I'd never seen a corpse before I got that job and to tell you the truth, I only ever looked one in the face once. They were always covered up when I went to get them. One time, not long after I started, I gave in to temptation and lifted the sheet when no one was looking. I'd collected the body from Men's Medical, so I thought it would be an old geezer who'd croaked from lung cancer or throat cancer or some other kind of geriatric disease. I pulled back the sheet and when I saw saw a young face on the trolley, it shocked me rigid. I was expecting to see something ugly and horrible, something I could describe to my mates so we could laugh at the awfulness of it. Instead I saw a young guy lying there, his face bluish-pale and fixed, like a china statue. His face looked peaceful lying there, as though dying had been just fine. I thought young people only died by accident, getting stabbed, or crushed in a car crash or wiped out by some other kind of violent event. I was young then, still a kid. I knew bugger all about life. Or death.

I met Dave after I'd been at the Royal Imperial for three weeks or so. I was queueing for lunch in the canteen and he was two places ahead of me, just another white man's head-back. I was standing there, looking around, feeling hungry, wondering what was on the menu and hoping there'd be chips left by the time I reached the counter. The canteen was full and noisy, roaring chatter interrupted by the chink of knives and forks and the occasional clatter of metal as one of the canteen ladies dropped a pan lid. Suddenly there was a commotion, and there was this guy in front of me bawling his head off at a weaseley-looking character.

"You ignorant shit!" he was yelling. "Have you got nothing better to do than abuse women old enough to be your mother? Apologise to the lady, you racist pig!"

Weasel-face just picked up his plate and marched off, as though no-one had spoken. Instead of just keeping cool and letting the incident blow over, the guy started apologising to the attendants, three older black women, as though he had to make up for the weasel's rudeness.

"Never min', soul," said one of the women in a broad Bajan accent. "He'll be up here again sometime, and when he come, we'll fix him!" She smiled broadly, flashing a gold tooth at him and winked.

I was watching him while all this was going on. White, with longish, curly dark hair. Foreign-looking, could be Jewish. He wore a white coat over jeans and a sweater, but he didn't look like a doctor. He was about my age. He looked and sounded like one of those trendy lefty anti-racist types who like to interfere in black people's business.

We sat at the same table. I began my meal, eyes down, not really wanting to get into a conversation. I mean, who wants to talk about racism over lunch?

"Those fuckers think they rule the world!" he said angrily, to the top of my head.

"Yeah," I said, just to be polite. Even though I agreed with him, I did not want to chat. I was keen to finish my hamburger and chips and leave the table.

"If I can find out his name, I'm going to lodge a complaint against that bastard to the health authority. He's National Front, I bet you any money."

"Don't waste your time," I said, letting myself be drawn into talking. "You heard what the dinner lady said. Let them fix him."

"What do you think they'll do?" he asked, looking a me, curious.

"Oh, they'll obeah him, or something like that."

"Obeah?" He looked puzzled.

"Voodoo." I looked him straight in the face, dead serious. "Or maybe they'll set aside a special pot of gravy for him, and piss in it."

"Really?" His eyebrows disappeared under his hair. "That's amazing."

He laughed as though the idea pleased him, then held out his hand across the table.

" I'm David Horowitz. I work in the lab. I'm a temporary assistant."

"Steve Erskine. Mortuary assistant."

He laughed again.

"You're kidding!"

"No joke." I laughed as well, amused by my own wit.

I kept bucking up on him in the canteen quite often after that. He was quite a laugh, really. We started swapping stories about work, and soon we had an on-going competition running, to see who could tell the most gruesome tale, or the funniest.

"How come you're temping?" I asked him. We were having a quick pint after work in the pub across the road from the hospital. The place was rammed with doctors knocking back vodka and tonics. The bar was always lined with them, from when the doors opened till closing time.

"I dropped out of college," he said. "I needed to earn some money, so here I am!" He grinned cheerfully, like he was trying to convince me that working as a lab assistant was his life's ambition.

"What were you studying? "

"Medicine. At Cambridge."

He didn't say it boastfully, or anything. I kinda got the feeling he was embarrassed to tell me, as though he thought it would make me feel jealous, or inferior. I didn't feel anything. After all, my sister went to university, and she ain't all that clever. I reckon I'm a lot sharper than her. I could've gone to university if I'd wanted. I just wasn't into wasting away my life stuck in a classroom year in, year out with a bunch of bookworms.

"Why did ya chuck it in?" I asked.

He thought for a moment.

"There were just too many things I couldn't deal with. Like Cambridge itself, the university." He stopped talking to take a swig from his glass.

"Have you ever been there?" he asked.

"Naa," I shook my head. Stupid fucking question.

"That place is still in the dark ages," he was getting heated, just thinking about it. "Talk about seat of learning! Most of the students I came across were pig-ignorant about the realities of life in Britain in the 1980s. I'd never met so many fucking Tories in one place! They genuinely believed that Thatcher is the best thing to happen to this country since Winston Churchill! I got into a fight once, with a first-class twat from Nottingham who was organising a national campaign to get support for the government's proposal to repatriate all unemployed immigrants!"

This guy needs some real problems, I thought.

"Then there was medicine, the subject, and the way it was taught. I guess Cambridge is not much different to any other School of Medicine in this respect."

"How d'ya mean?" I was trying to sound interested.

"I thought I'd learn about healing, about making people well and whole. What actually happened was that I spent all my time studying disease, disorders and malfunctions and cutting up preserved corpses!"

He noticed the way I winced with distaste.

"Oh yes," nodding his head sarcastically. "You think it's grim having to push them on a trolley, covered up with a sheet? Imagine having to cut one of them open and scrutinise the contents!"

I made as if to vomit on the floor.

"That's just how I felt most of the time. The smell of formaldehyde made me nauseous. It made my head ache. The anatomy lecturer, an old relic from the time of dinosaurs, used to ask me if I was really cut out to study medecine. Well after one year, I decided the answer was, no. So I quit."

We sat in silence for a while, supping our drinks. Three girls came and sat at the next table, giggling and scraping their chairs, trying to pretend they weren't eyeballing us. One of them wasn't bad-looking, a redhead with see-through skin and frizzed out-hair. Dave obviously thought so too. He turned round and stared straight at her and then smiled, sending all three of them into a fit of giggles.

"Well," he said, turning his back on the redhead, "I don't suppose you want to spend the rest of your life at the Royal Imperial!"

"Nah," I said.

"D'you have any plans? Hopes? Dreams?"

"Not really. When I get some bread together I want to go an' check out the sensimilia in Jamaica. And I wouldn't mind a car. A neat little BMW sedan would do nicely, thank you."

Later on I found out that Dave's parents had thrown him out when he told them he wasn't going back to Cambridge. He'd packed up his things and moved into a squat with some of his mates on Haverstock Hill, in one of those huge, dilapidated old houses. I'd often wondered what kind of people lived in houses like that, and now I knew.

Looking back, I always knew the scene I had with Angie was too good to last. The time came when were arguing over foolishness, ending up not speaking to each other for days. I was good at that. I'd just go out a lot and make sure I didn't get home till she was in bed. We went on like that for a few months before I reached the point where I felt I had to move out. She just got silly over some girl who fancied me. It was nothing serious, nothing to make a fuss about. Just a little flirtation, really, but Angie got all dramatic about it, crying and yelling, the way they do on TV. That's the problem with a lot of females, I reckon. They watch too much trash on TV. You try and talk to them, to explain things, and they go on about how you're taking them for granted, how you're using them. Anyhow, I told Angie a million times there was nothing going on with this girl, and when she didn't let up, I moved out and went to cotch with Cicero for a while. Which wasn't a very smart move. I can see that now, but it was my only option at the time. I gave up that nice flat, that cosy life style, without thinking twice. It's funny how sometimes you only appreciate something after it's long over and done with.

Moving in with Cicero was a mistake, even though I'd only intended to stay until I found a room of my own. Cicero had a neat little bedsit in Tottenham, not all that far from Seven Sister's tube station. He shared the house with five other students from the college just down the road. He'd done well for himself, had Cicero. He got quite a few "O" levels at school, five or six. I was surprised, I never knew he had any brains, but Roy said it was obvious that Cicero was ambitious, that he was going places in life. You would never think so to look at him. He was skinny and had pimples and buck teeth. And he wore glasses that looked like binoculars, the lenses were so thick. He had no luck at all with women. I guess that's why he spent so much time studying.

They say you never know someone until you live with them. Well, I don't know whether to be glad or sorry about getting to know Cicero. I mean, it's good to know who your friends really are, but it's upsetting to find out that someone you rated is a total shit.

There was Cicero, living in this not very special house, with these five not very special white kids. His room wasn't bad, but it was the smallest in the house, and next to the bathroom which everyone shared. We could hear everything that went on in there. We knew everyone's toilet habits—who sat for a long time on the throne, who used a lot of paper, who washed their hands and who didn't. I never could eat anything the girl Roberta cooked, and decency kept me from telling her why.

Cicero was a little grudging about allowing me to crash by him, but he definitely said it was OK so long as I didn't stretch out my stay for too long. I had no problem with that. After all, the room was small, barely big enough for his mattress. I tried to keep out of Cicero's way as much as possible so that he could get on with his studying and all that. I was being considerate, I thought. One night I came back to the house quite late after hanging out with Roy at his mum's place. I could tell something was up as soon as I set eyes on Cicero. I didn't have to wait long to find out what it was. He blasted me as soon as I walked in.

"Where's my raincoat, you thieving bastard? I saw it this morning, it was hanging right here behind the door!"

Talk about innocent until proved guilty! I could've got mad then and there, but I didn't. I mean, the raincoat was gone, so I could understand the guy feeling upset. It was a designer raincoat; it cost him a packet.

"It wasn't me, man. I didn't take your raincoat."

"Who else coulda done it?" he yelled at me, his eyes bulging frog-like behind his glasses.

"What do I want with a designer raincoat? Check me, man, I'm roots. In any case, I'm not the only fucking person in this house." I was beginning to get angry.

"No-one's ever had anything nicked in this house! An' you're always on the scrounge! You've probably flogged it already, you shithouse!"

"Fuck you!" I yelled back at him and walked out, slamming the room door and the front door hard behind me. Could you believe this git! Just 'cos he's going to college and hanging out with honkies he thinks he's king of the dungheap! Fuck him!

I walked down the High Road as far as McDonalds where I stopped and bought a bag of fries. It was late, but the place was full, black people mainly, young girls and youths. I ate my fries and by the time I'd finished, I was cool again and feeling more like reasoning with Cicero. I walked back to the house rehearsing a few arguments in my mind, which was just a waste of valuable mental energy. On the doorstep I found my holdall with my clothes in it, and a note from Cicero pinned on it.

THIS IS NOT A FREE HOTEL. FUCK OFF AND FIND SOME OTHER SUCKER TO TAKE YOU IN.

I was not pleased by this message. It took every ounce of decency in me not to kick in the door and then kick in Cicero's head. I mean, what was eating him? We'd known each other for years! If he'd wanted me to pay rent, why didn't he say so? Maybe he'd invented that raincoat shit. If I was bugging him by being around him, why didn't he just say so, instead of leaving me out in the street at midnight with nowhere to go. That was what upset me most. Where was I gonna go? I couldn't go back to my old man's house, definitely not at that time of night. I could have phoned Roy and asked him to ask his mum if I could stay the night, but I didn't want her to think I was some kind of vagabond drifting around the place.

I picked up my stuff and walked down the High Road, heading back towards McDonalds. I could sit there for a while and figure out what next. I'd only gone a few yards when I had a brainwave. I could go by my Uncle Matthew's house for the night! He lived near Bruce Grove, just down the road, a couple of bus stops away. I could walk it in no time.

I hadn't seen Uncle Matthew for ages. Not for three years, maybe four, but I was certain he'd be in that same house. He'd been there for ever, with Auntie Annie and all them kids. Seven of them, if I remembered right. When me and Tess were living with Aunt Vera, years ago now, when I was about four or five, we used to go over there often to play with our cousins. We didn't visit that much after we left Aunt Vera's, but no matter how much time had passed, Uncle Matthew was always glad to see us. Still, I was kind of nervous just turning up on his doorstep in the middle of the night.

As it turned out, he was cool. He always said the same thing whenever he saw me: "Stevie, mi bwoy, how yu do? Is a long time mi noh sii yu! Yu turn big man pon mi now!"

He and my cousin Winston were up watching wrestling on telly; everyone else had gone to bed. He drew me into the house, made me take off my jacket, sat me down on the settee. The TV set was huge, its screen filled the room, distracting me from what my uncle was saying. Winston was so absorbed in it, he hardly spoke a word to me after saying hi. Uncle Matthew offered me a beer and something to eat, which was pretty decent of him, considering. I could just imagine how my old man would've behaved if I'd gone to him. He'd have started yelling at me as soon as I got through the front door, just to make sure I didn't hang around too long.

I explained my problem to Uncle Matthew without giving too many details. I told him I'd had a disagreement with my flatmate, which was almost the truth. Of course I could stay the night! he said. He couldn't let "im sista pickni" wander the streets of London, not in these dangerous times. I could stay as long as I wanted, he said, as long as it took to find somewhere else to live. He boosted my faith in human nature, I can tell you. I mean, he was just about the only older man I knew who was decent to the youth. Most of them are like my Dad, sick in the head where young people were concerned. Put a black male under thirty in front of them, and they behave like demented robots stuck in destruct mode.

My Dad never liked Uncle Matthew much, but then, he didn't like any of my mum's family. The only one he got on with was Aunt Vera, the one who looked after me and Tess for a bit after our mum left us. We had another aunt who died not so long ago, but he hated her; like poison, he used to say. I hardly knew her, though Tess told me she used to live in our house before I was born, and that we used to visit her a lot when I was small. Aunt Molly, her name was. From what I've heard about her, she was a strange character. She used to wonder around Finsbury Park with her Bible tucked under her arm, accosting people passing by and offering to show them the way to Jesus. She crumpled up outside the Seven Day Adventist church on Tollington Park Road one Saturday afternoon and died.

Roy's mum had a picture in her living room which made me think of Aunt Molly, a white Jesus with long hair and flowing robes holding out his arms. A hole in his chest showed a heart, satin-pink and ringed with fire, aflame with love, I suppose. The caption at the foot of the picture read, "God heals the broken hearted and binds up their wounds." It made me think of Aunt Molly, middle-aged and decent, taking to the street to show people the way to love, but never finding it herself. Going to church faithfully every Saturday and praying to a God who left her to die like a dog, in the middle of the street. What a waste of a life! Tess, she thought it was OK, she thought Aunt Molly went out doing something she loved doing. But then Tess had her own way of seeing things. She had a way of not seeing some of the uglier things in life.

I was fond of Aunt Vera and she loved us. She would have kept us with her if my Dad had let her. We stayed with her for about a year, but then he took us back. He told us she had problems with her head and didn't want his kids raised by any nut case. When I was about twelve years old, she went completely off her rocker and was shut up in a mental hospital. She attacked a white woman with a brick down by Bruce Grove in the middle of the Saturday shopping rush. The woman was a witch, she said. The woman was using magic to steal her husband away. Aunt Vera had every intention of cracking the woman's head open, my dad told us; it took six men to hold her down, she was so wild. When Tess and me went to visit her in hospital, she just lay in bed like a bundle, eyes shut, limp and tame like any other sick middle-aged woman. She had plasters on both temples where they'd put electric wires to shock her back to sanity. Like Frankenstein, I said to Tess, who glared at me, put her finger on her lips and said shush. When Aunt Vera got better, her husband took her back to Jamaica, bought a house out there and put her in it, then hurried back to Tottenham. Last I heard he was shacked up with a woman he'd been carrying on with for years. Probably the same one my aunt had wanted to do in.

※ ※ ※

Auntie Annie was even more welcoming than my uncle, if that was possible. She didn't turn a hair when she found me asleep in her living room, she didn't even ask how I came to be there. She touched my head with her hand, and said it was good to see me, an what did I eat for breakfast? I loved it. It made me feel good.

I stayed by Uncle Matthew longer than I had intended, three weeks in all. I slept on the settee at night, got up in the morning and headed for Hampstead. I was careful this time. I made sure I came in early enough at night, and on weekends I gave my aunt money, even though she tried to refuse it. I insisted she took it; I didn't want them thinking I was a scrounger.

It really is true what they say about living with people. I mean my uncle was good to me, really kind and understanding and all that. But man, you should hear him with my cousins. Especially Errol the youngest. He was as bad as my old man! Pure cussin and murderation. At the time, Errol, was about ten and not too bright. He got on everyone's nerves a bit. But with Uncle Matthew, he was like a red rag to a bull. Uncle Matthew had this thing about being decent, behaving right, proving that you were somebody, that you were better than the English. I guess that's why his kids were the way they were. Real Londoners. Seriously into Tottenham Hotspur, the Royal family and the Sun. Poor Errol. He was the black sheep, literally the darkest one in the family. I guess that made it harder for him to be English.

It was Dave who came to my rescue. I didn't talk to him much about my personal life, but he picked up that I was having difficulty with accommodation. He told me there was a vacant room in his flat and that it wouldn't cost me anything to live there since it was a squat. I wasn't all that keen, but I moved in all the same. I had no choice, had I?

Chapter 14

LORETTA'S FLAT WAS IN ONE of those neat, two-story blocks on Belsize Park Road, just before the junction at Swiss Cottage. The block blended so well with the posh-looking buildings in the street I would never have guessed it was council. It was all very clean and pretty, so much so that I felt conspicuous being there, like a beetle in a box of fairy cakes.

We'd been seeing each other for three months before she invited me back to her place. Three whole months. I was beginning to think she was hiding something from me. Maybe she had a bloke living there and not her sister as she'd told me. Maybe there was a reason for us spending all that time and energy traipsing over Primrose Hill or the Heath. Maybe she had herpes, or VD, or worse.

As it turned out, all she had was a flat full of second-hand furniture she had bought from junk shops, and plants everywhere. Diana, Loretta's sister, was crazy about plants. She had a six-foot-tall Swiss cheese plant in the hallway and a ficus the size of a small tree by the living room window recess. There were plants in the bathroom and more in the kitchen. It seemed as though every space that wasn't occupied by a piece of furniture had a plant in it.

"They just love it here," said Loretta, "this flat gets a lotta sun." This was true. Evening sunshine lit up the living room, exposing every mark on the light brown carpet and every stain on the three-piece suite. A hefty old table, so big and dark it swallowed up most of the space in the room, sat like a hole in a corner. It was the ugliest piece of junk I'd ever set eyes on, but I didn't pass any remarks. Loretta had probably paid a bomb for it.

We sat watching TV while Kaya tottered around systematically assaulting the furniture with her Barbie doll. The noise got on my nerves.

"Christ!" I couldn't keep it in. "Don't she ever go to sleep?"

"Yeah, when she's ready."

"Kid her age should be in bed by now!"

"Know a lot about child care, do ya?" She could be quite sarcastic at times.

"Not much," I admitted. "It's just common sense, ain't it? I mean, don't you ever want time to yourself? A bit of privacy now and then?"

Every time I saw her Kaya was with us. Sometimes I felt that all she wanted me for was to push Kaya's stroller when she took her out for walks.

When she finally invited me round it was done casually, like it was no big deal. She made me nervous, this female. No girl I'd ever been with had waited this long to jump my bones. Most of them had their hands in my pants at the first opportunity. This one was different; I never really knew what she felt about me. A lot of the time she treated me like a pal she wasn't all that excited about. Then, just when I reached the point of chucking it in, she'd pout those luscious lips at me and get all warm and inviting, like she was really into me. If I had any sense I'd have packed it in ages ago. Instead I let her dangle me like a helpless fish squirming at the end of a line, hooked.

Loretta made a pot of tea and brought out a packet of ginger nuts. We switched off the telly and tried talking, which was difficult. Kaya was making more noise than a demolition crew and every five minutes Loretta had to rescue an object at risk. How was I ever going to get to know her better with this kid around? I already knew a bit about her family. Her mum was Irish and her father Nigerian. They'd split up when she was a kid and she'd grown up with her mum, whom she adored.

"What's it like, having a mum?" It was a real dumb question, but it came out before I could stop it. She stared at me, completely surprised.

"Dunno," she said, shrugging her shoulders. "Never thought 'bout it. Why d'you ask?" She stared at me hard, eyes bright and interested. "What happened to yours?"

"She deserted us when I was a kid, not much older than Kaya. I haven't seen 'er since. Not that I worry much about it." I didn't want her to think I had hang-ups about my mum.

"I dunno why people like my dad and your mum have kids," she said, relaxing against the settee and stretching out her legs, as though this new bit of information had somehow set her mind at rest about me. "Your mum sounds special, though. I've never 'eard of a woman leaving 'er kids before. How did yer dad cope?"

"He didn't! He didn't even try to cope with Tess and me. He was too busy living his own life. We grew up on our own, like weeds. We took more care of him than he did of us."

I had a flashback of Tess and me as kids, doing housework, cooking, washing, managing the best we could. Memories of anxious nights when Dad didn't come home, and of all those nights when he came home drunk, unable to make it to his bed without our help. Even after he got married again and we moved in with Pearl, his wife, we used to have to get up out of our beds and help him upstairs in case he slipped and fell on the staircase and broke his back or his neck. Our stepmother wouldn't lift a finger to help him when he was drunk. Can't say I blamed her either.

"My dad weren't all that bad, I suppose." She was staring into her mug as though she could see her dad's face in the bottom. "He used to come and visit us regular. He always brought money for clothes and stuff. I never felt he loved Diana and me, though. Not like mum. Men are all like that, ain't they?" She put her mug down, looking at me as though she expected a confession.

"Kaya's dad Keith is like that. Diana's bloke Delroy is like that. He even knocks 'er around, and she puts up with it, like an idiot. All they wanna do is get their end off, and once they've done it, they're gone."

She was getting angry thinking about all the rotten men she knew.

"Keith's been to see Kaya once! Once since she was born two years ago! What am I gonna tell her when she starts asking for her daddy? That he was a complete and utter good-for-nothing piece of shit?"

She'd worked herself up into a temper and I hadn't the foggiest idea what to say. I was glad when Kaya made a grab for her mug, distracting her attention for a while. What could I say? Yeah, some blokes behave like dogs, but not all of us. I reckon it's up to women to be careful, be selective. I kept quiet since she obviously wasn't in the mood to see reason and I didn't want her to get mad at me as well Keith and her dad.

While Loretta cleared away the mugs and the half-eaten pack of biscuits, I got down on the floor with Kaya who was banging away at her activity centre. The kid was really cute. She looked a lot like her mother, but darker. She was bold like her mum, too, stomping when she walked, grabbing at every interesting-looking object and flattening anything that got in her way. Just like her mum.

"Have you got any kids?" The question was on her lips as she came through the door. It was my turn to look surprised.

"Nah," I said, shaking my head as if to say, I wouldn't do anything that stupid.

"How come?" She sat on the floor beside Kaya, cross-legged.

"I ain't got round to it yet. Never given kids a moment's thought, as a matter of fact." That was the truth. "Why? You wanna have one more, or something?" I shot her a suggestive glance.

"Are you outta your mind? Once bitten, twice shy, that's me."

Aha. So that's her problem. Can't trust anybody. Well, I've got time and patience. She'll come round if I stick around.

I was right on that count. After that first visit, she invited me round quite often. We had to give up the park walks in any case. Summer was over, and it was cold and wet most of the time. I could have invited her round my place, but the squat was no place for a girl like Loretta. It was too much of a mess, too depressing, to tell the truth. I preferred going by her place.

I got to know Diana, the sister, fairly well. A slightly older, sightly fatter version of Loretta, but without the dreadlocks and Loretta's daring clothes sense. She was pretty, but ordinary, and she talked too much.

"I like everybody," she said, trying to impress me. "I'm a people person." Whatever that meant.

"I lo-o-ve these programmes about foreign places and people," she'd warble as we sat round the TV watching some boring documentary about man-eating pygmies in the Amazon jungle. "People are so-o-o interesting!"

She got a bit too carried away by her interest at times. She asked too many questions—about my friends, where I lived, what I did "in my spare time". I got fed up with it and asked her if she was on the police payroll, whether they'd hired her to spy on decent, law-abiding, young black citizens like myself. She took offence and went cold on me for a while. I didn't mind at all. My ears enjoyed the break.

Just when I had reasoned myself into accepting that Loretta and me were never going to be more than platonic friends, it happened. On Guy Fawkes Night. We were all supposed to be going to watch a firework display on the Heath. Outside was chilly and damp, typical November weather, and I wore an extra T-shirt and sweater to make sure I'd keep warm. The moment Loretta opened the front door I knew she had something else planned. She stood in the doorway in a long black dress with buttons all the way down the front, unbuttoned to mid-thigh. Quite a change from the jeans and sweater she usually wore at home. She had on big hoop earrings and bright red lipstick and the flowerey scent I loved. She looked sensational. I could tell from her smile and the way her eyes sparkled excitedly that she knew the impact she was making and it turned her on.

"Going somewhere special, are we?" I joked to hide my nervousness.

"If you like," she answered, tossing back her locks and shooting me a look worthy of Mae West at her best.

Diane was out at a bonfire party and Kaya was staying over with Loretta's mum. Loretta had planned it all carefully.

We ate dinner by candlelight; steak and kidney pie with mashed potatoes and peas, followed by trifle with ice cream. We demolished a whole pie and washed it down with a large bottle of sweet sparkling wine, Loretta's favourite drink. We stood by the window watching fireworks explode against the night sky like miniature bombs. Trails of stars blazed and dazzled, then fell, disintegrating slowly. Huge clusters of chrysanthemum flowers glowed like coloured lightning, electrifying the sky for one beautiful second before fading into their own shadows. Fireworks always made me sad. All that drama, all that beauty, all that glamour, gone in a flash, turned to dust in the space of a blink.

What with the wine and her scent and the gleam in her eye, I couldn't keep my hands off Loretta and she didn't seem to mind. We started undressing each other right in front of the window, then moved to her bedroom and sank into her soft duvet which smelled of flowers, like her. She finished taking off her clothes and started kissing my face, my neck, my chest, everything, everywhere. I'd dreamed about this. I'd waited so long for it to happen, I'd given up believing it ever would. And yet there I was, in her bed, in her arms, burrowing into her as deeply as I could while she ground her hips against me, wound her legs around me, moaning like a cat in heat. I came like a storm, heart crashing, blood pounding, burning and trembling, swept away by bliss.

Before I gave in to sleep, I eased up onto my elbow and looked at her face, hoping to see that soft happy look women have when they are satisfied. Her face was smooth and composed, eyes closed, though I knew she wasn't asleep. I lay back, feeling spent all of a sudden, like a burned out Roman candle. I let sleep take me away from the knowledge that Loretta had made me feel more than I'd ever felt with a woman—and the fear that for her, it had been just another fuck.

The next morning Loretta slid out of bed while I was still asleep. Her movement woke me, but I snuggled under the duvet, half-dozing, half-expecting her to come back with a cup of tea. By the time I was fully awake I could hear that she was busy elsewhere in the flat. I could hear Capital Radio playing and the soft thud of her feet as she moved around. Her room was chilly and I gathered my clothes together and put them on as fast as possible. The living room was much brighter, warmed a little by the sunlight shining through the window. I stood in the doorway watching for a while as she tidied up, putting away Kaya's toys, dusting, watering plants. I was kind of scared to speak to her. I wanted to hold on to last night's feeling. It lingered in the air, mingling with the faint smell of gunpowder and ashes which came drifting through the half-open window, leftovers from last night's show.

"Hi," she said, smiling briefly at me over her shoulder. She was standing by the window sill, dead-heading a pot of African violets. I walked up to her and put my arms around her, hugging her from behind. I wanted to share the glowing feeling inside me with her. Maybe she felt it too, maybe not. From her lack of reaction, I'd say not. She carried on picking at the pot of flowers.

"What's for breakfast?" I asked, more for something to say than anything else. I wasn't all that hungry. Loretta turned and looked at me. I could see sharp words forming in her mouth, see them in her eyes. I got the message loud and clear. We'd had sex, but that didn't give me the right to expect anything, not even something to eat next morning. Fair enough.

"I'll make it," I volunteered hastily. I wanted to show her that I was cool, that I was no male chauvinist pig.

"Nah," she said, relenting. "I'll get it. What d'ya want?"

"A cuppa tea will do nicely, thanks."

I gave up any ideas I'd had about getting cosy and morning-afterish. I figured the best thing I could do was to drink my tea and beat it.

※ ※ ※

Loretta stayed on my mind for most of that day. I re-ran the events of the previous night and the following morning. Something about the way she was worried me. Not just the way she was the night before, the way she always was. Or rather, the way she changed from hot to cold, affectionate one day, frosty or even hostile another. I went back in time, remembering Loretta dancing in front of me, eyes burning, face glowing, hot and feverish with excitement. Then I recalled sitting with her watching TV and catching her watching me with cold, hard, eyes, more than once. Those oval eyes could look reptilian, could give me the shivers.

You're worrying about nothing, I told myself, trying to shake off the dull, flat feeling that had come over me. She's probably the moody type. Maybe she had hormone problems, PMS, or something like that. The thing that mattered most was that I really was her bloke now, consummated, official almost. Maybe I ought to make more of an effort, break up the routine we'd got into, invite her round to my place and fix dinner for her. I wasn't much of a cook, but I could boil spaghetti and open tins. Yeah, that was it. Maybe I needed to pamper her a bit and show her that I rated her.

My room in the flat was huge, with a high moulded ceiling and big drafty windows. Although the paint was peeling off the walls and windows frames and the old floorboards were crusted with caked-up dirt, I could see it had potential. All it needed was a good clean and a coat of paint, and maybe something more stylish than old sheets hanging at the windows. Dave had painted his room in red, black and white. White ceiling and doors, red walls and black floor, very dramatic. He had the best room, at the back of the house with huge windows looking out on the jungle that was once a garden. He was in there playing some horrible-sounding music on his stereo, volume turned up high. I banged on his door.

"Hey, Steve! What's happening?" He had to shout to be heard above the dreadful noise coming out of the speakers.

"I'm thinking of decorating my room" I shouted back. He turned down the volume, inviting me to take a seat.

"Any practical hints?" I was hoping he'd have paint brushes and rollers, maybe even some left over paint.

"Well, paint is cheaper than wallpaper." He sank back into a deep black canvas chair and locked his hands behind his head. He had the air of a friendly schoolmaster. "You'll probably have to do some stripping first, though, which is a bit of a bore." He paused and I shrugged resignedly.

"I've got some white paint left, if you need any."

"Good lad. Got any brushes?" I was eager to get started right away.

"No, only rollers. The brushes all fell apart. You'll find everything I have in the cupboard under the stairs." He picked up a book from beside his chair and opened it. I took the hint and got up to leave.

I was trying to visualise how a red, gold, and green colour scheme would work. Yellow walls, green floor and red woodwork. Ceiling and door would remain white.

"By the way, Brian's moving out. He's going to shack up with one of his girlfriends."

"Oh yeah?" Brian was an ugly, nasty piece of shit. On the rare occassions he stayed in the flat he left trails of filth behind him, mess in the kitchen and worse mess in the bathroom. Fortunately, I hardly ever saw him and I don't think I ever spoke more than ten words to him.

"A friend of mine's moving in. You'll get on with him, I think. He's black too."

"Great!" I said. I was in a good mood so I let myself sound enthusiastic. "We'll be the ethnic majority in here then, won't we? That'll be a nice change." I could never resist taking the piss out of David.

I headed out to find a hardware shop selling cheap paint. One thing about me, once I make up my mind to do something, I get on with it. I was going to make my room look clean and decent, and when it was ready, I was going to invite Loretta over.

Chapter 15

B EN MOVED IN VERY LATE one cold, damp night not long after Guy
Fawkes Night. I was coming home after spending the evening round
at Loretta's and I bucked up on Ben by the gate. He was carrying an
open carton box and I could see that a load of clothes had been thrown
into it anyhow.

"Wh'happen, spar?" His smile was wide and friendly. "Feel like giving me a hand?" I didn't, but I could hardly say no. The beaten-up
BMW parked in front of the gate was packed full of stuff. I carried in
a few boxes for him then disappeared into my room, straight into bed.
I felt sorry for him, moving into the mess left behind by Brian, but that
was his problem.

Ben was a surprise to me. What I mean is, I expected a student type,
someone more like David. Someone like Cicero, maybe. Ben was more
like me. He was a bit older, and judging from his car and his clothes he
had more money than me, but he was a regular street negro on the
make, like me.

The morning after he moved in, he tried to flog me an ancient
colour TV. We were in the kitchen; I was waiting for the kettle to boil
for my morning cup of tea, and he was clearing out his part of the food

cupboard, making noises of disgust as he cleared away Brian's remains. How we got onto the subject of TVs I can't recall, but before I could make my tea and leave, he was telling me about a set a mate of his had given him to sell. He was decent enough to warn me that the TV only showed black and white, but I wasn't interested.

I asked what he did for a living.

" Buying and selling," he said, with a wink. "A little bit of hustling here and there." I thought as much. A few days later he was offering me a spliff deal, which was much more interesting. I soon sussed that dealing was his main livelihood, which was cool by me. At least I would know where my next draw was coming from.

I figured that weed was the connection between Ben and David, though I never found out for sure. It was hard to see what else they had in common. But then, anyone looking at me would say the same. I wondered sometimes whether David genuinely checked for me, or whether he was just doing good, doing the politically correct thing and befriending one of the underprivileged. Not that I had any complaints about him. Apart from his obsession with racism, capitalism, sexism and the like, and tendency to quote Karl Marx in the middle of otherwise reasonable discussions, he was cool.

From the time he moved into the squat Ben had a lot of visitors. People came knocking at the door all hours of the day and night. All kinds of people: white, black, student types, street types, professional types. He called them business contacts. I figured he was dealing in something more serious than weed and I wondered if Dave realised what he was taking on, letting Ben move in.

"I wish Ben wouldn't have people knocking at the door at two o'clock at night! That bloke last night made a racket loud enough to wake up the whole of Belsize Park!" Dave and me were walking down Haverstock Hill, crunching through piles of dead leaves on our way to the hospital. "They bang on the door as if they're trying to rouse the dead."

"Well, they are, almost. He sleeps like a corpse! He never hears a knock, even though it's nearly always for him."

"It happens too often. It'll draw attention to the place, if you know what I mean." I knew what he meant. If you live in a squat, you try to avoid attracting the attention of the boys in blue, who just loved making people like us homeless.

"You gonna say anything to him?" I didn't mind the comings and goings that much, though I could see the dangers of too many night-time visitors. The flat was a more lively place since Ben moved in. He was a lot more pleasant than Brian. In fact he was a laugh, he was OK. I didn't mind him at all.

I went out for a drink with him one night when we had nothing bet-ter to do. We ended up in a trendy cafe on Rosslyn Hill, one of those smart places crammed with little round tables and rickety chairs and bright with mirrors. It wasn't my scene at all. I preferred the dinge and funk of the local pub, but this spot was popular with the Hampstead in-crowd. It was rammed with people drinking coffee, or wine or sparkling mineral water that cost more for a glass than a pint of beer. Ben and me were the only black faces to be seen, though I could hear more than one foreign language being spoken.

"A lot of the people I do business with hang out here. Know what I mean?" Ben grinned and winked at me. "Not to mention the girls." I'd been looking at the girls, and I must admit, some of them looked quite tasty. I noticed a little blonde piece perched on a bar stool looking at me. I was tempted to shoot her one of my dazzling smiles, but I didn't. I never felt comfortable in this kind of place because I didn't know the people. I couldn't tell how that girl would react if I went and chatted her up. Some of those snobby types wear out their eyeballs sending you sexy looks, then act like you're gonna rape them if you so much as breathe in their direction.

"Known Dave long?" Ben leaned back in his chair and scratched his belly, like he was at home.

"Few months. Met 'im at the hospital."

"Enjoy that kinda work, do you? " He was mocking me, but I didn't rise to the bait.

"It's a job. It pays. If anything better comes up, I'll take it."

He shook his head with a sigh. "Oh, the innocence of youth. You expect something better to just float along and land in your lap?"

I shrugged.

"Nah, mate, that's not how it goes. Not for the likes of you and me.

We gotta make our own opportunities in this life. Otherwise we get screwed every which way."

"Oh yeah?" I was gazing round the room counting all the pretty women.

"Yeah. You gotta get entrepreneurial. Do your own thing."

"I get it! We all gotta be like you! What a wonderful prospect!" His know-it-all attitude was pissing me off. "And what's your line of business?" I hoped I sounded really sarcastic. Who the hell was he to preach to anybody?

"I'm into buying and selling, as you know. Nothing wrong with a bit of honest retailing." He chose to ignore my sarcasm. "Same as all them shops on the high road. Except I carry the goods direct to the customer. You name it, if it's available, I'll sell it."

"You make livin' out of it? So how come you're living in a squat?" I was getting bored with this conversation. My eyes were watching the little blonde wriggle her way through the crowd to the ladies toilet.

"Business goes up, business goes down. I had some bad luck last year, but I'm past that now. Business is on the up again, and the bread is multiplying. In fact, I could use a little help."

He was leaning forward, elbows on the table, looking straight at me. He had one of those faces that smiled round the lips but was cold round the eyes. He looked hard. He could get mean, I could tell. But then, I guess he had to be in his line of business.

"D'you want another beer?" I offered. I wanted to change the subject anyhow. I didn't see myself getting into drug dealing, but I didn't want Ben to think I was chicken either. He nodded and I got up and pushed my way through layers of chattering bodies to the bar.

By the time I got back to the table, there was a woman sitting in my chair talking to Ben. Not my type, but quite a looker all the same. Mature, no make-up, nice clothes.

"Steve, this is Celia." I nodded and she said hello. I pulled up another chair and sat down, passing Ben his beer. Celia was drinking red wine.

"Celia is a social worker." You could have fooled me. I thought social workers all wore jeans and guernseys.

"We're old friends," she said, smiling at me and tipping her head towards Ben. I could tell I had interrupted a private conversation by the way they just sat sipping their drinks. After a few minutes of silence Celia stood up and said she'd better get back to her table, she'd see Ben around, and it was nice meeting me.

"So you been in trouble, have you?" I asked when she'd passed out of earshot.

He shrugged. "Yeah," he said, "who hasn't? It was no big deal." He took a long swig of beer. "I had a spot of bother with the law. But all that's over now."

Sure, I thought to myself. I'm no entrepreneur, but I know that once the law gets its talons into you, you've had it. They'll never be far away from your tail. Especially if you're black.

"What does your dad think of your profession?" That second beer was going to my head. I was beginning to feel bold. He surprised me by laughing out loud, one big helluva laugh.

"My mum and dad went back to Antigua ten, no, eleven years ago. They left me here with my uncle, so I could get a good education, they said. That's a joke in itself! My uncle is in the business too! That's how I got into it; I learned from him. That was my education." He was gazing into his beer, a half-smile on his mouth.

"He's done very well for himself, my uncle. Owns three houses, spends half the year back home. That's me a few years from now. Watch me."

I wanted to finish my drink and get out of this place. The bright lights, the tittering and chattering, the blonde with the flirty eyes, Ben's hard face and know-it-all attitude, were getting on my nerves. Why did people like him think they had all the answers? Him, Roy, Cicero. They all thought they were better than me, even though none of them had done anything particularly great. I knew I would've been something by now if things had been different. If it weren't for my dad, I'd probably be playing ice hockey for England. I'd be famous, making money, instead of pushing corpses on a trolley. Fucking parents. Who needs 'em! They're more of a hindrance in life than anything else.

※ ※ ※

My room looked like another place when I finished painting it, even if it was a bit bright. The yellow walls, the red and green woodwork, were a bit psychdelic, but stylish all the same. I stopped short of painting the floor. The room couldn't cope with any more colour, Dave said. He liked it, said all that was needed was something colourful at the window, maybe an Indian bedspread, so I told him he could give me one for Christmas if he had money to spare. No amount of paint could make that room warm, though. I bought an electric night storage heater second hand, and fixed the electricity meter so I could leave it on all day and night without having to pay a fortune. If it made a difference to the temperature, I didn't notice. When I woke up in the morning the first thing I felt was cold. As winter wore on my lips cracked and my skin shrivelled. I had to wear layers of clothes, I had to put on nearly every garment I possessed just to keep my circulation going. I missed Angela's place with its central heating and non-stop supply of hot water. I tell you, I thought of going back to her more than once over that winter. If I could have worked out a way of going back while continuing to see Loretta, I'd have done it. The necessary flash of genius failed to strike, so I contented myself with spending as much time as I could at Roy's place which, next to Loretta's, was the warmest option available.

You'd think Loretta would've been glad for me to spend time over at her place, but no such thing. Man. I know females are hard to understand sometimes, but this one beats the Sunday Times crossword. Like, I'm her bloke, and we've been going round together for a decent while, right? You'd kind of take it for granted that I'd visit when I liked, that I'd spend a lot of time by her, wouldn't you? And you'd think she'd like that, right? Not this one. I felt like she had me timetabled. Twice a week, but no Wednesday nights, Thursday nights, or Sundays. Not quite that bad, but almost. I figured she was punishing me for not going round there for two weeks after Guy Fawkes Night. I told her I was busy fixing up my room so she could spend time by me, but she wasn't convinced. She came over kind of sarky and mean, which I cannot take at all. So I fell in with the routine and only went there once or twice a week. I got bored with it after a while, like you do with anything predictable, I suppose.

That year, the first snow of winter came in March. It had been a cold bastard of a winter, but we thought we'd been spared the misery of snow. Well, the first Saturday night of the month it snowed all night while we slept innocently in our beds. That Sunday morning, the whole city went mad. From my bed I could hear screams and yells as morons on sledges went careening down Haverstock Hill. Ben and Dave got up before nine, a lifetime record for both of them, and went to throw snowballs. Can you believe it? I've never understood why people go wild over snow. Yeah, it looks nice and clean and pretty just after it's fallen and no-one has walked in it. Like some fairy waved a wand and presto! London was covered in sparkly white make-up, hiding its dirty streets, its ugly buildings, its rubbish dumps. But when it all turns dirty grey and slushy, when the make-up begins to rub off, the real world looks even grimmer and the blemishes even worse.

I didn't join the other two in their frolics. I eventually gave up trying to keep warm in bed, got up and got dressed and drank a cup of tea, trying to decide where I could go to keep warm. I'd been round Roy's mum's place just a few nights before, so I couldn't go there. I could go round my dad's, but I didn't fancy it. I could go round Tess's place, but that was a bus ride and a longish walk away. I'd freeze on the way. It had to be Loretta's, I decided.

It was about two o'clock when I knocked on her door, not too early to pay someone a visit, or so I thought. She took a long time opening the door, and when I saw her face, I wished she hadn't bothered. She looked like Dracula's wife. She looked all pinched and withered, almost white, with huge purple shadows under her eyes. She looked like she'd spent all night outside in the snow.

She opened her mouth and screamed at me. I saw the words coming at me, in slow motion.

"What the fuck are you doing here? What makes you think you can come 'ere when you please? Fuck off out of it!"

I was shocked, I was surprised, but I didn't lose my cool.

"What kind of a welcome is that?" I tried to sound jokey and held my ground. "Are feeling OK? You look like death warmed up!"

She opened her mouth to cuss me some more, but at that moment Diane appeared behind her, pulled her inside and stood facing me. She didn't look too friendly either.

"Look Steve," she said, "You're not Lorretta's favourite person right now. And she's not feeling all that well, either." She stood square in the doorway, almost filling the frame, glaring at me like I'd done something really evil.

"What the fuck's going on? I've only come to visit! Is that some kinda crime? If something's wrong with her, all you gotta do is tell me!"

I heard the door of the flat opposite creak open and so did Diane.

"Don't make such a racket!" She was whispering now. "You're bothering the neighbours! Don't you have no manners?"

"I'm not the one with no fucking manners; it's you lot!" That was it. I was finished with them. I turned and started walking downstairs. I'd only taken a few steps when she called me back.

"Look, I'm sorry, but you shouldn't have come." She was quiet now, like the anger had just vanished.

"I wish you'd tell me what the big deal is. All I've done is come to look for my girl. Is she ill or something?"

Diane went all quiet for a moment. She stood on the landing hugging herself to keep warm. She looked worried and that bothered me.

"Loretta's not well, Steve. She should have told you 'bout it long ago. Matter of fact, I'm amazed she's kept it from you for so long." A cold draft was blowing down my back. I didn't like the sound of this.

"What's the matter with her? How long has she been ill?" I was shouting, but I couldn't help it.

"She's been ill for years, Steve. She gets depressed. You know. Really bad spells."

"Depression! What's so top secret about that! We all get depressed now and again!"

Diane didn't answer me. She didn't go back inside either. We stood on the freezing landing for I don't know how long, not saying anything. Then she turned and stepped back into the flat.

"I think you'd better go now, Steve," she said, still not looking me in the face, and shut the door.

I walked down the stairs and out into the snow. No-one had left these flats and none but me had come in. Mine were the only footprints along the front path and I retraced them step for step, down to the road. I was thinking about Loretta and wondering how depression could make her look half dead. Part of me felt kind of relieved that there was a reason for all that weirdness. Another part of me didn't like it. I didn't understand it and I didn't know what it meant for me and Loretta.

※ ※ ※

I got back to the flat to find that Ben and Dave had built a snowman in the front yard. They'd used stones for his eyes and stuck a piece of stick where his mouth was supposed be, to look like a spliff, I figured.

Dave was in the kitchen cooking something that smelled delicious. I have to give him credit there, he took good care of himself, cooked meals regularly, even fed me sometimes. Me, I couldn't be bothered with shopping and the hassle of preparing food. During the week I ate a big meal at lunchtime in the hospital canteen, and at weekends I either got take-aways or ate out of tins and packets. On a cold day like this one I fancied a good hot Sunday lunch. Rice and peas and chicken would've gone down great. It was too late now to go to my dad's for lunch; he and his wife had their Sunday meal at three o'clock, without fail. I stuck my head round the kitchen door and looked hungry, hoping Dave would take pity on me.

"I've got just enough steak for me, you scrounging bastard, but you can have some of this rice and some of the spinach." Not quite what I'd hoped for; I don't like plain rice much, spinach neither. The steak smelled so good, so rich and juicy and tasty, the sides of my stomach started banging together. I changed my mind about staying in. I declined Dave's offer and headed straight through the front door. I was going to check Tess. Even if getting to her place was a hassle, once I got there I'd be warm and I'd get food. Even if she'd had dinner, she'd make something for me. She was good like that.

Tess lived in one of those streets off the Stroud Green Road, not all that far from Angie. I took the underground to Finsbury Park Station then walked down the Stroud Green Road, heading towards Hanley Road. A freezing wind tried to get inside my bomber jacket. I hunched my shoulders and crossed my arms over my chest to keep it out.

I knew the Stroud Green Road like the back of my hand, from the days when I lived with Angie and we used to come down here to shop for food, or to get take-aways from Biwi's West Indian restaurant. I could have demolished a fish roti then and there and followed it with a chunk of cornmeal pudding. I felt at home down here, even on a windy, snowy Sunday afternoon.

In the short time since I moved away, whole streets, whole blocks of real estate had changed. Finsbury Park used to be such a dump that only blacks and Cypriots wanted live there. These days it's des res and everyone is moving in. The whole area was under scaffolding. Where are the blacks and Cypriots going to live now?

I was relieved to see Tess's face peeking out behind the front door in answer to my ring on her bell.

"Hi, stranger!" She looked pleased to see me, and gave me a hug. "You're freezing!"

Inside, her place was as warm as toast. I hung up my jacket and stretched out on the settee in front of a blazing gas fire. A lot of people would have liked the way she'd decorated the place: magnolia paint on the walls, off-white settee and big cushions everywhere. You could tell she'd spent money on it, though you wouldn't know she was well-off from looking at her. Sweatpants, sweater, short Afro haircut. She looked really straight, almost old-fashioned. No make-up, no jewellery. Nothing fancy about her at all.

"So, what's happening?" She had nice eyes, clear and bright. They looked straight at you.

"Not a lot." I sank further back into the cushions, enjoying the tingling feeling of my toes defrosting.

"Are you still at the Royal Imperial?" She always had this long list of questions about what I was doing but I never told her much. There was never all that much to tell, anyhow.

"Yeah. It's getting boring, though. Don't know if I can stick it much longer."

"Stevie, I wish you would decide what you really want to do. You ought to get some training, get yourself a decent job, do something you like."

"Yeah, I know." She meant well. She just wanted to see me in a nice job with a nice place to live. But she got on my nerves all the same.

"Got anything to eat?"

She went into the kitchen and came back with a plate of food on a tray set with knife and fork and paper napkin. Rice and peas, vegetable curry and salad. I was so hungry I could have swallowed it all in one go. Instead I ate like I had manners, like I really appreciated the food. Which I did. When I finished cleaning off the plate, she bought me a mug of tea and two slices of ginger cake. By the time I finished eating I felt human again.

"Have you been to see Dad lately?" I asked, just to make conversation.

"I went over there last week. He's OK; the same as usual. As miserable as usual." We both laughed. "He was asking about you. He says he hasn't seen you for months."

"I don't like going round there, you know that." She nodded. "He nags me more than you do!" We laughed again. She was all right, really. We were just different, that's all. We always were different. I could remember when I was a kid, I wanted to go out and play with kids on the street, just to run up and down and let off steam, and she always wanted to stay in and read. She always had her nose in a book. Yeah, she was older than me, but it wasn't just that. We were different.

"How's your social life?" She always asked, every time.

"I'm still seein' Loretta."

"You've been seeing her quite a while now. This looks serious." She gave me a knowing look. Or what she thought was a knowing look.

"Nah, not really. She's got one or two problems." I didn't mean to say that; it just came out.

"What kind of problems?"

I didn't answer for a while. I pretended to concentrate on the TV, which was showing "Songs of Praise". Gripping stuff.

"She gets depressed about things sometimes."

I was beginning to wish I hadn't mentioned Loretta's problem.

"Can you deal with her depression, Stevie?" Tess was looking at me with an I'm-really-concerned-about-you expression.

"I don't have to deal with it, do I?" I was beginning to feel irritated. "It ain't my problem!"

"Depressed people need a lot of support, Stevie and a lot of understanding." Christ, she sounded like a fucking schoolteacher at times.

"Yeah, yeah, yeah. I know!" I'd heard it all before, that stuff about support. Angie was always going on about it. How I never gave her anything, not even support. When I asked her what kind of support she wanted, she didn't know.

"Got any videos?" I asked. I wanted to change the subject. I also wanted to watch something a little more interesting than the usual Sunday evening TV programme. I was glad when she slotted an action movie into the VCR.

I left as soon as the film ended. It was dark by that time and really cold. Part of me wanted to stay in the warmth, but I knew I couldn't. Not without getting preached at, anyway, and who needs it?

Chapter 16

IF SOMEONE WERE TO SAY to me, Stevie, who is your best friend in life? without hesitation I'd answer, Roy. Roy's my best mate, always has been. And I'd mean it. All the same, I don't know what happened with me and Roy. We were still bredrin and everything, but I saw less of him from when I started going with Loretta. And even less after he started going with Jumani.

I was with him the first time he met Jumani. He made me go with him to a show at a community centre in Shepherd's Bush of African music and dance. The drumming would be wicked, he promised, the vibe would be irie.

The place was packed, row upon row of black faces, the odd white one dotted here and there. Dreads grouped by the entrance and at the back of the small hall,surveying the gathering crowd. I never saw so many women in headwraps, wearing African cloth, walking tall like princesses. Kids were everywhere, running up and down wherever there was space. The aroma of herb was so strong I felt a lift just from breathing. The vibe was powerful and it moved me.

I knew Jumani by sight. She's not the kind of woman you'd easily forget: tall and slim with a long, long neck and gleaming black skin.

She wore her locks wrapped in a white cloth like a crown on the top of her head. She watched everything around her out of cool, almost round eyes, spoke out of sweet, almost round lips. I felt Roy react the instant he set eyes on her.

"Man," he said, completely bowled over, "this is my ebony queen in the flesh."

By the end of the first half of the show, he'd found a way to talk to her. I watched them—him all serious, trying too hard to say the right thing; her, tilting her head to one side, just listening with a smile at the corner of her lips. It was going to work out for him, I could feel it in my gut. He had all the luck.

From the first day he met Jumani, Roy spent a lot of time over at her place in Kilburn. Three months later he moved in with her. I got the feeling Jumani didn't like me much. She looked at me like she had me figured out and she didn't quite like what she saw. Not that she ever said anything, nah, she was always friendly, polite and concerned, like a considerate auntie or big sister. A bit like Tess.

Ever since the Sunday it snowed, Loretta was off with me. I mean cold, like she was really mad at me. It was a few weeks before I went round there again. She sat at the big ugly table by the window gazing out at the white-grey street outside. On the table in front of her was a large sheet of paper covered with odd bits of paper and cloth some of them stuck down—magazine cuttings, photographs, a picture of a golden yellow beach and blue sea and palm trees. A Mars bar wrapper, a bus ticket. Her fingers fiddled with the tube of glue while she gazed out of the window, ignoring me. I apologised for turning up unexpected, I told her I was sorry, even though all the while I was thinking, this is crazy, why do I have to apologise for visiting my girlfriend? I apologised all the same. I wanted to ask her what was wrong, I wanted to ask her if I could help.

"Well," she said in a hard voice, looking at me, her eyes black in her pale face, "at least I don't have to pretend any more."

"You didn't ever have to pretend. You could've told me. It doesn't matter."

"Oh yes it does! Oh yes it does matter! If I'd told you at the beginning you'd have run like friggin' greased lightening! You'd have disappeared faster than a tenner someone forgot in McDonalds!"

I shook my head. No, I wouldn't have. I wouldn't have. Would I?

"D'you know how it feels to wake up in the mornin', scared? So scared you can smell it on yourself, in the sheets, in your clothes? So scared your kid can see it and starts bawling as soon as she sets eyes on you and bawls all day 'cos she's scared too?"

I said something about doctors; couldn't they help? She smiled sofly at me, stretching her soft pink lips, like I was a fool.

"The pills do help," she said, nodding, sorting through the cuttings on the table in front of her. "They stop me feeling scared. They stop me feeling anything."

I kept going round to see her, but everything had changed. Things between us were much, much worse. A whole month of evenings passed without her speaking to me. Each time I went round Diane would do the talking, or we'd watch TV, or play with Kaya to fill the silence. Then, unexpectedly, she'd take me by surprise, she'd greet me at the door smiling and happy, she'd chat and laugh, alive and funny and bold, lighting up her living room like a bright red flower in a cold place.

I never plucked up enough courage to ask her what caused it. I was scared to ask and I didn't know why. I tried to figure it out for myself. Maybe it was her dad, leaving her mum and everything, but then, Diane was OK. Maybe it was Keith. Maybe it was London, England, the whole fucking world. Maybe it was life.

I asked Dave. After all, he'd studied medicine.

"I don't know much about depression," he said, scratching his head. "You need to ask a psychologist or someone in the psychiatric field. I know that women get it more than men. Something to do with hormonal imbalance. But it can have other causes too." He looked at me, wrinkling his eyebrows in curiosity. "You're not depressed, are you?"

Nah. I wasn't depressed. But pushing trolleys day in, day out, look-ing down at bodies covered in hospital green—invalid bodies, sick bod-ies, anaesthetised bodies, dead bodies—it was getting to me. But I wasn't depressed. I mean, I'd stuck it for ages, longer than any job before or since. All because of Dave. I can see it now. By the time he left the lab, by the time he moved out of the squat, I'd had as much as I could take of the stink and the drudgery of pushing trolleys.

Out of the blue Dave announced he was going to film school. He was going to spend three years in college learning to make movies for morons like me to go to cinemas and gawp at. It came as quite a shock when he told me. A fuse blew in my head, I got angry, all of a sudden, everything went red, and my ears buzzed. I wanted to hit him. What a fucking stupid thing to do! I thought. Real people didn't do things like that. Not real people who care about the underprivileged, who wanted to fight racism and sexism and you name it, everysinglefuckingism. That's what I told him when my head cooled down enough and I could speak.

"Man, someone's got to make movies! What would all those people—including you—do on Friday and Saturday nights if no one made movies? Besides, film is a powerful tool, the best medium for reaching people. I can use film to say important things, stimulate social change. It's a really powerful tool."

Yeah.

He packed up his stuff in boxes and moved out with the help of two of his student-type friends. It was a fast move, one Friday evening in late summer, normally a pleasant time of year on Haverstock Hill. Outside was warm and breezy. Dave and his friends scurried in and out of the house carrying boxes, like ants transporting unwieldy burdens, through the door, down the path, through the gate, into a battered old Bedford van. I couldn't see them, but I could hear them. I lay collapsed on my mattress, light-headed from the lunchtime booze-up, Dave's farewell from the Royal. I lay on my back without moving, my hands under my head, seeing out this time, seeing Dave off without saying a word to him, breathing in the green smell of trees and grass and the scent of roses mixed with petrol fumes blowing in through the front door.

I wanted to move into Dave's room, but Ben got there first. The very night Dave moved out, as a matter of fact. I was mad. I told him: "I've been here longer than you, you should've asked me first, found out what I wanted!" He just stretched his lips in that alligator grin of his, creased up his face and his eyes, and said, "Tough shit!"

Next thing, he moved in a mate of his, a long-legged thug with a crew-cut called Spider. The guy gave me the creeps. He was black, in theory if not in actual colour, but he looked like a skinhead, like a paid up member of the NF. Tight jeans, big, heavy Doc Martins, moronic grin and rotten teeth and all. He stomped around the place, spreading his long legs and their over-size boots everywhere. He made a lot of noise, too, blaring music out of his system, worse than Brian. I wouldn't have minded if he played decent music instead of all that techno funk shit. It made me mad, mad as hell.

"What the fuck d'you mean, moving this creep in without even saying a word to me?" I had a right to complain, didn't I? So I cornered Ben and told him what I thought. "You're fucking out of order! This ain't your flat, y'know. You're not on the only one living here!"

"Oh yeah?" he says, cool as a snake getting ready to bite. "So whose flat is it?"

"Who's here longest has rights. That's how its been. That's how Dave ran things."

"Yeah, well honky's not here no more. So if you think you can run things, go right ahead." He grinned nastily. I didn't like him. I didn't like feeling outnumbered in the flat, either. He and Spider were tight, and I was on my own. I was ready to just keep to myself, just go about my business and stick to my room and fuck them. But Ben surprised me, he gave me a nice little stash of weed as a peace offering, so I accepted it in the spirit it was given and buried the hatchet.

※ ※ ※

The first time they gave a party, I thought it was a great idea. Get a decent system in one Saturday night, wire speakers into every room. Buy some crates of Red Stripe, charge an entrance fee, and split the proceeds. They'd share the lion's portion, and I'd get a cut for the inconvenience. I liked the idea. We'd just clear our belongings away and use the whole space.

I invited everyone I knew—Roy, Jumani, Roy's sisters, a few of the fellas I talked to at the Royal, Loretta, Diane, and a few others. I told them all to invite their friends. I even thought of inviting Tess, but thought the better of it. I'd never given a party before and I was excited. It was September, autumn, but still warm. I opened up the french doors in Ben's room so that people could wander out into the night.

There's nothing like being out in the warm night air with a spliff in your hand and some sounds in your head. The garden was a mess, it looked like a jungle in the daylight, but no-one would be able to see it in the dark. The three of us pulled together so smoothly getting this party organised, it was surprising.

Man, the people just kept coming. Spider and me were on the door, and I swear, people poured in non-stop all night, all different types, lots of them white, lots of them female, and lots of them gorgeous. I wasn't sure that Loretta would come. She liked parties and shebeens but I felt she was suspicious of this one because I was involved. If you understand what I mean. Like she thought because I was involved, this party had to be a wash-out. That's the feeling I got from her. As the people piled in and the fug got thicker and the vibes got bluesier, I got more excited. I just wanted her to come and see what we'd done.

She came with Diane and two of their girlfriends, girls I knew by sight, white girls who hang around a lot with dreads. She looked wicked, all in white under her big black leather bomber jacket. Tight white mini-dress, sexy white tights with big holes and shiny black Doc Martens, shiny red lips. I saw Spider swallow hard when I introduced him to her, and I felt good that this was my woman. I wished I could have stayed with her but I had to stay on the door.

Roy and Jumani arrived late into the night in a group with some dreads from Kilburn, Jumani's posse. I was glad to see them come, I hailed them up like the bredrin they were. It was like, these were my people, my tribe here at last. They too melted into the loud, heaving warmth of the party, out of sight.

I left the door at around three o'clock and went inside looking for Loretta. I'd been smoking all night and I was well red, I was mellow and I wanted to dance with my woman. I spotted Roy and Jumani dancing close and quiet in a corner in my room. I wondered through the other rooms, peering through the smoke and the dark, but I couldn't find Loretta, even though I spotted Diane and the girls they came with dancing together in a clump.

I pushed my way through the crowd in the back room, scanning the faces as best I could in the half-dark. The atmosphere in the room was heavy and rich-smelling. Nuff herb was being smoked. I'd seen Ben in the hallway earlier on, handing over a tiny package and I'd figured that this party must be a great business opportunity for him. I shouldered my way through the room and out into the backyard. Loretta's white dress caught my eye right away. She was leaning up against the wall, eyes gleaming, smiling into the face of Ben. They both turned their heads and watched me approach them, Loretta no longer smiling.

"I didn't know you knew this ne'er-do-well," she said, nodding her head in Ben's direction. He laughed as though she'd just cracked the funniest joke he'd ever heard.

"I didn't know *you* knew 'im." I wasn't sure why, but I wasn't amused.

"Known 'im for ages, ain't I, Ben? Everyone round these parts knows 'im, eh? Eh?" She was nudging him in the ribs with her elbow and laughing at him. What was so amusing? I wondered if I'd missed something. Whatever it was, it had her gleaming and glowing, eyes bright, smile brilliant, the Loretta I'd fallen for but hardly ever saw these days.

"D'you feel like dancing?" I felt a real idiot asking her with Ben smirking beside me, but I couldn't just stand there with the two of them giggling like two kids over a secret. They both kept on laughing, but she came with me back into the flat. We danced together for a bit, but something was wrong. Maybe the DJ was playing the wrong music, maybe the people were all wrong, but the vibe I thought I felt earlier had vanished. Loretta held me while we danced and shared a spliff with me. She wasn't having one of her off nights, so why did I have a cold feeling in my stomach?

※ ※ ※

The party was a success businesswise. We made nearly two thousand pounds on the door and on beer sales, and I figured Ben had done really well with his merchandise. Two hundred and fifty went to the sounds man, and we split the rest between us. I got two hundred and fifty, which I reckoned was less than my fair share, but I didn't make a fuss about it. What really pissed me off, though, was the damage to my room. The walls looked as though an army had marched halfway up, then turned back again. The mess of cans, fag-ends, roaches and even a used Durex half-filled a black garbage bag. Yeah, Ben's room and Spider's were messed up too, but they hadn't spent money and sweat decorating theirs.

We all woke up late next day, well into the afternoon, in fact. By the time we'd finished with sweeping and tidying up it was evening, and I was starving. I was going out for a take-away, but I couldn't find my jacket any place. I remembered taking it down from the peg behind the door along with a couple of grubby sweatshirts, and stuffing them into the cupboard in my room. The sweatshirts were there, creased and stale-smelling, but not the jacket. It was the only coldproof garment I had. I'd paid fifty quid for it, a lot of money for me. Some bastard had nicked it. One of Ben's junkies probably, nicked it so he could flog it. And what did Ben say when I told him?

"Sorry, man, that's tough. These things happen at parties."

Easy for him to say, it wasn't his coat. No more parties for me, I decided. Not in my place, anyway. Never mind the bread. Too much mess, and I don't want anything else stolen. I told them both, that was it with parties.

I had a dream that same Sunday night. In the dream I'm a kid again, back in primary school and I'm playing on the floor in a corner with a girl who looks like Kaya. We're building ships with Lego. The girl works faster than me and in no time at all her ship is huge, twice the size of mine. How do you do it? I ask her. She says nothing, she just keeps on adding blocks and the ship keeps growing till it's as high as the ceiling and as wide as the classroom. The teacher appears, she hugs the girl, then turns and looks at me and says, "Where's yours, Stevie?" She starts laughing at my ship which gets smaller and smaller, shrinking before my eyes. Then I realise that I'm shrinking too, even faster than my ship and I shout out: "It's not fair, it's not fair, I'm too small." I'm so small I'm almost invisible, a speck of dust on the floor. I'm fading fast but I keep on screaming and noboddy hears me.

I woke up and sat up in bed, soaked in sweat, my heart pounding in my head, feeling scared, so scared I couldn't stop shivering.

Chapter 17

A FEW PEOPLE I'VE COME across in life I wish I'd never met, and Ben is one of them. I never trusted that sod. I admit that to begin with I was quite impressed by the way he operated. He was smart and he was slick, no doubt about that. And he was always so friendly, you could easily be taken in and believe he was nice guy. He'd be knifing you in the guts and he'd smile and crack a joke while he did it.

In the beginning I thought Spider was the one to be wary of. It was his bovver-boy haircut, his rotten teeth and those heavy, clomping boots he wore; when he stomped through the flat, the floor shook and the walls trembled as though a contingent of Nazis was marching through. I was wrong about them both, it turned out.

After the party, Ben was buzzing around like a blue-arsed fly, busy, busy, busy. He was going through a prosperous phase, as he described it. Business boomed. People banged on our door at all hours of the day and night, looking for Ben and his goodies. Roy asked me how I felt about living with a cocaine dealer, like how cocaine was a truly evil substance that messed up your brain. I told him it didn't bother me that much, not at all, in fact, as long as he didn't try to tempt me with it. I was strictly a weed man myself. And Ben was pretty generous with the herb. I got to sample all sorts but sensi was always my favourite, cool and mellow, as sweet on the spirit as a dream of home.

I helped him make deliveries now and again. Not just weed; anything you could name. TVs, stereo components, radios, leather jackets, watches. Most times it was weed, though once or twice I suspected he was giving me blow to carry. I did it without asking any questions. As long as he paid me for it, and didn't do it too often, I didn't mind.

By the time Christmas came round again I was earning a fair amount doing deliveries for Ben, so it made sense to give up working at the Royal. After all, I'd been there a long time. I'd been there more than eighteen months. Eighteen months pushing corpses and sick human bodies around, breathing in the stink of disinfectant and disease. I can't believe I'd stuck it for that long. I'd just got used to it, I suppose. It became a habit, like anything you do regularly for long enough.

The strangest thing of all was that I missed it at first. I'd wake up in the morning, dreading having to get up and get dressed in the cold, psyching myself up for it before I remembered that I didn't have to. I was free to lie in my bed and frowse for as long as I liked. I could get up whenever I wanted, spend as much time as I wanted doing nothing but feel cold.

The days were long and passed slowly; there wasn't all that much to do, really. I'd start the day with a spliff, and listen to the radio for a bit. Later I'd go out and maybe make a delivery. Maybe I'd go out for a take-away or have a meal in one of those cheap cafes around Camden Town. Or maybe I'd go and check Loretta. I was seeing her more now I wasn't working. Sometimes I'd go shopping with her in the afternoons and push the trolley round Sainsbury's for her, dodging the mums with their kids dragging behind them. They were lethal with a trolley, those women. Sometimes we'd take Kaya for walks, on the Heath or Primrose Hill like we used to do when we were first going out. It was boring, boring as fuck, but I went along all the same.

I was seeing Loretta more but I was enjoying it less. I mean who could enjoy such a misery? Most of the time she was with me she was didn't say a word, but I told myself it was just her depression. She wouldn't talk to me, sometimes she wouldn't even look at me, like she was blanking me out. And she hardly ever wanted to have sex with me.

"Why d'you keep coming here?" She asked me that more than once. "What d'you get out of it?"

"I'm never gonna let you move in, you know. Never." Another of her songs. Anyone would think I was putting pressure on her to let me move in when the fact was that I'd never asked her. Silly bitch. OK, it would've been nice living with her and Kaya like we were a family. The flat was big enough. It could've been great. I'd have kept on working; I wouldn't have left the Royal. Or so I told her when she went on at me about me quitting. Nagged me worse than my dad, she did, went on about it for weeks. I was surprised. I never knew it mattered to her.

It got me down, though, the way she went on, it got me mad sometimes. Her not talking, her getting angry with me for every little thing. Sometimes I felt she thought her depression was all my fault, that she was blaming me for the way she felt. I couldn't make her see that I wanted to make her happy. I wanted to be around her and to look after her. She just wouldn't give me the chance. I thought about chucking it in with her more than once. I mean, what was I getting out of it? Not even sex, these days. There was a whole heap of women out there. Women were easy to get, nice ones, too. I didn't have to put up with Loretta's shit.

The Babylon had always kept their eye on the flat, even before there were illegal activities going on. I thought it was funny how Dave was always anxious about keeping on the right side of the law, and keeping everything looking regular and normal, yet he was the one who brought in Ben. And I must admit, I didn't worry all that much about the law. I never saw them. Spider was the one who was always getting anxious about the car parked outside, getting all worked up about it, pacing up and down like a giant long-legged insect. Understandable, I suppose. He'd been inside more than once, from what I could gather. I never knew exactly what Spider was up to. I mean, I knew he was a hustler like Ben and they did a lot of business together but that was all I knew.

Spider went out of town a lot, up to Birmingham and Manchester and Leeds. A proper travelling salesman, I called him. I even went on a trip up to Birmingham with him once, at his expense. It was my first visit to Birmingham. Actually, it was my first trip out of London. We took the train from Euston, really early one morning so we could get a cheap ticket. When we left home dawn hadn't yet broken and Belsize Park was still peaceful under a dim sky. No cars, no buses, no noise at all except the pounding of Spider's boots on the pavement, very little movement other than the odd cat prowling around and the quiet scurry of litter disturbed by the chilly morning wind. It felt weird, like Spider and me were the only inhabitants of a deserted city. Even the underground station was peaceful, just one other person waiting on the platform, hunched into his coat to keep warm, waiting on the first tube.

Euston Station was alive and bustling and warm, a return to normality. We bought coffee and two expensive croissants from a kiosk. The girl behind the counter moved like a zombie and looked at me glassy-eyed when I spoke to her. I knew how she felt; some jobs have that effect on a person. We ate our breakfast on the train and Spider yelled at me for dunking my croissant in my coffee. At the top of his voice he called me an ignorant nigger and asked me which tree I'd just climbed down from. I pretended to get mad and grabbed him across the table, calling him a dumb half-breed and offering to spread his brains across the carriage. Two men in suits sitting next to us got up and left, giving us space to spread out. Passengers in the seats across the corridoor were eyeing us nervously, obviously trying to decide whether we were just noisy louts or dangerous delinquents. Apart from snarling at each other every now and again, we gave this particular game a rest and settled down to doze away the journey.

Spider slept while I gazed out the window, letting north London pass in front of my eyes at one hundred and twenty miles per hour. London was one helluva big city. But what a mess! Compared to the country, it was a pain, a huge splinter in my eye. Even though the country had never appealed to me. Say "country" and I'd think of little villages with pretty cottages inhabited by white people wearing smocks who ate nothing but Hovis. I was seeing real country for the first time. From the train I saw a quilt of green and brown touched with mist and frost; the odd field with sheep sleeping, crouched on curled-up legs on the cold ground; the odd house, set off the road, surrounded by trees, dangerously secluded. Or maybe not. The places we stopped were tiny toy towns; we whizzed in and out of them in no time at all. And in no time at all we were in Birmingham.

What a shock I got when we stepped from the station into this ugly concrete apology of a city centre. So this was the second city! Thank God I lived in London. Spider must have had something wrong with his brain; he rated Birmingham highly. It's the people, man, he said. They're real. They're more human up here. In what way? I asked. They're not as prejudiced, he said. They're not as snobby. Well, I must've been looking particularly handsome that day, 'cos every other white person who passed us gave me the eyeball. And not always friendly either.

We took a taxi to Handsworth, passing out of the city centre in no time at all, passing through prosperous-looking whites-only suburbs in order to reach ghettoland. The high street looked as though a bomb had hit it yesterday. Then I remembered the riots they'd had up here a while ago. I wondered again what it was about the place that Spider rated so much? One thing for sure; I was glad I didn't live here.

We stopped outside a tiny two-up-two-down on a street with no gardens. The bloke Spider came to see was a smooth young Nigerian wearing beige patent shoes, sharp camel trousers, and an expensive-looking patterned sweater. He was the smiling, jovial type; he thumped me on the back saying, "My name is Tunje, welcome, welcome." I sat huddled up in a brown plastic armchair in the front room nursing a can of beer while they talked business in the kitchen. The room was choc-a-bloc with loot: huge piles of African fabric, shirts and sweaters in plastic bags, carton boxes full of wallets, handbags and heaven knows what else. From the look of him and the goods all around me, I could tell Tunje was doing good business.

We had something to eat in an Indian restaurant on the high road before heading back to the station. Spider was in a good mood; his talks with Tunje must have gone really well. He ordered tandoori chicken, pilaou rice, dhal and fried okras, and a couple of beers. I remember the taste of those okras, like nothing I'd ever had before. It was the best Indian meal I'd ever had. Birmingham rose a notch in my estimation.

Back on the train going home, I bought us both a beer and supped mine while Spider chatted on about good times he'd had in

Birmingham. About Liverpool and what a great place that was, even better than Birmingham. Oh yeah? So how come you're living in London? I thought it, but didn't say it. He talked about Ben and how he met him, years ago in Birmingham. They were teenagers at the time, but Ben was already well into hustling. Ben was his role model, he said, he'd learned everything he knew from Ben.

He asked me a very strange question. My girl Loretta, did she ever say anything to me about Ben? I told him she'd said she'd been seeing him around for years. Well, said Spider, you could put it like that. I wanted to ask him what the fuck he meant, but I didn't. I just sat back in my seat and looked out the window at the neat green English landscape flashing by, holding onto my can of beer and trying to ignore the cold, heavy feeling creeping through my guts.

I went to see Loretta that very evening.

"What the fuck are you doing 'ere!" she said when she saw me on the doorstep.

"What a way to greet a friend!" I tried to smile; after all, I wanted her to let me in so we could talk. "Can I come in a minute? I won't stay long."

The grudging way she opened the door really got to me. She was one mean bitch, no two ways about it.

As usual, Diane was transfixed by some rubbish on the TV. Kaya was sitting beside her on the settee, tearing a magazine to shreds.

"Can we go in the kitchen? I wanna talk to you about something." She screwed up her face, but followed me into her mess of a kitchen and leaned back against the sink, arms crossed on her chest, ready for anything. I knew what I wanted to ask, but I didn't know the words to say to this hard-eyed female who faced me, glaring into my eyes. Anyway, she took the matter out of my hands.

What d'you keep coming 'ere for? I'm sick of you coming round 'ere whenever you feel like it!"

"C'mon, Loretta, don't be like that! I wanna talk to you, that's why I came."

"So why the fuck don't you talk!" She was yelling now, loud and harsh.

"I wanted to ask you about Ben" I began, timid even to my own ears, but she jumped down my throat before I could finish my sentence.

"I don't have nothin' to say to you 'bout Ben, nothin'. So don't even ask!" Her eyes glinted hard and cold like frostbitten earth. "Spider said something to you 'bout Ben and me, didn't he? I knew he would sooner or later. Fuckin' creep! So what did 'e tell you?"

"He didn't tell me nothing." I sounded cowardly to my own ears and felt ashamed. This wasn't how it was meant to go. "He just said you've known Ben for a long time."

"I told you that already, didn't I? What more d'you want to know?" She was mocking me, the bitch, and it was making me mad. I felt like slapping that nasty smile off her face once and for all. I didn't, though.

"You wanna know if I'm screwing 'im? Yes, I am! And you wanna know something else? Something to really make you happy? He's the best. You should take lessons from 'im, learn what to do with that thing between your legs."

Her voice was quiet now, quiet in my ears but ringing in my head like an alarm you can't turn off. I looked at her face, her eyes, her beautiful locks. I could have smashed in that face, pulled out those dreadlocks one by one. Even though I loved all of her, she made me want to obliterate her, stamp on her, put her out like the fag-end she really was. I felt water on my face and burned with shame that I was crying so she could see. There was nothing I could do now, nothing she could do or say either. The best thing was to go, get the fuck out of it before temptation got the better of me and I did something I'd regret.

Outside, my head cooled a bit. What was the point in getting worked up about a bitch like her? It was just time to move on, forget about her. There were lots more where she came from.

※ ※ ※

That winter was one of the longest and coldest I could remember. It was still freezing in April, still cold in May. I reckon I survived by sleeping a lot. I got to the stage where I was staying in bed till three, four o'clock in the afternoon. I'd just curl up under the blankets and ignore the noise of traffic coming in from the street, ignore the daylight seeping round the edges of the window hangings. I'd get up when I could bear the gnawing in my guts no longer to search for food in the kitchen.

I didn't care whose it was. Ben's baked beans were as good as Spider's rancid bacon. I ate was what there, and sometimes there was nothing.

I did a lot of walking too. Everyday I went out and walked for hours. I walked the streets of Belsize Park and Hampstead. I walked round Camden Town, down to Kentish Town and Tufnell Park. Now and again I'd stop by Roy's Mum. She was always glad to see me. She'd make me a cup of tea and give me something to eat. I could sit and watch the TV with her and feel warm and normal for a while before hitting the road again.

I stopped by my Dad's once or twice but each time was a nightmare. Pure yelling and shouting. "Look pon di kandishun of! Look pon yu head! Look how yu stink!" I mean what was the point? What was the point of putting myself through that, even if I did get a dinner out of him? I walked over to Finsbury Park now and again and stopped by Tess. She got on my nerves with her questions: "What are you doing, Stevie? Where are you getting money from? Are you feeling OK?" Even while she was interrogating me and I was getting mad, I'd hear a voice saying, keep your cool, Stevie, play it right. Yeah, she gave me money. She bought a coat for me, a big navy blue, quilted winter coat that would've been great for the winter, but by the time I got it summer was around again.

I didn't like going to Finsbury Park much. I didn't like the way people on the street looked at me; it made me feel funny, like they were really watching me. As though they knew me. Well, maybe they did, seeing as how I was born in there and seeing as how I used to live in Hornsey, not far off. The time I went to see Tess, the time when she gave me the coat, I asked her about when we lived in Hornsey; what our house was like, what it was like living with our mum.

"She was a horrible person," said Tess. I remember her sitting on her cream settee and looking at me, saying, she was a horrible person.

She gave me directions to the house, the one we used to live in, and you know what? I went there. I walked from Tess's flat, along Stapleton Hall Road, up the hill and turned right, and there was number one. Our old house. One big fucking house! We used to live in that big fucking house, almost as big as a house on Haverstock Hill. I stood outside the gate looking at it. I leaned up against the broad trunk of a tree and looked at our old house, trying to imagine the people who lived there now. It was smartly painted, dark green door, sparking white window frames. White people. Rich people. I felt like knocking and telling whoever answered that my dad used to own this house and I used to live there, but I didn't. I stood under a tree for quite a while, just looking at the house until I got cold and had to start walking to stop my legs from freezing up.

All the way back to Hanley Road I noticed people staring at me. It got on my nerves. I stopped an old white woman wearing a red felt hat and asked her what the fuck she was looking at. I told her I used to live in a big fucking house with gardens at the front and back. Yes, I did, I said. I could see she didn't believe me, stupid old bitch. No point in wasting time on her, so I just walked on. On Hanley Road, I saw another woman looking at me. I saw her coming straight towards me, a middle-aged black woman in a pink satin dress. She must have been cold. I'd have lent her my jacket if I'd had another one. She was staring at me all the while she was walking towards me and I felt like turning and running away from her. When she came close I could see she was smiling at me and I felt better, I smiled back at her, and she said, "Mi have sumt'ing fi yu daalin," and she held out her hand and there it was, red, dripping, steaming, pumping and bloody. A heart, lying in her hand, throbbing. I heard screams as I ran, tearing down Hanley Road as fast as I could, cutting through backstreets, heading for Holloway Road. People turned and stared at me. I ran till my legs were tearing out of my groin and my lungs were on fire, not stopping to look behind me. As I ran I could hear screams like sirens in my ears, reverberating in my head, and all the while I felt the woman in the pink dress right behind me.

At Holloway Road I jumped on a bus heading for Tufnell Park. I was panting and sweating and in pain. At Tufnell Park I got off and straight away got onto a 137 going towards Camden Town. The young black conductress looked at me, half suspicious, half nervous. I used the fiver Tess had given me to pay my fare and went upstairs and collapsed in a seat at the back of the bus. I couldn't hear the screaming any more, but something was telling me, be careful, Stevie, she's out there waiting for you, while another voice was telling me, "All she wanted to give you was love, Stevie, all you need is love."

It was getting dark, but I strained my eyes to see if she was following the bus, but she wasn't. At Kentish Town I got off the bus and headed for Roy's mum's house, walking as fast as I could, glancing over my shoulder as I walked. I rang the doorbell hard; I wanted to be let in right away, no waiting. Mrs Henry looked vexed as she opened the door but her expression changed when she saw me.

"Stevie, what happen to yu, why yu pantin so?."

"I've been running," I told her. I walked straight into the empty living room and sat down on the settee, fixing my eyes on the TV. Mrs Henry followed me into the room and stood beside the settee looking at me, frowning.

"Stevie, you sure you all right? You don't look well to me."

"I'm alright, Mrs Henry," I said. The way she was watching me was getting on my nerves. "Just let me sit here a bit and watch the telly. All I want to do is sit here for a bit. And watch telly. You don't mind do you? I'm all right, really, I am."

Back at the flat all I could think of was how I wanted to kill that cunt Ben. I'd visualise him with Loretta, picture the two of them together laughing at my expense. God, didn't I let them play me for a fool! Those off-limits nights. Those cold, angry moods of hers. The signs were there, plain as the nose on my face to anyone with twopenny worth of sense. If I'd had anywhere to go I'd have left that fucking hole of a flat long time ago and put that trash behind me.

I spent most of the time indoors in my bed. I didn't want to see Ben or talk to him. Just the sound of his voice through the walls got me going. I had plans to get rid of the filth. I was just waiting for the right moment. The pigs loitering in the squad car outside would just love to have some of the info I had on him. I could give them enough to put his arse away for years. I amused myself for hours running the fantasy over and over again in my mind. All I had to do was time it right.

My money situation was tough, but I tried not to let it get me down. I stopped doing that fucker's deliveries, so I had no real money coming in. I signed on down at Social Security giving my dad's address. The pittance I was getting from them kept me going, but I was hungry half the time. Spider kept knocking on my door wanting me to pay my share of the electricity bill. Seventy quid he wanted. Said my heater burned up a lot of power. So what about theirs? I asked him. What did theirs burn? Water? He wanted to argue but I just pulled the covers over my head and dozed off. If they didn't want to pay the bill, let them leave it. What the fuck did I care?

※ ※ ※

I was curled up in a nice, cosy space, safe, warm and comfortable, so safe I felt I was being held, though no one else was around. I was alone, but not lonely. I could have stayed there forever, sleeping when I wanted, waking up and stretching out my arms and legs, then turning over and going to sleep again. I heard a noise like quiet rain falling on trees, only deeper. I felt like getting up and seeing what was going on outside. But when I stood up I banged my head, and when I stretched out my arms and felt around me, I felt the walls slowly closing in around me. A cold feeling spread through my stomach. I felt for a door so I could get out. I felt all four walls top to bottom. I felt the ceiling, I felt the floor. The walls were moving in, the ceiling coming down, slowly, but creeping in on me. I had to bend over, kneel down and keep my arms close to my body. My room had become a box with walls moving in to crush me. I realised the sound I thought was rain was the noise of the sea, of waves calmly beating against the walls around me. My heart banged against my ribs, faster and faster and the sea pounded harder, drowning the sound of my heartbeat. I was curled up like a snail in its shell, barely able to move.

Then I saw a glimmer of light coming through a hole in the upper-right hand corner. I looked out and saw the sea, dark and murky as petrol, churning, tossing around the wooden chest which was my room. A ship appeared in the distance, a bright red and white lifeboat and it ploughed through the waves towards my box, fast. I could see a tall white man looking in my direction through a telescope. Thank God, give thanks and praises. I was going to be saved. I sat, knees bent, arms wrapped around knees, listening to the approaching boat, waiting to be lifted to safety.

The noise of something sharp hitting the box made me start. It came again, a crash this time, several crashes from different directions as though stones were raining on my box. Something hard, cold and metallic pierced the box not far from my head—the point of a spear. Another one came through, nicking my shoulder. Another gashed my neck, another pierced the side of my head and I screamed, that's my head, you've got my head, but another came right through the top of my skull and the hand that drove it twisted the point in my brain. My brain spurted a streaming red fountain. As I held my head to stop the flow, blood dripped though my fingers and into my eyes blinding me. My brain burst into flames, my head burned in agony, igniting my locks, burning the walls of my box. I stood among the waves, aflame in the water, holding my head and screaming to the white man on the boat *HELP ME, HELP ME, HELP ME HELP.*

I couldn't put out the fire, no matter what I did. I filled the bath with cold water and lay there for hours with the water in my hair, cooling my head. That bastard Ben tried to drag me out and I smashed him in the face with my fist. You're sick, man, he said and I said yeah, I'm sick of you, you shithouse. The look on his face was a treat, made me laugh like I hadn't done in years.

The heat of the summer was agony, I couldn't take it. I stayed in all day, lying on my matress naked, or in the bath, trying to keep cool. Spider clomped up to my door and knocked now and again, but I never answered. I didn't want to see him or anyone, for that matter. He got bold eventually and came in. What the fuck do you want? I said. He stood there looking down at me, so I pulled up the dirty sheet to my neck and turned over to face the wall. Thought you might like a smoke, he said. I didn't move. I lay still, staring at the wall. He sighed and marched back through the door. Good riddance. As I turned over and threw off the sheet, I saw a nicely rolled spliff on the floor beside the matress. I picked it up and sniffed it before I lit it. It smelled like good weed. What a treat. I hadn't had a smoke in months. A few puffs and I was feeling cool, like river water was running over me. It felt sweet, like calm, quiet music and I let it soothe me, let it lull me, let it put me to sleep.

I felt good when I woke up, better than I'd felt in ages. I wanted to

stretch my legs and flex my muscles, take some excercise. It was evening
and I fancied taking a walk through Hampstead. I hurried out of the
flat; I didn't want to lose a moment of this feeling, like everything was
really fine and cool and life would be so sweet if I could just make the
moment last. I headed uphill, walking briskly, stretching out my legs
between steps, placing my heels firmly on the ground as I walked. Man,
I felt fit! Energy rose like heat up my body, shimmering around my
back and up into my head. People were looking at me and I smiled at
them, people turned their heads and watched me and I laughed and
shouted back telling them that I was God and they were lucky to see
me like this. I stopped outside the French place, the bar with all the
lights and mirrors, looking through the open doors at the tittering,
chattering crowd inside. Then I saw it! I knew the instant I clapped eyes
it, this was my jacket, the one that grinning blonde-haired fucker wearing it had nicked from my cupboard at Ben's party last year. I walked
straight in, pushing bodies aside with my elbows and grabbed his arm.
He was pretending I wasn't there talking to him, looking in the opposite direction, and I told him, that's my jacket you're wearing, sonny, I
want it back. I was gonna pull it right off him and leave, but he tried to
hit me, a great mistake, my lad. I had to defend myself, didn't I? I had to
smack him right on the nose and again round the head and when he
wouldn't give in, I kneed him in the groin but he still wouldn't give in
and they were trying to grab my arms but I was fit tonight, I quite fancied a fight, I shook them off and kneed him and biffed him again, and
they tried to grab me again, but I couldn't shake them off and I saw
the blue uniforms so I said, you're officers of the law, make him give
back my jacket and they said, you'd better come with us, my lad and I
said no fucking way. Two of them grabbed my arms and one of them
grabbed my legs but I gave them trouble, I kicked and twisted and
heaved and roared like a lion caught in a net. Nah, I wasn't gonna let
them take me without a fight.

Chapter 18

"TWENTY YEARS IS A LONG time to go without seeing your mother." Dr. Manson sat on a chair by my bed, frowning down at the clipboard he was holding. The paper was covered with scribbles. He looked tired and old. Who wouldn't, working in a dump like Friars Burnett Hospital, looking after a bunch of loonies?

"Would you like to see her?" He looked expectant, like he was hoping I'd bounce up and down on the bed with excitement at the thought of a visit from my mother. I was sorry to disappoint him. Not even a visit from Muhammad Ali could've got me excited at that point. They'd pumped so much medication into me that just opening my eyelids was a day's work. Most of the time my head felt like a concrete block, blank, heavy and completely unconnected to my body.

"Would you like to see her? I'll try to contact her if you'd like me to." He was more enthused by the idea than I could ever be. All the same I nodded, using every ounce of energy in my body, just to get him off my back. I felt better the moment he left the room. I couldn't cope with his questions, his probing and niggling. All those questions about my mum, my dad, my family. What was the point? I guess he was only doing what psychiatrists are supposed to do: trying to find out as much about me as he could, trying to figure out what made me tick. But how was that gonna help me get out of this place? All I wanted was for everyone, every striking one, to leave me in peace so I could get my head together again.

The police had got in touch with my dad after they took me in, but he didn't bother to pay me a visit while I was in the lock-up. He came a couple of days after they had me sent down to Friars, him and his wife. They sat beside my bed looking like they were keeping vigil over a corpse. He kept asking me if I felt all right, and I kept trying to nod. Even if I'd been capable of talking to them, which I wasn't, I wouldn't have done. I'd bet a tenner that if I'd shown a few more signs of life, he'd have gone on about how mi let him down and how mi no have no shyame, mi let dem put me inna mental institushun. As for her, she didn't say a word. She just sat there looking hard and sour, like a dumpling from last Saturday's soup. I was relieved when they left. That was their one and only visit and I was glad about that as well.

Tess came on Saturday afternoons. At first, when I was going through the zombie phase, she would creep up to my bed and sit beside me holding my hand and looking like she wanted to cry. I wanted to ask her, what the fuck do you have to cry about? She didn't have a single thing to worry about. Everything was cool for her. She had no problems, none whatsoever. Bloody women and their emotions!

Visits were less of an ordeal later on, after they reduced the amount of medication. Man that made a difference! My head felt like part of me again. I could move my lips, my arms and legs. I was alive again! She brought me food, brown rice and curried vegetables, stuff like that, and she brought me cigarettes. We went for walks in the hospital grounds, strolling on the lawn surrounding the red brick hospital buidings. She asked me a lot of questions I found it hard to answer; although I felt better, conversation was still an effort.

"What does your doctor say about your breakdown?"

"He don't say nothin'."

"Nothing at all?" She thought I was hiding something.

"He doesn't call it a breakdown. He calls it an episode."

She chewed on that for a while.

"He wants to get our mum to come and see me."

"WHAT!" she yelled. "What good does he think that's going to do? He must be out of his mind! I'm going to talk to him!"

Her yelling made me nervous. My hands began to shake and my mouth trembled. I told her I didn't want to talk any more and she shut up.

※ ※ ※

Who knows why I cracked up? It could have been for any number of reasons. I've always had trouble with my head. When I was a kid, about six or seven, another kid chucked a stone at me in the playground at school. It caught me bang in the middle of the forehead and cut my head open. Blood spurted everywhere. Later on I fell over playing hockey and cracked my skull on the ice. I was about fifteen at the time. My head ached for months afterwards. Maybe some damage had been done. Maybe it had been there all the time and was only beginning to show now.

I knew one thing for sure. Friars was the worst experience of my life and I couldn't wait to get out. The place didn't bother me much at first; I didn't take in all that much to begin with. I mean, I was out of it for nearly a month. As I got better, I took in more and more and it began to get to me. The dingy grey-green walls. The grimy windows. The damp, frowsy smell of the bedding, like hamsters drying out after a bath in Dettol. The place was a dump. It made the Royal look like the Ritz in comparison.

I was in a room on my own to begin with, but later on they put me on a ward with seven other beds, all of them occupied. The very first time I sat up and looked around me, the bloke from the bed beside mine came hurrying over.

"Welcome back to the land of the living," he said with a trembly smile, like he really wanted to cry but was making a huge effort not to. "My name is Terry." His big eyes stared at me without blinking. He was see-through-white and bone skinny. Kind of nervous-looking, like an overgrown young bird. He was friendly though, and quite chatty.

"I'm quite an oldtimer here," he told me, like it was something to be proud of. "This is my fourth stint."

Bully for you, mate, what's your problem?

Terry knew everything about the others on our ward. He knew all the staff as well and was full of stories about which nurse had done what to whom and under what circumstances. I didn't mind a bit of chat now and again, but Terry got on my nerves a lot. That's how I fell into the habit of walking around the grounds. I spent hours out there when the weather was fine. The staff didn't like it, more work for them, I guess, having to check to find out where I was. Dr. Manson told them it was OK, it was doing me good. I was the athletic type, he told them, I needed plenty of excercise.

There was another black guy on the ward, a good-looking hunk in his thirties who never spoke to anyone. He spent most of the time lying on his bed staring at the wall, or in the common room, sitting in a chair by the window staring outside.

"Oh, that's Lancelot! He's from St Kitts. He came not long before you. He's a solicitor or accountant, or something like that. He tried to gas himself."

I wondered how Terry knew so much about Lancelot, since he didn't talk to anyone, but I soon learned that Terry had his sources. Just looking at Lance, you would never guess someone like him would have problems so heavy he'd want to top himself. Educated, a proper job, a future. A nice-looking woman came to visit quite regularly; his girlfriend, Terry said. This guy had everything to live for: more than me at any rate.

I was sitting in the common room watching Top of the Pops when Dr. Manson came bouncing in.

"Ah, Steven! I've got some wonderful news for you." I turned my attention from the bodies gyrating on the TV screen to his face. He was so excited, the vein in the middle of his forehead was standing out. I felt like telling him to calm down and take it easy, but I didn't.

"I've managed to make contact with your mother. She's willing to visit, if you want her to! Would you like that?"

Would I like that? What the fuck did I know? I couldn't remember the woman, I hadn't seen her face for twenty-odd years. Maybe I wouldn't like it. Maybe I wouldn't like *her*.

"It might help, Steve. It really might." Well I didn't have the first clue what it might help, but I said yes anyway. It could be interesting. It would be good to see what she looked like. My dad burned all the photographs he had of her, so I didn't even know what her face looked like. In any case, I didn't have to talk to her if I didn't want to. I could just turn and stare at the wall like Lance if I didn't like her. So I said yeah, OK. Let her come.

Rain poured out of the sky in gallon-sized drops the day she came. It was a Saturday. Dr. Manson called me into his office a little after midday, which pissed me off a bit. It was nearly lunchtime and the food was usually good on Saturday; shepherd's pie and baked beans. It would all be gone by the time I got back to the dining room.

She was sitting in front of Dr Manson's desk, her back to the door, a short, stocky figure in a black coat, topped by straightened, reddish hair. I sat in the chair beside her and looked at her face. She looked a bit like Tess. Or rather, Tess looked a bit like her, which was odd, since I'd always thought Tess resembled my dad. I'd always thought that was why he preferred her to me.

She didn't look at me and she didn't speak so I just sat watching her. Looking at the thick make-up covering her skin like butter spread thick on bread, at the blue eyeshadow that didn't go with anything and the dark red lipstick that bled into the corners of her mouth. Her hair looked as though not one atom of rain had touched it: still straight, styled in neat waves and curls. She looked like no-one I'd ever met before. She looked unreal.

Dr. Manson cleared his throat and took charge of things.

"Well Steve, well Mrs Brewster. We finally managed to get the two of you together. This is quite a momentous day, eh?"

The two of us nodded.

"I've talked to your mother a bit, Steve, and I've explained a little about why you're here and why I thought it might help for the two of you to meet. I've told her you're not up to much conversation at the moment, but maybe you'd like a few minutes alone together? Eh?"

I wanted to shake my head, to say no, don't leave me alone with her, but she was nodding and he was rising to his feet, so I didn't. My head felt heavy and my eyelids began to droop. My brain couldn't cope.

Dr Manson glanced at me.

"I'll be in the room across the corridor if you need me," he said and left the room, closing the door softly behind him.

We sat in silence for what seemed like ages, but was probably only a few minutes. Then she shifted in her chair and fixed me with a beady look, neither friendly nor hostile. It was my turn to look down at my hands which were sandwiched between my knees for warmth.

"So Stevie, how are you feeling?"

"Better than I was." Not at this moment, though. I wished I was back in bed.

"It's a long time since I saw you last."

"Yeah." Oh Christ. Spare me.

Her accent was strange, part cockney, part Jamaican, part American. Not like my dad's, which was pure Jamaican.

"Have been to America?" I felt I should try to make conversation.

"No. Why you ask?"

"Oh, nothin'. Just wondered."

She moved in her seat again and I noticed her shoes. Black with high, spiky heels, pointed toes and narrow straps fastened at the side with silver buckles. Wild. Not motherly shoes at all.

"Like your shoes," I said, and she smiled cat-like and lifted a leg, twisting it left and right to give me a better look. Silence again.

"Do you need anything? Can I bring you anything?" She crossed her ankles under the chair and fixed me with her bright eyes.

Did I need anything? What kind of thing? I had to think.

"Yeah. Cigarettes. I need cigarettes."

She opened her handbag, a big, hard leather bag rather like the ones doctors carried around. She took out a pack of twenty Benson and Hedges and handed them to me.

"I need some new underwear as well. You know, briefs." Why should I feel embarrassed to ask her for briefs? She was my mother, after all.

Dr. Manson came back into the room at that point and relief fell over me like a comfort blanket. I could stop trying to think of things to say now. Maybe I could get back to the dining room in time for some food.

"Maybe next time Steve will be up to a longer visit, Mrs Brewster," said Manson, bringing my ordeal to an end. "You better hurry, Steve, or you'll miss lunch." I stood up and mumbled goodbye, thanks for coming, and headed for the door without really looking my mother in the face. I didn't feel like lunch any more. I just wanted to lie down and sleep for a long time.

Tess came later on that afternoon while I was still in bed. I didn't want to tell her about our mum's visit. I knew she'd get worked up and start asking questions and probably go charging off to talk to Dr Manson. So I waited a bit before I told her. I waited until I knew she was about to leave, then I casually mentioned that Mrs. Brewster had dropped in to see me.

"Mrs. Brewster?" She crinkled her eyebrows together trying to place the name. "Who's she?"

"Our mum!" I would have quite enjoyed the dramatic effect if I'd felt more lively. "She didn't stay long and we didn't talk much. She asked me if I needed anything and I told her I needed cigarettes and briefs."

"You should have told her you needed a childhood, you needed some maternal care and nurturing!"

I shut off at that point, closed my eyes. I wasn't interested in Tess's half-baked opinions. I reckoned I didn't need anything from a woman who put on her make-up with a trowel and ponced around in spike-toed shoes.

Time passed slowly at Friars, slow and monotonous like the boring plink-plonk of water dripping from a faulty tap. After I'd been there a few weeks, I started occupational therapy. I wasn't keen on the idea, but it turned out not so bad. I quite enjoyed macrame and I was good at weaving. I made some table mats for Tess out of stips of coloured cloth woven together with yarn. They came out really nice, even if I say so myself. Susan, the instructor, wanted me to weave stripes, black/white, red/yellow, blue/green, but I wanted colours blending and mixing into each other. I mixed pale sky-blue and turquoise and sea-blue green and navy with a silver thread. I mixed all the greens and added some tiny blobs of white and yellow, Primrose Hill speckled with daisies. I mixed red and orange and purple and black, bad dream colours, but they looked good on a mat. I mixed yellow and orange and brown and khaki to make a mat like the autumn leaves covering the grounds outside.

Tess was thrilled with them, quite bowled over. She never knew I was so artistic, she said. I didn't either, I said.

I was in the middle of an afternoon macrame session when Spider walked in. I was so amazed I almost dropped the pot-holder I was making. Spider, of all people. I hadn't thought about him in ages. Nor Ben. Not much, at any rate. He clomped into the common room in his ten-league boots, grinning and showing his rotten teeth, looking every inch a villain.

"Is he a friend of yours?" asked Terry, inclining his head anxiously toward the door.

"Yeah," I said, standing up. "Yeah. He's my bredrin."

I noticed some of the others looking at him nervously, as though he'd come purposely to mug them or put the boot into their heads while they sat innocently doing their macrame. I put down my work and asked Susan to excuse me for a minute.

"How did ya know I was in 'ere?" He followed me down the corridor and out the back door into the open. It was chilly outside and I only had on a sweater, but I didn't care. I was glad to see him. It made me feel as close as I'd come to feeling good to know that he'd bothered to find me, bothered to come.

"I went up to the cop shop and made enquiries. They told me you were over 'ere." We crunched through the dry leaves covering the road, keeping a steady pace. "They came to the flat, snooping around, askin' 'bout you. The Babylon, that is. Must've been soon after they took you in. Said you'd been disturbing the peace, assaulting innocent citizens. How're you feelin' now, mate? If you don't mind me sayin', you don't look too lively."

"I'm all right. Better than I was." The less said about the events leading to my being admitted, the better.

"They busted the flat, you know. They got Ben."

"Yer kiddin' me!" Ha! That bastard! He had it coming!

"Yeah. Not long after your little adventure." I noticed he was watching my face. "You didn't have anythin' to do wiv it, did ya?"

I almost laughed. "Nah. I was out of it for weeks, one way or another. They're turning me into a junkie, they are. You should see the amount of stuff they pump into me. See my fingers?" I held up my hands for him to inspect. "I can move them now, but for the first coupla weeks, they wouldn't budge, they wouldn't shift. I was walking around like this, like Frankenstein." I imitated the stiff, wooden movements of a monster. Spider watched, not smiling.

"Musta been rough, man. Musta been real rough."

"Yeah," I said, " it was. It still is."

We walked to the boundary wall and back again, smoking, him doing most of the talking. He told me what he was doing, the new deals he was setting up. He was living in Kilburn, he said, shacked up with some girl. It was OK he said. It would do for now. He was trying to keep Ben's business going and keep a low profile as well. He had to be careful. The cops were watching him.

When he ran out of things to say I walked him to the gate and watched as he loped off down the road towards the bus stop. He said he'd visit again and I said yeah, thanks. That would be good.

A couple of weeks later, Roy and his mum came. I was sitting on a bench outside, taking in what warmth I could from a feeble, late-afternoon sun. I spotted them walking up the drive, both of them looking subdued, and went to meet them. They hugged me up, both of them, so long and so hard I began to feel bad, all tired, weary.

"Stevie! We never know where to find the I! We a-worry bout you! I buck up on the one Spider the other day, and is him tell me you in here!"

"Is true, Stevie, mi did worry 'bout you plenty from dat time you came by me lookin so distress. Mi did know from den, someting was wrong!"

They brought me clothes: a shirt and a sweater, some underwear and some socks. They brought food: rice and peas and chicken, and a banana cake Jumani had baked. They asked how I was, what it was like in the hospital, what kind of care I was getting. I wanted to tell them it was all right, as good as you could expect. I wanted to tell them I was getting better, I was feeling better. I wanted to tell them I was glad to see them, thanks for the food, I was longing to eat some rice and peas. But my neck let me down, my throat gave in on me. It choked up solid, like a blocked drain, so I could hardly breathe. It refused to support my head. I had to let my head fall onto my hands, and hold it that way, sitting between Roy and his mum, my hands on my lap and head resting on them. I didn't want them to see me like this. I wanted them to know I was better, a lot better than I was a few months ago, but even if I had said so, seeing me like that, bent double and dumb, they wouldn't have believed me.

I don't know how long we sat there, huddled together, each of them with an arm around me. It was dark when the nurse Patrick appeared in front of us and announced it was time for my medication. We all stood up together and Mrs Henry hugged me.

"You make sure you take good care of im!" Mrs Henry jabbed Patrick in the chest with her finger almost angrily, as though he was personally responsible for me. Patrick looked at her as though she was crazy, but nodded all the same.

"I give tanks fi know where the I a-rest. Now I know, I'll come visit," Roy gripped my shoulder with one hand, patted my arm with the other.

"Yeahman. Thanks," I said. I stood by the door and watched them walk slowly down the drive and disappear into the darkness beyond the hospital gates.

※ ※ ※

"You've made good progress, Steve. You're in much better shape now than when you came to us. How do you feel?"

"All right," I said, nodding for emphasis. I really was feeling better.

"Last time I asked if you felt ready to leave us, you said you weren't sure. How do you feel about it now?"

I had to think. I felt better for sure and I was well and truly fed up of Friars. Fed up of the wet, tasteless food, fed up of the damp, unhealthy smell. Terry was getting on my nerves as well, him and his nurse crony Malcolm. I'd moved bed to get away from him. I felt sorry for the poor sod who came in after me, a young black guy, a soldier, a private in the army. Schizophrenia, they said he was suffering from. Mind you, he was out of it most of the time so he was safe from Terry for the time being.

"How would you like to be home for Christmas?" Only five more shopping days to go. Better to be out, I reckoned, better than sitting around the common room with a bunch of head cases pretending to have a merry time. Yeah, I told him, I'd like to be home for Christmas.

"Good!" He looked satisfied, mission accomplished, one more off his back. "I'll arrange for a social worker to visit your father and make sure everything is OK at that end." He pulled a note pad towards him and scribbled on it energetically, crossing his t's and dotting his i's with vigour.

"It's a pity your mother didn't come again," he said pensively, looking up from the note pad. Pity for who? She'd sent a parcel with some vests and briefs and some more cigarettes. Inside the package was a letter in a kid's handwriting telling me to stay in touch and to let her know if I needed anything. I could call her number at home weekends or evenings. Take care. Mum.

"I'll still need to see you regularly, of course. You'll need to come in for your injections. And for group therapy sessions."

Oh please. Gimme a break. Group therapy was a total waste of time. Sitting around in a circle listening to Terry drone on about his childhood. Terry was the only one who spoke much. Everyone else switched off. I definitely did. What was the point of it all? Talking about a dad I'd prefer not to think about and a mum I don't even know. What was the point? The psychologist who sat with us was all right, a motherly, middle-aged type. I wouldn't have minded talking to her on my own, but not with those others listening. Still, once I was out, they couldn't force me to turn up for therapy, could they?

Once I knew for sure I was leaving, I began to feel quite excited about it. The others were envious, those who were well enough to understand that I was going.

"I'll be going soon, too," said Terry wistfully.

"Sure, mate," I said, though I knew he had nowhere to go to. His mum was crazier than he was, spent her life going in and out of hospital. He didn't know where his dad was. Poor bugger.

When I told Lancelot I was going he looked at me and rocked back and forwards, not saying anything. He was better than he had been. These days he looked at you when you talked to him, even spoke the odd word now and again.

Three days after my chat with Dr. Manson I was out, back at my dad's. The social worker arranged it. If I had any problems, I was to contact her immediately, she said. Was I sure I wanted to go home? she asked several times. She was a young black woman, quite pretty, trendy-looking. Yeah, I told her, I was sure.

My dad was out at work when I arrived at the house. My stepmother let me in and led me into the kitchen and gave me lunch. One thing I had to say about her, she was a great cook. I sat at the table watching her as she dished out steamed fish, peas and potatoes. Shortish, plump, very neat and tidy, she was quite a good-looking woman in her own way. I never felt comfortable with her, though. I just knew she didn't like me. It showed in a dozen different ways. Like the way she sat at the table while I ate, droning on about how my dad worried about me and how I ought to show more appreciation.

"Wi hope you going to turn over a new leaf now, Stevie. Yuh Faada, him looking to see yu get a job and start mekin a decent livin. Yu still young, yu still have time to straiten up yuself."

I'd heard it all before. When I finished eating I went straight up to my room, my old room at the back of the house. It was exactly the same as I remembered it, chockful of furniture: bed, dressing table, two wardrobes, a battered, pale blue ottoman. Maroon-and-gold-flocked wall paper, brown and cream brocade curtains framed a view of the high wall at the end of our tiny back garden. I unpacked my few pieces of clothing and made space in one of the wardrobes to hang up my spare trousers and shirts. Both wardrobes were full of my stepmother's stuff—old clothes, new, unworn clothes, things her son had given her to store. There was barely room for my things.

I was in bed when my dad got home, not sleeping, just lying there staring at the ceiling. I was tired. I really didn't feel like it, but I got up and went down to see him, just to be polite. He was sitting at the table with my stepmother, eating his dinner and watching the telly, like he always did when he came home. Dinner and the six o'clock news, that was his home-coming routine.

"So yu get betta at last!" he said as I joined them at the table. "Yu fiil aal right now?"

"I feel better," I said. It would have been a lie to say I felt all right.

"Thanks for taking me in." I mean, he didn't have to, did he? I'd left home years ago. He was doing me a favour taking me in. If he hadn't, I'd have been like Terry, with nowhere to go.

"Well," he said, pausing from eating to look at me, though not in my face, "yu is mi son, afta aal. Mi haffi try wid yu." He put a forkful of food in his mouth and transferred his attention back to his plate. "Mi onli hope yu will try an mek somting ov yusself dis time. Fram what di docta tell mi, yu was livin a daag's life, livin likkl betta than a criminal!"

"It wasn't that bad, Dad! I had a job most of the time. I was working, I was OK. I wasn't committing any crime." I mean, I had to defend myself, didn't I?

"Well, di social worker seh yu will need a likkl time to straiten yusself out. But afta dat, mi want yu to get a diicent job an liv like a diicent smaddi!"

My stepmother was nodding, her head going up and down like it was on a spring. What did it have to do with her, anyway? Listening to him made me feel weary, I couldn't take it. I got up and told him I was tired, I was going upstairs to sleep.

Chapter 19

I**F I PROPPED MYSELF UP** on two pillows and looked out my bedroom window I could see the wall at the end of our garden and the top of a cherry tree in the garden beyond. I spent so many hours gazing out that window I got to know the wall really well. I could close my eyes and picture in detail the patterns made by mortar and brick, shades of rust and beige, contrasting and alternating. I grew intimate with the chips and cracks where moss took root and tried to spread, to break up and and soften its face. I knew where the diagonal stripe of morning shadow would fall, leaving the top left-hand side in darkness. Countless times I watched the sun take on the shadow and slowly push it back, slowly, like an arm wrestler forcing back his opponent's wrist, inch by inch, leaving the wall whole again.

On good days I'd go out, go walking on Parliament Hill fields, just round the corner from my Dad's house. There was a special spot I liked, a wooden bench by a big old tree, not far from the running track. I'd sit on the bench, resting my eyes on the green space spread out in front of me and slowly smoke a couple of fags, savouring the peace. Out here, nothing forced itself on me, no-one talked to me or expected me to answer them. Only the occasional dog bounding by, its tongue hanging out excitedly, made any demands on my attention.

I measured the slow-passing winter by changes in the trees around my bench. First, sticky buds appeared, then small green leaves, bright with new life. The trees on Parliament Hill transformed overnight, tall brown skeletons suddenly clothed in luminous, velvety green. Spring came and stirred everything up. There was brightness everywhere and in everything animal, vegetable and human. Except in me. I didn't have blood in my veins any more. I didn't know what kept me going. I guess it was drugs. At that point I was still going to Friars regularly and having large doses pumped into me. I couldn't respond to springtime, not even when it burst all around me; in the daffodils and hyacinths flowering cheerfully in our neighbours' front gardens; in the faces of people I passed on the street; in the loud shrieks and laughter of kids playing on Parliament Hill.

Spring even affected my Dad, though not for the better. It put new wind in him and life into that old song of his—when was I going to get a hold of myself, get a job and start making life?

For my own good I started avoiding him. I left the house late in the afternoon so I wasn't home when he came in, and I'd get back around ten, after he'd gone to bed. I passed time away visiting friends. I went by my uncle regularly. I went by Tess sometimes too. One thing about Tess, she always tried to cheer me up. I knew she was trying even though she didn't succeed, and I didn't pretend; if she asked how I was feeling and I told her. I told her as much as I could find words to explain. I found out she wasn't as stupid as I thought; she understood things, she understood the way I felt about our dad and his nagging, how I felt about being in Friars, about Dr Manson and Terry. She understood.

We went over our Mum's visit again and again again, what she said, how she looked, what she was wearing. Tess got mad over it every time and I kept telling her, it was no big deal, it didn't bother me all that much. I told her I was glad I'd met her.

I never told her that I telephoned our mum a few times. Every now and then I got the urge to call, so I did. We didn't talk much. She'd ask about my health, she'd ask about my dad. How's that shit treating you, she'd say. She definitely didn't like him. Can't say I blame her, either. Once, she asked about Tess and I told she's OK, she's fine, doing well in life. She kept saying I should come by and visit, but I knew she never really meant it. In any case, she lived over in Acton, past White City, way out in the middle of nowhere. There was no way I was gonna haul myself all that distance to see her.

Months later, Uncle Matthew told me my mum had moved back to Jamaica with her new husband. She left without a word.

I saw Loretta one day, while I was on a bus going to Kilburn to look for Roy. I saw her walking along the high road, with Kaya trotting beside her, hanging onto her hand. She was looking stunning, as usual. That full length sheepskin coat she had on must have cost a fortune. She wore it with a red, gold and green tam on her head. Very hip, I had to hand it to her. She was walking fast, weaving her way through the people on the sidewalk and I felt sorry for Kaya, who obviously was having difficulty keeping up. The high road was congested with traffic, the bus inched along, moving slowly in the same direction as Loretta, almost beside her, allowing me to watch her unseen. It was a good way to see her again. This way I could take in the things about her I liked without having to deal with the rest. I was on the upper deck, out of her range of vision, thank God. I wouldn't have liked her to see me as I was, all fat and puffy and crumpled, my clothes old and mashed up.

By the time the bus speeded up and left her behind I'd got over how good she looked. I couldn't forget the real Loretta for very long, even though the rottenness didn't show itself on that smooth, beautiful face. Even as I turned to look at her one more time I knew there would be dozens after me, poor suckers who'd get taken in by those sultry eyes and succulent lips. Poor sods. Just thinking about her brought back that heavy, near-dead numbness I dreaded. It made me wish I hadn't seen her. It made me wish I'd never ever set eyes on her.

Just about the only thing that gave me a lift these days was a puff. I looked forward to getting my invalidity benefit so I could go down to Camden Town and pick up a deal. I wasn't supposed to smoke weed or take any drug other than the one prescribed for me at Friars. But the odd draw wasn't gonna do me any harm. In fact I could feel it doing me good. For one thing, it melted the ice in my veins, brought me back to life for a while. If I'd had more money I'd probably have smoked more. But I didn't.

It worried Roy a bit at first.

"The I must know what im can handle an what im cannot. The I must try use im sense in this matter."

When he saw for himself it did me no harm, he relaxed though he kept warning me to go easy.

It eventually dawned on me that turning up at Friars and giving up my arm to their needles was completely stupid. I was asking for punishment. It was obvious that without medication I'd feel normal again. So I stopped going to Friars. And I did feel normal, to begin with.

I didn't tell anybody about it. I just carried on from day to day like before. And I really did come back to life. It was just great to get my head back, get my body back. Man, I felt happy again, so happy I woke up in the morning laughing and sprang out of bed, in a hurry to put on my clothes and go out.

"Where im a-go, so early a-maanin?" I heard my stepmother asking herself as she stood in the kitchen watching me march out the front door. She never asked me. She hardly ever spoke to me directly, which was fine by me, since I had nothing at all to say to her. If she'd asked me, I'd have told her I was going to look a job. Which wasn't exactly true. But that's what I told my dad when he asked.

"Where yu a-goh evriday soh, Stevie?" Sunday dinnertime was virtually the only time we came face-to-face. The rest of the time I just heard him. I heard him grumbling about me in a loud voice as he walked past my room. I heard him and my stepmother talking about me in their room, which adjoined mine, talking about me loud enough for me to hear every word. Conversations where he spoke and then allowed me to reply were reserved for Sundays, against the noise from the TV and witnessed always by my stepmother.

"Enh? Where yu a-go?"

I'd been watching him eat his food while struggling to keep his false teeth in place. Bottom lip, top lip, even his nose were brought into play. He probably thought I was smiling at him and being friendly, but I was just trying hard not to laugh out loud.

"I'm looking a job, Dad. I'm going all over the place trying to find a decent job."

Well, the last part was true. I *was* going all over the place. I was getting maximum benefit from my invalid's travel pass, travelling all over London on the buses and tubes. I went down south, to Brixton, Elephant and Castle, to Camberwell and Crystal Palace. I went out East to Mile End and Stepney and Whitechapel, parts of London I'd never been to even though I'd lived in the city my whole life. It was summer, it was warm and I had plenty of time. If I wanted to make a stop, if I wanted to get off the bus and sit in a park or look in a shop or anything like that, I just did. I didn't bother anybody and nobody bothered me.

❋ ❋ ❋

I told the doctor at Friars I didn't notice myself going off, but I was lying. I couldn't help but notice. You can't help but notice when you're just walking along the road as calm as anything and suddenly, your heart goes off like a bomb in your ears, starts pounding fit to bust, and you feel something grabbing you, taking hold of your whole body, like a boa constrictor squeezing the life out of you, suffocating you. You know something is wrong, you can tell, if only by the way people passing on the street look at you and keep their distance. You know something is amiss when you can't get to sleep at night because your head is like Brixton Market on a bad Saturday, a din of arguing, cantankerous voices. Or when your bed is full of thorns and you burn, sweat spurting from your pores like a million tiny fountains, drenching you in wet heat and saturating the sheets. And when you do get to sleep, the dreams you have, dreams of hell that make you want to die, just so you don't ever have another one.

My dad was no fool, he figured somthing was up with me. I knew he could hear me at night when I got up and went downstairs and paced up and down in the kitchen, trying to cool down. I knew because he had always been a light sleeper, he never missed a sound in that house, no matter what time of night. I knew from the way he looked at me when we met on the stairs or in the kitchen. He looked at me but didn't say anything. That was a sign in itself. On the morning of my birthday he came into my room before going to work, looking awkward and uncomfortable, chewing his lips like he was nervous. I was awake but I lay on my back and looked at him, waiting for him to speak. He sat on the edge of the bed, back towards me, his hands clasped between his knees and his head bowed, as if in shame.

"Stevie. Mi bwoy." He paused, like he didn't know what to say, and sighed.

" Stevie, di way yu karryin on...di way yu runnin in an out of di hous and maachin up and down in di middle ov di night...Mi an Pearl, wi wonderin if di siknis kommin down pon yu agen."

"I'm all right Dad. I am." I sat up and smoothed my locks with my hands, trying to straighten up and look normal. " I'm just having difficulty sleeping at the moment, that's all."

"When last yu sii a docta, Stevie? When last yu go fi yuh medicine?" He was looking at me now and I was shaking my head. I didn't want to see any more doctors. I'd had enough of hospital.

"I'm all right Dad, there's nothing to worry about. This is just a bad spell. It'll pass."

He was looking at me and from his expression I knew I didn't look all right. I knew my face was pasty with sweaty grease; I knew my lips were ash grey and dry and cracked from night fever. I knew I looked terrible. After all, I saw my face in the bathroom mirror every morning. I knew how I looked. He was no fool, my Dad. That same day, my birthday, he got in touch with my social worker and between the two of them, they put me back in Friars.

The ward looked the same, smelled the same, Patrick was still on the day shift, but everyone else was different, patients and doctors included. My new doctor, Dr. Richardson, didn't smile like Dr. Manson used to. Skinny and lanky with balding blonde hair and a boyish face, I didn't take to him at all. It didn't take long to figure out that he had even less sense than Dr. Manson, and he talked to me like I was a moron.

"It wasn't very bright of you to skip your appointments, now, was it?" He spoke crisp and loud, like I was hard of hearing.

"It's very hard for us to help you when you don't cooperate. You know that, don't you?" I just nodded. Since he thought I was a moron, I might as well behave like one. I must have been very convincing, because he gave me very little of his time, unlike Dr. Manson who never missed one of our weekly interrogation sessions. I used to think it was all a stupid waste of time, but at least Manson made me feel like he knew who I was, made me feel like a patient under his care like any of the others. The way this Richardson treated, or rather, didn't treat me was a fucking insult.

Getting back into the old routine was easy. Numb from the dope, I just did what was wanted of me, like a zombie. To be honest, it wan't as bad as the last time when they'd pumped knockout doses into me. I was with it enough to notice that the terrors had left me. I didn't hear voices or my heart hammering in my ears. I slept easily enough, a lot of the time, actually. I could close my eyes in bed at night without dreading that I was going to fall into the heat and clamour of a technicolour hell. That was a definite improvement.

I was the only oldtimer on my ward, which gave me a bit of status amongst the other patients. A psychiatric ward was never going to be lively place, but two of the other guys were quite decent, which made the place a bit more tolerable. Andrew, a young black kid who'd been at Friars a couple of months, took quite a shine to me. He didn't talk much, but I put two and two together and figured out he had similar problems to me. He'd freaked out one night and run naked out of his parents' house, run like a greyhound up the hill from Archway to Highgate, up Highgate High Street in broad daylight, completely starkers. The cops had picked him up and kept him at the station for two days before his parents came for him. They couldn't find out who he was or where he lived, the cops said. Bastards.

Then there was Barry, a balding cockney from Enfield. Used to box when he was a lad, he said. Caught one punch too many in his head, must have damaged his brain. He had one of those mushy, bleary-eyed faces, like the flesh had been pulped too often to regain its proper shape. It gave him a soft, babyish look. He walked up and down a lot, like me, but he mumbled to himself as he walked, a non-stop stream of senseless drivel. He left his bed at nights to roam the corridors. The nurses used to try and stop him, but gave up when they realised all he wanted to do was walk. He was the athletic type, I told them, he needed the excercise.

My Dad came to visit once, on a warm Sunday afternoon a week or so after I'd been admitted. I was out in the grounds when he arrived, taking in some summer sunshine. He came on his own, bringing me some new clothes he'd bought for me and some food: fish and peas and mashed potatoes, bananas and grapes. I suppose he meant well. I ate the food then and there, sitting on the old white bench with him there beside me, kind of stiff and silent, like I was doing something he didn't approve of. Well, I didn't give a toss. He asked me how I was feeling and I told him; better than I was. He asked if they were going to keep me in long, and I said I didn't know. I should have told him that I was no more eager to get back to his house than he was to have me back. I should have put his mind at rest on that score, but I didn't. I was polite. I thanked him for the clothes and for the food. I even asked after my stepmother. That done, I had nothing more to say, and no energy left to find anything.

Tess came every Saturday, like before, and Roy came three times. I suppose Roy was the reason my second term at Friars was cut short. The second time he came we were just sitting in the common room not saying much, watching the TV, watching the others, gazing out the window.

"You know what would be nice now?" I looked at him, wondering if he'd guess. He did.

"Yeahman. A nice cool draw." He grinned, shaking his head at me.

"Don't suppose they prescribe it on the National Health."

On his next visit three weeks later, he presented me with a beautifully rolled spliff.

"Dis one nice and light. Roll special for you."

It *was* nice. We went outside and I had a few puffs, enjoying the lift it gave me. I offered Roy some but he wouldn't take any.

"All yours man. But tek it easy. You don't want to smell of it."

I smoked less than half of it and put the rest in my pocket. I clean forgot about it until later in the week, one evening when I was sitting in the common room, in my usual spot by the window watching the telly. All of a sudden I remembered the spliff, shoved my hand into my pocket and found it.

"Eh, Andrew, Barry. Let's go outside a minute. I got something to show you!" I don't know what made me think of sharing my spliff with these two. Maybe I was just feeling generous. Maybe I thought it would do them as much good as it did me. For whatever reason, it seemed a good idea at the time.

"I ain't never had any o' that stuff before," Barry shook his head nervously when I offered him a puff. I'd taken them to my favourite spot round the back, to the old white bench. "Not sure it'd agree wiv me. Not sure at all. You go ahead, don't mind me."

Andrew was clearly no stranger to the weed. He took a deep, long draw, so long and deep I had to tap him on the shoulder and tell him to take it easy.

"Oh Steve. Man. Oh man." That's all he said, but his face told the story. He was feeling fine.

"All right then," piped up Barry. "Can't let you two have all the fun. Let's give it a try."

"Don't pull too deep or inhale," I warned him, "just take a gentle draw and see how it goes."

He pulled feebly on the spliff, then sat back waiting for something to happen, like a kid with his first cigarette.

"Don't feel a thing," he said, looking at Andrew's relaxed faced with envy. I let him take another puff. It got to him this time.

"I like this," he said, tilting his head from side to side and chuckling like a naughty child. It was the first time I'd seen him smile. I let him take another pull, and that was it, the spliff was done. Barry didn't stop there, though. The weed really went to his head. He got up and started trotting around, a bit unsteadily, waving his arms, talking and giggling like a drunk.

"Eh Barry, cool it. You don't want the staff getting wind of anything." We'd have to stay out here until he calmed down. One glimpse of him and they'd know instantly something was up.

He paid me not the slightest bit of mind. He went dancing off toward the back door before I realised where he was going, he was back in the common room before I could stop him, prancing around like a goon, like he'd completely lost his head. Well, that was it. There was no way the staff could fail to notice him.

The next morning I was called to Dr. Richardson's office as soon as I'd finished breakfast. News of our little escapade had spread round the other wards, making celebrities out of the three of us. I was the only one called into Dr. Richardson's office, though. Bright and early, straight after breakfast, the staff nurse came for me.

Richardson sat behind his desk with Matron on his right, and plump young white woman I'd never seen before on his left. He waved his hand at a vacant chair in front of his desk.

"Stephen, I've asked you here to discuss a very serious matter," he began sounding really formal, like a magistrate or someone very official. "You know Matron, of course, and this is Mrs. Mortenson, one of our social workers."

He paused while I glanced at Mrs. Mortenson. She moved her head slightly to one side, acknowledging me without enthusiasm.

"We understand that you gave Andrew Campbell and Barry Jones marijuana to smoke yesterday evening, on hospital premises, outside in the hospital grounds. Is that correct?"

I nodded. No point in denying it, after all.

"Do you know that the use of illegal drugs on hospital premises is a very serious misdemeanour?"

I shook my head without speaking. What could I say? That I didn't know having a smoke was all that serious? That I wasn't doing anyone any harm? That we were all on drugs anyway, the weed made us feel a lot better than the dope they pumped into us? I suppose I could have said all of that but what good would it have done?

"I'm afraid we're going to have to discharge you from this hospital, though in view of your condition, we won't press criminal charges. We are going to return you to your family home as soon as arrangments can be made."

So that really was it. They were turning me out, like a criminal. I felt shame creep across my skin like cold, damp slime. What was my dad going to say? He would go berserk. He would rant on about it for days without end. Just the thought of it brought a pain to my chest.

"Mrs. Mortenson is going to get in touch with your father today to make arrangements for your discharge." That was all he had to say. He dismissed me with a nod. I left his office without having spoken a word and went back to the ward to lie down in bed.

On the afternoon of the following day I was summoned to Richardson's office again. As I walked through the door he and the social worker broke off their conversation and looked up, watching me with stern faces as I sank into the chair in front of the desk, facing them.

Richardson leaned forward, folding his arms on the desk and paused for a minute before speaking. I gazed out of the window behind him, noticing for the first time that the windows were filthy, so thick with grime that daylight came through with difficulty.

"Bad news, I'm afraid," announced Richardson in that headmaster's voce of his. "Your father has refused to take you back, Steven."

The words took a while to sink in. I'd been so caught up anticipating the dreadfulness of being back at home, my head had no space to consider any other course of events. It took me a while to register the meaning of Richardson's words.

"So what's gonna happen to me?" I blurted out, a slow panic rising through my guts.

"I've just been discussing that with Mrs. Mortenson." He turned his head and looked at her, and she nodded encouragingly at him. Something about her smooth, well-fed face jangled my vibes. I didn't like the look of her one bit. I got the impression the feeling was mutual.

"We've decided to place you in a sheltered hostel. Somewhere you can stay until you are well enough to move into your own accommodation."

A shiver moved quietly up my spine.

"I can't afford a place of my own."

"We'll help you with that, when the time comes." Mrs Mortenson spoke for the first time. She had a nice voice, deep and quiet and kind. Looks can be deceiving.

"There's a vacancy at St Denis's Hostel, near Camden Town. Not too far away from your family. They've agreed to take you on Friday. Mrs Mortenson will let you know what the arrangements are for your transfer."

He leaned back in his chair and folded his arms across his chest. I just sat there, not moving, not speaking, my mind completely blank. Any ideas I might have had about how the next day would be, or the next week, or the week after that, were blown away like bubbles in a blast.

Then a thought registered; what about what I want? The thought registered but I crushed it. No use complaining. Who cared what I wanted? Not Richardson and certainly not my Dad.

No need to worry, though. Mrs Mortenson was going to take care of things. No need at all for me to worry.

Part 4
ANOTHER COUNTRY

LONDON

1989

Chapter 20

THIS IS NOT A GOOD start to the week, Tessa thought, bracing herself before stepping into a sheet of drizzle. This is no weather for human beings. Not even birds venture out on mornings like this.

She hunched deep into a voluminous winter coat, pulling it close to her throat as she reluctantly closed her front door. She was tempted to take a bus rather than walk to the tube. On fine mornings she didn't mind the fifteen-minute trek; it gave her time to wake up fully, to adjust to the prospect of a crowded tube train and eight hours at the office. But if she walked through the drizzle she would arrive at Finsbury Park station damp, hair, face and clothing soiled by air-borne grime. And the sturdy brown leather attache case she carried was heavy with the weight of files and documents. It pulled uncomfortably at her shoulder, another reason to opt for the bus.

As she hesitated on the doorstep a tall figure in a light-coloured raincoat emerged from the door of the house opposite. He waved and caught her eye. She waved back, smiling, indecision resolved.

"Another miserable Monday!" he called out in greeting.

She nodded in agreement, still smiling and they fell into step, both feeling slightly better for having met.

She was looking good this morning. His quick appraising glance took in smooth skin the colour of dark toffee and a wide, soft mouth. Pity about the hair. He couldn't understand why a good-looking woman would want to crop her hair like a man. Hers was shorter than his.

"Are you warm enough in that raincoat?" Asked Tessa. She felt chilly even in a thick woollen coat.

"I have on a jacket and sweater and everything else underneath." He smiled with appreciation at her concern, eyes creasing at the corners behind rain-speckled glasses. Deep voice and Guyanese accent, close trimmed beard and shapely mouth over even, white teeth. No wonder she looked for him each morning.

"Besides, they overheat the college buildings; it hot like hell in the classrooms. Once I'm inside, all I need is a sweater."

"Lucky you! They're economising on heating at the Town Hall. If I didn't pad myself well, I'd freeze during the day."

Tessa had seen him first the day he moved into the house facing hers, seven months or so ago. He was unloading his belongings from a van, assisted by a shapely young woman with long braids. The house was owned by a black housing co-operative which, up until that day, had only women living there. Yes, she had thought, taking in the attractive details of his appearance, the neighbourhood is definitely looking up. Shame about the girlfriend. Or is she his wife?

She never saw the girl again. She saw others, equally attractive, none of them more than two or three times. Nothing unusual in that, though.

They came face-to-face for the first time over a trolley-ful of groceries in Tesco's on the Stroud Green Road. They nodded and smiled in mutual recognition. Did she know where the grape nuts were? Over there, near the entrance, she pointed. How was he settling into his new home? Well enough. He liked the neighbourhood. See you around.

They covered the distance to the station at a brisk pace, talking all the while. By the time the train pulled into Tessa's stop they were deep into a discussion about her job, Town Hall politics, local government.

Hmm, she thought, he's just too nice. A bundle of trouble, I bet. I wonder why he's single?

His eyes followed her progress along the crowded carriage. She's cute. Bright too. She looks lonely, though. Shame.

The glow from the morning encounter had faded by coffee time. By then she had sat through two tortuous hours of a management meeting chaired by the Chief Personnel Officer, Peter Russell. As she sat in her tiny office sipping the scalding, bitter coffee, Tess tried to figure out why she was always in the hot seat. Peter and his sidekick Trevor Clarke seemed to take pleasure in goading her. Did they just want to see her cry, like schoolyard bullies? Or did they hope to scare her into leaving her job so they could replace her with one of their cronies?

After more than five years in the division Tessa was desperate to leave. Each Wednesday morning she eagerly scanned the job advertisements in the public appointments section of The Guardian. There were always dozens of vacancies, variants of the job she already had. Some were at a higher level and offered more money but she was not tempted. In her line of work, more money also meant more stress, more Peter Russells and Trevor Clarkes.

She dreamed of something lighter, more creative, like a job with a magazine, something in publishing or television. At one time, months previously, she had written to The Voice, to Good Housekeeping, to The Guardian itself, to Thames TV, to the BBC, neatly presented, well-worded letters which barely concealed the fantasies of escape which inspired them. She received in response a disappointing batch of one-line refusals.

From her first day in the division she was aware of being watched by colleagues who, with varying degrees of eagerness, awaited her mistakes. She had told herself that as the Town Hall's first black Personnel Manager, she could expect little else.

Her boss Peter Russell had blazed into the department as a new recruit not long after her arrival, his reputation as a radical *enfant terrible* preceding him. He came with a mission: to transform the division, to make its workforce more effective, more efficient and fully representative of the local population. At their very first meeting his eyes had boldly tried to lock gaze with hers. She had evaded his glance.

He had called her into his office.

"This department is still in the dark ages you know. It needs a real shake-up," he said, leaning over his desk towards her, inviting intimacy.

"We need a new recruitment procedure, before anything else." He lowered his voice conspiratorially. "We could quadruple the number of blacks employed here."

"Oh yes? How do we do that?" added Tessa, cooly.

He sat back, frowning a little, wondering if he had misread her. He thought she knew the ropes. These Equal Opportunities people usually did.

"We introduce a new recruitment policy," he said, speaking slowly. "And we back it up with watertight procedures. Results guaranteed."

He was as good as his word. One year after his arrival the division wore a new face: more ethnic minority employees, more disabled employees, more women as managers. The change was quite dramatic.

The speed of change had unnerved Tessa. She watched with chagrin and a growing sense of failure as Peter's proposals gained support that hers failed to raise.

Then came Trevor Clarke, Senior Personnel Officer, a new recruit from a neighbouring borough and a former colleague of Peter's.

"Don't be fooled," said Peter, introducing Trevor to the management team, "Trevor has years of relevant experience. Started off in Maintenance and worked his way up through the ranks. Didn't you, Trevor?"

"Yeahman," said Trevor, nodding sagely.

"And he's well regarded within the borough's Afro-Caribbean community. Aren't you Trevor?"

"Yeahman," said Trevor, nodding once again.

Peter and Trevor were always together—in Peter's office, in the staff canteen, at meetings. Like Robinson Crusoe and his man Friday, thought Tess, bitterly.

Tess's relationship with Trevor Clarke was far from cordial. He knew very little about personnel work, but he excelled at the power games that were part of everyday business at the Town Hall. He engaged her in a covert, guerilla-style conflict for which she was poorly equipped. At every opportunity he challenged her. He picked at her composure gradually and publicly, interrupted her in meetings, contradicted and argued against her every suggestion, leeching her confidence.

She contemplated lodging a grievance against him, but with what charge? Sexual harassment? Could she convince a panel that he harassed her with his eyes, with vocal inflections and body-language? She thought not and dismissed the idea.

Her one defence, her shield and her weapon was her remarkable calm. No matter how he aggravated her or how flagrantly he leered at her, she retained a rock-like composure. It riled him and she knew it.

"Men like that aren't fit to work among women!"

Telephone conversations with Marvine over a sandwich lunch were oases of release.

"I know what you mean, love." Marvine's voice dropped low with sympathy. She knew all about Trevor Clarke. "Put a black woman in front of them and all they see is pum-pum!"

Marvine was friend and confidante, almost a sister. Twenty years of friendship bound them so firmly that not even Marvine's husband Kwesi could enter the intimate space between them. They talked every day on the telephone yet they met infrequently, constrained by distance, two demanding jobs and Marvine's young family.

"He's a fraud, and he knows you know. He'll get found out one of these days, just watch and see! You can't give up your perfectly good job over dregs like him!"

Marvine's words came to Tessa's mind during the walk home from the station. She took the backstreet route that evening, avoiding the bustle and clamour of Stroud Green Road. She mulled over the events of the day as her feet trod the familiar streets.

I still have plenty to be thankful for, she concluded as she climbed the flight of stairs leading to the door of her flat. Once inside she hastily hung her coat in the hallway and slipped off her shoes, then fell onto the sofa, sighing like a collapsing balloon.

She loved her flat. After years of decorating and fixing, it was just the way she wanted it. Pale soft colours on the walls, Berber carpets on the floors, not too much furniture and a few well-cared-for plants. She could pass an entire evening stretched out among the scatter cushions, just savouring the tranquil atmosphere she had created.

Yes, Marvine was right. She should just hang on and hold tight until the Peter problem resolved itself.

A familiar, painful twinge in the region of her stomach interrupted her train of thought. Intestinal pain was part of her life these days but food kept the pain at bay. Starches were best: pasta, rice, potatoes, comforting foods which filled an emptiness in her belly, leaving a feeling of repleteness. Years on a high-starch diet had rounded her hips and buttocks, filled out her breasts. Such lush flesh was more than she wanted, but any other kind of diet was out of the question for the time being.

The phone rang while she was spooning pasta shells onto a blue and white earthenware plate. She let it ring while adding a large mound of garlic-flavoured vegetables and a dusting of cheese. She answered the phone seated on the sofa, cradling the receiver between ear and shoulder, one hand holding the plate while the other blended pasta and vegetables together with a fork.

"Good evenin, Tess?"

Her father was always courteous on the phone.

"Hi Dad. What's happening?"

"Is dat good-fi-nottn bredda ov yours! Dat bwoy gwain send mi to mi grave bifore mi time!"

Emotion made fluent by alchohol shouted down the telephone. Tess put down the plate and took a firm hold of the receiver.

"What's he done now, Dad?"

"Im kom to the hous likkl while ago an yu shud sii im kandishun! Im look like one ov dem ole tramp yu sii sliipin pon striit! Im neva evn stop fi seh 'good evening'. Im just maach into di kichin an dimand moni. Seh im bruk an staavin, im no hav food to eat!"

"It would be hard for anyone to manage on the pittance Stevie gets for invalidity benefit, Dad."

Even as she spoke she knew she was wasting her breath. In this kind of mood her father was impervious to reason.

"Mi noh knuo what else fi seh to im. Yu hav to taak to im fi mi, Tess. Mi kyaan bodda wid im enimore. Mi nerves kyaan tek it!"

A sharp twinge in her belly made her shiver and a wave of fatigue enfolded her like a sombre cape. How many times had her father called in this state, emotional, bordering on hysterical? How many times had she told him there was nothing she could say or do to influence Stevie?

"There's no point getting upset, Dad. That won't achieve anything."

"Yu must kom an look fi mi. Mi kyaan tell when last mi sii yu!"

"You saw me ten days ago, Dad, remember?"

"Well kom look fi mi agen soon!"

She hung up the phone and picking up the plate of food, began to eat perfunctorily, appetite gone.

Deferring to her father was almost a habit with Tess. For most of her life she had accommodated his demands. After all, he was her father and they were close, in a strange way. She understood him better than anyone, even Pearl, his wife. At the same time, she needed breathing space. Moving away from home had created a natural distance which she strove hard to maintain. She kept in touch by phone, visited infrequently and briefly. This arrangement kept her out of her father's reach and she had been happy with it.

Stevie's breakdown upset all that. Her father began calling on the pretext of needing to talk about Stevie, covertly seeking to enlist her support against her brother. She tried to distance him with coolness, with detachment, even stonewalling, all to no effect. She was a cardboard box in the path of a tidal wave; he caught her up and swept her along, crushing all resistance.

Stevie was so unlike his father; he made no demands at all. He came by the flat now and again, stayed for an hour or so then left. She gave him money and food because he always looked hungry and frail, like a waif, even though he was a grown man, past thirty. If she cried after he left her or lay in bed, unable to sleep for worrying about him, it was no fault of his.

Her gut was a mulch of pain, despite the food. She cleared up in the kitchen then ran a deep, hot bath. She had read somewhere in a magazine that pampering was healing, that luxury was every woman's right, and she was lavish with herbal oils, with scented creams and lotions. She stripped off her clothes, sighing in anticipation of a long, fragrant soak, some soothing music and bed.

The following day Tessa stopped by her father's house on her way home from work.

"Tess! Yu kom look fi Dada at last!" The pleasure in his smile was unmistakable. She couldn't help smiling back.

He and Pearl were in the middle of a dinner of rice and peas and chicken. Pearl rose heavily to her feet, barely murmuring a greeting, and set a place for Tess.

"How are you keeping, Pearl?"

"No worse dan usual, tank God.

"You hear from Dexter lately? How is he?"

"Well, I hav to seh no news is good news."

At first meeting, years ago now, Tess hadn't liked her at all. Solid, stout Pearl, with a bosom like a deep shelf and small, moist eyes.

"Laad, Ray, mi neva knuo yuh daughter was so pretti! An how she resemble yu!"

Apart from this feeble attempt at flattery, Pearl had had little to say. She had barely noticed Stevie. Her attention was focussed exclusively on Ray.

Tessa had found something irritating in the way she draped herself around Ray. Her hand on his arm, on his knee, stroking his back, announced that he was her prize, her trophy. Her manner was already proprietory.

Stevie had disliked her on sight.

"Yu must learn to like er," Ray told them. "She's a good woman. Yu must treat er like she's yuh madda. How many woman wudda tek anodda woman pickni into her hous? Shi hav one son and him big, gone bout him bisnis. Shi shud hav finish wid pickni by now. Oonu own madda neva want oonu, just remember dat."

They did not make a happy family. From the start, Pearl and Stevie were at war and their mutual animosity filled the house with bad vibes.

Stevie had hated the house too.

"It smells like duppy," he used to say. "It smells like duppy that don't bathe."

Tessa and Stevie used to hear noises at night, which added to their unease. Stairs creaked, joists groaned and their imaginations fired. Maybe Pearl's dead husband was patrolling his property, Tessa would reason. Perhaps he was jealous of her new husband. Tessa was uneasy, but Stevie was afraid.

"I'm getting out of here as soon as I can," he would say. "Just watch me."

"Mi get a letta from yuh Aantie last wiik," Ray said, impatient for Tessa's attention.

"Aunt Vera? How is she?"

"Shi seh to ask yu when yu kommin to sii er." Twenty-four years since she last saw her aunt. Would she ever make it to Jamaica?

"I'll go one of these days. I've got to see Jamaica again. It's about time I did."

"Well I wudn't seh yu shudn't go look fi yuh aantie. But dat good-fi-nottn piis ov rock? Dem good-fi-notten piipl? Dem tiif like John-Crow! Dem wudda tiif mi shirt aaf mi bak if mi neva watch dem. Di only riisin I went bak to dat place was to bury mi madda. Yu not ketchin mi bak dere agen fi nottn!"

He bit into a chicken leg, chewing noisily on the flesh.

"How yu mean, yu wudn't go bak agen?" Pearl asked quietly. "What bout yuh land an yuh hous? Yu gwain let begga tek dem? Yu gwain spend di rest ov yu life siddung inna Inglish pub drinkin aaf yuh pension? Is dat yu kom to Inglan for?"

"Woman, yu noh unnerstan what yu taakin bout! Yu pik up yusself an go liv dere now, dem rob yu blind. An dem wud kill yu too, fi next to nottn, fi yu gold teet or yu gold ring. Kwik as a shot dem will kill yu!"

Tessa had been in the house less that fifteen minutes and already the tension was rising. Any reference to Jamaica stirred him up. The previous year he had gone there to build his mother's tomb and had returned with nothing to relate but tales of robbery, greed and malice. Neagarishness, he called it. He always talked this way about the island and it puzzled Tessa. Friends of hers had been to Jamaica and returned enthusing about its incredible natural beauty, its warm people. Yes, the tourist areas were tacky in parts, but the countryside was fabulous. And wasn't there crime everywhere in the world?

Pearl glanced at Tessa, rolling her eyes in exasperation. In tacit agreement, Tessa turned her attention to the food on her plate.

"Dat bwoy Steven."

"Dad, he's past thirty, hardly a boy!"

"Im is a wutless, good-fi-nottn bwoy! All im kyan do wid imself is waak di striit an beg piipl moni fi go buy dat stinkin weed im lov fi smoke!"

Tessa sighed and stood up to clear the empty plates from the table. Pearl was watching TV, apparently engrossed in the early evening soap opera.

"Yu always tek up for him gainst mi. Yu tink yu helpin im? Mek mi tell yu, yu mekin im worse!"

She spun round to face him, stung.

"*I'm* making him worse? All right then. I'm going to leave him to you in future. When he needs clothes, or money, I'm going to send him to you. All right?"

She turned back to the dirty dishes, fuming. She was annoyed with herself for letting him succeed in goading her to anger, but he was like a parasitic insect, he latched onto her flesh until he drew blood.

She finished stacking the dishes and stood by the table looking at her father.

"I came here tonight because I thought something was wrong. The way you carried on over the phone the other night I thought Stevie had done something terrible."

He averted his eyes, not speaking.

"Since you don't really need me, I'm going home. I had a rough day at work and I'm tired."

Pearl followed her into the hallway, speaking so low Tessa could hardly hear.

"Yu see what I hav to put up with, day in day out? Yu see how him stay?"

Tessa pecked her on the cheek, patted her arm sympathetically and stepped through the front door with a sigh of relief.

The underground was crowded, even though rush hour was long since past. Tessa hung on a strap in the hot space between two other work-weary bodies, arguing with herself in her mind. Every visit, every encounter with her father sparked this inner conflict which threw her into reverse, pulled her through a time tunnel back to the distant, vague past of childhood.

The past was a bad dream she wanted to blank out. Murky, ugly family stuff, all so long ago. She needed to leave all that behind and move on, running. Running, she was almost free when skilfully he tripped her, felled her, tearing skin and reopening scars.

Was there no escape from him, she wondered?

Chapter 21

"HEY MARVE, WHERE ARE WE going on Friday night?"

Tessa relaxed into her chair, phone in one hand, egg mayonnaise roll held aloft in the other. It was lunchtime.

"I haven't thought. I fancy a really good meal; what about the Africa Centre?"

"Do you feel like inviting Cindy? I haven't seen her for ages, not since before Christmas."

"Fine by me. Why don't you call her?

Tessa and Marvine went out on the town together on the last Friday of each month. Their monthly night out, as they called it, was a tradition of several years' standing, a friendship ritual, like the daily telephone calls. Sometimes they invited a mutual friend to share their evening. Other times, the two of them gossiped over dinner or saw a film or a play. Whatever the entertainment, their enjoyment of each other's company was a certainty, a sure pleasure both women looked forward to.

They chose to meet in the West End purely for convenience, as they lived in different parts of the city. The restaurant at the Africa Centre was one of Tessa's favourite eating places. She liked its atmosphere, rich with traces of the continent: dashikis, boubous, lively voices raised in speech, Yoruba, Ga, Wolof. It took her back to college days, to Africa Society meetings, where she, Marvine and Cindy would be the only women, and Cindy's would be the only white face.

Immediately after work on Friday evening, Tessa boarded a crowded Piccadilly Line train heading westwards.

I'm not the only one going out on the town tonight, she thought as she balanced in the crowded tube, crushed between two brightly dressed, highly scented young things.

The arrival of spring had a visible effect on Londoners. As soon as the temperature turned warm, swarms of them emerged from the long limb of winter to crowd the cafes and restaurants of the West End, pale, thirsty fugitives from frowst.

A mass of them rushed Tessa out of the underground station into the twilight. The evening was mild, almost summery. A soft breeze stirring above the heads of the crowd in the street had an intoxicating sweetness to it. Winter-weary eyes regained their sparkle, smiles beamed. The smart and the hip sashayed down the street, weaving their way through tourists, the odd shopper, couples from the suburbs in town for the evening. In the piazza, stalls and shops displayed summer wear: light dresses, pretty cotton knits, razor-sharp jackets. Earthy naturals were in vogue, soft and mouthwatering, every shade from brown to rosy beige. Tessa was tempted to try on an outfit displayed in one of the more expensive shops, an ankle-length linen skirt, the perfect shade of terracotta with a matching cable-knit sweater. She was dissuaded by her own reflection in the shop window. Those hips were too wide, the waist too thick and besides, when would she wear such a smart outfit?

She headed for the far side of the piazza, expansive mood thwarted by vague feeling of dissatisfaction. A pair of lovers walked ahead of her, young, black and stylish as models. They held hands and smiled admiringly into each other's face. She was touched by their warmth, even while envy piqued her. She walked faster and overtook them to put them out of sight.

She saw Cindy immediately she entered the restaurant. Seated at a table by the window, Cindy was hard to miss. Everything about her was strikingly large—body sheathed in black jersey, head capped with black, black hair—pale eyes with pockets beneath them, red, smiling mouth.

"Whatever happened to Ginger Rogers?" said Tessa, bending to kiss Cindy's cheek.

"Felt like a change." Cindy smoothed the neat black cap of hair proudly. "What do you think?"

"I like it. Makes you look sultry."

"That was the idea!" Cindy grinned wide, like a cat with a wicked secret.

"OK. What's his name and where did you meet him?" That smile usually meant there was a man in the offing.

"Hang on a minute; here's Marvine."

Marvine's shapely form weaved its way between tables crowded with diners, her ample curves drawing admiring glances.

"So who's the vampire?" she said settling into a chair.

"You mean, who's the victim! Come on Cindy, out with it." Tess folded her arms and leaned back expectantly, knowing Cindy had a story up her sleeve.

"Please! Don't rush the foreplay! There's a whole evening ahead! Let's have a drink, at least." While Cindy looked around for a waitress Tess and Marvine exchanged isn't-she-a-devil glances.

"It's not me this time. It's my Mum," announced Cindy dramatical-ly." She finally got it together to leave my Dad. After forty-four miserable fucking years."

"God, Cind. You're kidding us!" Marvine gaped in disbelief. "What made her do it?"

"For once, I'm not kidding you. She packed a nightie and a tooth-brush in a holdall and walked out. A month ago yesterday, to be exact. She's staying with my sister Megs for the time being."

Tessa and Marvine stared at Cindy, digesting the news.

"I can hardly believe it, Cind," said Tess. Tired old Mrs Taylor. Cindy's mum had been grey for the twenty-odd years Tessa had known her. Grey-haired, grey-faced, grey in spirit. "What made her do it?"

"That's the most incredible part. She said it dawned on her sudden-ly that she didn't have that much time left. And she didn't want to waste her last precious years on that miserable old bastard."

The waiter placed a bottle of white wine and three glasses on the table.

"You've been telling her to leave for years, haven't you?"

"We all have. We couldn't stand it, the way he treated her. Knocking her around like she was his own private punchbag. That bastard! We'll see how he manages without her!"

Cindy picked up the bottle, sniffed it, then carefully poured out the wine.

"Was it all his fault?" asked Tessa. "I mean, we always put the blame on the men. And it isn't always all their fault."

"You're thinking of your parents, aren't you?" said Marvine, "But your mum was a special case. I always thought there was something not quite right about your mum from what you said about her."

"I'm not sure what Tess's mum did was all that unusual!" cut in Cindy. "Men do what she did all the time. They have affairs; they walk out on their wife and kids. Your mum put her own life first. She gave priority to herself. I think more women should do the same."

"Sounds good, Cind, but what about the kids?" Marvine blinked hard in exasperation. Where did Cindy get this drivel? she wondered.

"The kids survive. Kids grow up. They get over it and get on with their lives, like Tess. The ones that don't would have messed up anyway."

Silence.

"Maybe Cindy has a point," said Tessa, delving into her memory.

When her mother left home, she had been relieved. And anxious. And scared. Afraid Dada wouldn't be able to cope. She had been afraid for years, years of moving from place to place, from one new girlfriend to another. Years of Dada not coping.

And Stevie? Was he born to go crazy? Was madness his destiny, written in his stars?

"White kids might recover, Cindy," Marvine was ready to do battle with Cindy; she always was. "But its harder for us. There's too much other shit out there for us to deal with."

"Is there such a thing as a happy marriage, do you think?" Tessa's question broke the brief silence, hung in the air awaiting Marvine's reaction.

"What d'you want me to say?" Marvine shrugged. "The only marriage I know about is mine, and that's going fine, thank you!" She took a mouthful of wine. "My parents seem to be doing OK as well. Maybe good marriages run in families."

Tessa nodded, mentally reviewing her family. Ray and Esme, divorced; Ray and Pearl, barely tolerating each other; Aunt Vera, divorced and banished to Jamaica; Aunt Molly, dead and never married. Only Uncle Matthew and Aunt Annie maintained anything like a happy relationship.

She herself had never considered marriage, never even dreamed of it, not even in the days of her one significant relationship. Years ago, it seemed. Three years getting to know each other, one year living together, then nothing. Diverging expectations clashed, were fought over, then it was over.

She was thirty-three when it finished and the field was barren of all but parings. These she accepted, for a time. A fling now and again, an occasional short, sweet affair. Stolen kisses, tainted love.

Adultery was really not her style. She found rivalry tiring, debilitating. Her conscience took the other's part, undermining herself, while self-blame sapped the sweetness out of romance. If nothing else solitude was peaceful, guilt-free.

"Our problem is choice," declared Tessa.

"Choice?" Marvine set down her glass with a crack. "Aren't you the one who's always griping about the shortage of choice, the lack of decent available men?"

Caught out, Tessa laughed.

"Yeah, but at least I can choose to remain single without being seen as a freak. It was different for Cindy's mum. Who knows, she might've been a raver like Cindy if she'd had the chance!"

"Dead right! You should see her now. Megs and Anna and me took her out shopping to celebrate the start of her new life, to get a new hairdo and some new clothes. We bought her a knock-out new wardrobe, and while I was dyeing my hair black, she was dying hers red!"

"Men of Huddersfield, watch out!" Marvine and Tessa giggled, imagining old Mrs Taylor in the role of vamp.

"I could do with a new look myself," Tessa sighed, remembering the delicious terracotta outfit in the shop window. "I feel as flat as a stale soda."

"You haven't been feeling well for a while now, Tess. How's your stomach?"

"Up and down. You know how it goes."

"What you need is a holiday!" A holiday was Cindy's prescription for every ill.

"What I need is a new job and a new life!"

"Have a good holiday and you'll feel better about your job *and* your life."

"How're you getting on with wonder boy these days?"

"Here comes the food." Tessa wanted to avoid discussing work this evening. She wanted to relax, have a laugh, have a good time. "I don't want to spoil your appetite with my work problems. Let's eat."

※ ※ ※

Tessa woke next morning with a fuzzy head and that pleasantly jaded feeling which sometimes follows an evening of too much drink, too much food and too much cigarette smoke. Dazzling rays of light crept round the edges of her bedroom curtains. Normally, such clear signs of a fine day would lure her out of bed, but she ignored them, choosing instead to snuggle into the warmth of her quilt.

Cindy had been on great form last evening. Marvine too. Marvine was down-to-earth and no-nonsense, a perfect foil for Cindy.

Cindy and her amours: married men, younger men, black men, white men. It was only a matter of time before she tried women, Marvine said. Cindy was always experimental. Back in Leeds where Tess first met her, she had worked her way through the members of the Africa Society like a frantic bumblebee in a room of exotic plants.

Marvine had disapproved of her even then. Africa Soc was *their* haven, hers and Tess's, a comforting black space; Cindy was always an outsider, an intruder, in Marvine's eyes.

When Cindy asked about her love life, Tessa had related her encounters with Derek, embroidering every detail of his charms. After all, he was just about the most romantic thing around her.

"You should invite him over for a neighbourly drink," Cindy advised. "You could wait forever if you wait on him to make the first move."

"Come on, Tess! What's there to lose?" For once, Marvine was in agreement with Cindy.

Tess was too shy to admit that she'd never taken that first step. The very thought made her shiver. She was a coward and she knew it.

I wonder if he'll be in Tesco's today? The thought leaped audaciously to her mind.

She sat up in bed and peered at the alarm clock which ticked quietly on the bedside cupboard. It was late, nearly noon. Time to get up and go out to the supermarket.

If you don't do it now, Tess girl, you'll never do it.

She climbed of bed, showered and dressed, all the while rehearsing mentally the conversation she would have with Derek when they met.

Come over for a drink some time.
Sure, he'd say, I'd love to.
How about tomorrow evening?
Fine by me.

It wasn't hard at all.

"You read a lot?" He was exploring the room. He examined her music collection at length, then flicked through her books, pausing now and then at an interesting-looking volume.

"Compulsively. Ever since I was a child."

"Hmm." He shot her a quizzical glance." What were you escaping from?"

"I wasn't escaping anything," she replied coolly, uncorking a bottle of Rioja. "I just loved to read."

He loomed large, disturbingly solid and male in the delicate pastel of her living room. Explorations completed, he folded his long limbs into an armchair.

"And you like jazz," he said, accepting a glass of wine. "I didn't expect that!"

He was teasing but she felt riled anyway.

"So what did you expect?" Her tone was not quite sweet.

He studied the glass for a moment before speaking, twirling it with his fingers and watching light play and sparkle on the rich red liquid.

"I didn't know what to expect," he said. "You look West Indian, but you don't sound West Indian. You say you're Jamaican, but there's nothing Jamaican about you. There's nothing Jamaican in here. You're ...well...so English!"

She opened her mouth to retort, but he forestalled her by holding up a hand like a policeman halting traffic.

"And why you all get mad when people say you English? Nothing wrong with being English! Is there?" He ducked, hand over glass, to avoid the cushion Tessa hurled at him.

"How long have you been in this country?" she demanded. "Haven't you learned yet that if you're black you can't be English? You have to be British and be grateful for that!"

"I don't understand how you all can accept that! You let people tell you who you are or what you are? No man! Once you start down that lane, where does it end? "

Tessa leaned back against the sofa, anger deflated.

"The fact is, we don't feel English. *I* don't feel English. I've lived her thirty-odd years, most of my life, and I don't feel English.

"You were born in Jamaica?"

She nodded.

"When did you last go back?"

She flushed with embarrassment and hoped he hadn't noticed.

"I haven't been back - yet."

She cringed inwardly at the ironic gleam in his eyes.

"You left when you were a baby, and you've never been back? And you say feel Jamaican?"

She nodded.

"Man!" He scatched his head, feigning puzzlement. "That sound very confuse to me!"

"I think a lot of us are confused," she said quietly. "A lot of us."

For a long moment they withdrew to their own thoughts.

"You should go back, you know, if only to take one look at the place you feel you belong to!"

It was her turn to raise her hand, declaring a truce.

"Do you know Jamaica, then?"

He leaned back and opened his arms wide as though embracing a lovely vision.

"I was an undergraduate in Jamaica. I lived there four years. Is a fabulous place!" He leaned forward now, face alight, accent deeply pronounced. "And fabulous people! With all their problems there is more beauty, more talent, more creativity in tiny Jamaica than in the whole of Britain! I tell you is a fabulous place. Almost as fabulous as Guyana!"

His enthusiasm amazed her. No one she knew had ever talked of Jamaica with so much affection. She'd heard about government corruption, poverty and violence. She'd heard about beautiful beaches and comfortable hotels—none of which had roused her interest like this man's enthusiasm. She said as much.

"People who run away from a place never have much good to say about it," he replied scornfully. "You can't trust their opinions at all. All they thinking of is Europe or the States. They thinking in western standards, they holding western values. You must go and see for yourself, with an open mind."

She rose to refill his glass and offer a dish of dry-roasted peanuts. She watched him tilt back his head and throw a handful of nuts into his mouth in a typically Caribbean gesture. He attracted her, so much so that she felt self-conscious standing beside him, as though the magnetic pull she felt in her solar plexus was something to be ashamed of.

"If Guyana is so great, what are you doing here?" she asked. He smiled up at her, making waves in her stomach.

"Girl, as soon as I finish my course, I gone home. I can't wait to get out of here!"

Resuming her seat at a safe distance, she asked about his studies. He told her about the adult literacy project he had set up to bring basic education to people in remote rural areas of Guyana.

"Guyana not like Jamaica," he explained. "It huge. It have rivers wide as the English Channel with islands as big as London in the middle. It have place man don't go yet, plant and insect man don't name yet. The country have so much potential, you can't imagine!"

She was entranced, captivated by the vivid pictures his words created. So she avoided the subject of politics, and galloping inflation and huge international debt. She would ask those questions another time.

It was late when he rose to take his leave. As she walked with him to the front door she told him how much she'd enjoyed hearing him talk about the Caribbean.

He paused on the front doorstep and looked at her face. In the dim light of a streetlamp he saw warmth and friendliness gleaming there. He liked her, he decided. She was strange, and a little prickly, but he liked the way she made him feel: relaxed, knowledgeable, interesting.

"You must come again," she said as he walked away.

"Yes," he nodded, agreeing with her. "I will."

※ ※ ※

Her desk was covered with so much paper, not even an inch of its tarnished wooden surface was visible. Stacks of application forms made up the bulk of the debris. There were eight job vacancies in the department and she was recruiting for five of them. She normally enjoyed the process, which was relatively straightforward, reading through the applications, weeding out the obvious ineligibles, organising shortlisting and interviews.

Despite repeated attempts to focus her thoughts she was finding it hard to keep her mind on the task. Fragments of Derek's conversation inveigled their way into her mind like a fast growing vine, distracting concentration from the work in front of her.

She sat back in her chair and let her mind have its way for a moment.

Strange, how she had misread him. She had underestimated him. His intelligence was unmistakable, but she had failed to recognise the depth: depth of thought, of understanding, of spirit.

And the world inside his head! An unknown country, an entirely new territory.

There was a poet on every street corner in Jamaica, he said. Talent so common, it was unremarkable.

She laughed silently in self-derision. A bottle of wine, some smooth lyrics, and there she was, ready to travel halfway across the world!

Even worse, like a complete idiot, she had forgotten to ask the important questions; was he married/attached/single?

Marvine was disgusted with her.

"When were you born? Yesterday or thirty-eight years ago?"

"It didn't seem appropriate, Marve. There was so much else to talk about."

"Tess, if he's not available, all that talking was pure waste of time."

"No Marve, it wasn't. I was interested in everything he had to say."

She could hear Marvine clucking in her throat at her foolishness. That was Marvine. Down to earth and straight to the point, stepping over priceless treasures on the way.

Tessa pulled her chair closer to the desk and picked up a form. It was neatly typed but the print kept sliding out of focus. I still have four weeks leave to use up, she was thinking. Maybe I should take a holiday.

She waited until she had the airline ticket in her possession before telling anybody. Like a miser gloating over a secret hoard, she kept her plan to herself, enjoyed it in secrecy, hugged herself privately in gleeful anticipation of its realisation.

The first person she told was Stevie. He came ringing on her bell, disrupting the stillness of a Sunday afternoon.

She was glad to see him, as always. She threw an arm affectionately across his shoulders as they climbed the staircase and told him she'd been thinking about him, wondering how he was, what he'd been doing. She spoke gently, consciously trying to soothe away the small signs of anxiety around his eyes.

She hung up his coat, offered food, a cup of tea, TV. There was an established pattern to their interaction, an etiquette which helped to bridge the trough of pain which surrounded him, into which they could both so easily slide.

"Are you hungry? Would you like some food?"

She set a tray and dished out the remains of her lunch, red peas stew, rice and spinach.

He ate hungrily, taking great swallows of food. When he finished he carried the tray out to the kitchen.

"That was good, Tess. Best meal I've had in weeks."

She saw the hunger in his face. He had the faded, tired look of someone in need of care. And he looked far older than his years. Just past thirty, yet his hair was greying, his face was lined, his body podgy and lacking in tone.

He turned on the TV and sat back in the sofa, hands locked behind his head.

"Stevie. I'm going on holiday next month."

"Yeah? Where're you going?"

"I'm going to Jamaica. Just for three weeks." Why did she feel so guilty telling him about it? Everything about Stevie affected her that way; the look of him, his voice, the way he walked with his shoulders hunched and head down, in a permanent state of submission.

"That's great, Tess. It's about time you went." He was looking at her now, a spark of interest lighting his eyes.

"Are you gonna see our mum?"

"Not if I can help it. Why should I? I'm going to stay with Aunt Vera."

"I wish I was going." His eyes went back to Match of the Day. After a few moments he said, "When I get better, I'm gonna go. I wouldn't mind living there, you know. It can't be worse than here, can it?"

"I don't know, Stevie," she said softly. There was sadness in his voice, a quiet hopelessness that was painful to hear. "I don't know what it's like there. I've heard it's rough."

"Yeah, well it's rough where I live. It don't come much rougher than a council estate in Kings Cross. It's like living in a cesspit. There's dog shit everywhere. Half the tenants are Pakistanis and the other half are fascists who hate their guts. Can't get a moment's peace. Can't even sleep at night for all the bawling and screaming and cussing."

It's not worth arguing about, she decided and refrained from mentioning healthcare and other social benefits, necessities which were not available in Jamaica.

"Why don't you ask for a transfer? That kind of environment can't be good for your health!"

"Wake up, Tess! D'you really think they care up there in the housing department? They'd move me to a different estate in another area, but it would be just as bad!"

He rose to his feet, ready to leave.

"What did Dad say when you told him?"

"I haven't told him yet."

"Tell him you're going to stay with our mum and maybe he'll have a heart attack!"

"Don't be like that, Stevie!"

"Why not?" he retorted, unrepentant. "We'd be better off without him around!"

She followed him to the front door and hugged him goodbye.

"Have a good time," he said. "Say hi to Aunt Vera. And bring me back some sensi." There was a ghost of a smile on his face as he turned and walked through the gate.

Chapter 22

TWO SHOTS OF VODKA AND tonic, dim lights, a blanket covering her reclining body: none of these things helped sleep to come.

The steady hum of the plane was the least of the noise which disturbed her. A baby lying on its mother's lap two seats behind droned montonously, setting Tessa's teeth on edge. A child of five or six on the other side of the cabin whimpered continuously, unresponsive to her mother's command to shut up or else. Three young women seated somewhere in the middle of the cabin chattered and giggled the hours away, raising their voices in order to be heard above the hum of the engine. In the neighbouring seat, a fiftyish woman dressed in Sunday-best black suit and cream lace blouse snored quietly, undisturbed by the racket.

Tessa gave up trying to sleep. She sat up, returning the back of her seat to an upright position and raised the shade covering the porthole beside her. Sunlight poured in, brilliant and refreshing.

She had actually slept for a few minutes and dreamed fitfully of her mother. Remembering the dream, she felt uneasy.

"Yu mus go look fi yu madda," her father told her that very morning when she called to say goodbye. "Shi gettin ole now, an mi hiir seh shi not too well."

She said nothing at the time but was vexed all the same. Did he really expect her to overlook three decades of neglect just like that? He was crazy. Maybe *he* was getting old, and senile with it.

The dream stayed with her, lingering like the aftertaste of undigested food. Tessa gazed vacantly ahead, seeing again the image of her mother standing on a riverbank in a beautiful, tropical valley, gazing wistfully at the river, while Tess floated on her back, arms raised to the sky which was visible in brilliant blue patches through a shifting, dappled screen made by overhanging trees.

A snapshot of a dream, it was over in seconds.

She had already made up her mind not to seek out her mother. If they met by chance, fine. She would be polite, say hello, how are you, I'm fine, Stevie's fine; and leave it at that.

Their last meeting seven years ago or so had not gone at all well.

 She had gone because of Stevie, mainly. When she called, introducing herself as Mrs. Brewster, Tess felt obliged to respond. Yes, it was good to hear her mother's voice. Yes, they should get together sometime. It was a strained, dishonest conversation which left her feeling oddly dislocated.

Yet she was curious. Tantalised by Stevie's elliptical account of his own reunion with their mother Tessa let herself to be drawn into meeting her.

It was a mistake. She knew it the moment she entered the over-furnished semi-datched house in a quiet backstreet of Acton, the moment her eyes locked gaze with her mother, whose hard, defiant look was in no way apologetic.

They sat through a strained hour of small-talk. Tessa inquired politely about her mother's youngest child, a daughter of about twenty. Was she in college? Was she working? What did she look like? In return, she answered questions about her job, her flat, even her love life. A mother had a right to ask, didn't she? her mother had said.

Tessa let that one go in a spirit of conciliation, but drew the line at calling the stranger facing her Mother.

"I prefer to call you Mrs. Brewster. It's your name, isn't it?"

"I'm yuh madda. Yu mus kaal mi dat. Madda, like you used to kaal me, or Mum or Mummy. Eni one."

Tessa shook her head firmly, smiling politely. "Oh no," she said, "No. I can't do that anymore."

Unable to rescue their conversation from a flailing silence, Tessa rose from the red plush sofa and took her leave.

She beat her head gently against the headrest as though trying to dislodge the dream and the memories it revived.

I'm going on holiday. I'm going to relax and enjoy it. She chanted the words under her breath, like a prayer.

"Aoa! Wi riich alredi?"

Tessa's neighbour straightened up in her seat, adjusted her clothing and smoothed her hair with busy hands.

Tessa smiled and shook her head.

"Another hour-and-a-half to go, I'm afraid."

"Well, dat nat soh bad. Mi did get quite a swiit piice ov sliip, an now mi hungri!"

Tessa watched her rummage in a carrier bag stowed under the seat in front and emerge with a small foil-wrapped package, which she opened and offered to Tessa.

"Bun an cheese. Yu want some?" Tessa refused, but she insisted. "Yu need somting fi giv yu strengt fi manij di airport."

Two hours later, standing in a stationary queue waiting to pass through immigration, Tessa appreciated the foresight of her travelling companion. The immigration area was crammed with arrivants, many of them visibly tired and uncomfortable. The heat was exhausting, debilitating. It killed the excitement of arrival.

Tessa was melting. Though suitably dressed in a light cotton frock and sandals, having shed sweater and tights before disembarking the plane, she could feel moisture gathering on her forehead, on her upper lip, in the valley betwen her breasts, at the back of her knees.

Gazing around her, she was relieved to see that others were suffering too. Perspiration shone on faces, young old, dark, light, white. Jackets and sweaters came peeling off, while fans materialised out of nowhere, fabricated from hats, or magazines or sheafs of travel papers.

A thin, grey-haired man in the neighbouring queue mopped his face with a capacious white cotton handkerchief, complaining audibly on behalf of the mass of people waiting in line about the heat and the slow progress of the queue.

"Mi hate fi paas tru dis iirport ya, God knuo. It too uncivilise!"

Several heads nodded and a few voices murmured agreements. The immigration officers, unnaturally cool in crisp white shirts, continued sifting through passports and stamping their approval with vigour, unperturbed by the atmosphere of disgruntlement.

When her turn came, Tessa presented her documents with an audible sigh of relief. The officer smiled slightly as he picked up the dark blue British passport and rifled through its pages.

"You were born in Jamaica?" he asked, unneccesarily, Tessa thought, since the passport declared that fact quite plainly.

"Yes," she said flatly, too hot and too tired to elaborate.

"Welcome home!" He smiled warmly as he handed back her papers, instantly restoring both her tired spirits and the excitement of returning.

She had never seen chaos quite like the baggage reclaim area. The inadequate floorspace was crowded with people, trolleys and unclaimed baggage from earlier flights. Porters heaved suitcases onto the moving platform, shouting and cursing at random either to let off steam or to maintain momentum. People bumped into each other, bumped into trolleys, fell over suitcases, and cursed.

Finding and collecting her baggage was one battle, getting through customs was another. By the time she joined a line, Tessa was in a trance induced by fatigue, heat, and extreme disorientation. Long queues like fat snakes extended in front of each customs officer, signifying further hours of waiting in steaming, harassed conditions.

Will I recognise Aunt Vera? Tessa wondered anxiously. Does she still look the same? What if we miss each other?

It was dark by the time Tessa emerged from the aiport building. She lurched after a sly-looking porter who had grabbed her bags, thrown them onto his trolley and raced towards the exit without as much as a glance at her. Stories of thieves making off with the belongings of unsuspecting tourists jostled with fears of being left stranded at Norman Manley Airport, confusing her mind so that she failed to notice the portly form of her aunt approaching.

"Tessa! Yu doan knuo mi? You doan rekanize yuh aantie?"

She was taken by the arms and pulled into a deep, soft hug.

"Aunt Vera!"

She looked just the same, perhaps a little stouter with a few more grey hairs. Tess held her tightly for one long, emotional moment before remembering the fleet-footed porter. "Aunt Vera, mind de porter tek aaf wid mi bag-dem!"

"Doan worri yuself daalin, Austin hav yu bag."

"Austin?" Who was Austin?

"Austin, yu kusin Angela bwoyfren," Aunt Vera explained. "Yu doan knuo Angela? Is yuh Uncle Matthew first daata!"

A statuesque young woman came forward and took Tessa's hand, smiling.

"I knuo yu doan remember me," she said through perfect red lips, "but wi use to run up and dun toggeda when wi was tots."

Tessa smiled back and shook her head, bemused. She let herself be led away from the mass of people swarming the Arrivals doorway towards an unlit carpark, where a barely visible Austin was loading her bags into the boot of an aged Ford Cortina.

"Yu must bi well tired," said Aunt Vera sympathetically as she squeezed her girth into the back seat beside Tessa.

"Exhausted!" Tessa sighed, then gurgled childishly, remembering a joke she used to share with her aunt long ago, "and starving!"

※ ※ ※

The landscape was an indeterminate mass of dark shapes, blurred by the speed of the car. Tessa peered though the passenger window as though effort alone would lift the cover of night so that she might see the countryside more clearly.

The journey from the airport through downtown Kingston had been a prolonged, clamorous shock. They had been trapped in rush-hour traffic, nearly asphyxiated by exhaust fumes. Twice Austin narrowly avoided collision with a dilapidated, overloaded bus which charged along the road ahead of them as though intent on damaging as many vehicles a possible before it was consigned to the scrap heap. Traffic crept at a snail's pace through downtown Kingston, obstructed by pedestrians who, too numerous to fit on the narrow strips passing as sidewalks, took to the road, taking their chances amid lines of carelessly driven vehicles. Aunt Vera and Angela were brimming with questions about folks back in England, which Tessa answered as briefly as possible, too tired to engage in conversation, too interested in the dark, mysterious new world outside the car.

Once free of Kingston, the car picked up speed, coughing and belching out a continuous stream of exhaust fumes until they entered Spanish Town.

"Mi noh knuo why Austin doan fix dis kyar," grumbled Angela to no one in particular. "It luk like im wan poison aaf di whole worl!"

Him and every other motorist, thought Tessa. For some reason she hadn't expected so many cars, so much traffic, such teeming numbers of people. The congestion they encountered in the centre of Spanish Town was ten times worse than Kingston. Austin drove bumper-to-tail through the narrow thoroughfares. Past the bus terminal teeming with commuters dazed and jaded after their rattling, helter-skelter bus ride from Kingston. Dodging pedestrians too tired and resentful for caution. Obstructed by beaten-up taxis whose drivers disregarded all other traffic and remained rooted to one spot until they were crammed to capacity with passengers. Tessa watched incredulously as the Lada ahead of them absorbed six people into its back and four in front, plus the driver.

"Yu wud go in one ov dem?" Aunt Vera was watching her, noting the changing expressions on her face.

"I guess so. If I have to."

"If wi go to town yu gwain hav to. But it nat so bad if yu travl earli!" Aunt Vera was smiling at her. Tessa realised she was being teased and smiled back.

Everyone sighed with relief when Austin pulled up outside a low, tree-shaded house and switched off the Cortina's labouring engine.

"Is nat much, but mi welkom yu to it," said Aunt Vera unlocking the white metal grille protecting the front door, and then the front door itself.

"Mi liiv Jean in di hous but yu kyaan trust shii fi keep evriting shut. She wi go chat wid er fren down di road an liiv di hous wide open! Mi neva kom krass a gyal so foolish yet!"

Tessa stepped into a small dimly-lit front room crammed to capacity with furniture. She recognised many of the pieces. The settee and matching armchairs and the mock-walnut sideboad had graced the much larger living room of her aunt's house in Tottenham years back.

She flopped onto the settee, leaving Austin and Angela to bring in her suitcases. Aunt Vera disappeared through a door at the far end of the room, returning moments later dragging a teenage girl by the arm.

"Jean, seh hallo to yu kosin Tessa from Inglan!"

Jean pulled away her arm, glowering at Aunt Vera, but managed to raise a sweet enough smile for Tessa before backing shyly out of the room.

"Is yu Uncle Paul daata by im first wife." Aunt Vera collapsed her bulk into an armchair and kicked off her shoes.

"My uncle Paul?" Who on earth was Uncle Paul? Tessa's tired mind could not place the name.

"Yu noh knuo bout Paul? Mi big bredda, dat follow Matthew? Yu must knuo bout im, Tessa man!"

"I don't think I've ever heard of him before now! Nor Angela either." Tessa gestured towards Angela who was sitting at the other end of the settee. "How many other relatives do I have that I've never heard of?"

"Daalin, yu hav a whole distrik ful ov famli!" Angela spoke up, though whether she intended to relieve Tessa's confusion or add to it wasn't clear.

"Evri odder smaddi inna Rocky Gap is yuh famli," Aunt Vera announced grandly. "Mi haffi tek you dun dere fi miit dem soon soon!"

Tessa closed her eyes as though overcome at the prospect. It was all too much to take in. The flight, the airport, the shock of Kingston and Spanish Town. The heat. Now there was the prospect of a regiment of relatives to deal with.

"Kom chile, mek mi show yu where yu gwain sliip. Yu mus wan fi tek a showa an chienj aaf, too! An I knuo yu hongri! Jean soon kom wid yuh dinna!"

Aunt Vera led her into a bedroom with its own small bathroom en suite, and then withdrew. Tessa fell onto the bed, intending to relax for a few moments before bathing. Instead she closed her eyes and drifted into a short, restless doze.

* * *

All she could see was blue. Soft lavender blue sky up above, graduating through azure to deep cobalt expanses over on the horizon. Delicate clusters of whispy white clung to the sky here and there, calmly resisting the force of a rampaging west wind. Gusts of air rocked the tops of two mango trees whose trunks supported the hammock she lay in. Streams of current encircled her, fanning her skin before rushing recklessly on to ruffle crotons, play with mango leaves, dance with palm fronds, artlessly rousing every green thing into cool, shimmering music. She sprawled in the hammock, her senses enthralled.

Aunt Vera sat on a low stool a few feet away shelling peas. Now and again her eye travelled to the supine form of her niece.

What a good ting mi mek Paul put up di hammok last time him stop by! she was thinking. Tessa luv dat ting, shi spen most of di laas four day inna it! Poor chile. Shi look like shi niid fi rilax. Shi was stiff, too tight. Evribaddi who kom fram Inglan wiir dat look; like dem have on armour an kyaan bend dem bak or flex dem lim. Same ting wid dem mind. Tight-up likkl mind dese blak Inglish piipl hav.

A mango fell, hitting the bare earth not far from the hammock with a soft thud. Tessa came to life, deftly alighting from her resting place in order to find the soft, ripe fruit she had so recently come to love.

She hadn't set foot through the front gate once since arriving. Sleep had eluded her the first few nights, adding to her backlog of fatigue. The bed was too soft, the room too close and hot. Mosquitoes tormented her, singing in her ears all night and biting her vulnerable flesh at random. Unable to rest at night she slept in the daytime in the tree-shaded haven of her aunt's backyard.

Aunt Vera watched her peel back the mango skin with her teeth and suck the golden flesh from the stone.

"Wid aal dem mango yu iitin, yu gwain go bak to Inglan lookin fat an nice!"

"That's the last thing I need. Look at the state of me already!"

"Yu hav likkl weight yes, but yu nat fat. Yu look to mi like yu niid buildin up." Aunt Vera smacked her own substantial thigh as though to illustrate her point. "Rememba seh yu kom fram fat briid!"

Tessa disposed of the mango remains and rinsed her hands under the standpipe in the middle of the yard.

"Well, with the way you and Jean feeding me, I'll go home looking like a fattened calf."

"I send Jean to market fi buy fish fi yu dinna today. Yuh like fish?" Dis chile soh haad to fiid, she thought. Bout shi nat iitin miit! Where shi get dat foolishness fram? Nuo wanda shi look so wiik and flabbi!

"I love fish. I don't eat enough of it." Touched by the older woman's attentiveness, Tessa bent over and hugged her, pressing an affectionate kiss on her soft, fleshy cheek.

"Mind yu nak ova di peas, beg yu!"

Tessa laughed and climbed back to the hammock, stretching like a contented cat.

"Yu gwain spen di whole haliday in dat hammok?"

"No. Angela and Austin coming to take me to beach weekend. And next week we going to country."

"Soh when yu gwain look fi yu madda?" Aunt Vera eased her bulk from the stool and disposed of the empty pea pods she had collected in her lap.

Tessa was silent a while, watching a yellow-breasted bird hopping on a branch directly above her head.

"I don't know," she said finally. "I don't know if I'm going at all." They had talked about her mother at length. They had talked about her father, about their break-up, their divorce. And about Stevie.

"Poor Stevie. Is a shame. Up till dis day mi kyaan figga out why Esme neva tek oonu wid er." Aunt Vera shook her head, clucking deep in her throat to register disapproval.

"Afta aal, shi knuo seh Ray kud neva manij di two ov yu. Shi run liiv im cos im drink an triit er bad, but shi neva worri bout how er two pickni wud survive!"

"He didn't treat her that bad. She drove him to it, anyway, with her moods. Not to mention that man!"

"Chile, yu noh knuo how it goh, yaa! Im used to batta er terribl! From yu was babi, im use to biit er. Mi neva biliiv she wudda folla him go Inglan! Mi did expek er fi jus let im galang an kyarri on er own life right here in Jamiaca! All ov wii in de famli, wi was shok when shi book passij an seh shi gaan cos Ray send fi er!"

"Well, even if he did beat her, that was no excuse. She just didn't care 'bout us."

"Knuo it mus siim like yu madda neva luv oonu..."

"She didn't, Aunt Vera, she didn't. She was awful to me for as long as I can remember, even before the problems started."

"Like mi seh, prablem staat long bifore yu realise! Esme was misrabl from shi was pickni! Bikaas shi was smaal an no hav nuo madda, is pure ill-treatment she get. Mi knuo, kaas mi did get it too!"

"But you never turned out like her!"

Aunt Vera was silent, pondering what to say to this child, so eaten up with bitterness and pain. How could she describe the life they led, she, Esme and the others? How to explain what that life had made of them?

Maybe she would understand a little better after visiting Rocky Gap. Maybe when she saw how hard life was in that place she would understand how just growing there could make people hard, twist their spirits and spoil their nature.

They rose at five to make sure they caught the early bus for Mandeville. If they missed that one, they would certainly miss the one bus a day which made the dusty, bumpy journey from Mandeville to Rocky Gap.

They walked the short distance to the main road in the soft early-morning light and waited amid a clump of fellow travellers. The road was already busy with pedestrians, cars, mini-vans and buses, most of them heading toward Kingston. A crowd of people waited at the stop on the other side of the road. Young women, shower-fresh and crisp in their office uniforms, sleepy-looking school children in khaki or blue poplin, men poised to rush forward when the bus eventually arrived.

"I can't believe how early rush hour starts here, Aunt V."

"Is not rush hour yet. Is piipl trying to riich Town *before* rush hour staat! Dem wan riich dem destinashun in half-hour insted of in two-and-half hour, which is how long it tek later on!"

The Mandeville bus lumbered to a halt in front of them, thankfully not too crowded inside. Aunt Vera skillfully manoeuvred her way to a seat, using elbows and hips as levers and took Tessa's travel bag on her lap. The bus was an old Tata model, and had probably never had much in the way of suspension or shock absorbers. It jolted and lurched along for three bone-rattling hours, yet could not completely distract Tessa's attention from the luscious green world they passed along the way.

By the time the bus shuddered to a grinding halt at the Mandeville terminus, Tessa's legs felt like partly dissolved jelly. She would have liked to stop for half an hour or so, sip a cold drink, take a look at Mandeville and recuperate. But her aunt hustled her on, out of the terminus and across the town square to the market.

"Wi kyaan jus arrive in Rocky Gap wid wi han lang an empti," Aunt Vera held firmly onto Tessa, guiding her across the road.

"Wi mus kyarri sum fish an sum food, yam an banana, maybi sum rice and two bundle ov callaloo. An wi mus hurri, kaas Rocky Gap bus soon kom!"

The Rocky Gap bus turned out to be a semi-derelict Bedford van with seating for sixteen passengers. Tessa's heart fell as she entered the van and saw that not only were all the seats occupied, but that the small spaces between the seats were crammed with bundles and baskets and a few standing passengers as well.

"Kom, mummi! Kom Inglish ladi! Plenti room in di bus still! Di bus haaf empti!"

Tessa hesitated at the door, unconvinced by the conductor's assurances, unable to see any standing room at all. A hand pressing firmly in the small of her back propelled her into the centre of the bus, though whether it was Aunt Vera's hand or the conductor's, she couldn't tell. Her progress was halted by a large, unyielding sack of something hard, yams, maybe, or sweet potatoes.

"Kom, mi-diir, let mi tek yu bag!" A sweet-faced woman sitting near her took the plastic carrier bag of provisions onto her lap, leaving Tessa with her travelling bag over her shoulder and hands free to cling to the nearest handrail. Not that she was in any danger of toppling over. Jammed between the sack of produce on one side and Aunt Vera's soft girth on the other, there was simply no room for her to fall.

Aunt Vera had found space under a seat for her bags. She planted her legs firmly astride and stood calmly, one hand on hip, the other resting on a rail, like this was the most comfortable position possible for travel. Once settled, she hailed a passing vendor through a window, and producing a twenty-dollar note from her bosom, bought two boxed drinks and two bags of peanuts, handing Tessa one of each.

They had finished their snack, and the bus had acquired five more passengers by the time the weary old van pulled out of the terminus.

"Aunt Vera, beg you, lets find somewhere to sit for a minute!" Her head was spinning and she was exhausted. Her legs wobbled, her back ached and she was damp with perspiration.

"Is not far to yuh aantie hous, jus a few yaads up dat road!"

The bus had left them at a T-junction on a hillside in the middle of nowhere. There was nothing in sight but a small white church over to their right, wild, bush-covered scrub along the road side, and the road itself, rising gently and finally disappearing over the crest of a hillock straight ahead.

"Kom, Tessa man, wi soon riich."

Resentfully mustering her last remaining grammes of energy, Tessa followed her Aunt, who had already began to walk up the hill.

"Mi knuo seh yu nat use to dis kin ov travellin, but what fi du? Mi noh hav kyar, an fi heiya one fi dis journey wudda kaas plenti moni. When yu wash up an cheinj aaf an drink a cuppa tea yu wi fiil betta. Noh tru?"

"Aunt V, all I can say is, I don't know how you manage it. Not just you. Everybody! "

"Choh! Is nuo great ting. Yu just haffi pripare yuself good, dat's aal."

As they approached the crest of the hill a house came into view.

"Sii dere! Is yuh Aunt Sarah hous dat."

It was set a few yards back from the road and screened by trees. Aunt Vera led the way through the gate, down a red dirt path, hard from years of passing feet, round the back of the house. There was no backyard as such but there was land under cultivation, a full two acres or so.

"Dis was yuh granfaada hous. Is here I was baan. Yuh madda too. Aal ov wii."

In a tiny zinc-covered enclosure, a woman was cooking over a coal fire.

"Patsy!" Aunt Vera called out loudly.

The woman spun round, surprised, then smiled widely.

"Aunt Vera! How yu du? Bwoy, mi glad fi si yu!"

"Patsy, mi bring yu kosin Tessa, from Inglan, fi look fi yu!"

"Mi knuo it was famili! Mi kud tell from er face!"

Me too, thought Tessa. She looks like me.

"Wi kommin strate from Spanish Town an wi tieyad bad!"

"Inhi, Tessa look like shi gwain drop. Mek mi bwile some waata an mek sum tea. Dat wi kiip yu till dinner readi?"

"That would be just great!" said Tessa, sounding absurdly English to her own ears.

Soon she was seated on the small veranda, washed, refreshed, and sipping a mug of sweet milky tea. She sat alone, as Patsy and Aunt Vera had gone to find Aunt Sarah who was down in one of the lower fields picking tomatoes.

She was glad to have a quiet moment. What a day it had been, and the afternoon had just begun! Aunt Vera was a marvel, a powerhouse of energy, and still on the go.

She rested her feet on the low verandah wall and allowed her eyes to roam around and take in everything, from house, to verandah, to yard, then to the fields beyond. There were fields as far as her eyes could see. Soft patches in greens and reddish browns, rolling gently down to a plain, stretching far into the horizon. A silvery glint in the distance suggested a river, or was it the sea? To the east was definitely sea, deep blue and hazy.

I never imagined anything like this, she mused. No sand. No palm trees. No jungle lushness. Just acre upon acre of dry, red dirt, tilled and laboured until fertile. And beautiful, in a humble, orderly way.

How could they have left this ?

Aunt Vera's voice preceded her, in lively argument with the quieter, more hesitant tones of her sister. Tessa eased her limbs out of the chair and went to meet this aunt she didn't even know about until a few days ago. What a family! she marvelled. Aunts, uncles and cousins by the dozen, and no-one told me about them!

Aunt Sarah was a little bit of a woman, easily half Aunt Vera's size and obviously quite a few years older. Yet she marched into the yard with the spring and vigour of a much younger woman.

"Kom, mi daalin, mek yu ole Aantie look pon yu! Now is who yu risemble?" Tessa was seized by the shoulders and closely inspected by a pair of bright eyes.

"Mi kyaan si so gud agen, but mi tink yu hav a look ov yu faada. But yu fat an nice like yu madda!" Tessa laughed and hugged the small frame, feeling glad to be in a place where her size was appreciated.

"Bwoy, all ov oonu ova in Inglan figat bout wi ova here!"

Embarrassed, Tessa opened her mouth to apologise.

"But neva mind, yu kom look fi mi now, an late is betta dan neva. Noh tru?"

Aunt Sarah darted about with the lightness and speed of a small, nimble insect. She spoke in the same manner, in quick fast sentences, frequently digressing to a fresh subject.

"Is a good ting I dig up some karrot. Patsy kyan mek joos fi yu hav wid yuh dinna."

"Now what bout yuh faada? When im kom laas yiir im tell mi seh im kommin bak to liv. When im gwain kom?"

"Choh man, Ray jus taakin." Unable to remain silent for very long, Aunt Vera interrupted. "Yu knuo how im luv fi chat big."

Aunt Sarah sat down on a verandah step, a plastic bucket full of water and carrots in front of her and an old tin basin to one side.

"Mek mi help yu wid dem tings." Aunt Vena joined her sister on the step. Together they washed, topped and tailed a pile of carrots, chattering all the while. Their attention drifted from Tessa, who was glad to just sit and listen to them exhanging news and gossip about other family members. Patsy, who was frying the fish brought from Mandeville, left the fire from time to time to listen in on the elders and add her two cents' worth to the conversation.

They had dinner sitting right there on the verandah. Darkness fell quickly, bringing with it a light, cool breeze, and night noises gathered in the background to fill in the silence of eating. The food was delicious, with a freshness and flavour that was almost intoxicating. She said as much to Patsy, who simply smiled and took away the empty plates.

"Patsy kyan kook good! Nat one grain ov sens, but shi kyan kook!" Aunt Sarah had polished off a huge mountain of food and licked her lips like a satisfied cat. "Mi glad fi hav er here wid me fi kiip mi compani, aal di same."

"She's not married, then?" Tessa asked tentatively, hoping she did not appear prying or fast.

"Shi did hav a fiance likkl while bak, but dem neva badda marri. Up till now mi no knuo why." Patsy left the dishes and came hurrying over to explain herself.

"Yu knuo seh mi neva redi, Mamma, yu knuo well! Soh noh badda stir up argument dis evenin!"

"So wen yu gwain redi? After de man pik up imself an gaan? Yu tan deh turn ole maid!"

Aunt Sarah turned her beady eyes from Patsy to Tessa.

"An wat bout yu? It siim yu noh tek afta yu madda at all where man kansern. How kom all dem rich man inna Inglan an yu nat married?"

"I'm not ready yet either," said Tessa, earning a grateful look from Patsy.

"So yu neva stop by yu madda in Mandeville?" Aunt Sarah asked with a piercing glance at Tessa.

Tessa shook her head.

"There wasn't time."

"Well, yu kyan stop on yu way bak den."

"Maybe."

"Meybi? How yu mean meybi! If yu faada kyan goh visit er, den yu mus kyan goh too!"

"My father *what*!

"Yu fada went up dere when im kom laas yiir," explained Aunt Vera, shooting a vexed look at her sister. "Esme husban was away, Nyoo Yaak or Nyoo Jersi or sumplace. So Ray jus hire kyar an drive up dere one day. Mi an him."

Tessa flushed hot with a mix of emotions.

Her pleasure in the evening was spoiled.

※ ※ ※

Tessa woke with a start, uncertain at first of where she was. In the moment before she recognised the sleeping form beside her as Patsy, she panicked. Just for a moment, while her eyes adjusted to the dull grey light and to Patsy's room, which she was sharing for that night.

Her first coherent thought was of Ray. Ray going to visit Esme in Mandeville while her husband was away. Getting his own back after twenty-eight years?

She almost laughed out loud at the irony of it, but gave way to gloom instead.

There was no escaping them, it seemed. Nowhere was she safe from their foolishness, their selfishness. They followed her like tendrils of a creeping plant, clinging to her limbs and impeding her escape.

She was on their ground now and the spirit of the place was weighing on her. Yet it was her ground also. The place of her childhood, which should have held innocent and joyous memories. She needed to find that joy, she craved it, like a sick man craved a cure.

Chapter 23

Iwalked with Aunt Vera to the centre of Rocky Gap in the soft, freshness of early morning. We didn't have far to go. A few hundred yards from Aunt Sarah's house, past a scattering of houses to right and left of the narrow asphalted road, and there we were, standing outside a low, barn-like building bearing the sign "PETER'S GENERAL STORE AND BAR". This, apparently, was the centre of Rocky Gap.

Aunt Vera was taking me to meet people. My uncle Paul, her favourite brother who wasn't on speaking terms with Aunt Sarah; cousins, friends of my parents, and whoever else we happened to encounter.

"Yu nat gwain remember eni ov dese piipl," she warned me, rather unneccesarily, "but dem knuo yu madda an faada, an aal ov fiwi side ov di famli."

Inside the store a stout, elderly man was stacking tins of sardines on a shelf behind a long counter.

"Good maanin, Maas Piita, how yu du?"

He turned to face us, breaking into a gold-studded smile at the sight of Aunt Vera.

"Wat a sight fi sore eye! Glad fi si yu, Vera; afta how lang?"

"Not soh lang, man. I was down here jus di odda day!"

"Soh who is dis lady wid yu?" Maas Peter was beaming so warmly at me, I beamed back, feeling I knew him. "Shi look like shi resemble smaddi mi knuo!"

"Who yu tink?"

He studied me carefully.

"Shi resemble yu a likkl...Laad G-man! Is Ray an Esmi daata! Tun big woman! Kom, hug-up di ole man! Doan feel shy, now, mi knuo yu fram yu baan!"

How could I feel shy of such a welcome?

Others came to the store, summoned by Maas Peter by heaven knows what means. Miss Ruby, Miss Hatty, my cousin Beanie, trailing his two small children, and Uncle Paul in muddy boots, coming straight from working his field, looking like an older, sunburned Uncle Matthew. Uncle Paul didn't speak a word, he just folded me to his chest in a bear hug, then held me at arms length, smiling with delight before hugging me tight again.

Of course I was a curiosity, a surprise come to break up the monotony of the day, an excuse to sit in Maas Peter's store drinking beer, to talk about old times, and get news of old friends gone to "foreign".

Miss Ruby kept laughing and pinching my cheek, amazed at how much I resembled my mother.

"Is mii use to look afta yu when yu barn, yu knuo! Mi use to wuk in yu faada hous from it build to when dem lef fi Inglan. Dem neva tell yu bout mi?"

"Maybe they did," I said, knowing full well they hadn't, "but I'm glad to know you again."

My childhood world was taking shape, forming in front of my eyes like a mirage. I was surprised, happily, joyfully surprised. I felt like I'd stumbled on lost treasures, treasures forgotten, erased from my memory before I ever knew their value.

Aunt Vera inveigled Maas Peter to drive us up the hill in his battered old pick-up, to visit my father's house.

"Kom noh, Piita, man! Mi kyaan manij dat-deh klime! An yu kyan drop us by Paul hous kommin bak."

"Aal right, aal right! Since is a speshal okaishun, I will dwiit!"

The two of them filled the space in the cabin with their combined girth, but I was happy to sit in the back, open to the sun and air, and above all, away from the constant stream of my aunt's chatter.

What would I find up there on the hilltop? I wondered as the pick-up wheezed its way along a a narrow, overgrown track. Obviously, no-one had gone up there lately.

"I doan tink enibaddi kom up ere since yu faada kom out de odda day!" Maas Peter called to me from inside the truck echoing my thoughts. He parked the car in the shade of a tree, helped Aunt Vera out of her seat and me out of the back, then settled into his seat to wait for us.

I walked the few remaining yards to the house with all senses on alert. I felt like an animal entering a strange place, taking in the lie of the land, the quality of light, the strength of the wind and the scent it carried.

Vegetation was rampant and an overgrowth of bushes made progress difficult, even painful. Vegetation covered what remained of the house—five stone steps and four cornerstones.

"Dem mussi tiif way di lumba an zinc. Dem ole neaga up ya, dem worse dan Jan Crow!"

I bareley heard my aunt muttering. She perched on a step while I walked around the square of stones which once supported the house. I saw nothing remarkable and gained nothing but scratches and bites on my legs. Turning away from the stones I followed the slope of the hill to a ledge, beyond which lay a sheer drop, straight down to the soft hazy blue of sea, so unexpected it frightened me, so beautiful, my heart stopped. I squatted on my haunches to avoid dizziness and gazed into the endless expanse of sea and sky.

By the time I rejoined Aunt Vera on the step I was angry, hot with it, choked up with it and ready to cry.

"Wh'happen, Tess, sumting trubbl yu?"

I shook my head, afraid that if I spoke, tears would burst out. In any case, I didn't know how to explain what I felt, or even why I was so upset. So I rose to my feet, looked around me once again and strode off towards the tree under which Maas Peter was parked, waiting to take us to visit Uncle Paul.

We did not call on my mother on the way through Mandeville. Instead, we clambered out of the same old Bedford van that had taken us to Rocky Gap and hurried to board the Spanish Town bus. Strangely, Aunt Vera didn't even mention it. Maybe she was alarmed by my reaction up at the house. Or maybe she sensed that I simply wasn't ready to see my mother just yet.

※ ※ ※

"It seem like wheneva piipl go liv in Inglan, wen dem kom bak to Jamaica, mad head tek dem!"

We were sitting at her dining table, having just finished dinner. Jean was clearing up in the kitchen while Aunt Vera and I sat back in our chairs, allowing our food to digest.

"Wid mii, now, it was diffrent," she continued, a laugh beginning at the corners of her mouth, "mad hed tek mi when I riich Inglan!"

Catching Jean's eye I laughed so hard I got cramp in my groin. Did she know, I wondered, that the people in the neighbourhood called her Mad Miss V from Inglan? To them she was just another crazy returnee, according to Jean.

"Do you think it runs in the family?" I mused out loud. "Mental illness, I mean. You had it. Stevie's got it. Maybe its genetic."

"Beg yu pliis doan bodda mi hed wid dat foolishniss! Is nuo "illness"! Mi hed krak due to presha an stress an pure bad triitment inna dat kontri! An di same ting wid yu bredda!"

"He would like it here, you know. Especially country. He would love Rocky Gap."

"Den nex time yu kom, bring im wid yu."

Bright eyes beamed kindness out of her soft, plump face. I had forgotten how close we used to be. I had missed her all these years without realising it, her stories, her bursts of drama and her wicked sense of humour.

"How have you been since you came back? Healthwise, I mean."

"Well, chile, I was sik one time, soh bad dem lock mi up inna Bellevue. Dat was soon afta I kom bak. But since dat time I haadli hav any trubbl at all wid mi hed.

"Is like mi seh. In Inglan, evriting siim nice. Moni plenti, wuk plenti, so evribaddi tink it easi fi mek progress in life. But is not soh it go at all! Nuff blak piipl sick and ded ova dere yu knuo, from haad life an bad triitment. An koal wedda. Yu tink mi jokin?"

I could recall my father saying something similar about friends of his who had suffered illness or died.

"Let mi tell yu seh life haad inna Jamaica today! I kyan sii yu tink sun shine evri day so evrithing swiit..."

"No, Aunt Vera, I can see its not easy to survive here. But I can see you're managing fine, better than most."

I reached across the table and took her hand for a moment, visualising her pushing and shoving her way into a bus, perspiring with effort. I saw her haggling with the fish vendor in Mandeville market, bargaining for two pounds of snapper. I saw Aunt Sarah coming from the field, carrying a sackful of produce which I couldn't even lift, bathing in cold water she drew from a neighbour's tank, cooking on a coal fire, lighting her house with kerosene lamps. No, there was no way I could think that everything on this island was sweet.

"Life ova here *haad*, mi not tellin yu nuo lie. But di good ting is, if yu mind yu own bisniss, nobaddi but tief gwain trubbl yu. Yu might ded fi hongri if yu unluki, but yu not gwain go mad!"

Jean had finished in the kitchen and joined us at the table, chin on her elbows, engrossed in our conversation.

"What about my father's family, Aunt V? I know my uncle Tiny went to the States a long time ago, and I know my grandmother died last year. Is there nobody else around on his side?"

"Nuo, mi-diir, haadli any ov di Erskine dem liiv. Yu knuo seh yuh Aunt Becca did ded long time. Yu knuo how di stori go, Jean?"

"Inhi. Shi ded fram growt in er belli!"

"Growth? You mean cancer?"

"Nuo. I mean growth. Er belli jus swell up an bapse! Shi ded!"

"Shi was yung too," said Aunt Vera regretfully. "But yuh faada neva hav much famili from time. Dem scatta scatta, aal ova. Im neva evn knuo fi-him faada. I tink dat is why im did kling to wii so haad. Wi was like famli to him."

I remembered him cussing the Partridge family, cussing Aunt Molly and Uncle Matthew and consigning them to hell. He didn't seem all that fond of them to me.

"Yes, dat is why him hold on to Esmi fi so long."

"Hold on? What do you mean?"

"Im shudda lef her long time bifore shi lef him! Fi yiirs im did knuo bout shi an Junior, but im neva do nottn but thump er up now an den."

"He didn't know, Aunt V. I was there, I saw it all! He didn't know!"

"Chile, lissen to what I tell yu; im did knuo. From bifore dem liiv Jamaica im knuo. Nuff odda piipl did knuo too, an plenti ov dem did tell im bout Esmi an er triks!"

"So why didn't he leave her? Or throw her out? Why did he put up with her all those years?"

She was quiet for a while, searching her thoughts. In the silence I could hear my heart thumping, feel sweat gathering under my arms, feel my whole body tense, ready to spring to my father's defense.

"Yu knuo what I tink?" She spoke slowly, and with deliberation. "I tink im kudn't manij widout er. Evriting im had in im life kom wid her. Evriting. Im neva hav nottn or nobaddi fi imself. Dat is why im did hold on to yu an Stevie afta shi liiv. Di two ov yu was aal im did hav."

I had to leave the table. I got up and went into the bathroom, where I splashed my face with water. I patted my face dry with a towel, watching myself in the mirror above the washbasin. I looked calm to my own eyes. I felt like I was floating, adrift, yet I could see that I was not.

I left the bathroom and looked around for some postcards I had bought, intending to scribble something trite and send them to friends, to Marvine, Cindy, maybe Derek, and a few others. Do it now, I told myself. Reach for the safe part of your life. This part here, this island part is shaking, cracking, tearing down the middle like a rotten piece of fabric, is sinking fast and taking you with it.

Chapter 24

RAY ERSKINE WAS LOOKING FORWARD to seeing his daughter again. Every evening he reclined in his bedroom with one eye on the TV and one ear listening for her ring on the doorbell. She had only been away three weeks, but he missed her.

"How yu soh stupid?" Pearl demanded scornfully. "An foolish. When shi is here, yu ongle si er once in a while. Now shi gone fi just trii wiik an yu iitin out yu haart lakka hungri daag. Pure foolishniss."

"Yu gwaan bout yu bisniss, woman!" He picked up his favourite tabloid, preparing to bury himself in the horse-racing section. "Yu jus jealous ov mi pickni-dem!"

She pressed her lips together in a thin line and lay back against the mound of pillows on their bed. Had she felt in an argumentative mood, she would have questioned him about his son, the son he couldn't stand to see or to have in the house.

Yu luv dat one too? She wanted to ask him.

As for shi, dat *gyal*, why was he killin up imself ova er? Shi was nottn speshal. Shi hav one likkl job, buy one flat. Shi noh hav nuo husban; mussi kyaan kech man. Aal dat educashun an shi still doan knuo how fi kech man. What kind ov woman dat? Neida chik nor chile shi hav. Not even kyar shi hav.

Pearl kissed her teeth long and loud. She pulled the bedcovers up to her chin and turned over on her side, presenting him with her back.

Mek im gwan, yaa.

The day after Tessa's return, he called her on the telephone.

"Good evenin. Is dat Tessa?"

"Yes Dad. What's up?"

"How yu kom back so lang an yu doan kom look fi mi yet?"

"I've only been back one day! What's the urgency!"

"Mi long fi see yu! Kom look fi mi soon."

He hung up the phone.

Tess brought them gifts to remind them of home—snapper fried in coconut oil, carefully wrapped in kitchen foil to keep in the juices; breadfruit roasted by Jean; green gungu peas grown by Aunt Vera; coconut drops made by Angela. And a bottle of overproof white rum, of course.

Ray noticed something different in Tessa immediately. He thought at first it was the tan. The deeper colour emphasised the V-shaped shadows on either side of her nose, the narrow bar of shade between bottom lip and chin. Her face looked thinner.

They sat at the dining table, Ray bright-eyed and lively, a glass of rum in front of him. So what did she think of her birthplace? That rat-ridden island in the sun! He grinned with a trace of malice. She liked it? She was welcome to it! He was ready to chat and joke and jibe at length. Talk loud, get angry, let loose his demons on his daughter as he could with no one else.

Tessa sat facing him, her expression calm, or so she hoped. She was aware that only an overdeveloped sense of duty made her give in to his demand to see her. She wasn't ready to see him, yet here she was, humouring him, forcing back irritation and letting him amuse himself at her expense. Here she was, faking pleasantness despite the ache in her guts from the effort of pretending.

She could feel her control slipping. She was smoldering someplace inside, and her head felt heavy, as though filled with dense smoke. These mornings, she woke with a hangover Alka Seltzer could not disperse. Marvine had advised her to see a doctor. Maybe you picked up something on holiday, she said. Malaria or something like that.

She gave her father a skeleton account of her holiday; where she went, who with, who she met.

"Yu mean to seh yu *like* Rocky Gap? Dat God-forsaken place?"

"Yes, I loved it. It felt like home."

"Gyal yu mad! Yu mussi pik up yu Aantie hed siknis!"

"How come you never told me I had so many relatives over there? Auntie Sarah, Uncle Paul and all those cousins?"

He kissed his teeth.

"Dem piipl is bad briid, yaa. Evri one ov dem. Yu betta aaf widout dem. Mu ongle sorri seh yu go buck up on dem now!"

"Yu *sorri*? That I met my *family*? I can't believe you!"

She bit her lip. He refilled his glass, mouth twisting petulantly.

"I hear you visited my mother when you were over there," she said.

"An who tell yu dat?" His tone was irate, but his eyes avoided hers.

"Auntie Sarah," replied Tessa.

"An what if mi did goh look fi er? Shii was mi wife, mi pickni madda. Mi noh sii nottn rong wid it."

"You're so selfish!" The words emerged calmly, surprising her. "You want to keep me away from my mother and her family, don't you? You want me to be alone, don't you? Alone and lonely."

Even as she spoke, she expected him to storm back at her, but he was silent, a hurt look in his eyes. Then his chin began to tremble.

"Dat is wat yu aantie tell yu fi seh? Dat bitch! Shi always wanted to tek yu from mi. Always."

He's pathetic, she thought. Pitiful. She could hardly stand to look at his face.

She left soon after and hastened home like a rabbit bolting for the safety of its warren.

※ ※ ※

Returning to work turned out to be surprisingly painless. Her desk was just as she had left it, clear of memos, files, circulars and all other office currency. On the one hand this was an encouraging state of things; she could make a fresh start on work without the encumbrance of a backlog. Yet the sight of the empty desk made her uneasy. She saw a challenge in it, an accusation: you've been away for three weeks and look, we managed fine without you.

She flopped in the swivel chair, legs stretched out under the desk, hands behind her head, rocking from side to side while she psyched herself up to go and see Peter. She could just imagine the smirk on his face as he recounted the crises and dramas he and Trevor had effortlessly dealt with in her absence.

I give myself till next summer to get out of here, she resolved. Till the end of June. If I haven't found a job by then, I'm not worth ten pence.

She decided to drop by the general office and catch up on the departmental gossip. Of course, everyone in there would marvel at her tan, comment on how different she looked this darker shade and want to know all about the holiday. Her story was prepared, already polished by several tellings.

By the time she returned to her room, her head was reeling. She had expected the latest staff gossip—romances, pregnancies, resignations, appointments, dirt on Trevor and Peter, the men all the admin workers loved to hate. All that had paled into insignificance, overshadowed by the news of forthcoming cuts. There had been rumours going around the Town Hall for months, but now there was a definite plan, agreed by the council and ready for implementation. Everyone was worried about their job.

None of this really surprised Tess; after all, town hall staff in two neighbouring boroughs had already been decimated in the name of efficiency. She resolved to find out fast how the division would be affected. Would there be more work for personnel officers, dealing with redundancies and so forth, or less? Would she soon find herself out of a job?

The sound of the tea-trolley drew her into the corridor, mug in hand. She was the first to reach the trolley, followed closely by Trevor Clarke, who strolled up and stood beside her, hands in pockets.

"Morning, Trevor." Why did she get the feeling he was gloating over something?

"So the traveller returns!" He crossed his arms over his chest and shifted his weight on to one hip. "What you bring for me from yard?"

Didn't he know short men look ridiculous when they try to pose?

"I bring good vibes for everybody, Trevor. Even you," she said, flashing a blatantly insincere smile.

A leer flitted across his face.

"Bwoy, it look like Jamaica sugar sweeten you a likkl," he said, baring his teeth. "Yeahman, you look nice."

She was watching Bernice pour her mug of tea but noticed a movement of his arm out of the corner of her eye. She felt a lingering pat on her right buttock and froze. She looked down in shocked disbelief in time to see his hand retreating guiltily into his trouser pocket.

"I can't believe you did that," she said looking him straight in the eye.

He shrugged dismissively.

"Choh man, I neva mean notten."

By now a few others were by the trolley waiting for service. Tess turned to the tea lady.

"Did you see that Bernice?"

Bernice nodded.

"Mmhmm. I saw it." She handed Tess her mug and turned towards Trevor, hands on hips. "Im put im han pon yu backside!"

People behind them in the queue were looking curious, wondering what was going on. Tess walked past them and into her office, shutting the door firmly. She put down her mug and went to the bookcase on the wall facing her desk. She pulled out the staff procedures manual and sat down, picking up the phone even as she flicked through the pages searching for the guidance she needed.

She had to tell Marvine about *this* right away.

She knew that lodging a grievance against Trevor Clarke was taking on trouble. There was bound to be talk, speculation, taking of sides. Besides Elise, her secretary, she wasn't sure who to count on for support. Trevor's enemies would probably back her, the general office staff also too. But some black colleagues would react as though she was letting the side down.

Was she? she asked herself over and over again. She went back over the times that she and Trevor had clashed, reliving every slight. Was she overreacting?

Peter Russell surprised her. He summoned her to his office hours after she handed her written complaint in a sealed envelope to the secretary of the Division Director.

"Come in. Sit down. I thought we needed to have a chat." He sat with elbows resting on the arms of his chair, fingertips together, cradling his chin. He looked concerned, grave and pensive. He spoke gently, as though breaking bad news to an invalid.

"I'm surprised you didn't bring your complaint to me in the first instance. I could have dealt with it. I could have gotten an apology from Trevor and avoided the fuss of a grievance."

Tess sat straight and still, hands clasped together on her lap.

"Are you telling me I didn't follow the correct procedure, Peter?"

His eyebrows shot up.

"No. I'm saying there was an easier way to settle your complaint and I'm surprised you didn't take it."

She gazed out of the window and up at the sky, without speaking.

"The racists in this place are going to love this, you know."

He leaned forward earnestly. "Two black managers in conflict; I can just see them lapping it up."

He winced, as though the very thought caused him pain.

"And the Black Workers Group. They won't like it one bit! They'll probably support Trevor, you know that."

She smiled grimly.

"You mean the men will. The women might see it differently."

He threw up his hands in a gesture of surrender.

"I'm only doing this out of consideration for you, Tessa. You might be absolutely in the right, but the reality of it is that going through a grievance is a nasty business, and nobody emerges unscathed. This whole affair could damage your career. I'm sure you know that."

She might have been taken in by this display of sincere concern if she didn't know him.

"I couldn't believe his gall!" she told Marvine. "He was warning me off, the slimy bastard."

"Well, it's not going to reflect too well on him to have the entire

Town Hall know that his protégé, his Senior Personnel Officer, has gone and broken the code of conduct!"

"You're right. I didn't see it that way. I thought he was just looking out for his buddy!"

"Nah. His type don't give a shit 'bout anyone but themselves."

The mist in her head continued to spread. It gathered mass daily, seeping through her skin from the inside out, enveloping her like a dark cloud. The flare of triumph at striking out at Trevor was all too brief, quenched like a small flame in a fog. The Department's procedures for investigating a grievance was a lengthy one, and the waiting made her ill. Anxiety sucked at her, gnawed at her insides and drained the fight out of her. She was sleeping badly, four, five hours a night at most. In the early hours of every morning sleep left her with a jolt, like a lover's sudden departure. She lay on her back in the dark, hands on her stomach, nursing her pain and weeping like a desolate child. In the morning she looked at the drawn face and shadowed eyes in the mirror and wondered what was wrong with her.

Do I have a ghost on my back? Did I pick up a duppy in Rocky Gap and bring it home? Maybe something my mother sent to plague me out of spite, to punish me?

Maybe I should see a doctor, get something to help me sleep. Get some pills. Uppers, downers, vitamins, sleeping pills?

Maybe I should see a therapist.

She worried about Stevie too. Three weeks, six weeks, ten weeks passed, and still no visit from him. This had happened before, months had passed without her seeing him. Sometimes, most times, he'd been in hospital, committed by his social worker for his own good, or by the police for the good of the general public.

She felt stupid not knowing where her own brother lived. She had his address, and she knew the locality, but he made such a big issue about not wanting anyone barging in on him that she had never dared to go there.

Memories of the holiday were fading, shadowy now, like underexposed film. If she didn't see him soon she would forget it all. She was certain he would want to know about the family she'd found, the places, the food, the hammock under Aunt Vera's mango tree. She closed her eyes and travelled back to Rocky Gap, to vague images of Aunt Sarah's verandah, Maas Peter's store, and Aunt Vera's love, permanent and warm, like Rocky Gap's dry red earth.

She chose a light, early spring evening to go look for him, hoping the bright sky and mild air would soothe away any objections he might have to her arrival on his doorstep. Clayton Mansions was a 1950s housing estate in the council-owned no-man's-land between elite Bloomsbury and seedy Kings Cross. A dusty, meagre street led up to the main entrance which gave way to row upon row of four-story red-brick blocks of flats. A map of the estate posted by the entrance revealed that No 179 was at the far end of the estate, near the back exit. Tessa started walking.

It was quiet on the ground. An Asian woman wearing a shalwar kameez covered by a raincoat hurried past clutching a shopping bag, not risking even a glance in Tessa's direction. A young white man was walking an ugly-looking pitbull terrier on a leash too long for control. Tessa stopped by a staircase to let them pass. While waiting she helped a white girl with dyed blonde hair and tired eyes lift a baby in a buggy up three flights of stairs. The girl muttered "ta" and disappeared down the walkway with the speed and stealth of a fugitive.

The smell of cooking followed Tess as she made her way through the estate: bacon, garlic, curry, fish fingers, an odd, conflicting blend of aromas.

She was struck by the silence. No children were playing, no boys and girls careering on bicycles, no youths kicking footballs. She understood why when she read the graffitti which covered every accessible wall, bold and neon-bright.

"NIGGERS OUT!" "DEATH TO ALL PAKIS!" "BOTHA FOR PRIME MINISTER!"

Spray paint shouting out loud that someone somewhere in Clayton Mansions was having fun of the hateful kind.

By the time she reached Stevie's flat on the top floor of the very last block, Tessa was scared, so much so she was glad there was no answer to her knock on the door. So much so that she ran back down the end-less flights of stairs and out through the back exit, without knowing where she would end up. Head down, shoulders hunched aginst the fast-descending night, she aimed for Bloomsbury but found herself on Pentonville Road, hailing a cab.

Home, in the calm of her pristine flat, she crumbled and fell on her bed still wearing coat and shoes, body exhausted while mind galloped aimlessly like a restive horse.

She should have knocked at the flat next door to Stevie's and asked if anyone had seen him lately. Why hadn't she? The worst that could have happened was the door shutting in her face. Or not opening at all. A blue eye peeking through the letter box and seeing a dark face out there in the night probably would not have opened up. Not in a place like Clayton Mansions where fear walked, ugly and powerful as a hun-gry pitbull stalking a frail young woman in a shalwar kameez pushing a buggy with a baby in it.

Her belly ached from all that hate.

And where was the love? Any kind. The kind you reach for calm-ly with both arms and rest against, warm and smiling. Even the hot, frantic kind would do. The kind you chase thirstily in the night, barefooted, not minding the blood on the pavement or the lonely heart pounding fit to burst. No quiet with this kind, no healing. Like a fragment of a blissful dream, you catch it, you lose it, you chase it all over again.

She had seen Derek just a few nights before, leaving his house with a woman on his arm. He had caught her eye and waved, left the woman for a moment and crossed the road, smiling and saying:

I've been meaning to call by and find out how it was. Your journey home, I mean.

She loved the way the glossy hair of his moustache caressed the edge of his top lip.

It's not too late, she said, smiling up at him more brightly than she felt, aware of the woman watching and frowning.

I'll do that, he said, turning to cross the road again and waving a promise.

Some days later on her way home from work she saw him ahead of her striding down Stroud Green Road and almost ran to catch up with him.

"So how did you really find Jamaica?" he asked as she fell in step with him.

"I loved it. I can't wait to go back again!"

"Are you serious?" His eyebrows rose in mock surpise. "You loved all the violence, all the poverty, the heat..."

"I loved the countryside, the beauty of it. I loved seeing my aunt again and meeting my family. I felt at home. I felt I belonged, and I loved that too. I'm going there again as soon as I can..."

She was silenced by the feel of his arm falling around her shoulders in a brief, affectionate squeeze.

"That's my girl," he said, smiling approvingly into her eyes. "You're not as lost as I thought you were."

She was tempted to argue, to pretend she didn't know what he meant, but decided against it.

"I might be in Jamaica myself later this year," he continued. "I've applied for a research post in the Education Department at the university, to start in September. So, you never know, maybe we'll meet up over there."

"Well," she said, suddenly breathless. "Well. You never know."

※ ※ ※

The phone ringing at 7am startled Tessa, who was awake but hardly alert, having slept very badly. She picked up the phone anticipating bad news.

Pearl was on the line, brusque as a cold shower.

"Tessa. Sorri to wake yu but yu faada ask mi to phone yu."

"Where is he? What's happened to him."

"Is not him. Is Stevie. Im in hospital. Di Royal Imperial."

"Oh no. He's sick again?"

"Not dis time. Not wid im hed, enihow. Siim like im miit sum kinda aksident, mi noh knuo what. Di poliis jus kaal ten minit ago."

"Let me speak to my Dad, please, Pearl."

"Im in di baatroom righ now. Im nat pliis bout dis, mek mi tell yu! Is one more triyal pon im hed! But im going to di hospital aal di same."

"Tell him I'll go with him. Tell him to wait for me in the hospital lobby."

She was familiar with the Royal Imperial from the outside. All glass and concrete and gleaming synthetic flooring, the building looked more like an office block than a hospital.

Her father was waiting in the entrance lobby, perched on the edge of a red plastic chair, hands clasped between his knees. Dressed in suit and tie and bright white shirt, he looked every inch the respectable, concerned parent.

"What happened to him, Dada? How is he?"

He kissed his teeth and shook his head, as though irritated beyond expression.

"Mi no knuo, yaa! Poliis seh im kech fight wid some bwoy and dem biit im up."

"Stevie get in a fight? I don't believe it!"

"It look like yu doan knuo dat bwoy! Im nuo good! Not one good bone in im baddi!"

Anger rose like a hot flush and loosened her tongue.

"Stop it, Dad! Just stop it! I can't stand the way you go on about Stevie!"

He watched with surprise in his eyes as she turned on her heel and approached the enquiries desk to find out Stevie's whereabouts. Men's Medical 3, she was told. Take the lift to the third floor.

An absurdly young-looking nurse accosted them as they entered the ward.

"Umm, yes, I am Mr. Erskine," began Ray.

"We've come to see Steven Erskine," Tess interjected briskly.

"He's in the corner bed, the one with the curtains drawn. He's sleeping right now, but you can pop in for a moment so long as you don't disturb him."

They stood in shocked silence on either side of the bed. Was this Stevie? Shaven, lockless and beardless, head wrapped and crossed in a bandage like a fencer's helmet. One eye was covered with gauze and so was most of his right cheek. Both hands lying on top of the green-striped hospital coverlet were bandaged, leaving only the fingertips visible, purplish brown and oddly vulnerable.

The sound of choking broke the long silence, a deep, retching sound, like someone wanted to vomit.

"What are you so upset about," demanded Tessa in a harsh whisper. "Don't you realize this is your fault?" she said, resting a hand on one of Stevie's. "You threw him out on the street at a time when he couldn't fend for himself. And now you have the nerve to stand there and cry, as though you care one jot about him! You make me sick!" She stared into Ray's face, her expression hard and angry.

Stevie slept on while his father groped his way out of the cubicle and staggered through the ward under the curious gaze of eleven sick men, Tessa following, looking furious.

The nurse stopped Ray at the door, took him by the arm and led him into her office.

"Here, Mr. Erskine, sit here a while," she said, gently easing him into a chair. "I'll get you some water," she said and left the room.

There are times when a little kindness can undermine a man's efforts at composure. Ray Erskine doubled over in the red plastic chair, grasped his head in both hands and howled, choking out grief in great rasping gobs.

"God help mi," he sobbed. "Mi du di best mi kud du. God knuo, mi du mi best."

Sitting beside him, hands rising and falling helplessly in the air, Tessa felt anger roll off her skin and slide way.

By the time the nurse returned bearing two glasses of water Ray was upright, though still crying.

"He's not as bad as he looks, you know," the nurse said, referring to Stevie. "Its the bandages. They make him look like a war victim."

"When he's recovered from his injuries, we're going to move him to the psychatric wing for a while. Just to make sure he recovers properly from the shock. And you, Mr. Erskine," she said smiling softly at him, "you go home and have a nice hot drink and a good rest."

Stevie stayed in hospital the entire summer. Virtually every day, Tessa made the trek to the hospital from her workplace or, at weekends, her home. She quite enjoyed the daily walk from Hampstead station, down the tree-lined hill past smart shops and crowded, cheerful eateries.

Stevie mended fast, and once he was able to move around they spent visiting time together in the hospital canteen, chatting over cups of tea and plates of chips.

"Remember when I used to work here?" he asked.

"Oh yes. Quite a while ago, wasn't it?"

"Yeah," he said with a short, bitter laugh. "I was a porter. My longest job ever. And my last."

"Maybe not your last, Stevie. You'll get well. You'll be able to live a normal life."

"Who are you kidding, Tess? I'm never going to be 'normal'! Never again!"

Looked into his face at the scars which had not yet healed; at his eyes, cloudy from too much suffering; at his hair which was greying like an old man's; at his hands, swollen and trembling from the medication he took, Tessa had to acknowledge that he was right.

"Have you seen the old man lately?"

"No," replied Tessa, "I haven't. Not since the day after you were admitted."

"He's passed by here a few times, which is quite a record for him," said Stevie.

"Well, well, well. He's making an effort at last!" said Tessa sarcastically.

"Have you two fallen out, or something?" asked Stevie, glancing nervously at Tessa.

"Yes, we have. I finally told him what I think of him and the way he carries on, like he's some kind of martyr. He makes me sick."

"I've been trying to tell you about him for years but you wouldn't listen," said Stevie.

"I know, I know, " said Tessa quietly. "And I'm sorry I didn't listen to you. I'm sorry I was such a dupe for so long..."

"Well, at least you've seen the light now," said Stevie, visibly uneasy with Tessa's disclosures. "Better late than never, eh?" Then, to change the subject, he said, "They nearly killed me, you know. They nearly did me in."

"Did you recognise any of them? Were any of them from the estate?"

"Nah. It was dark, and I wasn't in my right mind anyway. The cops said there were no witnesses, so they've nothing to go on. No chance of catching any of them."

He was silent for a while, and then said, "I wouldn't mind living in Jamaica, you know."

"I think you'd like Jamaica," she said, chosing her words carefully, "but its a hard place to live, Stevie."

"It can't be harder than this."

"That's what Aunt Vera says. She said 'If yu noh trubbl nobaddi, nobaddi gwain trubbl yu, an nottn deh ya fi sen yu mad!'"

Stevie smiled faintly.

I should help him get out there when he's better, thought Tess. It would help him, just being over there. There's nothing here for him. Not one thing.

Stevie was discharged three weeks later to St Dennis's Hostel in Tufnell Park. He called her from there on his first night in residence, sounding almost cheerful.

"I was here before, you know. After my first breakdown. It's not bad here, not bad at all...Better than Clayton Mansions, at any rate."

*   *   *

Tess was so preoccupied with Stevie during his hospitalisation that she had little anxiety to spare for her own problems. The petty trials of the department faded into insignificance, put firmly into perspective by Stevie's much larger difficulties.

The official hearing of her grievance against Trevor Clarke passed successfully, yet she felt no burst of jubilation. She waited in vain for joy to come, for a sense of triumph to arrive. She saw Trevor several times a day, each time aware that he was watching defensively for signs of ego-inflation on her part. Not that there was anything he could have done, having been placed on probation for one year.

She fell into a shallow rhythm, treading a lonely, monotonous path from home to work and back again. She felt listless, like a convalescent no longer weak from sickness, but lacking the vibrancy of full health.

Of course, she walked past the office notice board several times each working day. The board hung on the right-hand wall of the entrance lobby, a little way past the double swing doors and opposite the photo-copying machine. Her eyes flickered on it, over it, past it, countless numbers of times each day.

Much later in time she would wonder why it took two months for her to read the Director's memo to the deparment on the subject of staff cuts which was posted on the board.

Voluntary redundancies: Special payments.
Applications from staff wishing to take voluntary redun-
dancy should be made in writing to the Director.

After reading these magic words, she danced back to her office, grin-ning like a madwoman. Even as she picked up the phone to call Marvine, she knew what she was going to do.

EPILOGUE

※ ※ ※ ※ ※ ※ ※ ※ ※ ※

JAMAICA 1990

AN UNACCUSTOMED SENSATION OF WARMTH woke her. She opened her eyes, still half-asleep, wondering: why was the sheet beneath her damp? Why had moisture gathered in the creases behind her knees, under her arms and between her breasts?

A mosquito cruising close to her ear answered her. With a gurgle of excitement she leaped out of the too-hot bed, drew aside the fleecy nylon curtains covering her aunt's bedroom windows and opened the louvres. Sunlight burst into the room, brilliant, glorious, dazzling. A cool current of air brushed her face as she stood gazing onto the back-yard, seeing with fresh eyes sunlight and morning breeze dancing together, shimmering gracefully in the leaves of the coconut tree.

Noises of the morning filled her ears, cock-crow, birdsong and human voices, cawking, tweeting and humming against the dense background rustle of foliage. She felt the warmth of light on her skin, deep, gentle warmth, beaming from a radiant sun in a perfect morning-blue sky. She fell back on the bed, stretching voluptuously in a pool of light, in complete surrender to the beauty of the moment.

An old Timex alarm clock on the dressing table showed eight-thirty. Half-past-one London time, she thought gleefully, an image of colleagues back at the office flashing across her mind. It was strange to think that only forty-eight hours ago she had been there herself, immersed in that grey, drudging existence. At this moment the office, London, England seemed like another universe.

The sound of a step outside the bedroom door made her sit up and brace herself. The door opened and Aunt Vera came gently into the room.

"Maanin! Mi tink yu was still sliipin!" Tessa shook her head and smiled, reflecting back the affectionate glow that warmed and softened her aunt's face. Aunt Vera hadn't changed. A little plumper, maybe a bit more grey on her head, but still alert, still lively, still incorrigibly talkative.

"I put a towel in di baatroom fi yu." Aunt Vera sat on the bed beside her. "An I lite a Destroyer so di miskito-dem doan nyam yu to piices!"

"It's too late." Tess rubbed a cluster of red bumps near her right elbow. "Dem staat alreddi!"

"What!" Aunt Vera threw up her hands, feigning outrage. "Dem haaf-staavin brute! Wach mi an dem and Destroyer tonite!" They both laughed in anticipation of mass slaughter.

"Jean kookin kallaloo and banana fi yuh brekfaas. Yu still luv kallaloo?"

"Oh yes!" Tessa sprang up and headed for the bathroom, now eager for food. "I still love callaloo!"